Under the CIRCUMSTANCES

A Novel

Susan Middleton

CLASS
Publishing Division

Under the Circumstances
by Susan Yandle Middleton

ISBN 978-1-955095-37-2

Published in the United States by

Publishing Division
P.O. Box 2884
Pawleys Island, SC 29585
www.ClassAtPawleys.com

Dedication to
Lillian Moore Sharpton
1902-1929

Acknowledgments with gratitude to

LaVerle McAdams and Adair Middleton who were willing over many months to read weekly installments of Millie's story,

Mary Whitfield who read the church scenes for authenticity,

and my writers' group who were willing to hear Millie's voice every month.

Chapter 1

In 1925 Millie Martin, age fifteen, was a pretty little thing growing up in Gaston, Georgia, such a small place it was better to simply say she was from Thompson County, Georgia.

Her long, light brown hair fell in soft curls to her shoulders. Her big blue eyes had a scared-deer look, but Millie had a coy way of using them, looking up and cocking her head as she cast her gaze toward whoever was speaking to her. She also had a nervous habit of licking her lips and then parting them slightly, not realizing how that affected men.

Tom Stapleton had seen her on Sundays sitting in church with her ma, Widow Martin. Millie's pa had died when she was just four and took with him his minimal farming skills. Widow Martin lacked the skills or the drive to run a farm and also had tuberculosis. She mostly kept to herself in her bedroom in an effort to stay away from Millie.

If it hadn't been for the Thompsons — and Gaston was full of them — Millie and her ma would have starved to death. So, when Tom Stapleton, aged twenty-three, proposed marriage to Millie, she and her ma said yes.

Widow Martin thought maybe he would give her a good life, take care of Millie after she was gone.

It was not much over a year later when Millie, then age sixteen, gave birth to a baby girl and Tom Stapleton left Gaston. Talk was he'd moved to Savannah and was working at the port there. He left Millie and Widow Martin worse off than they had been. Now there were three mouths to feed.

Again, they depended on their good neighbors and stumbled along for about a year. It was early fall in 1927 when Millie sat her ma down and took her hands. "Listen Ma," she said, "This TB thing is just gonna get worse. I can leave Gaston, go to some place bigger and get a job, that way I can send you money. You know, help you and Louise. And once I'm settled, I'll come back and get Louise."

Her mother had slowly nodded her head. "Millie, maybe you're right. I can get some help from Mildred," she said, referring to her friend at the next farm over. "Maybe she can even take Louise for a spell now and then when my coughin' is real bad. You go on. You're still young and pretty. Maybe you can get a job in a big store or somethin'."

Millie packed a small cardboard suitcase. One of the Thompsons gave her a ride to the main highway. She thanked him and stood there in her faded cotton dress with her cardboard suitcase waiting for a ride north. The trucker who stopped told her he was headed to Mason, the big town 125 miles north of Gaston. Good a place as any, Millie thought as she climbed in.

She held her suitcase in her lap, squeezing it against her as if to protect herself, as if to hide that she was a woman, a shapely one at that.

The truck driver introduced himself as Buck Wilson from Chatham County, near Savannah. He wasn't a big man, but well-muscled from his work of loading and unloading a truck. He had red hair and freckles.

Millie had no idea how old he was, but there was a soft sadness about his eyes which made her less anxious. The only man she had ever been with was Tom and his way, while not abusive, had been rough. She knew how a man's body hunger could make him act. She squeezed the cardboard suitcase even closer to her chest.

Millie just stared straight ahead.

"Well, what's yo name?" Buck asked.

"Millie." She saw no need to tell him more. And he didn't ask for more.

He told her that he was hauling supplies for small general stores: fabric, notions, nails, hammers, canned goods, some fresh produce like bananas.

He added, "Just serving those small general stores before the big chain grocers take over like the A & P." There would be stops along the way, he said, including Kellyville, Eureka, and Montrose, before they got to Mason. It was as if he knew how scared she was, so he was trying to chat things up.

"I want to go to Mason," Millie said.

"Where do you want to go in Mason?"

"I don't know, I mean, I don't have any kin there. I'll need a place to stay and a job. I ain't got no money, suh," she responded. She looked at him casting her coy upward gaze, as she licked her lips and parted them.

"Why yo leavin' home then?" he asked.

"Too many mouths to feed there," she said. "Leavin' means one less mouth." She turned her head and began to gaze out the window. Pine trees were all she saw. She had brought her ma's pair of scissors just in case she needed them. She had already used them to cut her hair into a short bob. She had strong arms and knew that if she needed to, she could sink those scissors deep into a man's arm.

She had not intended to, but she drifted off to sleep and when she woke up, she was alone in the paneled delivery truck and Buck was unloading merchandise at a general store. She had no idea where she was.

"Wanna banana?" Buck stuck the fruit in through the window. Millie took it. She had never had a banana. Buck saw her quizzical expression. He took the banana and began peeling. He handed it back.

"You'll like it. Try some."

"Where are we?" Millie asked.

"We're in Mason. This is my last stop. I'll be spending the night at Miss Sarah's on Maple Street. Do you want to meet her? She's always needing help. She runs a boarding house."

Millie just nodded, eating the banana. It was so good. She ate slowly, making the soft, sweet pieces last. She even pinched off a piece so she could feel its squishy softness between her fingers.

A warm breeze blew across Millie's face tossing the soft curls of her bob. Maybe Mason would be a good place to live.

Buck jumped back into the truck and cranked her up. With a jolt they moved forward. Maple Street was not far off and before she knew it, they pulled up in front of a well-maintained 19th-century three-story house with a rounded turret at one end. The window boxes were filled with yellow chrysanthemums and clean, sheer curtains fluttered at the open windows. A white picket fence framed the manicured front yard. It looked like a mansion to Millie. On the front porch were white painted wooden rockers.

"Come on, Millie, I'll be staying here tonight before going back to Savannah." Buck reached up to take her hand. She just looked at him and slid to the ground without his help.

"You need to meet Miss Sarah," he continued walking toward the front door. "You'll like her." He looked back at Millie who had now stepped onto the sidewalk, her wrinkled cotton dress wrapping around her legs. As she stood on the sidewalk, the sun behind her, Buck got a clear look at her legs, lean and shapely. You have more than you know, he said to himself.

Miss Sarah stood on her front porch. She was a fine-looking woman, if a little old-fashioned, wearing her dark silver-flecked hair piled high on her head. Her Gibson Girl figure was enhanced by the tailor-made dark blue gabardine dress that she wore. Her only jewelry was a modest cameo brooch centered at her neck. Her clothes and her demeanor told Millie that this was her house, her business, her rules.

Buck gave a slight bow as he took the steps.

"Ah, Miss Sarah, this is Millie. She needs a job and a place to stay."

Miss Sarah raised one eyebrow.

"Now Buck, I never told you that I needed another girl. What made you bring this baby to me?"

Millie stood at the foot of the front steps head cocked, but chin slightly up. She looked Miss Sarah in the eye. There's something about this little string of a girl, Miss Sarah thought. Millie licked her lips and then parted them slightly.

"Can you cook, baby?"

"Yes, ma'am. I can cook and clean."

"Go on in the kitchen. See Miss Cora. She'll put you to work. Supper's served at 5:30 sharp. My men folks come here hungry."

Her girls, her men folk. Millie wondered what that meant. She slipped past Miss Sarah and Buck as they fell into conversation about something involving a city ordinance and boarding houses.

The front screen door opened into a hallway. Straight ahead was a red carpeted staircase. To the right was a sitting room which smelled slightly of cigars and had an upright piano positioned against one wall. To the left was a dining room with a long table, covered in a white tablecloth. Millie was certain that she had never been in such an elegant place. Above her head hung a multi-layered chandelier. Millie just stood there, head up, watching the sunlight catch the prisms and splash colors on the papered wall. What was this place? Millie wondered. Well, it was the place where she had landed. She'd stay here at least for the night.

Millie followed the smell of cornbread and turnips coming from down the hallway by the stairs. "Swing low, sweet chariot, comin' for to carry me home" sung full and loud was the sound Millie heard as she slipped into the kitchen. She set her suitcase by the door as she entered.

"Well, look here, Magdala, Miss Sarah has sent us some help. What's your name, chile?"

"I'm Millie from Gaston, Georgia. I need a job and a place to stay. My husband left me and my baby and my ma. Ain't got no pa. He died when I was four." What am I doing? Millie thought to herself. But the early fall breeze was fluttering the curtains, and the smell of cornbread and turnips was filling the air. Her mouth watered.

"You know how to wash pots and pans?" Miss Cora asked as she wiped her hands on her apron. Perspiration was just beginning to form on her forehead. She picked up a clean dish towel and wiped her face. Millie marveled at this beautiful black woman, her skin, a cream-and-coffee shade, was so smooth and blemish-free. She had a dimple in her right cheek and when she smiled her eyes twinkled. She had her hair bound up in a dark blue cotton kerchief. Millie knew immediately that she was a lean, spry type who could bustle around quickly in a kitchen. She wore a beautiful, starched white blouse with a deep lace-trimmed yoke that peeked from under her equally starched apron.

"Come over here. Magdala will show you how we do it." Miss Cora gently directed Millie to the sink as she patted her shoulder.

Magdala, Miss Cora's fourteen-year-old daughter, joined Millie at the sink. She was darker skinned than her ma and her tight-curled short hair framed her face. Her eyes were hazel, like her ma's and she had a dimple in her right cheek like her ma.

"I'll show you how, Millie," Magdala giggled.

The kitchen sink faced a window that looked out into the back yard. Millie could see a carriage house behind the big house. Magdala saw Millie looking out the window at what must once have been a carriage house.

"That's where we live, Millie. Ma, Pa, and me. You can come see it sometime."

The backyard was as tidy as the front but included a fenced-in vegetable garden. There was row after row of turnips. Millie could see the back entrance to the house. The window above the sink was open and that same soft fall breeze again found Millie's face.

Miss Cora's work had already produced a pile of dirty bowls, pans, and big spoons.

"Since I know where everything goes, I'll dry. You wash," said Magdala.

The dish pan was filled with hot water and soap, and bubbles like prisms broke the light into rainbows on the wall. This place is full of rainbows, Millie thought.

Miss Cora began singing again and before Millie knew it, she had begun weaving harmony notes into the melody: "I looked over Jordan and what did I see. Comin' for to carry me home. A band of angels…"

"A band of angels…" Millie looked up and saw four of the most beautiful young women she had ever seen giggling and jostling their way up the back steps. Each one was dressed to perfection, and each had a shopping bag labeled "Zimmerman's."

Something had struck them as funny, and they were coyly laughing behind their gloved hands. Their cloche hats were a shade lighter than their dresses, each dress a different color in a crepe de chine fabric: navy blue, magenta, deep orange, and purple. And Millie was certain that they each wore a slip under the dresses since the dropped waists fell smoothly from the top to bottom. Millie had never owned a slip, but she had seen them in the Sears catalogs and according to the ads a slip was an essential garment if you wanted to be a real lady and have your dress fall smooth and not have your legs show through a sheer fabric.

"Oh, Miss Cora, that cornbread smells divine!" the first angel cooed.

"I'm also making your favorite, Hazel: banana puddin'," Miss Cora told her, smiling.

The other three angels fell in behind her.

"Who's helping Magdala?" another one asked.

"Oh, that's Millie. She rode up from Savannah way with Buck. She needs a place to stay and a job."

Miss Cora turned from her work toward Millie.

"Millie, meet Hazel, Corine, Lucy, and Gladys. They live here with Miss Sarah."

Millie was still in awe of their grace, their style, their beauty. The best she could muster was a nod of her head. A curl had fallen over one eye and as she reached to push it away, she left bubbles from the dish pan linger on her face.

The girls giggled more. "Millie, you don't have to wash your face in a dish pan. We'll show you how to wash your face and apply creams," Hazel smiled. "We'll be busy tonight, but maybe tomorrow we'll give you a make-over."

The four turned to leave, but over their shoulders they said almost in unison, "We love your banana puddin', Miss Cora!" And then they giggled and headed up the back staircase that led to the upper floors from the kitchen.

"Millie, when was the last time you ate?" Miss Cora asked.

"I ate a banana today," was all Millie knew to say.

Miss Cora laughed. "Come here, chile. I'll fix you a bowl

of cornbread and turnips. We'll be servin' in the dining room soon and you'll need your strength."

Millie wiped her hands on a dishcloth and sat down at the little wooden kitchen table in the middle of the room. Painted white with four sturdy legs and four matching chairs, it filled the center of the room, the hub of the kitchen, a place where things simply made sense.

Miss Cora set the bowl in front of her. Millie leaned toward it, taking in the aroma of the fat back-seasoned turnip greens. Miss Cora had even included one turnip root, soaked through with the pot liquor. The cornbread square perched on top was golden and crisp on the edges, a large glob of butter sitting on top.

Yes, surely, I have found a home, thought Millie as she hungrily devoured the cornbread and greens. She finished up by lifting the bowl to her lips and drinking the leftover pot liquor.

At five-fifteen Miss Cora began giving orders like a field marshal readying her troops for battle. "Millie, you take the cornbread on into the dining room, then come back and get the sweet potatoes."

Millie picked up the plate of cornbread and walked across the back hallway into the dining room. Four men were already seated at the table. Each one was wearing a white shirt and fresh collar, their faces freshly scrubbed, and they were smiling. Millie almost didn't recognize Buck now that he was one of the freshly scrubbed. She set the plate down.

Just as she turned to leave, the angels, the four she had met earlier, began gliding into the room. Millie's jaw dropped. Each one wore a beaded slip dress featuring an uneven hem that ended in fringe the color of the dress, each a different jewel tone: red, green, purple, and blue.

Millie was speechless as she studied the outfits created by these young women. Drop earrings dangled and twinkled in the light, jeweled headbands held back just a bit of their bobbed hair, and each one wore a long strand of pearls knotted at the end. And the fragrance that came from them as they moved across the floor.

Millie looked closely at their beautiful faces, eyes accented with soft, tinted eyeshadow and heart-shaped lips perfectly covered with red lipstick.

Miss Cora's voice broke the mood. "Millie, get yourself back in the kitchen and bring the sweet potatoes." She spoke sternly but, understanding that Millie was seeing feminine elegance for the first time, she smiled.

Millie returned to the kitchen to get the sweet potatoes and found a colored man seated at the kitchen table, a plate of food piled high in front of him.

"I'm Millie," was all she knew to say.

"And I'm Lester Butterfield, Cora's husband," he replied. "Pleased to meet you." Lester was a handsome man with a head full of curly dark hair, skin the color of milk chocolate. His most remarkable feature, however, was his blue eyes. Millie had known colored folk all her life, but never had she known one to have blue eyes. She was momentarily mesmerized, but snapped out of it when she remembered Miss Cora had given her a job to do.

"I better get the sweet potatoes, Mr. Lester, suh," Millie nodded as she spoke.

"That might be smart," Mr. Lester smiled.

Back in the dining room Millie set the bowl down wherever she could find a spot. And then she stepped back, leaning against the floor-to-ceiling china cabinet, and just stood there and looked at the vision before her. Miss Sarah sat at the head of the table, hair piled high, and dressed in a white lace dress. The rest were arranged in an alternating pattern of gentleman and lady.

The smell of the food — cornbread, fried pork chops,

sweet potatoes, turnips — combined with the smell of the newly washed and pomaded men and the glamorous and sweetly scented women was intoxicating.

Millie could have stood and watched them the entire meal, but Miss Cora would have none of that, taking her by the elbow and leading her back to the kitchen.

"I guess you've met my husband, Millie," Miss Cora smiled as she leaned in to give him a quick hug. "Want some banana puddin', honey?"

"I'd love that," Mr. Lester responded as he held up his plate. "See, I cleaned my plate."

"You better have cleaned that plate!" Miss Cora muttered. "Not gonna waste this good food I've toiled over all afternoon." She patted his cheek as she took the plate.

"Listen, baby, I'm gonna head home after I eat my puddin'. I'm beat. I had to trench out the entire floor of a bathroom today to get to a busted pipe. I'm whipped. May already be in the bed when you get home. But I'll take a bath first," Lester winked as he dug into the large bowl of banana pudding. Millie could only think, What a handsome couple. He really does love Miss Cora.

Magdala had already fixed her plate and was eating at the table with her pa. The early fall breeze whispered through the open windows. Millie felt her heart swell and a deep sense of well-being swept over her as she also filled her plate.

Miss Cora turned to Magdala, "After you and Millie eat your supper, take her up to the turret room. Show her where everything she'll need is and then come right back. I can clean up tonight. You need to get your homework done, so you can go on home with your pa." Magdala nodded. Millie had enjoyed the sights and smells of the dining room, but she had an idea this table in the kitchen would be her favorite place.

Mr. Lester entertained Millie and Magdala with tales about

unclogging stopped pipes, explaining to Millie his slogan, "A flush every time," which included a drawing of a poker hand, a royal flush, on the side of his paneled truck.

When they had finished their supper, Millie grabbed her suitcase from the hallway and followed Magdala up three floors to the turret.

The room was small, but just right for a young, lost country girl. From the windows Millie could see the lights from downtown Mason. Magdala showed Millie the small adjoining bathroom which had a toilet, sink, and a bathtub with claw feet. This would be the first indoor bathroom Millie had ever had. She couldn't believe her luck.

After Magdala left, Millie washed her face and fell into the bed. She fell asleep listening to the crickets and feeling that same soft fall breeze that had welcomed her to Miss Sarah's.

Chapter 2

Awakened from a deep sleep by a sharp rap at the door to her turret bedroom, Millie sat up, pulling the bedclothes around her shoulders. Miss Sarah came in, moving as if on wheels. She had a tray which she set down on a small table by the fireplace.

"Get up, Millie. It's five-thirty. Bathe and wash your hair. Put on these clean clothes. Eat some breakfast and then come down one floor to my rooms. My study is at the end of the hall. We'll talk about your job here at my boarding house."

"Yes, ma'am," was all Millie knew to say, but the words "your job" gave her a start. Oh, my goodness, was all she could think.

Miss Sarah left as smoothly as she had come in, gently closing the door behind her.

Millie could smell the freshly baked biscuit and fried bacon. Suddenly she was ravenously hungry. Miss Sarah had laid out breakfast on a tray lined with a linen napkin: a golden-brown biscuit slathered in butter and two crisply fried strips of bacon. A cup of coffee lightened by milk, but still steaming, was set alongside the biscuit and bacon. Millie stuffed one strip into her mouth. Oh, how good it tasted.

She was determined to make the biscuit last, so she tore off small bits, even letting the sweet butter run down her hand as she ate. Washing it all down with the coffee, she finished up, wiping her hands and lips with the linen napkin.

Miss Sarah had left a neat pile of clothes: a chemise, step-ins, and a cotton drop-waist dress. New clothes. All Millie knew to do was to press the pile into her nose and breathe in their freshness.

In the bathroom she filled the tub with warm water and stripping down she stepped into the warmth. She lay completely flat in the tub letting the warm water soften and stretch her curls. She bathed quickly, knowing that Miss Sarah was waiting for her downstairs. She dried her body and fluffed her hair, causing the soft curls to reappear.

The bedroom was chilled from the early fall cool night, so Millie quickly dressed, smoothing down the front of her dress once finished. She slipped on her one pair of shoes, scuffed black tee-straps with holes in their soles.

One floor down Millie entered Miss Sarah's living quarters, which included a parlor, bedroom, study, and bathroom, each entered off the hallway. Windows facing the front of the house let in the soft morning light. Decorative prisms hanging from the sashes broke the light into rainbows that bounced against the walls.

The doors to the parlor, bedroom and bathroom were closed, so it was easy for Millie to find Miss Sarah's study.

She hesitated at the door. "Come on in, Millie," Miss Sarah greeted her. "Have a seat."

The walls were paneled with lightly stained pine. On one wall was a floor-to-ceiling bookcase, filled with books. Millie had never seen so many books. Her one-room schoolhouse in Gaston had barely had enough for each child.

Miss Sarah had a green banker's lamp on her desk which lit up a clutter of papers and envelopes. Once Millie was seated, Miss Sarah began.

"Millie, I want to give you a job. I'll pay you $2.00 a week. In addition, you'll have room and board and I'll also supply some clothes at the start of your employment."

"Yes, ma'am," was all Millie knew to say.

"You'll clean my rooms every day, sweeping, mopping, dusting, and cleaning the bathroom. Start out doing what you think is a good job. I'll tell you if it's not good enough. You will also help Miss Cora in the kitchen, same as you did yesterday. She'll tell you what she needs."

Millie nodded.

Miss Sarah looked her straight in the eyes and her tone became stern. "Now, I want to make some things clear. This is a boarding house. If anyone asks you about what goes on here, you will say, 'It's a boarding house like the sign out front says.' If anyone asks you more questions about my boarding house, you simply refer them to me. Understood?"

Millie nodded again.

There was a high window above Miss Sarah, the light from which cast a beam on her head. She sat there anointed by the light. Millie was in awe. Am I now one of her "girls"? she wondered.

Miss Sarah continued in the same stern voice, "You are not to go to the second floor, unless one of the girls invites you. They take care of keeping the rooms on their floor clean."

Her face softened a bit. "Because you are now working for me, I'll have some say in what you wear. I have asked Lucy to take you to town and buy you at least three outfits: two for work-a-day and one Sunday-go-to-meetin' dress. She'll also get you a toothbrush and deodorant. And an alarm clock. You should get up at five o'clock sharp every morning, so you can be downstairs in the kitchen by five-thirty."

Millie nodded.

"Now go on downstairs. Miss Cora is in the kitchen and will tell you what she needs this morning. You can start cleaning my rooms tomorrow. As soon as Lucy gets up, she'll find you in the kitchen and take you to town."

Lucy. Who's Lucy? Oh, yes, she's one of Miss Sarah's girls. One of the angels I saw yesterday, Millie mused.

Millie was not certain that she had been dismissed, so she continued to sit in the chair she had taken in front of Miss Sarah's desk.

"Well, go on now, girl," Miss Sarah said, a bit sharply.

Millie jumped up, tripping on the chair leg, but she quickly recovered her balance and left the room, wondering if she should have curtseyed like you do for a queen.

Taking the backstairs to the kitchen, same as she had come up the night before, Millie found Miss Cora bustling around. "Good morning, country girl," she greeted Millie. "Breakfast gets served at seven o'clock, so we have to shake a leg," she said as she cut biscuits and lined them up on a large cookie sheet. The bacon had already been fried and was stacked in a warm, fragrant pile in the middle of the kitchen table.

As if knowing what Millie's question would be, Miss Cora explained, "You'll be washing pots, pans, dishes, glasses, well, just whatever is dirty and fills that big sink. I'm guessing that you watched where Magdala put things."

Millie filled the sink with warm water. She reached for the big square box of Oxydol soap with its familiar half circles of dark green and yellow, same kind of dry soap she and her ma had used to wash everything — clothes, pots, pans, and themselves. She sprinkled the Oxydol on the water's surface and then made the water churn with the movement of her hands. Making bubbles. She couldn't resist popping a few with her fingers.

For a few seconds she thought of her baby, Louise. She remembered filling the kitchen sink back home with water warmed on the wood stove. And the pure joy of her baby splashing the bubbles. She felt a lump growing in her throat, but quickly reassured herself. Ma will take good care of her. I'll be making $2.00 a week. I can send some home.

She filled the sink with the clutter of pots, pans, dishes, and spoons lying beside it. She had been careful to put on an apron. She didn't want to spoil her dress, new to her, but soon to be one of her work dresses. She felt proud. She had a job; she had a new dress.

The warm fall sun streamed in through the window filling the room with soft morning sunlight. Millie could smell a fresh batch of biscuits coming out of the oven and eggs Miss Cora was now frying to go with the bacon and biscuits. A pot of grits was bubbling on the stove.

"Hi, doll," Mr. Lester greeted Miss Cora as he came through the back door and let the screen door slam. "Got a spare biscuit for your lovin' man?"

"All you gotta do is set yourself down," Miss Cora said without even turning from her frying pan.

"Mornin', Millie. Cora got you workin' for your bread and board?" Mr. Lester warmly greeted Millie.

"Yes, suh," Millie smiled.

Mr. Lester quickly finished his breakfast. "Say, Millie, may I drop my hands into your dishwater so's I can wash them. Need to head on out. No time to go back to the house." Millie stepped to one side. As he turned to leave Mr. Lester tapped his forehead as if in salute to Millie. "Thanks, Miss Millie."

By seven-thirty Millie found herself alone in the kitchen, as Miss Cora was busy tending to the men folk in the dining room and beginning to clear the plates. Breakfast was not a leisurely meal at Miss Sarah's. Each of the four men had things to do, places to be.

Busy in the kitchen, Millie had no way of knowing but only the men were at the table; the girls — or the angels, as Millie thought of them — were still in their rooms upstairs.

Millie was just finishing up washing and drying the pots and pans, setting them on the table as she did, when Miss Cora came through the door. "Millie, it's time you learned how to clean up the dining room. Come along now."

"I didn't know where to put anything, so I just dried 'em and put 'em here," Millie said as she pointed to the table.

"Never mind that, girl. We'll tend to that later."

Millie followed Miss Cora into the dining room. The aroma of eggs, biscuits, and bacon still floated in the air. A bit of morning light was slipping through the front windows, passing through the sheer curtains and falling on the dark oak face of the china cabinet.

Miss Cora set out two square pans on the table, one of which she had filled with warm soapy water, a slight steam rising. "Now, Millie, scrape all the leftovers into this pan," she said as she pointed to the empty pan. "Stack the plates and put the silverware into the pan with soapy water." She continued, "Don't stack the plates too high. Don't want to have you drop and break a stack. Lord only knows what it would cost to replace Miss Sarah's Buttercup china."

Millie held up a dinner plate admiring the delicate yellow blossoms that filled the center and covered the rim. Just holding the plate made her feel rich.

Miss Cora left Millie to the work. All the scraping and stacking made her feel important, accomplished, and prosperous. Knowing she would earn $2.00 by week's end, Millie, made fast work of clearing the plates and silverware and serving dishes.

In the kitchen Miss Cora was stationed at the sink. Much to Millie's relief Miss Cora told her the china washing would be her task, so Millie deposited the stacks near the sink and on the table.

Following Miss Cora's other instructions, Millie rolled up the linen tablecloth, took it to the back yard and gave it a real good shake. The chickens were out of their coop roaming and pecking in the backyard. They clucked and fluttered their way to Millie and began pecking at the remnants of biscuit and bacon floating down from the shaken tablecloth. Millie could tell that this was their morning routine. The hens clucked to each other, talking among themselves about the quality of the biscuits and the new girl.

Millie balled up the tablecloth, leaving it on the back porch near a pot-bellied washing machine. Back in the dining room the morning sun now spread across the long oak table. Using a slightly damp rag, Millie wiped the table down, sliding it across and catching crumbs in a pan. Then she went across the table again with a dry cloth with just the slightest bit of polish on it. As if rewarding her for the work, the morning sun filled the room reflecting off the table, the pine oil smell of the polish now filling the air.

When Millie returned to the kitchen, Lucy, one of the angels, was at the kitchen table nibbling on a cold biscuit and sipping on a steamy cup of milk-lightened coffee. She had one foot propped up on the rung of another chair and was reading a magazine, head tilted, her blonde bob already perfectly coiffed.

Closing the magazine, Lucy looked up. What caught Millie's eye on the cover of the *Redbook* magazine was an article's title and description: "The Girls' Rebellion: A startling and revealing story of the 'younger generation' that everyone should read." What in the world is that? Millie wondered.

"Ready to go shopping?" Lucy asked as she looked squarely at Millie and tossed her head, blonde curls bouncing.

"Uh, I guess so," was all Millie could get out, in awe of this confident, beautiful girl who read about things "startling" and "revealing."

"Well, let's go. We're going to Zimmerman's. It's not far. Miss Sarah has an account there, so we can get whatever you need, plus maybe some extras," Lucy added, winking at Millie.

Millie turned toward Miss Cora who was busy at the sink with her precious china. Miss Cora glanced her way, "Get on outta here, girl. I got this." Millie nodded and turned back to Lucy.

"Thanks, Miss Cora, "Millie said, removing her apron.

They left through the back way, screen door slamming behind them. The warm morning sun kissed their faces, landing on their matching bobs, one light brown, the other blonde.

They walked down Maple Street and made a left turn onto Third Street, Millie reading the sign as they crossed.

They were five blocks away, Lucy explained. Lucy was a few inches taller than Millie, so she strode along stretching her long legs. Millie almost had to skip to keep up.

"Hey, Lucy, wanna a ride?" A truck had slowed down and the man inside leaned across the front passenger seat as he spoke.

"No thanks, Joe. I need the exercise," Lucy responded.

Lucy faced forward and kept walking. Millie did the same.

"Okay, Baby." Joe gave a slight salute and revving the motor headed on into town.

Another truck coming from the opposite direction slowed and the driver shouted, "Good to see you this morning, Miss Lucy. Lookin' good!"

Lucy simply tossed her head and made a slight wave in his direction.

Millie, head down, kept walking.

At Poplar and Third, Millie looked ahead and read "Zimmerman's" on a huge marque across the top of a building. Zimmerman's filled one corner of the intersection of Poplar and Third. Both streets had split lanes with parks that filled the in-between. Walkways ran the length of the parks complete with wrought iron benches every few feet.

Millie and Lucy scampered across the double lanes before the traffic light turned red. A bit out of breath, they giggled as they hopped to the curb and with that hop a strap on one of Millie's shoes broke. Now I really feel "country," she thought.

Lucy looked down when Millie gasped. "We got here just in time. We'll start with new shoes!" she said encouragingly.

Store windows faced Poplar and Third, wrapping the store front. At one end was a mannequin dressed as a mechanic with a satisfied look on his face and a hand resting on a new tire.

There were baby carriages, children's clothing, and toys filling the rest of that double window. Along the front of the store and what immediately caught Millie's eye were the lady and gentleman mannequins dressed to perfection, head to toe. He was wearing a dark gray fedora, lighter gray suit and polished two-toned gray and black shoes. A fine-looking man.

But what held Millie's attention was the female mannequin. She was dressed in a black silk georgette crepe dress, the sleeves sheer crepe to the wrist. Under the dress, neck to hem, was a black and dark brown-patterned slip. The dress was further accented by a faux belt with a rhinestone buckle at the dropped waist. And the shoes were black leather with dark brown straps and trim.

Millie could not stop looking at this vision of feminine couture.

"Millie, come on. We don't have all day," Lucy whispered as she urged Millie forward to the door. Millie shook her head as if to break the spell and nodded in Lucy's direction.

Lucy was all but dragging Millie at this point, as Millie limped along hoping to keep both shoes on her feet.

The big double doors opened into the first floor of Zimmerman's, with cosmetics, jewelry, and perfumes at the front, followed by men's ready-to-wear, shoes and hats, and at the rear piece goods and notions. Midway was the elevator, run by a uniformed young colored woman wearing a cap and white gloves and asking, "What floor, please?"

By now, Millie's shoe had completely given way, so she wore one shoe and held the other. Millie and Lucy pushed their way to the back of the elevator and Lucy with a confident and commanding tone answered, "Ladies ready-to-wear and SHOES. Pronto!" Millie lowered her head and pressed herself into the back corner of the elevator.

The elevator operator pushed the number two button and with a jerk the elevator began to move upward. Millie gasped. A woman in front turned, looked at Millie holding a shoe, her bare foot obvious, and just grunted, "Humph."

Fortunately for Millie, ladies' shoes was the first department as she and Lucy left the elevator. "Okay, just take a seat. I'll look around and see what I think might be the best shoe for you. Maybe we'll get a couple of pairs: one for work and one for dress up!" Lucy was definitely in her element, knowing as she did the fashion world of Zimmerman's.

As Lucy walked away a tall, skinny gentleman wearing a dress shirt, black pants, and a red bowtie came forward and asked if he might assist Millie in fitting her shoes. "I guess so," is all she knew to say.

"Well, now," he began cheerfully "just put your foot up on this slanted part of this here front of the shoe stand and I'll measure your feet length and width, while your friend looks for the styles she thinks might work." Millie just nodded.

Mr. Bowtie made quick work of the measurements and had just finished when Lucy returned bearing two very different types of shoes. One was a black lace-up oxford, the other a sleek tee-strap with cut-out designs on the sides just below the strap.

Lucy announced, "Let's try her size in these two shoes. Do you have some footies she can wear with the oxfords?"

Mr. Bowtie found the shoes in the right size, slipped nylon footies on her feet, and soon Millie was well shod in black oxfords, not the most beautiful shoes, but definitely the most comfortable shoes she had ever worn. She left the department carrying a bag with one empty box and one filled with her dress shoes. Mr. Bowtie had said he'd dispose of Millie's old shoes, holding them as if they were carrion.

The rest of the shopping trip was a whirlwind with Lucy pulling dresses off the racks and handing them to the saleswoman who then dutifully placed the soon-to-be purchases on the sales table. Millie was relieved to be freed from this process, since she had no idea what she needed or how to put together outfits for work or Sunday once she found a church. She'd look everything over, including the gloves, underwear, hose, and garter belt, when she got home and was alone in her turret room.

They had two more stops, one for that all-important purchase, the alarm clock, on the third floor, and the other, toiletries, on the first floor. So back into the elevator with their arms full of the newly purchased finery, they headed to the third floor, the housewares and furniture departments.

"Here, Millie, hold all this," Lucy directed, handing off the purchases she was toting. "I need both hands in order to properly examine these alarm clocks." Just as with the dresses, there were way too many choices for Millie, so she deferred to Lucy, who had now taken on the role of master shopper.

The alarm clocks had similar faces, some with white letters on a black background, some with black letters on a white background. But what Lucy was looking for was the one that would have the loudest sounding alarm. She settled on a blue one with the biggest bell, a bell that sat atop the clock like a big round hat. "Trust me, Millie. You don't want to be late at Miss Sarah's," Lucy said as she raised an eyebrow. "Don't worry. I'll show you how to set it." Millie just nodded.

Back on the elevator, arms loaded, now including a sack with the clock in it, Lucy and Millie bustled out on the ground floor and walked to the personal care department just behind the cosmetics and perfumes. Again, Lucy told Millie what she needed which now included, in addition to the toiletries Miss Sarah had mentioned, a package of sanitary napkins and sanitary belt which Lucy explained she would use during her time of the month. How? was all Millie could think.

All done, they trudged toward the front door. Millie was exhausted. It was now 1:00 p.m. according to the clock above the front door of Zimmerman's. Millie had to be back in the kitchen by 4:00 p.m. That left just enough time to walk home and take her treasures to her turret room, examine them, and maybe grab a cold leftover biscuit in the kitchen before she started her evening chores. Can it really have only been one day since I arrived at Miss Sarah's? Millie mused.

At this point she simply wanted to be alone and quiet, but Lucy jabbered all the way back about her inspired purchases for Millie, how much better Millie was going to look and feel in the new clothes, and how now all Millie needed was a few make-up and hair care tips.

In no time they were retracing their steps up the back stairs at Miss Sarah's and entering Miss Cora's kitchen.

Miss Cora was already there and, to Millie's relief, helped her break free of Lucy. "Now, ladies, you've brought a load of fine things to this house. But I don't have time to hear about your shopping trip, and you, Miss Millie, don't have time to tell me. Get on up to your room with that finery and then come on back down to me. And Lucy, leave her be. You've got things to do too."

Millie turned to Lucy, "Oh, Miss Lucy, you will never

know how much I appreciate what you've done for me today. Maybe I'll be a fine lady like you one day."

"Well, for starters, don't call me 'Miss Lucy.' I'm just Lucy. We're not that much different in age. That 'Miss' thing makes me feel old!" And that ended that. With a toss of her blonde bob, she turned to head up the back stairs. But, before she began to climb the stairs, she winked and asked, "Millie, don't you want to be a blonde like me?"

"Too much for the first day, Lucy. Get on outa here," Miss Cora said as she popped Lucy on the bottom with her dish towel. They all laughed, with Miss Cora shaking her head.

Millie gave Lucy a few minutes to head up the stairs. Miss Cora with her hand on her hip, looked at Millie. "Don't leave the country behind just yet, Millie. Keep your eyes peeled and your thinking cap on. Not everything that glitters is gold."

Millie had no idea what that meant as she climbed the stairs. But no need to figure it out right now. She had treasures to open. Hmmm…she might even brush her teeth before going back down to the kitchen.

In her turret retreat Millie opened the Zimmerman bags and cardboard carry cases. Lucy had purchased three dresses: two for every day and one for special occasions. Millie wanted first to see what Lucy had chosen for those dress-up times. And there folded neatly in the carry case was the same dress featured in the store window with a few minor differences.

Same sheer sleeves, but the dress was a lovely sky blue, with matching sky-blue slip. Same rhinestone buckle but at the drop waist, instead of a smooth skirt, the dress fell into soft pleats.

And in the soft folds of the dress was a cloche hat and gloves the same color as the dress. Millie gasped. She had not even noticed that Lucy had slipped this hat in with the other purchases.

Millie simply couldn't help herself. She hugged the dress, a perfect Sunday dress, a lady's dress. Maybe I'll go to church somewhere this comin' Sunday, she thought.

In her room was a rolling dress rack with five wooden hangers. She carefully placed the slip and then the dress atop the slip on the hanger. She caressed the fabric. "For me," she said aloud. Then she gently laid the cloche hat and the gloves on the shelf above the rack.

The day dresses were serviceable, but tasteful. Both were of plain cotton fabric, one dark blue, the other dark green. Each had lace trim around the neck and on the wrists. Both had drop waists but had no belt accent. Millie hugged them, too.

They would be her everyday dresses, but she treated them like the wardrobe of a queen, carefully hanging each on its own hanger. She left the dress shoes in their shoe box. No need for dust to spoil the finish.

Counting the dress Miss Sarah had given her, Millie now had three everyday dresses, plus a very comfortable pair of work shoes for every day. She would keep her "country" dress as a spare.

At Zimmerman's Lucy had set and wound Millie's alarm clock which now clearly showed 3:30 p.m. Millie decided she'd take the clock to Miss Cora to make certain an alarm had been set for 5:00 a.m.

She had just enough time now to brush her teeth. She scrambled to the bathroom, toothbrush and paste in hand.

She smiled and brushed and smiled and brushed. I have beautiful teeth, even if I am just a bit bucktoothed, she thought as she spat the last bit of toothpaste into the sink. This was the first time Millie had used real toothpaste. At home she had brushed her teeth with a mixture of salt and baking soda, using a frayed stick as a brush.

Alarm clock in hand, Millie scurried down the stairs, humming the tune of her favorite hymn, "Amazing Grace."

Miss Cora looked up from the chicken pieces she was dredging in flour. "Well, country girl, if you can hum, you can sing."

"Not right now, Miss Cora," Millie began. "I need you to check the alarm clock Lucy bought and make sure it's set all proper now."

Miss Cora walked across the kitchen to the sink and stuck her hands into the hot soapy water with the dirty pots and pans Magdala was beginning to wash.

Wiping her hands on her apron, Miss Cora reached out for the clock. Turning it over, she examined the back. "See here these two stems. One is to wind up the time and the other is to wind up the alarm." Miss Cora tested the stems and announced, "They're both fully wound. You'll have to do this every day. Now look here on the back. See the words 'pull alarm'?"

At this point Magdala had joined the lesson in clock design, so all three of them were now studying the back of the small blue alarm clock.

"So," Miss Cora continued, "you pull this out to make the alarm work. It's already pulled, and you'll need it like that for every day except Sunday. Maybe just leave it like it is even for Sunday. Now these other two things here set the alarm and set the clock. Just read the back here: 'set alarm' and 'set time'."

She finished up, saying, "All I got time for now, chile. Go take your clock back upstairs and hurry back."

Millie was up and back in a flash. "Lord, chile, you got some fast legs!" Miss Cora commented, looking up from the chicken pieces, drumsticks, breasts, wings, and thighs, now floured up and lined up in neat rows ready to become crispy, tender delicious fried chicken after a passage through the hot bubbling lard in the heavy black cast iron skillets.

"Millie, you're going to learn how to make fried potatoes. Let me show you how to cut these spuds."

Miss Cora produced a broad-bladed chef's knife and taking one of the freshly washed and scrubbed russets cut the potato crosswise and lengthwise. Then with the skill of many years and many spuds, she whacked away, producing eight wedges.

Millie looked on, wide-eyed. Miss Cora, knife in hand, turned toward Millie. "Here you go," she started, but she hesitated. Lips parted and then licked Millie was now looking from knife to potato and then to Miss Cora.

Millie squinting her eyes and raising her shoulders, close to a shrug, reached for the knife, but Miss Cora moved her arm back, and glancing at the iron skillets and floured chicken parts, shook her head and asked, "Do you know how to fry chicken, 'cause I don't want your blood all over my russets?"

"Uh-huh," Millie answered, as her shoulders relaxed.

"Well, then," Miss Cora continued, "I'll put the first batch in the grease. Thighs and drumsticks take longer, so you'll fry them together," she explained as she placed chicken thighs and drumsticks in the first frying pan. "Breasts and wings go together. They fry up faster. There now. Here's a long-handled two-pronged fork." She paused. "Put on an apron, girl. Keep your dress nice."

Millie nodded.

The fall weather in Mason was unpredictable. It could be chilly in the morning and turn hot by afternoon. This was one of those days. Standing over the frying chicken, Millie began to sweat. Between the turns of thighs, drumsticks, breasts, and wings, she reached up to wipe her forehead.

Putting the knife down, Miss Cora, picked up a long dish towel. "Sit down in that chair," she directed Millie. Millie complied. Spreading the towel smooth across Millie's forehead, Miss Cora wrapped it around the back and finished up in front where she tied it in a knot. Now Millie's curly bob popped out from under the white towel which now caught the sweat.

"Better?" Miss Cora asked. "Now you're really one of us," she winked at Millie.

Yes, I am, Millie thought. Yes, I am.

Soon the chicken lay crisp and brown on a china platter. Pushing Millie aside and into a chair with a gentle nudge, Miss Cora took command of the iron skillets. She scooped up a spoon of white lard from a Crisco can and dropped it into the chicken grease. From a can atop the stove she added bacon grease saved from breakfast.

Miss Cora stirred the melting shortening and bacon fat until all dissolved into clear, hot grease. Satisfied, Miss Cora dumped the freshly cut potatoes into the grease.

The combination of smells — fried bacon and potato — made Millie's mouth water and her stomach churn. Her last meal had been the biscuit at breakfast.

"Wanna try one?" Miss Cora set a plate of fried potatoes in front of Millie. "You'll need to wait a bit or you'll burn your mouth."

Millie leaned over the potatoes and drew in the richness of those solid, now brown and crispy chunks. Once the pieces were not hot to the touch, she began to nibble the crispy edges. Oh, my, she thought. This is the best thing I have ever put in my mouth. As soon as she could safely take a bite, she did. And one after the other the five pieces of fried spuds disappeared.

"Rest time over, Millie," Miss Cora said, "Get back here to the frying pan and finish up these here potatoes. I need to get the rolls in the oven."

It was now five o'clock and Millie knew that the gentlemen guests would soon be making their way to the dining room. Magdala had finished washing the sink full of pots and pans and was beginning to pour freshly brewed tea into nine thick-walled crystal glasses. She had already chipped ice from the huge block in the ice box. She carefully placed chips into every glass, popping a few into her mouth and offering some to Millie.

"Millie, take that dish towel off your head before you start taking platters into the dining room."

Millie thought that odd, but she complied. "Yes, Miss Cora."

Millie carried the tray filled with tea glasses to the table and placed them just above the tips of the knives as Miss Cora had shown her.

It was all coming together now, and Millie marveled at how Miss Cora could make every part of the meal get done at the same time.

Magdala and Millie carried platters of food into the dining room. Just as before four gentlemen, freshly washed, coiffed, and smelling of Old Spice cologne, were seated at the table.

Miss Cora made a grand entrance with the fried potatoes. Those familiar with this dish spoke up. "Oh, Miss Cora. I sure came at the right time. Can't wait to get my mouth around a few of these!" And "Miss Cora, these are a perfect match for your famous fried chicken!"

Millie stood behind Miss Sarah holding a pitcher of tea, ready to replenish the glasses as needed. From this spot she could survey the room and clearly see the girls as they glided in, resplendent in their beautiful dresses.

But as Millie scanned the room her eyes fell on a particular gentleman; in fact, he was the one sitting closest to Miss Sarah. He was young. In fact, Millie was certain he must be around her age, sixteen or seventeen, and he looked terrified.

His dark black hair was parted and slicked down. Sweat was forming on his forehead and, head down, he was just moving food around on his plate rather than eating. One of the girls sat down next to him and he just turned her way and nodded. It was Lucy, never at a loss for words. She was chattering away, and he seemed a bit relieved that he would not have to talk. In fact, he was even trying one of the fried potatoes.

At that point he looked up and saw Millie looking his way. As if reading his mind, Millie just smiled and nodded. Millie recognized his pained expression which clearly said, "Please get me out of here." He sighed and began nibbling at the drumstick on his plate. Millie thought, He must not want to be with all these grown folks. He's bashful.

"Millie, you can begin removing the serving plates now," Miss Cora directed as she came up behind Millie. "And bring in the dessert plates for the chocolate cake. I'll get the cake."

"Yes, ma'am."

In the kitchen Millie again found Lester Butterfield at the table, his plate full of chicken, potatoes, string beans, and rolls.

"You ladies made a fine meal tonight," Mr. Lester said as he winked at Millie, his blue eyes sparkling. "Guess I'll have to wait on getting some chocolate cake. She ain't cut it yet."

Miss Cora came in right behind Millie, lifting the cake plate from the kitchen counter and pivoting to return to the dining room. She looked back at Mr. Lester. "Honey, I made two cakes, so don't you worry none about getting a big, fine piece. Just let me cut it. I don't want you tearing up my cake with your slicin' like a plumber."

"Okay, baby. I can wait," Mr. Lester smiled.

It was all winding down now. Millie stood by the china cabinet as Miss Cora cut the cake and Magdala passed pieces to everyone at the table.

Miss Sarah stood and as she did, she looked around the table, saying, "Brandy and cigars in the parlor, gentlemen. Hazel has some beautiful selections prepared for us on the piano."

Making small talk as they left the dining room, they made their way to the parlor. Millie was left alone in the dining room. She knew what to do. First, she returned to the kitchen and filled one pan with hot, soapy water for the silver. Then she set that pan inside another pan which she would use to scrape leftovers from the plates. Finally, she would carefully stack the fine china and take that to the kitchen.

She kept thinking about the boy and his terrified look. She wished the two of them could have sat on the back steps and looked for fireflies, maybe there would have been a few flitting over the back garden.

It was almost seven o'clock. Magdala had gone home with Mr. Lester, so she could get her homework done. Miss Cora was at the sink finishing up washing the china plates and silver. The rest of the kitchen had been tidied up, the iron skillets wiped out and resting on the stove awaiting the morning's bacon and egg frying.

"Miss Cora, is there anything else you need me to do?" Millie asked as she stood by the back stairs, hoping her day was almost done.

"No, chile. You've had a big day. All of this will get easier. Go on up to bed now. Five o'clock in the morning comes early. I'll see you down here around five-thirty. Good night and God bless." Miss Cora never turned around from her sink full of suds and dishes.

"Thank you, Miss Cora, for being so kind to me."

"Go on now, Millie. I'm grateful, too." Then Miss Cora began to sing, "Go down, Moses, way down in Egypt land. Tell ole Pharo---a---ro. Let my people go."

Millie walked up the stairs to her turret room. Grateful. That is how I feel. I just wish I had a pencil and paper. I'd write a letter to Ma and Louise. Well, I'd better bathe so I'll be ready to head to the kitchen at five-thirty tomorrow.

She slipped off her clothes in the bathroom. Filling the

tub with hot water she stepped in and lay down, taking her underclothes with her to wash out in her bath water. Just as she had done earlier that day, she lay down flat in the tub of hot water and rested there. In her mind she began to compose a letter to her mother and her daughter.

Dear Ma and Louise,

I am living in Mason now and I have a job. I clean and cook for a fine lady named Miss Sarah. I've been here one day and already I have new clothes. I'll be paid $2.00 every week. I'll send some home to you. Maybe Buck, he's the man who brought me here, can deliver the money to you on his way home. He lives in Savannah.

Louise, you mind your grandma now, you hear. I love you and miss you every day.

Your Ma,

Millie

I'll write it down tomorrow, Millie thought as she dried off and rinsed out her step-ins and chemise. After squeezing out all the water with her towel, she hung them on her clothes rack hoping the night breeze would dry them.

Lucy had bought her two more sets of underwear, but Millie wanted to save those for a bit. Instead she pulled on the threadbare nightgown she had brought from home.

She lay down in the bed, listening to the whippoorwills and owls calling out in the night. As the night wore on, she got colder and pulled the blanket up and tucked her head under the covers. Blessed rest.

Chapter 3

The little alarm clock did her job, clanging her bell at exactly 5:00 a.m. Millie rubbed her eyes, stretched, and made her way to the bathroom. Just enough time to wash her face, brush her teeth, and pee before getting dressed and heading downstairs to Miss Cora's kitchen.

In her usual efficient scurry, Miss Cora had bacon frying and biscuit dough ready for rolling and cutting. "Mornin', Millie. You look mighty chipper this mornin.' Gonna teach you how to cut biscuits today. Put that apron on now. Come here and stand by me and watch what I do." She put her long brown fingers into the dough and began to knead. Then, she flopped the ball of dough onto a dusting of flour on the kitchen table.

She took the rolling pin and after a few back and forths the ball was a smooth, flat expanse of dough. Taking a tea glass, she began cutting the dough and placing these big round pieces onto a baking sheet.

"Here, Millie, you finish up. I'll come re-roll the dough once you've cut this first batch." With that Miss Cora returned to the ever-present black cast iron skillet and began frying another batch of bacon.

By seven o'clock the meal was ready. Millie had already set

the table and started taking platters of bacon, eggs, grits, and biscuits into the dining room.

The gentlemen began to arrive, only three this time. The young one was not among them. Millie wondered if he had left last night and gone home. He sure looked like he didn't want to be at Miss Sarah's.

Millie helped serve the eggs, bacon, grits, and biscuits. The men made fast work of breakfast, smiling as they ate, satisfied with their stay at Miss Sarah's. "These are the best biscuits I've ever had," one of them cooed to Miss Cora, who, with hand on her hip and looking down at him, rolled her eyes. "Go on now, eat the rest of your eggs," she said laughing as she returned to the kitchen.

After the men were gone, Millie began the clean-up process she had learned the day before. She brought the two pans from the kitchen, one with hot soapy water, the other empty. She scraped plates into one and put the dirty silverware into the hot soapy water. Then she took a stack of china to Miss Cora who was at the sink washing the dishes.

Returning to the dining room she balled up the linen tablecloth. She hoped the hens would be out of the coop and at the foot of the back stairs. They were, and clucked and picked at the biscuit pieces falling from the tablecloth as Millie shook it. "Not gonna let you get any of the egg pieces. That'd just be wrong. Like eatin' your babies." The hens clucked a little more. One hen looked up at Millie and appeared to wink at her. Millie quickly named her Henny Penny after one of her favorite childhood stories. "Henny, it's the biscuits that are falling, not the sky," Millie told the hen.

She finished up in the kitchen and climbed the stairs to Miss Sarah's floor where she would start cleaning her rooms.

Miss Sarah was in her parlor when Millie arrived. Next to her was a contraption the likes of which Millie had only seen in catalogs. It was, Miss Sarah explained, a vacuum cleaner which would, with the power of electricity, suck up all the dirt that may have accumulated in the carpet.

"Millie, all you'll need for cleaning my rooms is right here. Rags, bucket, Oxydol soap. As I told you yesterday, do your best job, and I'll let you know how you can get better. But I will show you how to use the vacuum cleaner, so pay attention."

Miss Sarah walked across the room taking the long electric cord attached to the vacuum cleaner with her. She plugged it in at a wall socket.

"Now, Millie, if you forget how to turn it off or if something happens and you need to stop it real quick, remember, you can just pull this plug."

Millie studied the socket where the plug had been placed and nodded.

"I'm going to turn it on. It may be loud, so just watch what I do," Miss Sarah continued.

Using the left toe of her satin slipper, she hit the start button and the bag on the vacuum cleaner swelled up. Millie was fascinated. Miss Sarah then began to push the machine along. Millie could hear it eating up some loose dirt which crackled as it made its way to the bag. This will make my job so easy, Millie thought.

"Now, you try it, Millie," Miss Sarah said as she turned it over to her.

Millie pushed it along a bit and smiled.

"Easy, isn't it?" Miss Sarah said as she nodded. Millie nodded in return.

"Well, carry on, Millie," Miss Sarah said as she walked from the room.

Millie began to move the vacuum cleaner across the center of the rug. As she backed up to start another swath of the rug the machine caught the fringe and would no longer move.

Dropping the handle, Millie moved to the front of the

vacuum cleaner and pulled on the rug. The machine refused to let go. Millie then got down level with its square head, her nose to its nose. Putting one foot on each side of the vacuum cleaner's head she began pulling as hard as she could. The contraption began to whine and cough and smoke. Oh, Lawd, I'm killing it, Millie thought.

Just when she thought she couldn't pull any harder the vacuum cleaner stopped. Miss Sarah had come in and pulled its plug. There she saw Millie sprawled on the floor in mortal combat with the machine attempting to wrestle the rug from the thing's mouth.

Miss Sarah hid her smile with her hand and spoke harshly to Millie. "Get up off the floor, Millie. You may have just ruined my expensive vacuum cleaner. You will pay for the repair or if it can't be repaired you will pay for a new one. You will get no weekly pay until this thing is repaired. Now go downstairs and get a broom and dustpan. Then come back up here and get back to work."

Millie was crying so hard she was shaking, "Yes, ma'am," she muttered between sobs.

She stumbled downstairs to the kitchen. Miss Sarah just stood there shaking her head and smiling, If she can wrestle a machine like that, what in heaven's name would she do to a man?

Millie was relieved that Miss Cora was not in the kitchen, so she could retrieve the broom and dustpan without the shame of explaining her tear-stained face.

Back upstairs she was equally relieved that Miss Sarah had left her parlor and pulled the rug free from the vacuum cleaner and set the miserable machine in the corner of the room.

The morning sun was coming through the high windows and casting sunbeams along the floor. Millie moved from one beam to the next pretending to dance with her partner the broom. She was cheered by the sun. Looking up she whispered, "Thank you."

There was a trash can in the parlor which she used to empty her dustpan. Some of the dust floated through the sunbeams giving another dimension to those rays.

Millie made quick work of dusting the furniture in the room. She straightened the few books that lay on the low table fronting the sofa.

The next room was Miss Sarah's bathroom. Millie carried the bucket in which she had placed the Oxydol soap box and rags. She pushed open the door and could not believe what she saw.

The room seemed twice as large as Millie's turret bedroom. The floor was tiled in a pattern of eight grayish-white tiles surrounding one black tile of the same size. Looking straight ahead, Millie saw an elegant bathtub set in a fully tiled arched space which featured a circular window which now allowed those mischievous morning sunbeams to dart about the room. Just to the left of the tub was a clear door. What that room was for Millie could only guess.

To Millie's left was a pedestal lavatory with a large, framed mirror above it. To her right were two vanities with shiny glass tops and even larger framed mirrors hanging above them. On the vanities were combs and brushes with silver handles, in addition to various jars and bottles neatly lined up.

Millie stood there taking it all in as the morning sun fell on her soft, light brown curls. "One day I'll have a bathroom like this, and Louise can take a bath in the tub with bubbles from some fine soap, not Oxydol," Millie said aloud.

First Millie investigated the room with the clear door and found that it was a shower. She had never had one but knew that some folks did make them for outside out of garden hoses strapped to trees. You couldn't get naked when you used those, not like Miss Sarah's shower room. "I'll have one of those too," Millie sighed.

She scrubbed the tiles in the shower and around the tub. Then she scrubbed the tub, toilet, and lavatory. Finally, she wiped down the glass tops of the vanities and mopped the floor.

She still had one more room to clean, the bedroom. She didn't know about Miss Sarah's office, but it was further down the hall, just past the bedroom.

Millie opened the door to the bedroom carefully just in case Miss Sarah was in there. The room's focal point was a massive bed, headboard and footboard of stained fruitwood veneer, with metal ornamentation atop the ends of the footboard and bas-relief dark metal sculptures across the headboard.

Millie could not resist examining these. The figures on the footboard were cupids. Millie recognized the impish creatures from Valentines she had seen at the one country store in Gaston; she had never been able to buy any. The cupids had their bows and arrows ready and pointing toward the bed.

On either side of the headboard were identical sculptures. Again cupids, but this time there were multiples of cupids, each one with a bow and arrow chasing the other ones. And the center-most bas-relief featured people. A man dressed in a ruffled collar and vest was grabbing the arm of a woman and a sleeve of her off-the-shoulder dress was sliding off and exposing a bit of her breast. Next to her was a collection of cupids, some flying, some standing. All had their arrows aimed at the man and woman.

Millie gasped. She had never seen the likes of this. The room had a fireplace over which was a large oval mirror facing the bed. On one side of the room was a vanity, with a soft cushioned chair. On the other side was a four-drawered chest-of-drawers with lady chairs on each side. Another plat-formed mirror sat atop the chest-of-drawers.

There were two rugs on the wooden floor. Millie was relieved that she did not have to use the vacuum cleaner; she just knew she would have sucked the fringe on these right up.

She swept and dusted and straightened the room. The bed had been made, so she didn't have to do that. She'd need to ask Miss Sarah about that. But, based on the decorations on the bed, Millie was relieved that she didn't have to see the condition of the sheets.

It was almost 1:00 p.m., according to the clock in Miss Sarah's bedroom, so Millie packed up her bucket, Oxydol, rags, broom and dustpan and moved toward the stairs. She had already dumped the bucket water into the toilet and flushed it down. She hoped that would be okay. Tomorrow she'd ask Miss Sarah about when she should clean her office. She didn't have the courage to do that today. She stowed the cleaning gear in the closet in Miss Sarah's parlor where she had shown her.

Millie went to the kitchen and began looking around for something to eat. She saw a bowl of apples and selected one. That plus a cold biscuit and bacon would be her midday meal. She found leftover banana pudding in the refrigerator, that amazing box with the round cap atop that whirred. Millie had only seen them in the Sears catalog and now she had one…well sort of!

She found a small dish for the biscuit and a bowl for the pudding which she set out complete with a napkin and knife to spread the butter on her biscuit. She did enjoy these made-up meals, a bit of this, a bit of that. It was nearing two o'clock and she had just enough time to sit on the back steps for a while. The warm fall sun was kissing her cheeks. Millie drifted off to sleep leaning against a porch column. And that's where Cora found her at three o'clock when she came up the steps.

"Millie, wake up, chile, time to get supper started. You must have worked hard this morning or maybe that ole sun just put you to sleep, smiling down on you like he's doin'."

"Oh, Miss Cora, I'm so sorry, "Millie said as she stood and pressed her hands against her dress, smoothing it down.

Now in the kitchen Miss Cora began busying herself with supper preparation, beginning with the apple pies.

"Miss Cora," Millie hesitatingly began, "do you have paper and a pencil I could use to write my ma and my baby. I ain't got none."

Miss Cora, pausing from her work, walked over to the drawer of a desk tucked under the stairs.

"Here, chile, take what you need," she said as she handed Millie a box of stationery.

Millie wiped her hands on the napkin and then opened the stationery box. Inside she found pages of light blue stationery and envelopes. The sheets of paper were embellished with a sketch of Miss Sarah's house and the words "Miss Sarah's Boarding House" in a sweeping loopy font. Smaller letters stated: "Maple Street, Mason, Georgia." A smaller version of the house and smaller font decorated the left top of the envelope.

"Oh, Miss Cora, are you certain I can use this. It's so fancy."

"Yes, doll, free advertisin' for Miss Sarah, even if in some cases she doesn't want it. Special customers and all."

So there on the kitchen table in her favorite room at Miss Sarah's, Millie began to compose her letter.

Dear Ma,
I am here now. I gets paid once the thing I broke gets fixed.
Tell Louise to mind you. Kiss her for me. Please write me.
Love.
Millie

Millie signed her letter, folded it, and slipped it into an envelope. On the front she wrote: "Martha Martin, Rte. 1, Gaston, Georgia."

Looking up at Miss Cora, Millie asked, "May I also have a stamp, Miss Cora?"

"Look in the box, chile."

Millie found a red two-cent stamp with George Washington in profile. She licked it and stuck it on the front of the envelope.

"Now take it out front to the mailbox on the fence. Lift up the flag. It won't go today, but tomorrow for sure," Miss Cora told her.

Millie took her letter to the mailbox on the front picket fence. Opening the box, she slid her letter in, closed it and then carefully lifted the little red metal flag. She felt proud. She had a job. She had new clothes. Looking down at her feet she sighed, I have real nice shoes.

Sending a letter off felt almost like being back home in Gaston. She nodded her head, turned, and skipped up the front walk and bounced up the front stairs, taking two at a time.

Back in the kitchen Miss Cora announced to Millie, "We're havin' meatloaf, mashed potatoes, and green beans, with rolls and apple pie. Might even find a dollop of vanilla ice cream to plop on top." She placed big russet potatoes already peeled and cut into quarters into a pot of boiling water on top of the stove.

"You're gonna learn how to make mashed potatoes from scratch, Millie."

I have so much to learn, Millie thought, but I ain't been here long. Maybe there's hope for me after all.

Millie could smell the sweet brown sugar, butter, cinnamon, and apples that hung in the air as those delicious pies baked.

"This here is a potato smasher," Miss Cora said as she handed Millie a kitchen tool she had never seen. Millie could see how it would work, a red wooden handle attached to a flat open grate at the end.

"We always just used a fork at home," she said. "This'll be a lot easier."

"Once the spuds are done, you can start smashing 'em. Add butter and plenty of salt and pepper. You can put 'em in this here metal bakin' tin. We may have to keep 'em warm in the oven."

Millie sat down at the table and watched Miss Cora press the ground beef mixed with breadcrumbs and onions into several large loaves.

Sooner than she would have imagined, Millie had a big bowl filled with boiled pieces of russet potatoes. She knew that she had strong arms, so she began mashing, or as Miss Cora called it "smashing," the potatoes. Soon she had a bowl filled with soft, white, steamy potatoes. She piled in table-spoons full of butter and then, remembering what her mother always did, cupped her hand and filled the palm with salt.

"Miss Cora, would this be too much salt?"

Miss Cora paused and smiled, "No chile, that's about right."

Millie continued smashing potatoes until Miss Cora told her to stop. She then carefully scraped them into the deep baking dish Miss Cora had set on the table.

By then she could smell the onions and meat melding as the meatloaves simmered in the oven.

"Oh, chile, we runnin' out of time. I wish Magdala didn't have so much homework. We really need her help tonight. Get on in the dining room now and make sure the table is set."

Millie quickly pushed open the dining room door. She made certain that every place had a napkin, plate, knife, fork, and spoon. She could hear the men beginning to make their way from their rooms down the hall from the kitchen. They were talking and laughing. They were looking forward to a good meal and a good evening at Miss Sarah's.

Millie was beginning to understand the routine of supper time. She was confident now that she knew exactly how to help Miss Cora. Soon all the parts of the meal had made it to the table: meatloaves, mashed potatoes and gravy, green beans, and rolls.

"I've got apple pie and ice cream for you gents if you clean your plates," Miss Cora teased.

"I'll bet I could eat two pieces, Miss Cora. I'll clean my plate twice," a sandy-haired, heavyset gentleman quipped.

Just as she had done the previous two nights, Millie stood by with a pitcher of tea. The cracked ice was in a bowl on the shelf of the china cabinet. She scanned the room. The girls were each leaning in and chatting with their gentlemen, giggling now and then, and fluttering their lashes. Millie mentally practiced these moves which she believed demonstrated a lady's manners. She wanted to be a lady, too.

Soon Miss Sarah, the gentlemen, and the girls were strolling toward the parlor. One of the girls, whom Millie had learned was named Hazel, told them that she would be playing the piano for them. As Millie cleared the table, she could hear Hazel's beautifully played music. The group was settling into an enjoyable time. Millie smelled tobacco: some the sweet smell of pipes, some the acrid smell of cigars, both overpowering the smell of cigarettes she was certain was there as well.

And she heard the clink of glasses as the men toasted the evening and the brandy they were sipping, not easily obtained in these days of Prohibition.

When Millie returned to the kitchen for the last time, Mr. Lester was finishing up his second piece of pie. Miss Cora was at the sink. "Get yourself something to eat, Millie. Then you can finish up in the dining room."

Millie nodded and smiled. She was hungry and exhausted. She found a good chunk of meatloaf, not really a slice, but a crispy, browned end piece. The potatoes had gone cold but were still buttery. The green beans floating in the fat back seasoned juice had been sitting on the stove, so they were still soft, warm, delicious.

Mr. Lester was soon wiping his mouth and getting up. "Enjoyed watching you eat, Millie. A compliment to Miss Cora's cooking."

He walked over to Miss Cora, kissing her on the cheek, and gave her a light pat on her fanny. Without even looking his way, Miss Cora smiled, "Get on outta here, Lester. I'll be home in a bit."

"I'll be there," Mr. Lester said as he pushed through the back door into the cool fall night. "I'll be there. I may be asleep in my chair, but I'll be there," he chuckled as he left.

After cleaning her plate, Millie returned to the dining room and finished clearing the table and shaking out the linen tablecloth. When she returned to wipe down the dining room table, she heard singing coming from the parlor. The gentlemen and girls were singing as Hazel played. Millie recognized the song, "Swanee." She had heard that song on the radio.

It was nearing eight as Millie finished up. "Need anything else, Miss Cora?"

"No chile, go on to bed and don't forget to wind your clock."

"Yes, ma'am."

Legs aching, Millie trudged up the stairs.

After bathing, she filled the tub again and put all that she had worn into the warm soapy water. She'd let it soak overnight. Get the sweat out. She finished up by brushing and admiring her teeth. Look at me. I've got a store-bought toothbrush!

After she wound her clock, she looked at her clothes rack and selected her outfit for the next day. "Yes, I think I'll wear the new blue dress tomorrow," she said aloud.

She turned on her side in her bed and looked out the window at the stars and moon. Thinking of all her good fortune, she fell asleep, whispering, "Thank you, Lord."

Chapter 4

At five o'clock the little blue alarm clock woke up and began to chime with such enthusiasm she almost walked off the bedside table. In her eagerness to stop the racket Millie knocked the little timekeeper off the table.

But the little blue clock was built to withstand such a tumble. Millie pushed the alarm button in and picked up the clock which, with an almost audible sigh, stopped ringing.

Millie quickly dressed and fluffed her hair. Licking and slightly parting her lips, she looked in the mirror to admire the final results. "I'm a workin' lady. Yes, I am."

Downstairs Miss Cora was already busy. Millie knew the routine now and quickly set to work preparing the dining room for the gentlemen. She loved this time of day with the soft morning light touching her face and falling on the Buttercup china and linen tablecloth.

Now it all seemed to fly by in a flash. Cutting biscuits for baking, then serving the bacon, eggs, and grits. After that the sink filled with warm water, Oxydol, pots, pans, but no dishes. It would be a while before Millie would be washing the Buttercup dishes.

Millie had just finished shaking out the tablecloth and

clucking to her hen friends when she heard the girls whispering and giggling as they made their way down the stairs.

As they bounced into the kitchen, Hazel spoke first.

"Oh, Miss Cora, got any of your biscuits left. They're just the bee's knees!"

The other girls, Lucy, Gladys, and Corine, slipping in behind her, giggling, chimed in, "The bee's knees!"

"They're over yonder on the stove. May even still be a bit warm. And bacon is there too." Miss Cora never turned from washing her Buttercup china.

The girls made fast work of finding biscuits, butter, and bacon. Soon they had taken seats at the table.

"Come on, Millie, join us," Gladys offered.

Millie took a chair from the small kitchen desk and carried it to a corner of the kitchen table.

She sat down, daring to be one of the angels, the entertainers of men, the readers of *Redbook*, the wearers of makeup. Millie did not understand much of what they talked about, fascinated as she was by how they each looked: Lucy with her bleached blonde bob, Hazel with her head of tight red curls, Corine with her dark-banged page boy and Gladys with her light brown marcel waves.

The girls fingered their biscuits, breaking off and nibbling bits along with tiny pieces of bacon. Millie wasn't listening to what they were saying, enthralled as she was with their hands. Each one had superbly manicured nails, painted in dark red. They talked with their fingers, moving them like miniature ballet dancers, lithe and elegant. Millie was mesmerized. Each girl had multiple rings, each with a small stone, that caught the morning light, breaking it into rainbows that danced around the kitchen.

And then Millie caught on to the conversation, starting with Lucy.

"I'm telling you he had the biggest hairiest belly I've ever seen."

Gladys chimed in. "Mine had chest hair you could have combed."

Now all four girls began to giggle. Millie's eyes widened.

"You girls got a parlor upstairs. You can keep that talk out of my kitchen," Miss Cora interjected.

"Sorry, Miss Cora," the four said in unison and then started to giggle again.

By then their plates were empty except for a few crumbs. Corine turned toward Millie, "Millie, do you want to see our rooms. And since Miss Cora mentioned it — would you like to see our parlor?"

Millie almost said yes, but then remembered that she had to clean Miss Sarah's rooms. With a sigh, she said, "I need to clean Miss Sarah's rooms now."

"Well, then come to our floor after that. As long as it's not later than 2:00 in the afternoon. We all rest a bit before starting to get all gussied up for the evening," Hazel explained with a wink.

The girls cleared the kitchen table, even using their palms to catch the leftover crumbs as they swept the table clean with their hands.

Lucy spoke for the group, "Miss Cora, anything you need us to do before we go back upstairs to tidy up our rooms?"

"No, chile, just hand me your plates. I still got plenty of suds."

All the girls, including Millie, left by way of the dark stairway, which was still cool, even though the day was beginning to heat up. They reached the second floor and almost in unison cooed, "Later, Millie."

Millic halfway believed she was part of this little sorority as she finished the climb to the third floor.

She started by checking in with Miss Sarah whom she guessed would be in her study.

"Mornin', Miss Sarah," she began. "I thought I'd start with your bedroom unless you have other plans for me."

Head bent over her desk, Miss Sarah looked up, light falling on her face. Millie thought she was dignified and elegant. Certainly the epitome of an independent woman. Maybe I'll be like her one day, she imagined.

"Good morning, Millie. I'll be leaving shortly. Got some business in town. Go ahead and start with my parlor and work your way down the hall. I want you to sweep and dust in here today. Don't move anything. Just sweep and dust the best you can. Oh, and if you want to borrow a book, please do. Just write down the book title on this pad here on my desk. I like to keep up with my books."

Millie had stowed her broom, Johnson paste wax, dust rags, mop, bucket, and a box of Oxydol in a closet in Miss Sarah's parlor. She enjoyed cleaning these rooms. At times she imagined that the tables, sofas, doilies, lamps, and knick-knacks belonged to her as she touched each one.

In one corner of Miss Sarah's parlor was a sewing machine and neatly piled in a large basket to one side were pattern pieces attached to cut fabric. Millie had seen sewing machines; in fact, her ma owned a very old one, but Millie had never learned how to use it. Miss Sarah knows how to sew. All those beautiful dresses. She makes them. Maybe she'd teach me how. She then moved on to Miss Sarah's bedroom. Not much was needed. Miss Sarah had made her bed, so Millie just did her usual dusting and sweeping.

Then on to the bathroom where she straightened up Miss Sarah's collection of makeup and perfume atomizers on the dressing table. Millie took the time to arrange them all by size, taller bottles in the rear, squatty ones in the front. She cleaned the mirror and then stepped back to admire her work. "Nicely done, Millie," she whispered to herself. "Nicely done."

Finally, she made her way to Miss Sarah's study. Miss Sarah had been clear about what could and couldn't be touched, so Millie dusted, swept, and straightened the best she could.

Then she remembered Miss Sarah's offer to lend a book.

What book should I choose? she mused.

Lying on Miss Sarah's desk was a big book, its cover bearing the words *Webster's Dictionary*. Millie ran her fingers across the cover and then carefully opened it. All those words. I need more words. If I know lots of words, I'll sound smart.

She picked up a pencil and wrote in straight, clear letters, "Dictionary."

Millie left the dictionary on the desk, stowed her cleaning tools, returned to Miss Sarah's office, and took the big book with her.

It had taken her much longer than usual to clean Miss Sarah's quarters. It was close to two o'clock and she'd need to be back downstairs in the kitchen by four.

She had two hours to rest and look at her book, her dictionary. She scrambled back up the three flights to her turret retreat, fully intending to lie on her bed and try to read, but she fell asleep with the dictionary across her chest.

"Millie, Millie, wake up. Ma's upset with you. It's 4:30 and we've got to get supper ready."

She slowly opened her eyes. Magdala. Magdala? What's Magdala doing in my room.

Millie jumped up, dictionary tumbling to the floor. "Oh, Magdala, I'm going to get fired." Tears began to well up.

"No, Millie. It's okay. You've been workin' so hard. Come on now. Let's go." Magdala smiled sweetly as she nodded toward the door.

Millie and Magdala scurried down the back stairs to the kitchen. Miss Cora pretended to be angry. With one hand on her hip, she chided, "Millie, girl, am I gonna have to get you TWO alarm clocks?" But then she smiled and said, "We're having salmon croquettes, slaw and sliced tomatoes and lemon meringue pie. I've already made the slaw and slicin' the tomatoes won't take long, but I need both of you helping with the croquettes."

Magdala and Millie washed their hands and took seats at the table where Miss Cora had kitchen knives and big white onions to be sliced. Five cans of pink salmon had been emptied into a big bowl.

"Slice the onions first 'cause I need to give them a dip in the grease before they land in the croquettes. And mind you I don't want any fingers in my croquettes so cut with care."

Magdala and Millie began cutting the onions. Soon tears began to flow. They'd have to stop and wipe their faces on a dish towel and then go back to cutting. Pausing in her work, Millie leaned toward Magdala and joked, "This is the saddest work I've done all day." Magdala nodded and laughed. "We're just a couple of crybabies!"

Soon the onions were ready for their quick trip through the bacon grease. Miss Cora had already turned leftover biscuits into crumbs.

Now the making of the croquettes could begin. Millie and Magdala decided that another bowl would help speed things up. They both then had a nest of salmon and crumbs in their bowls awaiting the fried onions.

"Oh, Lord, I forgot the celery. Here chop this up real fast. Don't need much." Miss Cora handed each of them a celery stalk.

No tears for the celery. Millie and Magdala were soon ready for the onions, which Miss Cora dumped into each bowl.

"Salt and pepper, girls," Miss Cora reminded them.

Then it was time for the mashing together of all those

delicious parts. Millie believed that cooked onions always made any place smell like something truly delicious was being made. Her mind went back to the smell of her ma's dressing made for Thanksgiving Day. "You know, Magdala, I think home smells like cooked onions."

"Millie, you funny. I think home smells like my ma's biscuits."

They both began to giggle. Onions and biscuits…

Miss Cora wanted the croquettes shaped like patties, so the grease could crisp up the edges. She was now overseeing a pan full of them.

Millie had another idea about the smell of home. "Hey, Magdala, maybe home smells like anything that comes out of Miss Cora's iron skillet."

Now all three of them were laughing. The late afternoon was hot, but a slight breeze was lifting the curtains in the kitchen. Miss Cora began to sing, "Go down Moses, way down in Egypt land. Tell ole Pharoah, let my people go…"

She stopped singing to give more orders. "You girls get started on the dirty pots and pans. And clean up the table now. Lester will be here soon. I don't want him to have to eat amidst onion peels. He'll make some kind of crack about it."

Millie took up her post at the kitchen sink, filling it with hot water and topping it off with Oxydol. She loved fluffing up the water and making bubbles and popping a few.

Like all the other nights the pace began to pick up around five and peaked to a frenzy by five-thirty.

It was a different group from the previous nights, and these gentlemen, scrubbed, coiffed and slicked, were a jolly crowd, winking all round. "Gonna be a fine night," one of them laughed.

Millie and Magdala hauled platters of croquettes, slaw, and tomatoes to the table. Millie took up her station in front of the china cabinet, tea pitcher in hand.

One of the gents had a big round belly and Millie wondered if he was the one Lucy had spoken of at breakfast. She had to suppress a giggle.

She knew that Mr. Lester would be in his place in the kitchen when she returned and that Magdala would have gone home to her homework. Sure enough, Mr. Lester, at his place at the kitchen table, had a plate full of croquettes, slaw, tomatoes, and a big slice of lemon meringue pie on a dessert plate alongside his dinner plate.

But as Millie slipped into the kitchen, another man was coming through the back door, a tall white man wearing a uniform like the sheriff she had seen the time Willard Johnson got busted for making moonshine and was hauled through Gaston on his way to jail.

The big, tall white man had removed his big hat as he came through the door. He looked freshly bathed, his face still a bit red from the shaving and scrubbing. And he smelled fresh and spicy.

"Evenin', Lester"

"Evenin', Sheriff."

"I guess Sarah's still with her guests. I'm gonna slip on upstairs if you don't mind."

"Help yo'self, Sheriff," Mr. Lester never looked up from his plate, continuing to enjoy his sweet Cora's fine cooking.

The sheriff lumbered his way through the kitchen and disappeared up the stairway.

As if guessing her question, Mr. Lester looked up. "Yes, Millie, that was our sheriff, Sheriff Sparks. He's, uh, a friend of Miss Sarah's. Comes around about once or twice a week. But, Millie, we never saw him here. Understand?" Lester nodded, looking at Millie for an answering nod.

"Yes, suh, yes, Mr. Lester."

Millie busied herself with the rest of the kitchen clean-up.

When Miss Cora came back to the kitchen, Mr. Lester spoke, "Sheriff's here, Cora."

"Well, it's Thursday," Miss Cora replied. "Lord says, 'foxes have holes and birds of the air have nests.' Mind you, I like knowing where one ole fox is on Thursday nights."

Mr. Lester shook his head, "Cora, you are one wise woman. Maybe that's why I married you, or was it because of this fine lemon meringue pie?"

"You a fool, Lester Butterfield. Jus' a plain fool!" Miss Cora just stood there, hand on hip, shaking her head.

Mr. Lester held up an empty dessert plate. "Cora, dear, may this ole fool have another piece of this fine, divine, lemon pie?"

"Well, you know what, Lester. You can clean this pie plate. There's one piece left, and it has your name on it." Miss Cora handed Mr. Lester the pie plate and as she did their fingers touched.

"Thank you, darlin'," Mr. Lester said as he smiled at his wife.

Millie knew that she could now fix her plate and eat her supper, no longer waiting for Miss Cora's permission. She sat down to eat as Mr. Lester finished up his second piece of pie.

Soon, it was just Millie at the table and Miss Cora at the sink washing her precious Buttercup china. A cool breeze had picked up and Millie could hear the Mason night sounds wafting through the open windows: the crickets and farther downtown a truck downshifting as it made its way through town.

Millie sighed and dug into her slice of pie. Wonder how Louise is doing. Millie felt a catch in her throat and sternly told herself, Ma's takin' care of her. She's jus' fine.

Another day of work was done as Millie climbed up the back stairs following the route the sheriff had taken, but continuing up to her turret room past Miss Sarah's floor where she figured Miss Sarah was entertaining him.

Millie followed the same routine she had done the night before, placing her new blue dress in the fresh warm water she had run after her bath along with a bit of Oxydol soap she had brought up with her from the kitchen. Tomorrow she would wear her new green dress, she decided, and then back to her new-to-her dress from Miss Sarah.

She wound the little blue clock, fell into bed and fell asleep to the night sounds of a small Southern town: owls, crickets, and trucks up and down shifting gears.

Chapter 5

Once again, the little blue clock began chiming at 5:00. This time Millie easily reached her and stopped the chime. Today she was determined to get her work done so that she could visit the girls on the second floor.

Millie quickly rinsed out what she had left soaking in the tub. Squeezing out the water she hung it all on the clothes rack: step-ins, chemise, and dress. What she had worn two days earlier was now dry and ready to be worn again, but oh my, did that dress need the touch of an iron. "I'll ask Miss Cora," she said aloud.

She put on her other new dress, the green one. She smoothed and straightened the front, gave herself a nod and walked toward the door. But something had caught her eye. She had left the dictionary she had borrowed on the bureau, but that book had been replaced by a smaller version which was so worn the pages were held together by a rubber band. A note had been left.

Millie slowly read, "Millie, the dictionary you borrowed is one I use almost every day. I need it. Here's an older one, but it has lots of words, too. A dictionary is more than just a book of words. It's a book full of all kinds of knowledge. I'm glad you want to learn more." It was signed "Miss Sarah."

Millie held the book. It was a Miss Sarah discard. In a way she was a discard, too. Miss Sarah may not have wanted this old dictionary, but it was the first one Millie had ever had. She laid it down on the bureau and gave it a pat.

Soon she was in the kitchen, keeping pace with Miss Cora. As she rolled and cut biscuits, she asked, "Miss Cora, may I borrow an iron and ironing board?"

"You really settlin' in, aren't you, Millie? Not even a week and you really settlin' in. Yes, dear, look on the back porch. You can set up in here and iron after you clean Miss Sarah's floor, but best you be finished before four, 'cause I can't be navigatin' an ironin' board when I'm hoppin' round fixin' supper."

"Yes, ma'am, Miss Cora, ma'am."

Biscuits, bacon, grits, and eggs. Coffee, too. And today Miss Cora had some orange juice. Millie served it all, keeping the coffee cups full just as she did each night with the glasses of tea.

Soon all was done. The gentlemen had slipped away, headed to their work. By the time Millie had finished up in the dining room and was going out the back door to shake out the tablecloth, the girls had arrived and were nibbling on their biscuits.

What they were wearing shocked Millie. Each girl was wearing a one-piece, belted gym suit and soft-soled shoes. And on the floor beside them was a ball.

Hazel saw Millie's surprised look. "Oh, Millie, we're going to play volleyball over the clothesline. Wish you could, too. Come see us in our parlor after you clean for Miss Sarah."

Breakfast done, Lucy scooped up the ball and ran to the door. "Catch me if you can," she teased as she dashed outside.

Hazel, Corine, and Gladys followed her, laughing as they went. They formed teams of two. Lucy and Hazel, taller than Corine and Gladys, each took a side. Lucy gave the orders:

"Corine, you're with me today; Gladys you get on the other side with Hazel."

Each one had a different color bandana catching up her bob. Hazel's red curls were caught up with bright green, Lucy's with dark blue, Corine's yellow, and Gladys's purple.

Mouth gaping, Millie watched from the back door as they batted the ball over the clothesline, at times Lucy or Hazel spiking her shot to the ground.

The few clothes on the line swayed with each spike.

"Close your mouth, Millie, and get back to work," Miss Cora chided. "Those girls deserve a bit of childish fun."

Millie wondered at Miss Cora's meaning as she turned to climb the back stairs to Miss Sarah's rooms. It was still early morning, not yet as hot as it would be by noon on this late September day in Mason, Georgia.

"Never seen the likes of these girls," Millie spoke aloud. She had seen outfits like those the girls wore in the Sears catalogs, but she never dreamed that she would see someone wearing them. "Somethin' new every day 'round here."

Millie thought the girls were as beautiful playing volleyball as they had been when she saw them in all their elegance that first night at Miss Sarah's. Oh, to be like them, she mused. But Millie wondered about a dark side, a sad side. What did Miss Cora mean by "those girls deserve a bit of childish fun"? No matter. I want to finish up here in time to visit them in their parlor.

Millie headed to Miss Sarah's floor and quickly finished cleaning her parlor. And then on to her bedroom.

The bed looked as if someone had had a sleepless night. The bed spread and sheets were tangled, some of them even hanging off one side of the bed.

Millie didn't think that Miss Sarah smoked cigars, but still floating in the air was that acrid, sweet leathery smell of the carefully cured tobacco of a finely crafted cigar, not all together a bad smell. Millie sniffed. She looked around the room and found the remains of that smoke lying in an ash tray on a bedside table.

She dumped it into a small trash can she had been using as she swept and dust-panned the rooms. She hoped that by removing the cigar butt the smell might fade. Maybe she should ask Miss Sarah about ridding the room of that smell. No, she'd ask Miss Cora.

"The sheriff was here last night," Millie said to herself as she cleaned up. "Guess he smoked a cigar."

Millie did her usual thorough job, finishing up Miss Sarah's rooms around noon. She stowed her cleaning gear in the closet in the parlor and climbed to her turret room to freshen up a bit.

She washed her face and pinched her cheeks, hoping they'd look as if they were rouged. Taking a deep breath, Millie began the trip down two sets of stairs to the second floor and the girls' rooms.

The second-floor hallway, identical to Miss Sarah's floor, was dark wood paneled and even at noon still cool. The first room she entered was the girls' parlor. It was small, with one big window that looked out over a few oak trees and the driveway. Millie took it all in. She was alone in the room.

In one corner, placed kitty-corner to the wall, was an upright piano, keys uncovered. Next to the piano was an overstuffed chair near a floor-to-ceiling bookshelf filled with books. Across the opposite wall was a plush dark violet velvet three-cushioned sofa with a coffee table in front filled with *Redbook* magazines. Lucy must sit on this sofa, Millie mused. In the corner by the sofa was a radio. Music was coming from the radio, a brassy, jazzy sound.

What struck Millie as unusual however, was what she saw right in front of the open window: an easel and next to it a variety of brushes and tubes of oil paints.

Millie was standing by the easel when Corine came in the room. "You like my art studio?" Corine said with a chuckle. "The light is really good there. I turned the radio on. Once Hazel gets here, she'll be shutting it off so she can practice the piano." Corine rolled her eyes. "I'm glad you're here," she added as she moved to the easel and Millie moved away and took a seat on the sofa.

Corine continued, "Gladys, Lucy, and Hazel are getting cleaned up after the volleyball game. They'll be along in a bit, unless one of them decides to take a nap. That volleyball in the morning heat can sure take the starch outta you. I'm working on a painting. You're welcome to watch. I'm not one for chatting. Lucy's the one if you want to talk."

Feeling a bit awkward about even being in this room, Millie had sat down carefully on the sofa. She turned her attention to Corine and her careful preparations. She was selecting oils to be squeezed onto her palette. Millie watched her hands as she opened the tubes and squeezed blobs of paint out. I wonder if she ever scrubs floors? Millie mused as she looked at her own hands that were now reddened and rough.

Millie could hear Gladys, Hazel, and Lucy before she saw them as they chattered their way down the hall and came into the parlor in a scrum.

Hazel was the first to see Millie. "Millie! Glad you decided to drop by. I've got some new music to learn, so I'd love having an audience." With that Hazel turned off the radio, set the music on the music rack above the keys, and positioned herself on the piano stool. She began working through the piece measure by measure, at times backing up and starting again.

Lucy grabbed a *Redbook* magazine and flopped down next to Millie. "Wanna play 'favorites'. You'll have the page on the right; I'll have the page on the left. Then we each will say what is our 'favorite' thing on that page." Millie had wanted to be a bystander only. She licked and parted her lips and sighed, "Okay."

Gladys sat down in the overstuffed chair and picked up a book lying on the small table by the chair. Millie could just barely read the spine, *Wuthering Heights*.

Millie and Lucy were into their "favorites" game, laughing over each one's choices and flipping pages in the magazine, when Gladys, looking up from her book, asked, "Millie, what do you like to read?"

Millie looked up and said the first thing that popped into her head, "I have a dictionary I borrowed from Miss Sarah."

It was as if time stopped. Each of the angels paused, Corine at her easel, brush lifted; Hazel at the piano, one hand on her music; Gladys with her hand on her book, and even Lucy looked up from the magazine.

In unison all four said, "A dictionary!" And again, "A dictionary!" Followed by laughter.

Millie felt humiliated. Gladys knew immediately what they had done and started with, "Oh, Millie, that's a great book to start with. So much knowledge crammed in with those definitions."

"Of course," the other three added.

Gladys continued, "Would you like to bring your dictionary to our parlor next time, and you and I can read together?"

Tears trying to burn their way out of her eyes, Millie just nodded. She did not even have to glance at the clock on the wall, she knew it was time for her to go.

"I need to go. You ladies have to get ready for your, uh, evening."

With that Millie unfolded her legs, hopped up and was gone out the door and up the stairs before any one of the girls could object.

After it was clear that Millie was really gone, Gladys spoke,

"We gotta do better, ladies." The rest nodded and then each one went back to whatever lay beneath her hands.

Millie climbed the stairs to her turret room. She fell across her bed. Looking out her window, she berated herself, "They must think I'm the biggest country hick ever. Well, I guess I am. Hazel was nice to me. But, the others, well really all of them laughed at me. But I ain't gonna quit. I got to think about Louise and once the vacuum cleaner is fixed I'll start gettin' paid. I can save up. Send Ma some money for Louise so's Ma can buy her some fine store-bought clothes."

Mille sat up. "Okay, Jesus, let's you and me do some reading."

She picked up the ragged dictionary and took it to her bed where she propped it up and opened to page one.

There she saw the word, "aardvark" and a small picture of the strangest looking animal she had ever seen. To Millie its face looked like a cross between a rabbit and a pig.

She began struggling to read the lengthy definition. She read the words she could: "snout, tongue, claws, ears, and tail." Looking at the picture as she read, she added other words: "long, funny, strong, big, and floppy." She was certain that her words were not the ones on the page, but it was a start. She was sort of reading.

Millie glanced at the little blue clock. Its short hand pointed toward three, its long hand toward twelve.

Millie decided to take care of the ironing she needed to do. She grabbed her dress and down the stairs she went. She had an hour. She moved the iron and ironing board from the back porch then found a spot in the kitchen where she could set up. She had never used an electric iron. The only irons she had ever used were those cast-iron ones that you heated in a fireplace.

Fearing that she might kill the iron, just as she had the vacuum cleaner, Millie spread her dress out carefully on the ironing board and then began to press with all her strength. Nothing was happening. The dress remained as wrinkled as it had been. She leaned harder on the ironing board.

She heard a creak. The ironing board rocked and then fell over carrying the dress with it to the kitchen floor. Millie stood dumbfounded holding the cold iron. Miss Cora was just coming into the kitchen.

"Chile, what in heaven's name are you trying to do?"

Millie stood up straight, the iron at her side and the black cord running along the floor like some long, black snake.

"Give me that iron, girl. Let me show you how to get it hot enough to press out those wrinkles." Millie sheepishly handed it to Miss Cora.

In no time the iron was plugged in and heating up. She watched as Miss Cora licked one finger and tapped the iron. It sizzled. "Don't you go doing this, Millie. I think you're a bit accident-prone. Here now, iron your dress quick as you can. I've got an errand for you to run. I'm sending you to get our fish for supper."

Millie began gliding the iron back and forth across her dress and then finished up with her step-ins and chemise. "What do I do with the iron now, Miss Cora. I don't want to kill it like I did the vacuum cleaner."

"I'll take care of that, Millie. Now run your things up to your room and scurry back."

Coming back as quickly as she could, Millie was still on the last step of the stairway when she said, "Miss Cora, I'm back."

"Okay, now listen. Go out the front door and turn left, just like you did with Lucy when you went to Zimmerman's. Remember where you turned left to go to town?" Millie nodded. "Well, don't turn there. Keep walking two more blocks. Look right and you'll see 'Willie's Fish House.' Tell Willie that Miss Cora sent you. He knows what I need. I've already called over there. He'll have eight pounds of catfish wrapped up for you. You can take this bag to carry it in." Miss Cora handed Millie a small canvas bag. "You won't need any money. Willie will just bill Miss Sarah."

After her embarrassing time with the angels, Millie was eager to get out of the house just to walk and breathe. The afternoon had heated up, but there was a slight breeze which kissed her face as she headed in the direction Miss Cora had described.

Two blocks, cross Third Street and then two more blocks. There it was, Willie's Fish House.

Inside Millie asked for Mr. Willie. "I'm Willie," a dark-skinned colored man spoke up from behind the counter.

"Yes, suh, Mr. Willie. Miss Cora from up yonder at Miss Sarah's sent me to get her fish."

"'Up yonder'?" Mr. Willie grinned. "Where y'all from?"

"Gaston, Georgia, suh. I got here Monday."

"Well, country girl, welcome to Mason."

While Mr. Willie went to the back to get the order, Millie leaned in to gaze at the fish lying there in the ice, mouths open. "I'll bet someone had a fine time trying to land you," She murmured.

The smell of fish hung in the air. She liked that smell. It took her back to the smell of the fish she had caught down home on the Ohoopee River. The smell of nature, a pure, raw smell. A good smell. She breathed in deeply.

Mr. Willie was back and handed Millie the wrapped fish.

"Millie, you one of Miss Sarah's girls?" Mr. Willie asked.

Millie considered that question, remembering what Miss Sarah had told her about answering questions about the boarding house. By now she had taken the wrapped package of fish and put it in her bag. "Mr. Willie, suh, I mainly works for Miss Cora." Oh, Jesus, I hope I don't get in trouble for saying that. Millie cocked her head and licked and parted her lips. With a quick toss of her curly bob, she turned to leave. "Nice to make your acquaintance, Mr. Willie, suh." And she was out the door.

Shaking his head as he leaned into the display case and moved the ice around to cover his inventory, Mr. Willie muttered, "Not one yet, no sur-ree bob, not one yet."

Still pondering Mr. Willie's question and feeling concerned about her answer. Millie walked toward Miss Sarah's. As she approached Third Street, she noticed a big dump truck beginning to slow down. When she got to the stop light, the man in the truck leaned out. "Hey, pretty girl, didn't I see you with Lucy the other day. Where you headed?"

Flustered, Millie kept her head down and only glanced up long enough to answer, "Yes, I was with Lucy. I'm headed home now. I've got fish that needs to get inside before it spoils." Millie shifted the eight pounds of fish from one hand to the other.

"Well, go on with yo' fish now." The man slapped his steering wheel. "Maybe I'll see you at Miss Sarah's some time. Tell Lucy I'll see her tonight, okay?" He pulled on through the intersection, laughing.

The light turned green, and Millie hurriedly crossed Third Street. Sweat was now pouring down her red cheeks. This late September day had remembered that it lived in Mason, Georgia, and it had heated way up.

When she got to Miss Sarah's, she went straight to the kitchen. Miss Cora was at the table, two pans set before her: one with seasoned corn meal, the other filled with buttermilk.

"Now, missy, wash your hands and come help me dredge these cats up real good."

Millie washed her hands and looked at them afterward, red and rough. "Miss Cora, your hands are so smooth and soft. How do you do that. You work with your hands as hard as I do."

"Well, chile, see this can of Crisco. After I finish in here for the evening, I dip my hand in and take a tiny bit, rub it in. Crisco fries fish, softens hands." Cora smiled at Millie. "Now get those cats ready for the HOT Crisco."

Millie began to dredge the fish through the buttermilk and then through the cornmeal. She was happy to change the cats from slimy fish to properly dressed fillets ready for frying. The extra pan on the table filled up fast. "You're ready for the frying pan, fishies," Millie proudly declared.

Taking the pan of dressed fish to the stove, Miss Cora looked at Millie. "Now, Millie, put these in the grease careful like. Don't want to splash your dress with grease. Get one of those aprons off the back door." Millie took the first apron she saw. After wrapping the string around her waist twice she tied it in the front.

"You look like that bundle of catfish you brought in from Willie's, all wrapped 'round with that string," Miss Cora smiled and lifted her hands. "Now back to the catfish. Pick them up by the tail and put that broad part down first." Miss Cora watched Millie. "That's right. That's right. Use a fork to move the pieces around. Make room for more."

Soon Millie had a pan filled with breaded catfish swimming in the hot grease and starting to brown up. Miss Cora had finished the breading of the remaining fillets and joined Millie at the stove.

"Here now. Let me turn 'em over." Miss Cora quickly flipped the pieces. "Now just a minute and they'll be ready to come out."

Miss Cora had placed yet another pan on the counter next to the frying pan. Millie speared the browned, crispy catfish and carefully placed each piece in the pan.

In no time a mound of fried fish filled the pan. It was almost five o'clock.

"Millie, I've got the rest of the meal done," Miss Cora said.

"All 'cept the hush puppies. Can't have fried catfish without hush puppies."

Having said that, Miss Cora added more lard to the pan. "Here's the hush puppy dough. Jus' start makin' medium-sized balls and plop them right here in this ole iron skillet. I'll take care of the rest." Now the smell of fried cornmeal and onions filled the kitchen. Cooked onions, Millie's favorite "home" smell.

Sweat was beginning to pour down their foreheads as Miss Cora and Millie worked against the clock, but their teamwork paid off and by five-fifteen there was an equally high pile of hush puppies alongside the catfish.

Magdala came through the back door. "Ma, I'm here. I had basketball practice today. You remember I made the team."

"Of course, chile. Now come on and join this one."

"Yes, ma'am. Hey there, Millie. Those hush puppies smell so good!"

"Hey, Magdala. Glad to see you."

By five-thirty the meal had been served: catfish, hush puppies, cole slaw, sliced tomatoes, and lemon icebox pie. Millie had taken up her usual station with a pitcher of tea and a bowl of chipped ice nearby.

It was late September, some considered it fall, but it was still middle Georgia, and no breeze blew through the open windows. In the dining room Miss Sarah had set up a large pedestal fan which turned its head lethargically, blowing hot air across the table.

The gentlemen and the angels did not seem to notice, the men loading their plates with catfish and hush puppies and a few sliced tomatoes and just a dollop of cole slaw.

"You gents better eat my cole slaw. If you don't you know you'll see it again," Miss Cora scolded.

"Ah, Miss Cora, I'm saving room for lemon icebox pie that I just know is in your kitchen," one of the gents, a young, fresh-faced man with curly dark brown hair and dimples said as he smiled at Miss Cora.

Joe. That's who spoke to Lucy when we were on our way to town. And he's the one who spoke to me today, Millie mused. And sure enough Lucy was seated right next to him, picking at a single piece of fried fish. He is kinda cute, Millie thought. Lucy looks like she thinks so, too.

The fried fish tasted real good and was a big hit, but back in the kitchen the smell of lard, catfish, onions, and corn meal weighed heavily in the air.

Miss Cora tossed a bit of ground cinnamon into the flame on one lit burner on the stove. The burnt cinnamon smell competed with the fried fish smell. Really just one more bad smell.

It took a lot of Oxydol to clean the kitchen and Miss Cora was adamant about getting all the scrapings from the plates out of her kitchen, even recruiting Mr. Lester.

"Before you get that second piece of pie, Lester darlin', you'd better help us get all this fish smell outa my kitchen."

"Of course, darlin', that was my intention all along." Mr. Lester winked at Miss Cora and began bagging it all up in the brown paper bags Miss Cora had stacked on the back porch.

Magdala had already gone home when Miss Cora, Mr. Lester, and Millie finished up with the fried catfish purge. All three just flopped down at the kitchen table, that place of rest and conviviality. "You know it's almost not worth it. All you have to do in cleaning up after frying that catfish," Miss Cora said.

"I'll serve you two ladies." Mr. Lester stood behind them, a clean dish towel wrapped around his waist and one folded across his left arm. He bowed and set the remains of three lemon ice box pie pans on the table. He handed Miss Cora and Millie forks, keeping one for himself. There was just enough left in the three pans for each one to have a piece.

"Let's dig in, ladies. Startin' to smell better in here already." Mr. Lester leaned into Miss Cora and gave her a peck on the cheek.

This is my home now, Millie thought, taking a big bite of the delicious pie.

"Say, Millie, do you want to go to church with us Sunday?" Mr. Lester asked between bites. "Today's Friday, so that's just two days away. Thought I'd check in case you were makin' plans for the weekend."

"And I can wear my new dress," Millie began. "I mean, yes suh, Mr. Lester, that would be real fine. Will it be okay for me to go, my bein' white and all?"

Mr. Lester and Miss Cora looked at each other and smiled. Miss Cora spoke first. "Millie, anyone who wants to worship the Lord is welcome at First Baptist."

"Yes, Millie, and you get to ride in my Butterfield's Plumbing truck. We'll be uptown, girl. Real uptown," Mr. Lester added.

Millie just nodded. I'll get to wear my new dress and shoes! she thought again.

"Miss Cora, this pie is just the bee's knees," she proclaimed, trying out what she had heard the girls say earlier in the day.

With that they all three laughed out loud.

After he had finished his pie, Mr. Lester stood and handed the two dish towels to Miss Cora. "My time as your waiter is done. I'm going home now. See you in a bit, boss lady." Using one of the towels he had just given her, Miss Cora popped his behind as he left. "Get on outta here, you." She turned toward Millie.

"Millie, I'll finish up in here. Pretty much all that's left is the Buttercup china. And you know how I am about those precious plates." Miss Cora winked at Millie and then headed to the sink.

"Precious Lord, take my hand…," Miss Cora began singing as she washed the dishes.

"Night, Miss Cora. See you in the mornin'."

"Night, Millie. God bless."

Millie trudged up the stairs to her room. It had been a long day, but she wasn't quite ready for bed. Instead, she grabbed her dictionary and sat down on the bed.

"Oops. Better wind up little blue bell," Millie said, taking the small blue clock into her hands and winding the time and the alarm.

Back to her bed and the dictionary, Millie looked at the entry for "aardvark."

She decided to study the definition more closely. "Long snout" she understood, but the next phrase, "extensible tongue," she did not understand.

"Maybe I should look up that 'e' word and see if I can figure out what kind of tongue it means," Millie said, talking herself through this word study.

"Ex-ten-si-ble," Millie broke the word down and attempted to sound it out.

She flipped pages until she found it, "extensible." She read aloud, "capable of being extended. Oh, it means he has a long tongue that he can stick way out. 'Extensible.' I now know a new word," she said with a sigh. "But that's enough for one day. Good night, little aardvark with the long tongue."

Millie returned the dictionary to its place on the small table and made her way to the bathroom. It was still quite warm, and no breeze was blowing so her soak in the tub was refreshing. She made certain that she washed her hair real good to get all that fried fish smell out.

She chose not to dry herself completely, leaving just a bit of water all over her body. She pulled on a clean chemise, jumped into bed, and pulled the covers up tight. "Good night, Blue Bell," she said to her little clock. "Wake me up in time, now."

Chapter 6

At five o'clock Blue Bell did her job, chiming hard and bouncing along the side table. Millie jumped up and quieted her, punching in the alarm button.

Today Millie decided to wear the dress Miss Sarah had given her. She had washed and ironed it, so it was ready for her last workday of her first week at Miss Sarah's.

Outside her window, a Carolina wren was singing loud and clear. For some reason it made Millie think of her little daughter Louise. "Louise always liked to sit on the porch and watch the birds," she said aloud. "I wonder when I'll hear from Ma." She began putting on her shoes. "Well, it won't be a week until next Wednesday since I sent that letter. Just hasn't been enough time. No news is good news, right, Millie?"

Miss Cora was bustling around the kitchen when she arrived. Millie knew what to do. She had gotten really good at rolling out the biscuit dough and cutting biscuits out using a tea glass turned upside down. This made really big biscuits, the kind the gentlemen liked.

Pan after pan she filled and alternatingly put them in and took them out of the oven.

Miss Cora had her blue cotton scarf wrapped around her

head. Sweat beads were beginning to form on her forehead. It was already starting to heat up in the kitchen and there was no fall breeze blowing through the window to bring relief.

"Millie, after you clean Miss Sarah's rooms, I want you to go out and pull some turnips from the garden for supper. Do you know anything about turnip greens and roots?"

"Yes, ma'am. I love turnip roots and greens."

"Well, we'll be making an especially big batch so that you girls will have something to eat on Sunday. I'll fry up some extra bacon to go with the turnip greens and roots. Y'all can nibble away on that tomorrow. The only place I cook on Sundays is in my own kitchen."

"Yes, Miss Cora."

Miss Cora scrambled the eggs today and even sprinkled a bit of shredded cheese all across the top once she had spread them out on three serving plates. She also had strawberry jam dished up in several cut-glass bowls. The grits were bubbling in a big pot on a back burner.

The biscuits were coming out of the oven light brown and flaky. Oh, they smelled good. Millie was already planning her plate once she had served the men and cleared the table.

It was almost seven o'clock and Millie could hear the men talking their way into the dining room, some even laughing.

Miss Sarah was not in the dining room this morning. Sometimes she ate with the men, sometimes she didn't.

Millie had placed the last of the serving plates of biscuits, bacon, and scrambled eggs and the big bowl of grits with pats of butter melting on top on the table and filled the cups with coffee. Just as she did at supper with the tea pitcher, she stood by with the pot of coffee.

Usually, she was ignored by the men, but this morning one of them looked up at her and asked, "Say, Millie, are you Miss Sarah's spare girl. She keepin' you in reserve?" With that question the other men stopped eating and looked up, interested in what Millie's answer would be and looking her over head to toe.

Millie took her time to answer, licking her lips and parting them before she did. "I work in the kitchen with Miss Cora," she said, seeing no need to answer the question directly.

"Well, maybe one day Miss Sarah will add you to the offerings here at her boarding house," the gentleman said, putting emphasis on "boarding." That elicited a chuckle from the other men at the table.

Millie felt her face turning red and her pulse quickening. This man frightened her. "Excuse me, I need to go refill this pot with some more hot coffee," she said. She slipped out of the room.

She set the pot down on the kitchen table so hard it startled Miss Cora who was at the sink washing pots and pans. "Millie, is everything okay, chile?"

"Yes, Miss Cora. I just need to get some hot coffee."

Miss Cora turned and looked at her. "Well, you come on over here and take over with this dish washin'. I'll see to the coffee."

Millie was relieved that she did not have to go back into the dining room. She started washing what was in the sink and looking out the window at the garden, planted with one vegetable: turnips. It would be nice to be outside today. A slight breeze had picked up and blew through the open window above the sink and cooled her face.

As usual after finishing their breakfast the men would collect their belongings and be on their way. It was Saturday and they would each be going home or to their next stop, wherever that might be. The girls were still sleeping, and Miss Sarah was in her study. As if letting out a sigh, the big house went silent.

Miss Cora was soon back in the kitchen. Knowing that the men were gone, Millie returned to the dining room and began her routine of scraping and stacking the china. By the time she returned to the kitchen Miss Cora was at the sink full of fresh hot water and Oxydol ready to wash the Buttercup dishes.

Millie, carrying a stack of Buttercup china, dinner plates, and bread plates pushed her way into the kitchen. Still rankled by the men's comments and muttering under her breath, she made a misstep and for one second the stack was airborne and then in a crash was a scattering pile of broken china sliding across the floor.

Startled, Miss Cora jumped and then quickly turned from the sink. "Oh, no, Millie, not the Buttercup china!"

Millie sank into one of the kitchen chairs and putting her hands to her face began to cry, "Oh, Miss Cora, Miss Sarah's gonna fire me. I just know it."

"Not now, Millie. We gotta clean this mess up and you've got to get upstairs and start cleanin'. Get some paper bags from the back porch and we'll get the shards up. I'll tell Miss Sarah. You get on with your work."

So together, they began the cleanup. Soon, the pieces of Buttercup china had been bagged up and were lined up on the back porch like brown soldiers in review.

"Miss Cora, I killed her vacuum cleaner and now I've broken her Buttercup china. What can I do?" Millie asked, voice trembling.

"Clean Miss Sarah's rooms and then start pulling turnips. Now wipe your face and get to work." Miss Cora gave Millie a hug and then popped her bottom. "Now git!"

Millie shook out the linen tablecloth, telling her chicken friends all about the broken china. Henny Penny seemed especially concerned and sympathetic. Then, returning to the dining room, she wiped down and lightly waxed the dining room table.

Back in the kitchen Millie fixed herself a plate of bacon

strips, biscuit, and a small glob of grits. None of it was warm, but that really didn't matter to her. She felt despondent. She was certain that Miss Sarah was going to fire her and then what would she do?

Still washing dishes, Miss Cora began singing, "Amazing grace how sweet the sound that saved a wretch like me. I once was lost, but now I'm found…" That's me, Millie thought.

She began to sing as well and the sound became fuller and fuller, filling the kitchen. "When we've been there ten thousand years, bright shining as the sun. We've no less days to sing God's praise than when we first begun…"

"Oh, Miss Cora, let's sing it again!" And they did, this time with Millie weaving notes of harmony all around the tune Miss Cora was singing.

It was nearing nine o'clock when Millie began her trek up the back stairs. Unlike the main stairs, these stairs twisted and turned, wedged into the stairwell as if squeezed in as an afterthought.

The turns created blind spots. Millie heard the girls before she saw them and they all but ran into each other at one of the turns. The girls headed down; Millie headed up.

"Oh, Millie, we almost ran over you," Lucy laughed. They squeezed past each other, still laughing. Millie kept climbing.

After four days Millie knew how to clean Miss Sarah's rooms by rote. She could let her mind focus on other things. Forgetting the broken dishes, she chose to think about turnips, reminding herself how to clean 'em. She'd need to find a way to wash them outside. She thought about the big green turnip leaves and how she'd wash them carefully. Nothing worse than grit in your turnips.

Before she knew it, she was at Miss Sarah's study. Her bedroom had been easy. In fact, Miss Sarah had already made the bed this time, so Millie didn't have to bother with that. The sheriff definitely didn't come last night. The bed is smooth and there's no cigar smell, Millie mused.

Miss Sarah was not in her study, so Millie could work quickly.

It was almost noon when Millie finished. She had worked fast and now she was hungry. She stowed her cleaning utensils and made her way down to the kitchen. Miss Cora was not there. Millie found a cold biscuit and leftover bacon. She looked in the icebox and found a plate of sliced tomatoes.

Biscuit, bacon, sliced tomatoes, and a glass of cold sweet tea. To Millie's way of thinking, this was a fine meal. Mighty fine.

After she washed her plate, she went through the back screen door to the yard. The turnip patch was five rows wide and twenty-five turnip plants long. Millie found two buckets on the back porch. She planned to fill both with turnip greens and roots. Her first bucket was full by the time she reached the halfway point of the first row. In no time she had filled both buckets and one of the five rows now was nothing but holes.

Where will I wash these greens? she asked herself.

Mr. Lester was just coming out of his house when he saw Millie with her two buckets of turnips and a quizzical expression on her face.

"Look-a-here, Millie. Let me show you where the water spigot is. You see that green hose there?" Millie nodded her head. "Well, come over here and let me show you this little wheel." Mr. Lester motioned toward the spigot and its wheel. He turned it on, and water began flowing from the end of the green hose.

"Thank you, Mr. Lester. Do you think I've got enough turnips for supper?"

"Millie, I think we'll be eating turnips for the next week. Yes, you do have enough for supper. Maybe half a row would have been enough." Mr. Lester walked away shaking his head.

Millie set about cleaning each of the big green turnip leaves of the twenty-five plants she had pulled up. First, she dumped all the turnips on the ground near the spigot. It was a tedious task, but she was determined to wash away every last speck of dirt.

By the time she was done, her feet were wet, her dress was wet, and even her hair was wet, and her fingers were wrinkled. Oh, my, I do know how to make a mess.

She took one bucket at a time into the kitchen and to the sink. One bucketful filled the sink to overflowing. She did not know what to do with the second bucketful but to lay the turnips carefully out on the table.

It didn't look like that much outside, she fretted.

It was three o' clock. Miss Cora came through the back door. "Mercy, chile, we ain't feedin' an army!"

Miss Cora stood, hand on hip, finger to her cheek. "Well, let's get started. We have a lot of chopping to do." With that she retrieved a couple of kitchen knives from a drawer and handed one to Millie.

"Let's start by cutting off the roots. Here's a pot to put those in."

Millie started chopping the greens. The more she chopped the bigger the pile grew. It seemed that rather than becoming smaller the greens had minds of their own and were multiplying with each chop.

The girls could be heard coming down the back stairs, chatting and giggling. Once they had reached the bottom step and looked into the kitchen, they knew that the full-fledged turnip tempest happening in there was not what they had planned for a Saturday.

They turned, thinking that Miss Cora had not seen them, and they began to slowly climb back up the stairs. "Oh, no, you don't," Miss Cora began. "Get back in here. Grab a knife and start chopping."

Now the six of them, each one stationed at a different spot in the kitchen, were chopping turnips. Miss Cora cut up large pieces of fat back and they were soon beginning to roll around in the boiling water. She allowed the fat back to boil and fully season the water before plunking in the chopped turnips. And there were plenty of chopped turnips. But as Miss Cora was quick to tell the girls and Millie, turnips cook down real quick.

With military efficiency Miss Cora lined up the piles of chopped greens just to one side of the stove, so that more could be added to the pots. The kitchen was beginning to take on the fragrance of pork-seasoned turnips, a smell Millie found especially appetizing, but the girls found absolutely repulsive.

"My hair is gonna smell like turnips. Oh, Miss Cora, I need to head back upstairs." Lucy complained.

"Oh, Miss Cora, haven't we helped enough?" Hazel whined as Corine and Gladys nodded their heads.

"Oh, all right. Go on now. I've got it from here. You too, Millie, go get yourself a bath. You look a mess from your trip to the turnip patch." Miss Cora raised her hands and dismissed all five girls. "But Millie, I need you right back down here to make supper."

Millie scurried up the stairs with the girls, telling them good-bye as she climbed the last stairs to her room. It didn't take her long to bathe and wash her hair. She even had time to put her dress in the tub to soak.

Her shoes were pretty muddy so she was careful to scrape them off over the trash can. "I know I'll have to clean my room tonight after all of this. Haven't thought to do that all week!" she said aloud.

Back downstairs Millie found that Miss Cora had already begun the meal preparation. "Millie, we're having ground beef patties, grilled onions, mashed potatoes, TURNIPS, and more TURNIPS, rolls, and pound cake. I've put the potatoes on to boil, so you have just enough time to slice the onions."

Magdala came through the back door just in time to help with slicing the onions. Millie smiled, saying, "Magdala, you and I are going to have a real good cry."

In no time they had sliced up six onions. Miss Cora had finished up forming the patties. The onions would be grilled first, so she took the bowl filled with the slices and started piling them into the pan. Millie's favorite smell, cooked onions, began filling the room.

"Millie, you and Magdala, get yourselves a bowl each and start smashing these potatoes," Miss Cora ordered as she drained the boiled potatoes in the sink.

Millie loved smashing the potatoes. She and Magdala each had a big bowl filled. The meal was coming together. Miss Cora dismissed Millie and Magdala to set the table and fill the tea glasses. No ice yet, just tea.

Soon Millie heard what had become a familiar sound: the gentlemen coming down the hall from their rooms and making their way to the dining room.

It was a little after five when the hustle began. Millie, Magdala, and Miss Cora began bringing serving platters and bowls to the table. The smell of cooked onions, fried beef patties, brown gravy, and TURNIPS now filled the room.

The men were taking their seats, the girls had drifted in, and Miss Sarah was seated at the head of the table. This is just perfect, Millie sighed. Perfect.

In no time at all everything was happening in reverse. All back to the kitchen. And the girls, their gentlemen, and Miss Sarah had left the dining room and were in the parlor. Millie could already smell the cigars and pipes.

Mr. Lester was at his usual place at the kitchen table. His plate was piled high with grilled patties, topped with onions, potatoes covered in gravy. But his turnips were in a bowl all by themselves.

Millie and Magdala fixed their plates and sat down with him.

Looking at Millie, Mr. Lester remarked, "Millie, you must have known how much I love turnips. Why, girl, you pulled up one-fifth of the patch. We may even be eating turnips for breakfast!" All three of them began to laugh uproariously.

Just as the three of them began to regain their composure and set to eating their supper, the sheriff came through the back door.

"Evenin', Lester and ladies."

"Evenin', Sheriff."

By this time Miss Cora had returned to the kitchen.

"And Miss Cora. Smells like you made a mighty fine meal tonight."

"Thank you, Sheriff. Would you like a piece of pound cake to take with you upstairs?"

Miss Cora cut an especially large piece, put it on a Buttercup dessert plate with a silver fork and handed it to the sheriff.

"Thank you, kindly," the sheriff said, as he put the fork in his front pocket, no need to drop it in the dark going up those back stairs.

Once the sheriff was gone, they went back to their conversation.

"Millie, you have now learned how to prepare every meal we'll have here at Miss Sarah's. I don't change a thing. So, can you tell me what we ate this week? Just list the meats," Miss Cora smiled.

"Well, Miss Cora, Monday was pork chops, Tuesday, fried chicken, Wednesday, meat loaf, Thursday, salmon croquettes, Friday, catfish and Saturday, fried meat patties AND TURNIPS!"

Mr. Lester let out a whoop. "Millie, you nailed it. You really nailed it." And all four of them laughed some more.

It was late by the time they finished cleaning up. Since it was Saturday and Mr. Lester wouldn't be going to work the next day, he helped, too.

"Millie, you goin' with us to church tomorrow?" Miss Cora asked.

"Yes, ma'am, Miss Cora."

"Well, be here in the kitchen around ten-thirty. I'll send Magdala over to get you."

It had been a long day. Millie decided to just drop into the bed. She'd set her clock set for 7:00 a.m. She'd have plenty of time to bathe and dress in the morning. She had a church dress and now she was going to a church with the Butterfields.

She slipped out of her dress and fell into her bed. A cool fall breeze was blowing through the open window. Millie could see the stars and the moon and could hear the truck drivers shifting gears on their big rigs as they drove through Mason. "Thank you, Lord." And with that benediction Millie fell asleep.

Chapter 7

The little blue alarm clock chimed at 7:00 a.m. Knowing it was Sunday, Millie took her time getting out of bed. It was chilly, the temperature having dropped over night. She closed the windows and set off for the bathroom. There she rinsed the work dress that had soaked overnight.

Then she took her time bathing her body and washing her hair. She wanted to smell nice and look nice. She put on her clean step-ins and chemise.

Millie could hardly contain herself as she laid out the sky-blue georgette crepe dress, carefully separating the dress from the slip. She patted the dress and the slip affectionately. She had never owned such elegance. She carefully removed the black tee-straps from their shoe box and set them alongside the dress. Stockings and garter belt followed.

"Oh, Lord, no one has shown me how to use this garter belt," she worried. But the garter belt was attached to a card which clearly showed how it was supposed to work.

Millie decided to wait a bit before putting on her dress, giving her hair time to dry, and to fill the time by reading a word or two in her dictionary.

"Maybe I'll just open the book and drop a finger and see what word I get," she said out loud.

She opened the dictionary, closed her eyes, and dropped her finger. She opened her eyes and read the word aloud: "brothel." And then read the definition: "a house where men can visit prostitutes."

Considering the definition, Millie decided to look up the word "prostitutes."

She flipped forward in the dictionary until she came to "prostitute."

Again she read aloud, "a person, in particular a woman, who engages in sexual activity for payment."

She then put it all together: "A house where a man can visit a woman who engages in sexual activity for payment."

And then it dawned on Millie. She dropped the dictionary and, shaking her head as if to clear it, she again spoke aloud, adding another phrase to the definition: "Miss Sarah's boarding house is a house where men can visit women who engage in sexual activity for payment."

And then, "This house where I have a job and a place to live is…a BROTHEL. Lucy, Corine, Gladys, and Hazel are PROSTITUTES!"

She let this soak in for a moment, and then a thought entered her mind, something she had never considered until now: *Will Miss Sarah make me a prostitute, too?* She was shocked by the thought, but it was nearing nine-thirty and she had to be in the kitchen in an hour. She'd figure it out later.

She put the dictionary back on the little table by the door and then began the careful process of dressing. First the garter belt, then the stockings, one by one. She did remember that Lucy had told her to roll the stockings up before stuffing her feet in. Carefully Millie slipped first one and then the other stocking up her legs and attached each one to the front and back clips. She sat down, tried to bend her legs and, realizing that she had hooked the stockings too tightly, had to redo both and only then did she put on her new tee-strap dress shoes.

"This being a lady is a lot of work," she sighed as she stuck her legs out to admire her new tee-straps.

It was now getting close to 10 o'clock. She quickly put the slip on, and it fell perfectly down to her knees. The dress came next and there it was. She felt like a queen. Rushing into the bathroom she fluffed her hair while admiring how the sky blue made her blue eyes really shine. "I'm almost pretty," she remarked.

Finally, she took the cloche hat into the bathroom and pulled it over her head, leaving just a few light brown curls peeping out.

"I don't even have a Bible. Aw, maybe that'll be okay." With that Millie headed down to the kitchen.

She was hungry. She found the leftover pound cake and cut herself a slice. She decided to make herself a bowl of turnip greens too, but before she did that, she got an apron from the back porch and carefully covered up her dress.

"Now for some turnips. I'm certain I can find some." She carefully removed the covered pot from the refrigerator. Slowly now, Millie, she said to herself.

There it was. A fine breakfast of pound cake and cold turnips. Still nervous about getting turnip juice on her dress, Millie tied a clean dish towel around her neck.

So, that's how Magdala found her at ten-thirty, wrapped up like a mummy eating cake and turnips.

"Oh, Millie, you are the bee's knees!"

"Magdala, do I have time to run back upstairs to brush my teeth? Don't want to have turnip greens hanging from my teeth."

"Go on, Millie, and then come on to the driveway. We'll be getting in the truck."

Millie scurried back upstairs. This time she wrapped a

towel around her neck to keep toothpaste from falling on her dress. Now, she was ready.

She raced down the back stairs to the kitchen. There she slowed down, slid her hands down her dress front to smooth it, touched her hat, looked at her gloves covering those red housemaid hands, and took a breath. She opened the screen door and slowly moved down the back porch stairs.

Once down the steps, she looked to her left. The autumn morning sun was lighting the driveway and in the brilliant light stood the three, Miss Cora, Mr. Lester, and Magdala. Like a vision of fashion, each was dressed to perfection. Mr. Lester, looking like the mannequin in the Zimmerman's window, wore a dark gray fedora, a lighter gray suit with vest, and two-toned gray and black shoes. At the neck of his white shirt was a dark purple bowtie. Millie was certain that he was the handsomest, most well-dressed man she had ever seen.

Next to him Miss Cora was wearing a dress in a similar style as Millie's with sheer fabric for the sleeves, shoulder to wrist. But Miss Cora's was a dark, rich red which highlighted her coffee-creamed skin. Her hat had a big, wide brim encircled by a broad purple satin ribbon, the same color as Mr. Lester's bowtie. Her shoes were tee-straps the exact color of her dress. Millie's jaw dropped.

"Oh, Miss Cora, you look beautiful!" Miss Cora responded with a big smile which showed off her dimple.

"What about me?" Mr. Lester quipped.

"Oh, Mr. Lester, suh, you look beautiful, too. And so do you, Magdala."

"Come on, Millie. Let's stuff ourselves into Daddy's truck," Magdala urged Millie. She was dressed in a precious dark blue frock covered in white polka dots and set off with a wide, white collar and white sash. She had on white socks and black slippers. Her cloche hat, the same blue as her dress, had a broad white satin hat band.

They climbed into Mr. Lester's paneled plumbing company truck, emblazoned with the words "A Flush Every Time" with a picture of a poker hand, a royal flush. The front seat was wide, but not very long, so Millie and Magdala sat one a bit back, the other a bit front. Magdala, the one in front, had to hold onto the dashboard when Mr. Lester came to a stop sign. They giggled all the way to church.

First Baptist Church, or better known as First Baptist, black, had been organized in 1835, many years before emancipation. The building, a tall, imposing brick structure, had been built in 1887. Up the hill from this church at the top of Hill Street stood First Baptist Church, white. Two impressive buildings with active, faithful congregations. Both of them "firsts."

Mr. Lester pulled into a parking lot near the church. Millie and Magdala tumbled out, each pressing her hands down the front of her dress and touching her cloche hat.

Millie had never seen so many people moving toward a church building, in cars, from busses, by foot. So many colored people in one place.

They climbed the high front steps and were immediately greeted by gentlemen who manned both doors: "Good morning. Welcome to First Baptist. Glad to see you."

Millie and the Butterfields got caught up in a wave of people pushing forward toward the sanctuary. They began greeting each other —women calling each other's names, men just lifting a hand and nodding their heads toward each other.

The interior of the church was a dark, rich wood. Pews filled a center bounded by two aisles with two side sections on either side. Stained glass windows ran the length of each side, the bottom of which could be opened, and all of them were. The Mason fall morning was beginning to heat up. Pedestal fans were set along the sides blowing across the pews, fluttering bulletins and the feathers on ladies' hats. Their hum filled the air.

Miss Cora gave them directions. "Come on, let's get a seat under a window. Lord, it's gettin' hot in here." Mr. Lester, Magdala, and Millie followed her to a back row near a window and under a fan.

One woman sat at the far end of the pew. Evidently, she had gotten there early enough to get the prize seat, by a window, near a fan.

Millie slid in next to her, then Magdala, followed by Miss Cora and finally Mr. Lester, who ended up next to the aisle. He kept his nodding and greeting going on. Most of the First Baptist members were his customers. And those who hadn't been surely at some point were going to need his services. Even those who rented their homes had benefitted from Mr. Lester's skills because several of the white-owned rental agencies regularly hired Lester Butterfield.

Millie spoke to the woman she sat next to with a polite, "Good mornin', ma'am."

The woman just nodded. She was a wizened little woman. She seemed to rattle in her dark black, wrinkled skin. Her faded cotton dress had at one time been covered in flowers of various hues, but now the colors blurred, and the dress hung on her frame. Millie especially noted her hands, which were calloused and wrinkled. She wore slippers on her feet and her feet were as wrinkled as her hands. Her big black straw hat was limp, and the hat band stained with sweat. Millie knew that this woman must work hard for whatever pay she might receive. Her heart swelled.

The church service was getting started. The song leader announced the first hymn: "Leanin' on the Everlasting Arms." Millie knew this one. When the number was called, she opened the hymnal, offering to share it with the old woman. The woman nodded. They began to sing, "What a fellowship, what a joy divine, leanin' on the everlasting arms…. At the chorus Millie let loose in her best country voice, "Leanin',

leanin', leanin', on the everlasting arms." They sang all four verses.

The final verse struck Millie as applying to her right now, especially now that she knew Miss Sarah's place was a brothel. She sang out loud, "What have I to dread, what have I to fear, leaning on the everlasting arms…"

The song leader announced the second hymn, "Blessed Assurance." Millie was really enjoying all this singing and again this was one she knew. She turned to Magdala. They both smiled.

After "Blessed Assurance" the song leader motioned for them all to sit down. He told them that since an election was coming up in early November, the church had the privilege of having one of the candidates present who would make a few remarks.

Millie was agog. Coming up to the dais was none other than the sheriff, the man she had twice seen headed up the back stairs to visit Miss Sarah. Millie cut her eyes at Magdala, who just shrugged.

The congregation erupted in applause. The sheriff shook hands with the song leader and the Reverend and then stepped to the pulpit. "Good mornin' all. So glad to have the privilege of being with you at First Baptist." He glanced toward the Reverend. "I'll be brief because I know you all want to hear from your Reverend and not your sheriff." Laughter followed with a few amens.

"I'm asking for your vote on the first Tuesday of November. I believe that I've done a good job for you. Know that my door is always open to you. You are my eyes and ears in the community. Help ME serve YOU." He kept nodding, raising his arms. And then he sat down, to further applause.

Well, that beats all, Millie mused.

The congregation kept their seats. The choir stood. Every one of them, and Millie thought surely there were a hundred, were wearing flowing gold robes with a purple inset at the neck with the letters "FBC" embroidered on the inset.

The pianist began and then the organist followed, playing a version of "Come Thou Almighty King," a hymn tune Millie recognized. The choir began to sway in time with the music. And then an explosion of sound followed. Millie knew the hymn but had never heard it sung quite like this. The sound swelled and fell in accordance with the director who stood in front of the choir. "Come thou Al-mi-gh-tee King, help us, YES, help us sing."

Then the men sang, "Father all glorious" and the women answered, "O'er all victorious, come and reign over us."

Then with a shout, "Ancient of Days."

The choir sang that first verse a few more times, with a soloist adding the phrase "ancient of days" as a back-up. Finally, they reached the fourth verse, again the sound building as if to lift the rafters. "To thee, great One in three, eternal praises be, hence, evermore. Thy sovereign majesty may we in glory see, and to eternity love and adore." The "love and adore" rolled through the choir in a call and response fashion.

Millie was able to take in the entire room. She fixated on the women's hats in every shape and hue, some curved up, some down. Some had flowers, some had feathers that stuck straight out from the side of the hats.

The Reverend stood and announced his sermon topic: "Get Out of the Boat."

He intoned, "Our scripture comes today from the gospel according to St. Matthew." And he read aloud:

"And straightway Jesus constrained his disciples to get into a ship, and to go before him unto the other side, while he sent the multitudes away.

"And when he had sent the multitudes away, he went up into a mountain apart to pray; and when the evening was come, he was there alone.

"But the ship was now in the midst of the sea tossed with waves; for the wind was contrary.

"And in the fourth watch of the night Jesus went unto them, walking on the sea.

"And when the disciples saw him walking on the sea, they were troubled, saying it is a spirit; and they cried out for fear.

"But straightway Jesus spake unto them, saying, Be of good cheer; it is I; be not afraid.

"And Peter answered him and said, Lord, if it be thou, bid me come unto thee on the water.

"And he said, Come. And when Peter was come down out of the ship, he walked on the water, to go to Jesus.

"But when he saw the wind boisterous, he was afraid; and beginning to sink, he cried, saying, Lord save me. And immediately Jesus stretched forth his hand, and caught him, and said unto him, O thou of little faith, wherefore didst thou doubt?"

And then the Reverend began to teach. He started with a series of questions:

"Where was Peter?"

Someone from the congregation answered: "In the boat."

"Yes, and again I ask you, where was Peter?"

This time several voices answered, "In the boat."

"Yes," and now his voice began to rise. "And sisters and brothers, what did Peter have to do to get to the Lord?"

"Get out of the boat," was the answer.

"Yes, and again I ask you, what did Peter have to do to get to the Lord?"

Now more voices answered, "Get out of the boat."

And others murmured, "Amen."

The Reverend continued, "So if Peter wanted to get to the Lord, he had to get out of the boat and put his foot into, what? How did the Bible describe it? 'The sea tossed with waves.'"

Listening intently, Millie leaned forward. The Reverend was taking his time to lead the congregation. His message was as much his delivery, the cadence of the rise and fall of his voice, as it was the content of the sermon.

He continued, "So, was Peter stepping out onto a solid, firm surface. Was he assured that his feet would meet solid ground?"

The congregation was fully engaged now. Many voices joined to bellow, "No!"

Others shouted, "Come on now, Reverend."

"No, he was stepping into a sea tossed with waves. Any of you ever stepped out into a sea tossed with waves?"

Millie knew he did not mean that literally. What came to her mind again was that she had now landed herself in a brothel. Maybe that was her "sea tossed with waves."

"Yes, Reverend!" came the response.

"But Peter did get out of the boat. Didn't he. And Peter did step into the sea tossed with waves. And what did he do then. What did he do then?" with each repetition his voice because stronger and louder.

And then as one the congregation shouted, "He walked on the water!"

Now the organist was beginning to provide accompaniment to the sermon, moving with the Reverend, dramatizing the story.

"Yes, yes, he walked on water. But that's not the whole story, is it?"

"No!" was the response. "No!"

"Peter began to sink, didn't he?"

"Yes!"

"Hmm, let's review. Peter got out of the boat and stepped into the sea, that sea tossed with waves." The organist hit a chord.

"Well, now I ask you, where was Peter looking when he

stepped out of the boat?" The organist followed with more chords and a run.

"At the Lord!" was the response.

"Yes, yes, at the Lord. And Peter walked on the water and was getting closer to the Lord, BUT…" And here he paused and let the organ have a turn for a full minute.

"But then you know the story. Peter began to sink. Up to his knees, then to his waist."

"Yes, preach on!"

"What happened. Why did Peter sink? Where were his eyes?"

"On the water!" they shouted. "On the water!"

"But what did Jesus do. Did he leave Peter to drown?"

"No, no, no!"

"What did Jesus do?"

This time the Reverend answered his own question: "Immediately, listen now, immediately, not later, not tomorrow, immediately, he reached down and pulled Peter up!"

"Glory, glory!" was the shout from the congregation.

"Now, children, let's go back and talk about you. You are in that boat…"

The congregation became quiet, attentive. Millie's mind drifted back over her first week at Miss Sarah's. She looked to her right at Magdala, Miss Cora, and Mr. Lester. They were now like family to her. They weren't white like her. *What would Ma say?* she asked herself.

Here she was sitting in a black church with a black family whom she had met because she now worked at a brothel and there was the sheriff sitting on the front row, a customer of Miss Sarah at the brothel. Oh, goodness, I can't figure all this out, she thought. But — and this was a shock to her — I'm already out of the boat. I did that when I left Gaston. But what do I do now?

The church service was winding down. They sang two

more hymns: "What a Friend We Have in Jesus" and "Is Your All on the Altar?"

Millie turned to the old woman next to her, and said, "Thank you for sharing your song book with me."

The old woman took Millie's hand and said, "Bless you, dear."

A wave of people was moving toward the door. Mr. Lester served as the point of the spear and Miss Cora, Magdala, and Millie fell in behind. More head-nodding and greetings were exchanged as they pushed toward the front door. Reverend Edwards stood at the front door speaking to each one as the crowd flowed out and down the steps. When Millie got to him, Miss Cora stepped in and made the introduction, "Reverend, this is Millie. She works at Miss Sarah's. Helps me in the kitchen. Just moved to Mason from down South Georgia way." The Reverend, taking Millie's hand, spoke kindly to her. "Now, Miss Millie, don't let this be the first and last time you come to First Baptist. The Butterfields here are faithful members. You come with them every week. You hear?"

Millie nodded. "Thank you kindly, Mr. Reverend, suh, thank you kindly."

That was all. The wave was pushing them down the steps. Soon they were at the Butterfield Plumbing Company truck, all stuffed in and going home.

"Millie, you want to come home with us and have cold fried chicken and potato salad. And if you run back into Miss Sarah's kitchen and fetch that leftover pound cake, I'll fix us some strawberry short cake with vanilla ice cream."

"Oh, Miss Cora, that would be the best, the bee's knees!" Millie answered.

They all laughed.

Smiling, Mr. Lester shook his head. "I don't know about 'bee's knees,' but my Cora's fried chicken is some fine eatin'."

Once home they made their way to the side door entrance

to the carriage house. The front with its double doors had originally been designed to open out as an entrance to a large parking space for a carriage or two.

The first floor of the Butterfield home was a large open living space with room for a parlor, dining area, and kitchen. Light came through the windowpanes above what had once been the large carriage house doors. The light, cut by the shape of the windows, fell in patterns across the floor and on the dining room table. Light also streamed through the window above the kitchen sink along the rear wall. Softness, gentleness, light.

In the parlor section of the room was a small desk and chair, evidently where Magdala studied, Millie thought. Next to the desk was a radio on a small table and next to that was a soft, big comfortable chair and footstool. Littering the floor alongside that chair was a stack of newspapers.

There was one more chair finishing up the cozy corner: a lady chair. Millie just knew that must be where Miss Cora sat. Running a third of the length of the side wall and behind the chairs were bookshelves groaning with books, some even stacked in front of the shelves. It's like a school in here, Millie thought.

In charge in her home, just as she was in Miss Sarah's kitchen, Miss Cora began giving directions. "Millie, run over to the house and get what's left of the pound cake. Then I'm gonna show you how to make strawberry short cakes."

In no time Millie was cutting the pound cake into slices for the four dessert plates Miss Cora had set out. In the center of each plate was a large pink rose surrounded by leaves and other smaller flowers.

Millie held one plate up. "Oh, Miss Cora, these are so beautiful. Do they have a name like Miss Sarah's Buttercup china?"

"Yes, Millie, these are called 'Floral Nosegay.' That cluster of flowers in the center is what you call a 'nosegay,' a small bouquet. I guess you'd sniff it and be happy with the smell. Put your nose there and be gay." Millie carefully placed the plate back on the table and finished by covering every nosegay with a chunk of pound cake.

Miss Cora and Magdala had already brought the fried chicken, potato salad, and sliced tomatoes to the table.

"Millie, just leave those plates on the counter there until we finish our meal," Miss Cora instructed.

Mr. Lester had already taken his seat, ready for another fine meal prepared by his Cora. Then Millie took a seat, as did Miss Cora and Magdala.

Mr. Lester spoke, "Millie, we always hold hands when we say the blessing."

Millie nodded and reached for his hand on one side and Miss Cora's on the other. They all bowed their heads.

Mr. Lester began, "Oh, Lord, we are indeed grateful for the bounty of this table provided to us by your hand. We are grateful for our health, for our jobs, for our home. And Lord, thank you for sending Millie to us. Now bless this food to the nourishment of our bodies and us to your service. In Jesus' name, amen." He paused and then said with a smile, "Let's eat!"

And they did, biting down on the chicken thighs, legs, and breasts, drinking glasses of cold, sweet ice tea, and savoring potato salad made to perfection with sweet pickle relish and boiled egg chunks.

They laughed about the funny things that had happened the week before with Millie telling all the tales of her week: killing the vacuum cleaner, breaking Miss Sarah's Buttercup china, pulling up an entire row of turnips, and limping into Zimmerman's with one shoe on, one off. By the time she had finished they were all laughing. And Millie was thinking, *I belong, they're glad I'm here.*

Miss Cora, Millie, and Magdala finished making the

strawberry short cakes. Almost in assembly line fashion, Miss Cora put a scoop of sliced strawberries on each piece of pound cake, followed by Magdala's dropping a big spoonful of vanilla ice cream on the cake. And Millie proudly delivered each piece to the table.

"You wait for us to sit down now, Lester," Miss Cora admonished when from the corner of her eye she saw Mr. Lester lifting his fork.

"Yes, ma'am, but you better hurry. My ice cream's melting." Mr. Lester winked.

In no time the short cakes were gobbled up. Millie stayed to help clean up. She, Magdala, and Miss Cora knew how to work together by now. Once done, Millie looked from Miss Cora to Mr. Lester to Magdala, and said, "Thank you for taking me to church. It made me happy. I think I'll head back to my little turret room and maybe take a nap. Feeling a little sleepy."

Miss Cora spoke first, "Before you go, Millie, you have a Bible? You might want to have one to carry with you to First Baptist next time."

"No, ma'am, Miss Cora."

"Well, here you go," Miss Cora said as she walked over to the bookshelves. She handed Millie a small, black leather-covered Bible.

"Here, let me mark something for you to read." With swift hands Miss Cora flipped to the middle of the Bible and using the satin bookmark in the spine marked the passage, closed the book, and handed it back to Millie. "Read what I marked before you take that nap. You'll sleep better," she finished with a wink.

"See you tomorrow, Millie. Glad you went to church with us," Magdala said as she reached for and squeezed Millie's hand.

"See you at supper, maybe even breakfast, tomorrow,

Miss Millie," Mr. Lester added as he led her to the door and opened it for her.

Millie skipped up the back steps into the kitchen where she paused and just stood still in this place so strange a week ago and now so familiar.

Suddenly she felt so weary. She trudged up the back stairs, passing the girls' floor as she did. She could hear Hazel playing the piano. "Wonder where they went to church?" she asked aloud.

Once in her room she closed the door. It was warm. The day had heated up. She crossed the room and opened the window. A slight breeze began cooling the air.

In no time she had slipped off her tee-straps, stockings, garter belt, and Sunday dress, carefully hanging up the slip and the dress and returning the shoes to their box. Then she set the cloche hat and the gloves on the shelf above the rack.

She then went to the bathroom, brushed her teeth, and peed. Back in her bedroom she wound her little blue clock and reset the alarm for 5:00 a.m. "I think I could actually sleep until tomorrow," she chuckled.

Flopping on the bed, Millie opened the Bible to the place Miss Cora had marked, Psalm 23, and began to read:

"The Lord is my shepherd; I shall not want…" was as far as Millie got. She let the book slip from her hands and lay back. In seconds she was fast asleep. And indeed, that's where she was when the little blue clock began chiming her little head off at five o'clock the next morning.

Chapter 8

Millie could not believe that she had been asleep since mid-afternoon Sunday, but she felt so refreshed. As Ma would say, 'you must have needed it,' she thought.

"Maybe Miss Cora was right about reading the Bible before bed. I sure feel good and bouncy," she said aloud.

She filled the bathtub and climbing in, stretched out into the warm water. She quickly washed her hair and her body. As she dried herself, she wondered about the towel and wash cloth she had used the past week and where she might get clean ones. Miss Cora will know.

She dressed, smoothed out the bed covers and put the Bible on the table next to the little blue clock. Then she headed down the back stairs to the kitchen. She knew what she would find there and sure enough Miss Cora was bustling about, singing while she fried bacon.

"Good mornin', Millie. How'd you sleep last night?"

"Oh, Miss Cora, you were right. I started reading what you had marked in that Bible and the next thing I knew it was five o'clock and my alarm clock was ringing her head off."

"Must've needed that sleep, Millie."

"Miss Cora, that's exactly what my ma would have said.

And you know I do feel rested. Maybe you can show me how to do the laundry today. I think I need to wash my sheets and towels."

Millie quickly donned an apron, put flour and buttermilk in a big bowl and started to make biscuits.

"Sounds good, Millie. I'll show you what to do after you finish with Miss Sarah's rooms."

"Yes, ma'am." Millie was soon rolling out the dough and cutting the biscuits with a big tea glass turned upside down.

"Millie, four gentlemen checked in yesterday for two nights. They'll probably be real hungry, since we don't serve supper on Sunday nights. Might need two or three biscuits for each."

Millie nodded. "Miss Cora, could we sing one of the hymns from church yesterday?"

"Pick one, Millie and you start."

"What a friend we have in Jesus, all our sins and griefs to bear. What a privilege to carry everything to God in prayer...," Millie started.

And then Miss Cora lifted her strong, deep voice, "Oh, what peace we often forfeit, oh, what needless pain we bear, all because we do not carry everything to God in prayer."

Then together they finished that first verse with Millie adding harmony, "All because we do not carry everything to God in prayer."

"Put those biscuits in the oven now and go set the table, Millie," Cora said with a smile.

In the dining room Millie knew the routine. She set the table using Miss Sarah's Buttercup china. To her way of thinking it was pretty, but not as pretty as Miss Cora's nosegay china with the big pink rose in the center of a plate.

As she was finishing up, Miss Sarah came in. "Good mornin', Millie. Hope you're doing well."

"Yes, Miss Sarah, I am. Feelin' real bouncy this mornin'."

"Well, Millie, come to my study first thing after breakfast. The vacuum cleaner has been repaired and I want to watch you use it in my parlor. Also, I've decided to go ahead and pay you for last week. So, there'll be $2.00 waitin' for you too."

"Oh, Miss Sarah, thank you so much."

The four gentlemen were making their way into the dining room, so Millie hurried back to the kitchen to help Miss Cora get the breakfast on the table.

In no time there were platters of bacon, eggs, and biscuits on the table along with a big bowl of steamy grits. Millie filled coffee cups as the men filled their plates.

Miss Sarah introduced her. "Gentlemen, this is Millie. She's been with us about a week. She helps Cora in the kitchen."

Millie nodded and bowed her head. Suddenly, she felt their eyes reading her body up and down. She felt naked. She tried to remember to hold her shoulders up and stand tall like her ma always taught her, but all she wanted to do was slump over and keep her head down. She licked her lips, parted them, and looked across the table, her gaze not landing on anyone's face.

Only one of them spoke, saying, "Nice to meet you, Millie." The others just continued to eat their breakfast and crack jokes about life on the road. Millie guessed that maybe they were delivery men like Buck. She stood at her station by the china cabinet and only moved when one of them needed more coffee.

After clearing the table, shaking out the linen tablecloth, and clucking to her hen friends, Millie straightened up in the dining room. It was routine now, making, serving, and cleaning up after a meal. Millie liked the work and especially liked working with Miss Cora and feeling like she knew how to do something useful. Mr. Lester had come in while Millie was in the dining room, and he was finishing up his breakfast at the kitchen table.

"Mornin', Millie. Cora tells me that you made the biscuits today. Fine job, real fine job," Mr. Lester said as he wiped his mouth. After sticking his hands in Miss Cora's sink full of soapy water, he wiped them off on her apron.

"Go on now, Lester," Miss Cora said without even turning around.

"See you ladies tonight. And I bid you adieu," Mr. Lester bowed before slipping through the back door.

"Miss Cora, if you don't need me to do anything else I'll go on up to Miss Sarah's study. She wants to show me how to use the vacuum cleaner better than I did before when I killed it."

"You'll do fine, Millie. Come back here after you're done with Miss Sarah's rooms. If I'm not in here yet just come knock on my door at my house. I'll show you how to use the washing machine."

"Yes, ma'am, Miss Cora."

Millie made her way up the two flights of stairs and down the hall to Miss Sarah's study. She hop-skipped through the patterns of light on the floor all the way down the hall. She was a bit breathless when she turned in to the study. "Oh, good mornin' again, Miss Sarah."

"Have a seat, Millie. You are certainly happy today."

"Yes, ma'am. I'm bouncy. Happens to me sometimes."

"Here's your $2.00. Why don't you scurry up to your room and slip this into one of the small drawers of the vanity? And then meet me in my parlor."

Millie took the $2.00 and wrapped her fingers around the worn, soft bills. She climbed the stairs to her room. As if it had been waiting to be useful, even though a bit scuffed up, the dark, stained-oak vanity stood proudly with her hinged mirrors flared. The vanity had four drawers. Millie picked the upper left one and stashed her precious $2.00 there. "Maybe I'll see Buck today and he can take Ma a dollar to help with Louise. You're a handsome ole vanity," she said aloud. Millie turned and ran out the door and down to Miss Sarah's parlor.

Miss Sarah, in a starched white blouse and calf-length, dark blue skirt, was already there with the repaired and ready-for-duty vacuum cleaner. "Now Millie, watch while I demonstrate using this vacuum cleaner."

Miss Sarah started in the middle of the area rug and worked to the edge, being careful not to catch the fringe. Then back to the center and out to the fringe. "Do you see how this works, Millie?"

Millie just nodded.

"Now, see this switch. Always remember, you can turn it off any time."

Millie kept nodding.

"Here you go. I'll be in my study if you need me."

Millie was determined to make it work this time. So she started by speaking to the vacuum cleaner. "Now you listen here. Miss Sarah gave me my $2.00 for last week because she's a good-hearted woman. I'm still in her debt for your trip to the vacuum cleaner hospital. So, you better behave, you hear. I'll cut you off in a flash if I see you tryin' to gobble up any of that fringe. There now, let's get to work."

And they did. Millie followed Miss Sarah's instructions, even going over the section of the rug she had already done just to get the hang of it. This was certainly easier than sweeping, but just to make certain it all got cleaned Millie used the two in tandem: sweep a bit; vacuum up what got swept; repeat.

She moved down the hall to Miss Sarah's bedroom, which was tidy. Millie voiced her opinion, "Well, I guess when the sheriff comes on Saturday nights, Miss Sarah cleans up her room her own self. Thank you, Miss Sarah. Sure don't think he was here yesterday after being at First Baptist."

By the time Millie reached Miss Sarah's study, she was gone, so Millie was able to clean that room as well. As usual she stowed her cleaning materials in the closet in Miss Sarah's parlor.

She climbed the stairs back to her room, stripped her bed of its sheets and the pillow of its case and, gathering up the towels and bath cloth from the bathroom, she headed back downstairs to the kitchen.

The sun was close to overhead, and the fall day was heating up, but there was a slight breeze moving the curtains and almost cooling the kitchen. Millie dropped her pile of bed linens and towels on the floor and flopped down in a kitchen chair. I think I'll have a cold biscuit and bacon before I go get Miss Cora. I'm hungry, Millie decided.

Refreshed by her snack, she went out the back door, down the stairs to Miss Cora's house, and knocked on the door.

"Ready to wash now, Millie?" Miss Cora asked when she opened the door.

"Yes, ma'am. I didn't kill the vacuum cleaner again, so I guess I'm ready to learn how to use another machine."

They returned to the house through the back porch where Miss Cora paused. "Okay, Millie, let's roll 'er into the kitchen to the sink."

There in a corner of the back porch was a squat, round, white enameled fat-bellied washing machine with rollers on its feet.

"Okay now, Millie, you push, and I'll guide it to the sink."

The kitchen floor was slightly lower than the back porch and once they got the white machine over the threshold it began to roll faster and faster.

"Oh, Lord, Millie, come here. Get on this same side with me."

Now they were both on the same side holding onto the fat, round slick surface as they crashed into the kitchen table, which thankfully slowed the rolling. All that was left now was to push the thing over to the sink. The rollers were accommodating and in no time the washer was by the sink where it needed to be. Miss Cora pressed down the lock on one of the wheels. Then she pulled the electric cord to a plug.

"Watch now, Millie." Next Miss Cora attached a hose to the kitchen sink faucet and turned on the water. "See this line here, Millie? It reads 'water line.' Let the water run until it reaches that line. Then sprinkle some detergent in the water and put your sheets and towels in."

Millie was fascinated. She carefully followed Miss Cora's instructions and soon she had a tub filled with water and sheets and towels. "Now, Millie, put 'er into gear with this lever." Millie did.

The clothes began to move back and forth. All Millie knew to do was to watch in awe as the soap dissolved and then began to bubble and the machine began to agitate, swishing the sheets and towels back and forth.

Not one to remain idle, Miss Cora was busy making several banana puddings. "Okay, Millie, if you can get your head outta that tub, answer me this. What's the menu at Miss Sarah's on Monday?"

Millie looked up, paused, and then confidently described what would be on Miss Sarah's table that night. "Pork chops, turnips, sweet potatoes, rolls and banana puddin'."

"That's right." Miss Cora kept slicing bananas. "Now let me show you how to drain the water."

Draining, refilling, putting it into gear. Millie worked the machine and Miss Cora made her banana puddings. The machine completed its final rinse just as Miss Cora slid the puddings into the oven.

The final task was to use the wringer. Millie watched as Miss Cora let the wringer grab one sheet and pull it through. "Watch your fingers and if you panic you can hit this 'panic button' and the wringer will stop. I don't need you to squash your fingers."

"I could never have wrung the water outta this towel, but the wringer gets it out. They're almost dry," Millie marveled.

Neither Miss Cora nor Millie had noticed the man who now stood in the middle of the kitchen. When Millie looked up her face lit up. "Buck!"

Buck Wilson smiled at her, his face turning a shade of red close to the color of his curly hair. "I just wanted to check on you to see how you're doing. But you've become a city girl in one week. Usin' a washin' machine and all."

Miss Cora turned and looked up from the stove. "Now, Buck, you know you have no business in my kitchen. I'll let you slide this time, since I know you're just checkin' on this country girl you brought to us."

"Miss Cora, may I help Millie hang out these sheets?"

"Oh, okay, Buck, and then get outta my kitchen."

"Yes, ma'am."

The warm afternoon sun was ready for Millie's wash. As she and Buck worked to hang out the towels and sheets a warm breeze picked up and began pushing the linens around.

"These'll be dry by night fall, Millie. In fact, you'll want to take them in then even if they're a bit damp. Mornin' dew will wet 'em all down again." Buck laughed and gave Millie a big grin.

By the time Millie and Buck returned to the kitchen, Miss Cora had already rolled the washer back on the porch. "Now, Miss Cora, you know I'd have done that for you," Buck said.

"Yes, I know, Buck, and then you'd start thinkin' you belonged in MY kitchen." Miss Cora spoke firmly this time and looked Buck square in the eye with her hands on her hips.

"Oh, Miss Cora, can he stay just one more minute while I run up and gets a dollar for him to take to Ma?" Millie pleaded.

Miss Cora just nodded yes.

Millie raced up the back stairs to her room, pulled open the drawer to the vanity, and grabbed one of the dollars.

Back downstairs she reached out her hand to Buck. "Here, Buck, I got paid and I want to share it with Ma and Louise. Would you be able to drop by Ma's at Gaston. Ask anybody. They'll tell you which house belongs to Widow Martin. Will you?" Cocking her head, she licked her lips, parted them, and cast her clear blue eyes at him.

"Of course, Millie, of course," Buck said as he stuffed the dollar in his front pocket and patted it. "I'll keep it right here. Now, Miss Cora, I'm leaving your kitchen." Buck began backing out and bowing as he went. He bounced against the frame of the door leading to the hall, gave a little salute, and disappeared.

It was four o'clock now. The banana puddings were out of the oven and resting on the kitchen counter filling the room with a delicious blend of vanilla flavoring and bananas.

"Millie, I took care of pulling the turnips today," Miss Cora said. "Look here at the bunch I pulled and compare it to what you pulled up last week. Lesson learned, huh?"

On the stove the big pot of turnips, roots, and fat back was beginning to bubble, and the sweet potatoes' skins were beginning to crack as they baked their way to perfection in the oven. The kitchen was getting hot, and sweat was beginning to trickle down Millie's cheeks.

"Millie, you may have noticed that I wear a scarf here," Miss Cora said, touching her head. "You might want to do the same. It'll help keep that sweat from forming on your brow and running down your face. Also keeps our hair outta the food. There's an extra one on the hook with the aprons on the back porch."

Millie found a bright orange cotton scarf and wrapped it around her head, tying it in a knot just above her forehead.

"We're twins now, Miss Cora," Millie announced as she did her best Broadway pose with arms outstretched.

"Well, come on now, Miss Broadway, and shake a leg."

Miss Cora was now overseeing the pork chops lined up and frying in the skillet. She had already begun to stack them up. Once done, she would put them all in a pan and slide them into the oven to keep warm.

Sweet potatoes out and rolls in for some oven time.

Millie began her work in the dining room. Soon it was five-fifteen and the gentlemen were beginning to make their way to the table.

Magdala had come in and was at the sink that was filled with an assortment of plates, pans, and spoons. "Hello there, Millie. I like your orange head scarf. Very fashionable."

Millie touched her head and laughed. "You can take the scarf off, Millie, now that you'll be serving the table," Miss Cora said. "Don't want them thinking you are only kitchen help."

"Yes, Miss Cora, but I am kitchen help. I'm your help."

"Well, chile, I don't want any one of those men folk to say something you and I will both regret."

Millie looked confused, but this was not the time to ask Miss Cora what she meant. Too much to do.

Back in the dining room Miss Sarah was at her place presiding over it all. The four gentlemen and now the girls seemed to move in rhythm with Miss Sarah, each one handling forks, spoons, and knives as she did. Buck was there fresh and slicked, sitting next to Corine. He smiled at Millie. She decided that it would be best just to nod.

Millie served the tea and added cracked ice when asked. Looking around the room, she studied the face of each gentleman and wondered what they would have said about her head scarf. Somehow Millie knew that it had something to do with her being white and Miss Cora being colored. And

Millie felt both mad and sad, a combination of emotions she had never experienced.

The evening moved along as it would tonight and every night except Sunday at Miss Sarah's. The dining room was soon empty, and Millie heard Hazel playing the piano in the parlor and she smelled the cigars and pipes of the gentlemen.

Back in the kitchen Millie found Mr. Lester scooping up another bowl of banana pudding. "Good evenin', Miss Millie. How was your day?"

"Oh, Mr. Lester, I used Miss Sarah's vacuum cleaner and didn't even kill it. And I even washed a load of sheets and towels, and I didn't even flood the kitchen while doing it. And Miss Sarah paid me for last week even though I killed her vacuum cleaner! She ain't told me what she's gonna do about the dishes I smashed."

"Well, Millie, Miss Sarah has plenty of Buttercup china. She might not even notice. You might want to get your wash in before the dew starts to fall. It'll be wetter than it was when it first came outta the machine."

"Buck said the same thing. You know Buck. He's the one who brought me here. He came into the kitchen to check on me."

"My Lord, I bet he didn't stay long!" Mr. Lester winked at Miss Cora, who had made herself a plate and was sitting with him at the table. Magdala had already eaten and gone home.

"If it's okay, Miss Cora, I'm gonna get my wash off the line before I eat and before I finish the cleanup."

After Millie left to get her wash, Miss Cora turned to her husband. "Lester, I had Millie take the head scarf off that she wore while we made supper. I told her I didn't want one of those men to make an unfortunate comment. I know she didn't understand. I just knew one of those crackers would have called her a 'little nigger girl' and I just didn't want to deal with that. I know she was confused, but figure I'll just wait until she asks about it."

Mr. Lester patted her arm, "Let it go for now, Cora. Let it go."

Her face softened, "You know, Lester, I love you more each day." She leaned in and kissed him.

"Now my day is complete, banana puddin' and a sweet kiss." Mr. Lester leaned back in his chair and smiled.

Millie was at the back screen door. "Miss Cora, Mr. Lester, my arms are full, so could one of you open the door?"

Mr. Lester smiled. "Cora, wanna help our little white baby get in the house?" Miss Cora laughed, "Lester, I think we've had another daughter, come full grown this time. Yes, I'll help her." Miss Cora got up shaking her head.

"Come on in, Millie."

"Just smell 'em, Miss Cora. All of 'em smell so fresh. Don't you think they smell like sunshine?"

"They do, Millie." Now run them up to your room and come back so we can finish cleaning up.

"Yes, ma'am." She paused. "And Miss Cora, may I wear the orange scarf again tomorrow?"

Miss Cora nodded. "Yes, Millie, of course you can. Now get on."

"Well, Cora, I'm gonna 'get on' too." Mr. Lester rose, pushed his chair back under the table and then took his plate to the sink. "See you in a bit, Cora."

He paused at the door. "Let it go, Cora. Not good for your head to settle on that. Let it go."

"Yes, Lester."

Millie returned to the kitchen. She and Miss Cora worked like a house afire. Soon the kitchen was clean and shiny and ready for the next day when they would start all over again with the biscuits, bacon, eggs, and grits. All over again.

Exhausted, Millie headed to her room. There on the floor

was a small envelope that had been slipped under the door. Millie picked it up. Sitting on her bed, she opened it. Inside was a small card. The short message read: "Come see us tomorrow in our parlor, Millie, after you finish with Miss Sarah's rooms." It was signed "Lucy, Hazel, Corine, and Gladys."

How lovely, Millie thought. I'll do just that. It was late; the clock needed winding up and Millie needed winding down. She soaked for a while in the tub and then as had become her routine she wiped herself down with her clean towel that still smelled like sunshine. She left just a bit of water like dew on her body. Putting on fresh step-ins and a chemise, she dropped into bed and was asleep as soon as her head hit the pillow that she had just covered with the fresh pillowcase.

"I love my bed," was all she had strength to mutter and then she was asleep.

Chapter 9

Millie's day began as usual with kitchen duty and then up to Miss Sarah's floor to clean. Her morning work done, she could always count on finding a cold biscuit and bacon in the kitchen. She made herself a plate. Seeing the chocolate cake on the counter under a cake keeper, she decided to cut herself a slice. Miss Cora had made the icing thick and gooey so that after cutting the slice Millie couldn't resist sliding her finger down the knife and licking the chocolatey perfection off her finger. "Miss Cora certainly puts a lot of love in her chocolate cakes. Mmm," Millie said aloud over her plate.

After eating her meal and washing the plate and fork, Millie went back up the stairs one floor to the girls' parlor. The door to the parlor was open. They, all four of them, were in their favorite places: Corine at the window with her paints; Lucy sprawled on the sofa with her ladies' magazines; Hazel at the piano; and Gladys in her chair, book in hand.

Looking up from her book, early afternoon light falling on her light brown marcel waves, Gladys was the first to greet Millie. "Oh, Millie, I'm so glad you came for a visit."

Her smooth black page boy swinging as she turned, Corine spoke next. "Good afternoon, Millie. Come take a seat with Lucy. Just push her out of the way."

From what Millie could tell Lucy had reapplied the bleach to her bob. The color of her hair was now approaching white, but soft curls still formed around her face. "Sit here, Millie," Lucy offered as she moved some magazines.

Finally, Hazel stopped playing and turned to speak. "Millie, we were afraid we had upset you. So, we sent the note. Just wanted to make up for that."

Millie just nodded and sat down.

"What do you like to do when you have a break?" Hazel asked, cocking her head to one side and causing a shift in her red curls.

"I read the dictionary or the Bible," was all Millie knew to say. *That really sounds so stupid. They must think I'm a real ninny.* Millie sighed.

Trying to sound interested, Gladys asked, "Well, tell us what word you have read recently."

Before Millie could stop herself out it came, "Brothel."

Now she had their attention. "How in the world did you come upon that word?" Lucy asked, sitting upright on the sofa.

I'm in too far now. Gotta tell the truth. "I just opened to any ole page, closed my eyes, and dropped my finger. And there it was, 'brothel'."

The room fell silent, each of the girls looking anywhere but at Millie. She pressed on as only a seventeen-year-old country girl might, "Is Miss Sarah's boarding house a 'brothel'?"

"What do you think?" Hazel asked, looking straight at Millie.

"I just think that this is a boarding house where we, I mean mainly you, entertain men. I just make sure they get fed before you entertain them."

That comment broke the ice and the four, after glancing one to the other, began to giggle.

"Millie, I think your definition about sums it up," Gladys smiled.

Corine turned back to her palette and canvas by the window with the sun streaming in, making a long pattern across the room. Hazel, making a half circle on the piano stool, returned to her music, leaving Gladys and Lucy in conversation with Millie.

"Millie, we make $20.00 a week, even after sharing part of what we earn with Miss Sarah, who after all provides us room and board. Each one of us has plans for our futures," Gladys explained. "I figure I'll make over a thousand dollars this year. I even have a bank account. I figure in another year, I'll have enough to go to college somewhere." Lucy nodded in agreement.

Millie was flabbergasted. That was more money than she could ever have imagined.

Lucy took up the story. "Each one of us has a closet full of clothes. And since Miss Sarah controls the whiskey, the men are gentlemen mostly. And if we don't like the way they act with us, we tell Miss Sarah, and she won't let them stay ever again."

Millie had to make her mouth close. She was trying to act calm.

Gladys spoke up, "We are all on our own and need to earn what we can. It's really not that bad. And look here, we have our own floor, our own parlor. And Hazel has a piano. What more could we want?"

The rest of the afternoon was a blur for Millie as she listened to Lucy and Gladys tell about their work. They explained what they did to prevent pregnancy. Lucy even left the parlor returning with a long rubber thing which she explained that every man had to wear. And once used would be discarded. Millie's brain was beginning to buzz, and glancing at the clock on the wall, she realized that she needed to head to the kitchen. Thank goodness!

"Hmm, I guess you ladies need to get ready for your evening's, uh, work and I need to head to the kitchen," Millie said as she rose to leave.

"Come any time, Millie. You can look at my *Redbook* magazines," Lucy offered.

"And I want to read you a Shakespeare sonnet next time," Gladys smiled.

Millie slipped out the door and down the stairs. She muttered, "Twenty dollars a week. Twenty dollars a week."

Her head was spinning. For a brief time, she had entered the angels' world. It was clearer now just what they did with the gentlemen. And what the gentlemen paid for the "doing."

It was Tuesday so Miss Cora was already cutting up chicken, breading the pieces, and beginning to fry a skillet full. It was hot in the kitchen. "Millie, go ahead and start cutting up the potatoes for frying once I've finished with the chicken. I've got the oven heated up to keep the chicken warm," Miss Cora directed without even turning around. "Oh, and if you were the one who cut my chocolate cake before it was time, I forgive you, but don't do that again. You can have all the leftovers you want, but not the 'befores'."

Miss Cora paused. There was a quietness in the room. She turned and asked one question, "Millie, did you visit the girls today?"

"Yes, ma'am."

By now Millie had put on an apron and wrapped the orange scarf around her head, careful to tie it in front just like Miss Cora's. She knew how to cut the potatoes, halves, quarters, the quarters cut into thirds. The big bowl was filling up.

"Somethin' on your mind, Millie?"

Millie looked up. "Miss Cora, the girls make twenty dollars a week, even after giving Miss Sarah part. Twenty dollars. Miss Cora, Lucy and Gladys told me that they have closets full of dresses and shoes. Closets full. Miss Cora, I have one good dress and three work dresses and two pairs of shoes."

Miss Cora put her long-handled fork down and came to Millie, putting her arm around her. "Miss Cora, Gladys has a bank account. And she's planning on going to college. To college, Miss Cora."

"Be careful what you wish for, Millie. Think it through real good. Right now we need to get this meal ready. It's almost 4:30. We've got one hour."

The topic was shelved for the time being. Miss Cora figured it might come up again. She planned on getting prayed up before it did. But she knew if Miss Sarah needed another "girl" just where she'd be looking.

Millie got lost in the potatoes. She moved as if in a dream. Twenty dollars a week. How could that be. Could she do that every night. Magdala had joined them in the kitchen. She had to call Millie's name twice before Millie acknowledged her.

"Millie, Millie, need any help?"

"Oh, yeah, hey, Magdala. Sorry. Just have something on my mind."

They finished the spud cutting together, passing the bowl to Miss Cora who dumped them into the bubbling grease for that hot fry bath. Now all three of them moved as one loading platters, filling glasses with ice and sweet tea, pouring green beans into a big bowl. Millie knew Miss Cora would want it, so she pulled off the orange scarf before taking the platter of fried chicken to the dining room table.

"Oh, Miss Cora, I do love your fried potatoes AND your chicken," one of the gents commented.

"Why, thank you, sir," Miss Cora smiled as she placed the platter of crisp fried potatoes on the table.

Millie took up her post near the china cabinet, ready to add more ice and tea to the glasses. But, tonight, because of her talk with Lucy and Gladys, Millie closely watched the girls as they nibbled what little was on their Buttercup china plates and leaned into the gentleman seated nearest them.

Millie watched each of them exude charm, at times even batting their eyelashes and giggling. The men were eating it up, believing that all the attention and flattery was just for them. Each girl was completely devoted to her gentleman, the one she would bed down later.

Soon the supper plates had been removed. Back in the kitchen Miss Cora was cutting the chocolate cake and placing huge slices on the dessert plates. Millie put several plates on a tray and pushed her way through the door to the dining room. She served the cake from the left as Miss Cora had taught her.

Again, she watched the girls. They were now leaning into the men and touching their arms. Millie was cataloging it all.

Back in the kitchen Mr. Lester was finishing up his supper, getting ready to leave. "How be you, Millie?"

"Pretty good, Mr. Lester. A bit tired tonight. My bed is sure going to feel good."

"Know what you mean. Have a good evenin'." Miss Cora was at the sink washing the Buttercup china. Mr. Lester kissed her on the cheek.

"See you in a bit, baby," Miss Cora nodded.

Predictable. All day long that had been Millie's thought. Predictable. Making biscuits. Cleaning Miss Sarah's rooms. All predictable. Until she went to visit the girls. Now things were somewhere between predictable and unpredictable.

Millie shook out the tablecloth and wiped down the dining room table. She heard Hazel playing the piano; she smelled the cigars and pipes. Predictable.

Back in the kitchen she tidied up a bit more. "Miss Cora, anything else you need?"

Miss Cora turned from the sink, wiped her hands, and

looked at Millie. "Millie, you may be coming to a crossroad in your life. Make certain you pick the right path. And don't rule out going back home."

Millie could not move. "Oh, Miss Cora, I'm so confused." Tears began to pour down her cheeks. "I don't know what to do." She wiped her face with her apron.

"Go on to bed now. You're tired. Things will look better tomorrow. And read the Bible. You still have that spot marked, 23rd Psalm?"

"Yes, ma'am. I'll do that. And Miss Cora, may I go to church with you again on Sunday?"

"Of course, chile. Of course." Miss Cora turned back to her sink full of dishes.

Millie trudged upstairs. She bathed, brushed her teeth, and fell into bed. She picked up the little Bible and started to read again, "The Lord is my shepherd, I shall not want." And then just before falling to sleep, she thought, Twenty dollars a week.

Chapter 10

When Millie awoke the next morning, she found that the night's rest had cleared her mind. "Here I am," she announced as she hit the kitchen floor, jumping from the last step. Miss Cora looked up. "Well, that sleep sure perked you up."

Millie set to making the biscuits, humming "Amazing Grace." Soon they had been popped into the oven and their warm baked smell began to blend with the bacon. Mr. Lester slipped through the back door just in time to wait at the table with an empty plate and fork in hand. "Good morning, Lester, where you off to this morning?" Miss Cora asked as she spooned scrambled eggs and three pieces of bacon onto his plate.

"Aw, Anderson Realty has a list of jobs for me to start on today, may get home late tonight. I'll be tired and hungry. I know you'll save me a plate. And you know your cookin' is good hot or cold, so don't trouble your sweet self."

Millie was just getting the biscuits out of the oven. "Here you go, Mr. Lester. Is one enough?"

"Make it two, Millie. I'll need my strength today."

"Here's your coffee, Lester." Miss Cora set the cup down to the right of his plate.

Millie no longer had to be told when to start taking food to the dining room. After she left the room, Miss Cora turned to Mr. Lester. "She seems herself today, Lester."

"Not your problem, Cora. Not your problem." Lester was finishing up with a last bite of the biscuit and sliding his chair back. "See you tonight, Cora. I love you."

"Go on now, Lester. You know what you love. My cookin'."

"That, too," he bowed and slipped out the back door.

Miss Cora began cleaning up the kitchen, letting Millie handle everything in the dining room. Millie breezed in, "They need more biscuits, Miss Cora." She loaded the platter up with more biscuits. Miss Cora didn't even turn from her sink.

When Millie returned to the kitchen after tidying up the dining room, Miss Sarah was seated at the table. Miss Cora did not even turn from her sink full of Buttercup china, "Millie, Miss Sarah wants to talk to you."

Miss Sarah looked up. "Have a seat, Millie."

"Have I done something wrong, Miss Sarah. You told me I could go visit the girls if I was asked."

"No, Millie, nothing is wrong. This is your second week here and you have done a fine job cleaning my rooms and helping Miss Cora in the kitchen. In fact, Miss Cora and I have just been talking about you and what a hard worker you are."

"Thank you, Miss Sarah," Millie said.

"What I want to talk with you about are some additional duties for a bit more pay. The colored girl who had been doing some cleaning for me has moved out of Mason. So, Millie, I need you to start cleaning the first-floor rooms: the dining room, parlor, the four guest rooms and the two bathrooms. I'll add 50 cents to your pay. Starting this week, I'll pay you $2.50."

Millie nodded her head, but was thinking, *This isn't much pay for twice the work.*

"Now then," Miss Sarah began as she stood, "Take a few minutes to eat some breakfast. I'll meet you in the parlor. Hmm, let's say around 8:30." Millie glanced at the clock on the wall in the kitchen. *That was fifteen minutes away.*

Miss Sarah left. Millie made her plate of biscuit and bacon. She fixed a cup of coffee with a spatter of milk and sat down. Miss Cora wiped her hands on her apron, got a plate, and joined Millie with a biscuit and strip of bacon and a cup of coffee. "Take your time, Millie," she advised. "Miss Sarah ain't goin' nowhere far. And Millie, tell her you need an upstairs and downstairs vacuum cleaner, you hear." They finished their breakfasts in silence.

Picking up the plates before Millie had a chance, Miss Cora returned to her post at the sink. "I'm going to Miss Sarah's parlor, Miss Cora," Millie said. Miss Cora just nodded her head.

Millie headed for the parlor. She had never been in the room, only glimpsed it on the day she had arrived at Miss Sarah's. She marveled again at the chandelier that hung in the foyer. But now everything would be viewed as something to clean. "Will I have to clean that?" she wondered aloud.

The morning sun came through the floor-to-ceiling windows in the parlor, bathing the room in light. There was a fireplace directly across from the entrance covered with a screen. *Hope they don't burn logs there. I'll have to shovel the ash.* Against one wall was an upright piano. *That's where Hazel plays every night.* The furniture in the room was pulled close in an open circle around a beautiful rug. Millie studied the rug's edges, planning how she would vacuum it. The walls were papered with a light golden pattern, the squiggles of the design reflecting the sunshine. *Doesn't show dust. Thank goodness!*

There were three overstuffed chairs and a settee, three pillows wide. Behind the settee were two other chairs clustered around a small table. On either side of the piano were overstuffed chairs. The room was designed for comfort and conviviality. Ashtrays on pedestals were positioned near the chairs. Those'll have to be emptied every day. Oh, those cigars. They really stink up a room. She did not hear Miss Sarah enter the room so was startled when she heard her name.

"Millie, come with me," she said. "You've seen the dining room and parlor. Now let me show you two of the guest rooms. Two are occupied, but they are identical to the ones I'll show you."

Millie followed Miss Sarah down the main hallway. At the intersection with the back hallway, they turned right. Miss Sarah explained that there were four bedrooms, paired with a bathroom between the two.

They entered the first bedroom. It had simple furnishings, a small desk and chair near a window and a single black iron bed covered with a chenille bedspread.

A door along one wall led to the shared bathroom. Bathtub along one wall, toilet and sink along the other wall. Two sets of fresh towels were folded neatly on a shelf above the toilet.

"Millie, each day, you'll need to check with me to know which rooms are ready to be cleaned. You'll clean all of them every day, but there may be times when you'll have to wait an hour or so before a room is empty. Understand?"

"Yes, ma'am."

"Any questions so far?"

Thinking of her ordeal with the washing machine, Millie asked, "Will I need to wash their sheets and towels?"

"No, Millie, I have a colored girl who does all of that. She'll come by and get the laundry every day. Her name is Alice. Just leave the laundry piled up in the hallway. Alice will find it there. Wondering why you've never seen her. She comes while you're cleaning my floor."

She continued down the hallway. Summoning up her nerve, Millie said, "Miss Cora said we need a downstairs vacuum cleaner."

Miss Sarah gave a slight smile, "I'll think about it, now that I know you won't kill it." Millie blushed.

Miss Sarah showed Millie a closet in which were stored all sorts of cleaning solutions, rags, mops, and brooms.

"I think that about covers it. You'll do this cleaning after you clean my floor. You can certainly stop between jobs to eat if you wish. I do need the rooms cleaned and ready no later than three o'clock."

Millie sighed. No more time with the girls. Oh well.

Miss Sarah left Millie in the hall and went up the front stairs. Millie made her way to Miss Sarah's floor by way of the back stairs. The cleaning went quickly. Again, Miss Sarah's bedroom looked neat, the bed already made. Well, it'll be a sight after the sheriff's visit tomorrow night. Millie kept to her cleaning routine, finishing up around noon. Her rumbling stomach told her it was time to find a cold biscuit or two.

She loved the quiet of the kitchen this time of day. A slight warm breeze pushed the curtains aside and a mockingbird was running through his repertoire, sounding like he thought it was spring.

Millie found the leftover biscuits and took two this time, adding two slices of bacon. The iced tea pitcher in the refrigerator was always full of Miss Cora's dark, sweet tea. Millie filled a glass.

Taking her time with her meal, Millie plotted out her cleaning plan for the first floor. Think I'll start with the guest rooms.

After washing and drying the dish and putting it away,

Millie went to the back hallway and assembled what she would need. She figured that she'd start with the bathroom between the last two guest rooms.

There was a sink in the closet with the cleaning equipment, so Millie filled a bucket. A box of Oxydol sat on the shelf above the sink, so she sprinkled a bit of it in the bucket. Finding a mop that looked fairly clean, she went down the hall to the last guest room which she would enter to get to the bathroom.

Shouldering the door open, Millie leaned the mop against the door frame. Then bending down she picked up the bucket handle and started walking into the room.

"My, my, what do we have here? Room service?" A sturdy-built man with dark, slicked down hair parted down the middle and a pencil mustache came toward Millie.

"Oh, excuse me, suh. Didn't know someone was still here. I'm here to clean your room."

"Well, why don't you start with me?" he asked, moving even closer. Millie stepped backward, but the man had already grabbed her arm and was pulling her into the room.

"You need to let me go, suh."

"Oh, no I don't. I jus' want to get my money's worth. That little whore I had last night was too skinny. I'd say the two of you will about equal one really good one." Now he was squeezing Millie's left arm and trying to drag her into the room, but she had her feet spread apart and was pulling backward with all her might.

"You a feisty little thing. Another skinny one, but feisty. I like that in a whore." He yanked again, thinking that with one more pull she'd be in the room, and he could with one kick of his big leg close the door and with his free hand lock it.

But Millie had a surprise for him and with all the strength she could muster she swung the bucket filled with water and

Oxydol up and into the side of his head. Now he was covered in sudsy water, with some now burning his eyes and bubbles of Oxydol soap blowing out his nose.

With one "you little bitch!" he let Millie go and she turned and ran into Miss Sarah who was standing in the hallway.

Without even a pause to ask questions about what she was seeing, Miss Sarah dug into her pocket and pulled out a fist full of bills. "Sir, here's a refund for your trouble. Take this, please. Take this and don't ever plan to stay at my boarding house again."

"Gladly," the man sputtered as he wiped his face on his shirt sleeve. "Gladly. Your little whores don't even have enough flesh to hold onto. I like my whores soft, not bony." With that he grabbed his suitcase, set his fedora on his head, and stomped toward the front door in a huff.

Turning to Millie now, Miss Sarah reminded her about what she had told her earlier. "Now, Millie, what he just did was totally uncalled for, but in the future remember to check with me before you come to these rooms to clean. Understood?" Millie nodded. Miss Sarah patted her on the shoulder and winked. "You really put him in his place. I'm gonna tell the sheriff about how you swung that bucket. He'll get a good laugh outta that! Might even make you a deputy!"

Millie sighed with relief that she wasn't getting fired and that Miss Sarah had stepped in to protect her. When she looked at Miss Sarah, the humor of it all settled in and they both began to laugh and recap the whole scene with one "what-about-when" after another.

"I guess I'd better get to cleanin' while I can before the fresh ones come in, right, Miss Sarah?"

"Just hope they won't be as 'fresh' as this one," Miss Sarah responded and with that she glided down the hall, the picture of authority and grace.

Adrenalin pumping through her body from the bucket

battle, Millie made quick work of the guest rooms. After cleaning the bathroom between the rooms where the goon had been, she stripped the beds in those two rooms. Finding fresh linens in the utility closet, she made the beds and set out new towels in the bathroom. The other two rooms and bathroom had already been cleaned so Millie could now move on to the parlor and dining room.

The dining room was already hers. She knew it well. Cleaning it was almost like caring for a friend. Millie was done for the day. She decided to get some tea and see what time it was. She headed for the kitchen and as she entered, she heard uproarious laughter. She could not believe her eyes. Miss Cora and Miss Sarah were sitting at the kitchen table with a glass of tea each. "Oh, and Cora, you should have seen his face with those Oxydol bubbles comin' out his nose and mouth. Oh, he was mad."

Millie cleared her throat. They both turned. "Here she is, the lady of the hour!" Miss Cora smiled.

"Come here, Millie, get yourself some tea. You need a break." Miss Sarah pointed to a chair. "Sit down."

Millie looked at the clock first. It was 3:30. It had already been a long day. But here she was being invited to drink a glass of sweet tea with both Miss Cora and Miss Sarah, the queens of this castle. Millie just smiled.

"Tell me all about what he said. And don't hold anything back."

"Well, Miss Cora," Millie began. She didn't hold back. She repeated every word just as it was said, every "whore," every "bitch." She had never let these words pass her lips, but with Miss Cora and Miss Sarah there in the kitchen, it seemed all right. It seemed freeing.

Four o'clock came quickly and it was time to get to work. Miss Sarah excused herself saying that she needed to freshen up before supper.

"All right, Millie, what's on the menu tonight?" Miss Cora asked, testing just how well Millie could remember each night's fare.

"Miss Cora, it's Wednesday, so tonight we're having meat loaf, mashed potatoes, green beans, and apple pie."

"Indeed, we are. Remember how to fix the potatoes?"

"Yes, I do."

"Well, they're over here in a pot. So peel 'em and get to smashing."

Miss Cora began with the work on the meat loaves. She had already cut up the onions. Working at the counter, she began molding the ground beef into loaves, just the right size to cook through and not have any raw spots.

The apple pies were in the oven and the smell of cinnamon and cooked apples filled the kitchen. Millie had put on her orange head scarf, tying it in the front just like Miss Cora's.

Magdala came through the back door. "Hey, y'all."

"Hey, Magdala, wanna smash potatoes with me. Or maybe I'll start washing that sink full of dishes and you come smash some."

"Okay, Millie. I had a hard test today in geometry. I need to smash something."

So, Millie moved to the sink and Magdala took over with the potatoes.

"Millie, tell Magdala, about the goon in room four."

Millie told it all again, this time dramatizing it with voice changes and arm movements. "Tell it, Millie, don't act it out. We need those pots washed."

"Yes, ma'am, Miss Cora."

"Oh, Millie. Were you afraid?" Magdala said.

"Terrified. But there was no way he was going to get me in that room."

Five o'clock came quickly. "Time to set the table, Millie. And take that scarf off your head."

Millie was just wiping her hands getting ready to go to the dining room. She looked up and standing in the kitchen in all their elegance were the girls, all attired for the evening.

Lucy spoke for the group. "Millie, we can't stay, but we heard what you did to the old fart that Corine had to entertain last night. Good for you. We are so proud. Maybe you can come to our parlor tomorrow for a little bit. Ciao." With that the four slipped out, whispering and then giggling as they went.

"'Bitch', 'whore', 'old fart', 'ciao.' And I thought I needed a dictionary to learn new words." She shook her head and grinned.

Soon the meal was over. Miss Sarah, girls, and gentlemen were in the parlor. Now Millie could picture them. Hazel at the piano, Corine on the sofa, Lucy by the front window, Gladys near the piano and the gentlemen equally disbursed. Miss Sarah in one of the overstuffed chairs near the fireplace overseeing it all.

In the kitchen Millie saw Mr. Lester with a plate full of meatloaf, mashed potatoes, green beans, and rolls. An extra generous slice of apple pie to his right. He looked exhausted.

"Well, Millie, I hear you gave a rogue a lesson in decorum."

"Oh, Mr. Lester, I'll let Miss Cora tell you what words he used. I already feel like I need to wash my mouth out with soap."

At the sink Miss Cora just shook her head. "Lester, it was the damnedest thing I've ever heard. She taught that son-of-a-so-in-so that even a scrawny little country girl can take care of herself. I'll fill you in later."

"I'm outta here, Cora. My bath and bed are calling. Check on me. I may fall asleep in the tub and drown."

"Lester, you are a sight. Go on now." She leaned toward him for a kiss which he gave her full and soft on her lips.

Magdala had left once supper had been served. It was just Millie and Miss Cora now. Millie finished up. "Good night, Miss Cora."

"Good night, Millie. God bless."

Millie walked up the stairs to her room. Finishing up her bathroom routine, she slipped on clean step-ins and chemise, wound her little blue clock, and fell into bed. Her window was cracked just enough for her to hear the night sounds, an owl, crickets, and in the distance a truck gearing up and then down as it passed through Mason. She fell into a deep, satisfying sleep.

Chapter 11

Another day dawned and the routine of her chores had filled the morning. Millie had made herself a fine dinner from last night's supper: cold meat loaf, string beans, and apple pie. It was nearing 2:00 and she had enough time to visit the girls.

She found them in their usual places in their parlor. Hazel was playing "Alexander's Ragtime Band" and Gladys and Lucy were singing. Corine was at the window adding touches to a rabbit pictured in a beautiful meadow.

"Come on along, come on along, it's the best band in the land…"

"Hey there, Millie. Come on along." With that Lucy took Millie by the hand and they began to sashay around the room, Gladys clapping as they did. "The best band in the land…"

The afternoon sun was streaking through the window and heating up the room, so the dance only lasted until pearls of sweat started to form on Millie's and Lucy's foreheads. "Gotta stop," Lucy wiped her forehead. "I don't want to have to bathe again." She flopped down on the sofa and continued, "Hazel, stop that playing so's Millie can tell us about what she did to that asshole pee brain Jack Jones." Millie's eyes widened at the words "asshole" and "pee brain."

Corine even stopped painting, setting down her brush. "Tell, tell," Lucy urged. And Millie did from the first "whore" to the last "bitch." She stood in the middle of the room and acted out the whole thing. The girls clapped at every twist of the story. The part about Miss Sarah's standing just behind Millie brought an enthusiastic, "Hurrah!"

Not much time was left after Millie's theatrics, just enough to play a short game of "favorites" with Lucy, turning the pages of the latest *Redbook* magazine and pointing out what each of them liked the best. Millie loved hearing Lucy's opinion about fashion and her ideas about being an independent woman. Millie was determined to at least attempt some modicum of style like Lucy.

"I gotta go," she said finally. "I enjoyed my time with y'all." Corine waved with her brush; Hazel lifted one hand from the piano in a salute; both Gladys and Lucy smiled and in unison said, "Come any time, Millie."

When Millie came into the kitchen, Miss Cora was busy making lemon meringue pies. "Onion-cutting time, Millie. This time I want to give you a suggestion. Cut the fuzzy end off first. Don't cut the stem end, the other one at all. Just let it end up being what's left."

Miss Cora had already set out cutting boards, chef's knives, and onions on the kitchen table. About that time Magdala came through the back door. "Hey, Magdala, we don't have to cry this time as long as we cut the fuzzies first."

"I'll believe it when I see it," was Magdala's response.

With more precision than she had exercised the previous week, Millie attacked one onion after another. Magdala was keeping up with her, onion for onion.

The onions took a quick turn in the grease, and then bringing the frying pan to the table, Miss Cora spooned out the onions into the big bowls, one for Magdala, one for Millie. The canned pink salmon was already there so croquette making got under way.

As always five o'clock arrived way too soon. Working as one, Miss Cora, Magdala, and Millie soon had the croquettes, the cole slaw, sliced tomatoes, and rolls on the table. Millie was at her post watching the girls and their evening guests. Again she recognized Joe the truck driver seated next to Lucy. Something about the way they looked at each other told Millie that Lucy did not see Joe as just another evening's work and Joe looked at Lucy as if she was to be treasured and not just used. Millie wondered if these gentlemen guests ever married prostitutes. Not likely, she thought.

Tomorrow would be Friday with another fish meal, so when Millie got back in the kitchen, she asked Miss Cora about buying fish at Mr. Willie's.

"Yes, ma'am, that'll be on your agenda tomorrow, Millie." Miss Cora had already made her plate and was seated at the table with Mr. Lester.

"Millie, take a load off. Join us for supper." Mr. Lester pointed at the empty chair. Magdala had eaten and gone home.

"I believe I will, Mr. Lester." Millie quickly fixed her plate and sat down.

Just as they began to eat, the back screen door opened and in came the sheriff.

"Evenin', Lester, Cora, and I believe it's Millie, right?"

"That's right," Miss Cora answered.

The sheriff paused at the table. "Millie, Sarah told me about how you can be a real threat with a bucket. Give me a mind to deputize you. Here, this is a little badge I give to kids at school. Consider yourself one of my deputies." He handed Millie a small tin badge.

"Thank you, Mr. Sheriff, suh. I'm certain any self-respecting girl would have done the same thing when under a threat like I was. Oh, and Mr. Sheriff, I saw you at First Baptist Church last Sunday. That was you, right?"

Mr. Lester and Miss Cora both looked down and covered their mouths to keep from laughing.

"Ah, well, yeah, Millie, that was me. Ah, ah, glad you noticed. Good evenin' to all. I'll head on up to see Miss Sarah."

"Good evenin' to you, Sheriff." When the sheriff had left the room, Mr. Lester winked at Millie. "Millie, I think the sheriff wants to pretend that he's invisible here. Maybe best not to comment on where else you may have seen him."

"Yes, suh. I'll remember next time."

It was time to start cleaning up the dining room and kitchen. Mr. Lester slipped on out, leaving Miss Cora and Millie to clean up.

"'Night, Millie. See you in a bit, Cora. I'll save you a spot in my bed."

"Oh, Lester, you just won't do." He patted her back as he left.

This was another of the quiet times Millie enjoyed here at Miss Sarah's, she and Miss Cora lost in thought getting the kitchen ready for the next meal.

"Good night, Miss Cora, God bless you."

"And you as well, Millie. See you in the mornin'."

They had finished up at the same time tonight, so as Millie took the first step on the back stairs, Miss Cora turned out the kitchen light and left, back screen door slamming as she slipped on through.

The air was muggy tonight, the summer trying to hold on even into October. Millie did her usual, bathing but leaving just a dew of bath water on her body. She fell into her bed, but as she drifted off to sleep, she found herself wondering about Louise, her little girl, how she was. It had now been almost two weeks since she sent that letter to her mother.

Tomorrow would be Friday. She'd get out of the house even if it was just a trip to Mr. Willie's for fish. "Hope he doesn't ask me anything about Miss Sarah," she sighed as she went to sleep.

Chapter 12

Friday. Up at five. Dressed and down to the kitchen by 5:30. Miss Cora at her frying pan cooking bacon. Predictable. Millie put on an apron, wrapped her head in the orange scarf and went to work making the biscuits. "How'd you sleep last night, Millie?"

"Real well, Miss Cora. Thanks for askin'. Miss Cora, you guess I might get a letter from Ma today. It's been almost two weeks."

"That sounds about right, Millie."

They kept at it until the smell of bacon and biscuits filled the kitchen. Mr. Lester came through the back door. "I jus' followed the smell. Mornin', ladies. Is it too early for a warm biscuit? And not jus' one biscuit. How about two, plus bacon, eggs, and grits? My, my there's nothin' like my Cora's breakfast."

"Jus' sit yourself down, man of mine. 'Fore you sit, get yourself some coffee."

Millie had just pulled out the first pan of biscuits and pushed in another. In no time a plate just as he had described sat before him.

And it was time for the breakfast hustle. Millie finished setting the table and then she and Miss Cora brought it all to the dining room. Being Friday, the gentlemen seemed particularly focused on finishing up their meals and heading out.

Soon it was just Millie in the dining room cleaning up. It was as easy as breathing. Back in the kitchen she fixed herself a biscuit with bacon and coffee with a splash of milk.

"Millie, you'll need to go on to Willie's as soon as you finish up down here on the first floor. No time to waste. You remember the way to Willie's?"

"Yes, ma'am."

"I've already called and placed the order. You just need to get the fish."

Looking forward to getting out of the house, Millie finished up cleaning Miss Sarah's rooms. The sheriff must have been a bit less active the night before. The bed needed making, but at least the sheets weren't all twisted up. The cupids looked sad. "Sorry, little cupids. He'll be back on Saturday," Millie told them.

Back downstairs to the first floor, Millie tidied up the front rooms and then headed to the guest rooms. She had checked with Miss Sarah. All the gentlemen were gone.

It was now close to 3:00 p.m. Millie slipped back through the kitchen, grabbed a cold biscuit, and went out the back door. The October sky was brightest blue, flecked with a few wisps of white clouds. The day was warm, but not hot and the promise of cooler weather seemed to float along in the breeze.

Millie carried the small canvas bag Miss Cora had given her across her arm. She skipped her way to Third Street and waited for the light to change. Crossing Third Street, she decided that she needed to walk in a more dignified way these last two blocks. She didn't want Mr. Willie to see her skipping like a child. *I'm a working woman now.*

The bell above the door rang as Millie entered Willie's Fish House and Mr. Willie himself, wiping his hands on an apron slick with fish scales, came out from the back.

"Well, well, Miss Millie. This gone be a regular thing now. You don't mind makin' the trek every week?"

"Oh, no, Mr. Willie. Gets me outta the house. Miss Sarah has me cleanin' more of the house, but I get paid $2.50!"

"Good for you, young lady. Hey, Cora told me 'bout how you whomped up on that cracker. Wooo-eeee. Wish I coulda seen that. Don't mess with a country girl, right?"

Millie blushed. "I guess so, Mr. Willie." Cracker, what's a "cracker"? she wondered.

"Well, here you go, enough catfish to feed ten hungry men or maybe four at Miss Sarah's. Cora always knows exactly what she needs."

"Thank you, Mr. Willie. Maybe I'll see you next week. Bye now."

"See you next week, Millie. You take care and don't let any of those crackers get the best of you." Shaking his head, Mr. Willie headed back through the swinging door to the rear.

Millie kept a steady pace as she walked home. Occasionally looking up at the brilliant blue October sky, she breathed in the warm fall air. All seemed good to her. She went down the driveway and up the back stairs. "Here's the cats, Miss Cora." Millie handed off the canvas bag.

"You got some mail, Millie, and an envelope from Miss Sarah there on the table."

Millie sat down in front of the two envelopes. Which should she open first. She started with Miss Sarah's. Inside was her pay for the week, $2.50. In a bit she'd run upstairs and put it in the drawer with the dollar left from last week. But there was the other envelope post-marked "Gaston."

She held the letter for a moment and then tore into the envelope. Miss Cora was unwrapping the fish and beginning to slide them through the corn meal. Millie unfolded the letter and read silently:

Dear Millie,

That trucker from Savannah left the dollar you sent.

Not feeling very well. That TB is working on me. Had to take to bed for the week. Mildred saw to me for a while. You remember Mildred next farm up.

Tom came back last week. Took Louise with him back to Savannah. Said it was for the best.

Hope this letter finds you well there in Mason. Don't think I'm long for this world.

Keep your wits about you. Go to church when you can.

Love,

Ma

Millie dropped her head onto the table. "Took Louise with him to Savannah! I'll never see her again," she said with a moan. "She's gone forever. Oh, Jesus, whatever am I to do?" She began to weep.

Miss Cora turned from her work. "Millie, let me see the letter?"

Without even looking up Millie handed Miss Cora the letter. Miss Cora read it and sat down at the table. "Millie, you're here in Mason now. Louise needs a family that can do for her. You can't bring her here. Your mother is real sick. It's hard. I know. Living under the circumstances is hard, like carrying a load, a big load. We all have an 'under-the-circumstances' load we carry. But we carry on the best we can. Some days better than others. For now, Millie, it's time to fry these cats and make the hushpuppies. Those gents will be at the table in about half an hour."

Millie looked up, wiped her eyes, nodded her head. She went to the sink to wash her hands, splashed water on her face, and then began making the hushpuppies. She cut up the onions, not caring that they made more tears fall. She pressed the onions into the corn meal and in no time had rounded balls ready for the frying pan. Magdala had come in and was washing dishes.

Going through the motions, Millie finished up her duties. The gentlemen guests, the girls, and Miss Sarah seemed in a fine mood, eating, laughing. All so jolly. And in the kitchen, Mr. Lester at his place; Magdala gone home, Miss Cora now at the table with Mr. Lester.

"Millie, make yourself a plate and sit down."

"I'll sit down, Miss Cora, but I ain't hungry. Maybe a glass of sweet tea and a hushpuppy. That's all I want."

The three of them ate in silence. Finally wiping his mouth, Mr. Lester rose to leave. Looking at Millie, he said, "Millie, you got a family here. Remember that, you hear." He turned and slipped out the back door. Miss Cora reached over and patted Millie's arm.

Millie and Miss Cora finished cleaning up the kitchen which included a good wiping down with Oxydol and hot water, ridding the room of the fried fish smell. Miss Cora had given her husband a pass because he looked so tired.

Wiping her forehead with a dishtowel, Millie asked, "Anything else, Miss Cora?"

"No, baby. Go get yourself a good night's sleep. Everything will look better in the morning."

Exhausted, Millie trudged up the back stairs, almost dragging herself at times. In her bathroom she drew a bath of very warm water. Stretching out full length she let the warm water cover her whole body and her face, leaving only her head above the water level. "Oh, I could just die," she said aloud. "I could just die. But right now I'm too tired to die." Something about that thought struck her as funny, so she repeated the line louder now, incredulous at that thought. "Too tired to die. Millie, that's about the stupidest thing you've come up with yet."

She bathed her body and washed her hair. Getting out

of the tub, she dried just a bit, choosing as had become her habit to leave just enough water to cool her down before going to bed.

She opened the Bible Miss Cora had given her to the 23rd Psalm. Her eyes fell on verse four: "Yea, though I walk through the valley of the shadow of death, I will fear no evil; for thou art with me." She stopped there. "That's me, walking through the shadow of death, but too tired to die." She rested the Bible on her chest, closed her eyes and fell asleep.

Chapter 13

As usual the little blue clock announced the hour of 5:00 a.m. "Wake up, Millie," she seemed to say. Millie slowly opened her eyes and wondered, It's morning. Everything looks the same. Is that the 'better' Miss Cora was talking about?

"Yesterday we had fried fish, so today must be Saturday, turnips, and meat patties with gravy," she said aloud. "This time I won't pull an entire row of turnips. Gotta few minutes. Think I'll do a drop-finger dictionary search before I get dressed."

Millie brought the dictionary to her bed, opened it up and dropped her finger. Her finger fell on "forgive." She read aloud, "Stop feeling angry or resentful toward someone for an offense, flaw, or mistake." Humph, not yet, Tom Stapleton. I'm gonna live angry just so's I can survive. Yeah, my anger toward you, Tom Stapleton, you goon, you asshole, you rogue." She used every word she had learned. Two from the girls and one from Mr. Lester. "Yeah, you ASSHOLE."

Now she was ready to work. She dressed, brushed her beautiful teeth and with new resolve headed to the kitchen. Of course, Miss Cora was there, bacon frying, grits bubbling. Mille put on her apron, wrapped her head with her favorite orange scarf and started with the biscuits. "You better today, Millie?"

"Yes, Miss Cora. I'm a bit better. I'm gonna learn to live under those 'circumstances'." In no time Millie was pushing one pan of biscuits into the oven.

Soon Millie and Miss Cora were serving the gentlemen their biscuits, eggs, grits, and bacon. Millie got to moving so fast she forgot to remove her orange head scarf and Miss Cora failed to notice.

Millie was serving coffee when one man looked up and called to the other three. "Hey, fellows, look at Cora's little nigger girl with her head rag." The other three laughed.

The first man continued, "You better take that head rag off, little girl, or your skin will go black." Now all four of them began to laugh aloud. One in fact added, "You really told her, Jesse."

Millie, still fueled by her anger toward Tom Stapleton for taking Louise to Savannah, put down the coffee pot on the table so hard coffee spurted out the spout. "Listen here, mister, I'm proud to wear this here orange scarf. If I ever hear that word again from you, I might have to hit you in the head with a bucket. Where I come from, we don't talk like that. You, you, cracker." And with that she grabbed the coffee pot and left the room. She could hear the men laughing as she left, but she didn't care. She had stood up to those goons, rogues, assholes, and crackers, too.

Millie, muttering "Hit you in the head with a bucket" as she came back into the kitchen, got Miss Cora's attention. Millie again set the coffee pot down hard. "Miss Cora, what's a 'cracker'. I just called one of those gentlemen a 'cracker'."

"Well, Millie, I'll answer your question, but after that I want to know what just transpired in the dining room." Miss Cora paused. "Millie, a 'cracker' is what we black folk call a white person, mostly men, who are disrespectful and may have called us 'niggers.' Understand?"

"Well, Miss Cora, one of them called me a 'nigger' because I had this head scarf on. And I told that man, if he ever said that word again, I'd hit him in the head with a bucket. And then I called him a 'cracker.' Sounds like I picked the right word, right?"

Miss Cora had to sit down she was laughing so hard. "Oh, Millie, I think you got it right, but next time remember to remove that scarf. Those men pay our bills, and I don't want one of those bills bein' their doctor's bill."

"Yes, ma'am. But, you know, Miss Cora, it felt real good to say that word to them. CRACKER felt real good. Is that wrong?"

"Millie, you got some real tough news yesterday. You've got a load of anger now. Use it well, but don't throw more of it on folks than is necessary. I'd say it was necessary just now."

Millie just nodded.

"Now, little girl, get back to work."

The clean-up in the kitchen went fast. A gentle early fall breeze was blowing through the kitchen cooling it off from the heat of breakfast. Millie hung up her apron and put up her head scarf. "If you don't need anything else, Miss Cora, I'm going upstairs to clean Miss Sarah's rooms."

"See you around four, Millie," Miss Cora said from her sink full of Buttercup china.

Millie cleaned Miss Sarah's floor, checked with her about which rooms to clean on the first floor and then headed to the kitchen to find something to eat. There was leftover bacon and biscuits on the counter. Millie took a biscuit and a piece of bacon, then she looked in the refrigerator. One piece of lemon meringue still in the pie pan and a glass of sweet tea would finish up her meal. She ate her biscuit and bacon and then decided to eat the pie in layers, sliding her fork through the meringue and eating that first and then bite by bite savoring the lemon filling and flaky flour crust.

After washing her plate, the pie pan, and her glass, she decided to finish up her cleaning duties on the first floor. It was three o'clock when she finished and since she had to pull turnips before four, she figured she'd better go ahead and get that done. She might even have time for a bath before going back to the kitchen.

Millie enjoyed being in the turnip patch. A few lazy butterflies kept her company as she pulled half a row of turnips. She washed them real good without even getting herself wet. Back in the kitchen she left them in the sink, figuring that she'd have time to chop them up at four.

She had just enough time for a bath and a new dress. Back in her room she took her time stretching out in the tub and just letting the warm water do its work. She reflected that she enjoyed her work at Miss Sarah's, the feeling of accomplishment when a room got cleaned or a meal got prepared.

She dried completely this time and put on new step-ins and chemise. Finally, she chose the blue everyday dress because she thought it made her eyes look bluer. "There, Millie. You are ready to get the rest of your $2.50 earned for this week," she said.

Miss Cora was not in the kitchen when Millie returned, so she went ahead and started chopping the turnip greens just as she had seen Miss Cora do last week. Millie started singing, "Come on along, come on along…the best band in the land…"

Miss Cora came through the back door and joined in "Alexander's Ragtime Band." "Well, you're bouncy today, Millie."

"Yes, ma'am, I'm feeling bouncy."

"I almost forgot," Miss Cora said, "we have an extra guest for dinner. Set another place."

Chopped turnip greens and sliced roots were now simmering in the chunks of fat back and water in two big pots. Magdala had joined them and was helping Millie slice the onions. The meat patties were frying and soon Miss Cora would be making her famous gravy.

Once the onions were sliced Millie and Magdala moved on to mashing or, as Miss Cora called it, "smashing" the potatoes. The clock was ticking and soon it was five o'clock.

Millie pulled off her orange scarf and started carrying the platters of food to the dining room. Magdala was right behind her with more platters of food. Once the platters were on the table, Millie stationed herself at the spot near the china cabinet watching for empty tea glasses. It was then that she noticed that same boy, the one she had seen a week ago, the one who didn't seem to want to be there. The one Millie was certain was close to her same age. Miss Sarah had stationed him at her right.

Again, he gave that furtive look, the one that again seemed to say, "Get me out of here." Millie just smiled and nodded.

Soon the pound cake had been served and they all were sliding their chairs back and moving toward the parlor. Millie turned to head for the kitchen when Miss Sarah touched her arm. "Millie, wait just a minute."

Now it was just Millie and Miss Sarah in the dining room. "Millie, I need you to entertain that young man, the one who looks so scared. He's the mayor's son and well, normally I'd see to him, but, well, you know the sheriff will be visiting me tonight."

Oh, good lawd, she's gonna ask me to entertain him. Ask me to be a prostitute. Millie thought, eyes widened.

"His name is Alex. Go tell Miss Cora that you'll be in the parlor with us tonight. Then, when that part of the evening is done, you'll take Alex to your room. And well, you let him do what men do. Here, you'll need these. Hopefully not this many, but you might. He's only seventeen. This will be his first time and he may be, well, energetic." Miss Sarah handed Millie three packages of condoms. "Any questions?"

Am I becoming one of the girls. I guess I am. Millie thought.

Millie took the condoms and put them in the pocket of her dress. All she knew to ask was, "How much will I get paid for, uh, what I do tonight, Miss Sarah?"

"Millie, I will add $4.00 to your $2.50. I'll give that to you on Monday. See you in the parlor once you've explained to Cora where you'll be."

Four dollars! That's more than I make for my kitchen and cleanin' work for, well, two weeks. Millie mulled it over.

She went back to the kitchen. Mr. Lester was enjoying an extra wide slice of pound cake. "Good evenin', Millie. How was your day?"

"Well, Mr. Lester, I don't think it's over." Mr. Lester and Miss Cora were family to her now. She kept nothing from them. Millie reached in her pocket and showed Mr. Lester the three packages. "Mr. Lester, I'll be entertainin' tonight. Miss Sarah told me to come back here and tell Miss Cora."

Turning from her dish washing and looking at Millie, Miss Cora spoke, "Millie, we want you to go to church with us tomorrow. Understand?"

"Yes, ma'am. Well, I'd better go now." As she left the kitchen Miss Cora placed her hand on Mr. Lester's shoulder. "Not your problem, Cora," he told her. "What you said was all you could say. Get a glass of tea, sit down here, and have a slice of this delicious pound cake. I'm gonna help you clean up the kitchen tonight."

"Yes, Lester."

Well, I'm sure glad I took that bath, Millie thought as she headed to the parlor.

In the parlor Hazel was playing one of her new numbers

and everyone was smiling, the gentlemen were keeping time with the tune by patting their knees. But, under the surface was a tension that was building, each man knowing this is not what he came here for.

Millie took a seat next to Alex. He cut his eyes at her and sighed. She just nodded. The evening wore on and soon it was time. First Lucy, then Corine, next Gladys, and finally Hazel left, each one with her gentleman.

Not knowing quite how this was to go, Millie took Alex's hand and said, "Come on, Alex, I'll show you my turret room. We can go up the back stairs." Millie was in charge now. Alex didn't have time to even think. All he could get out was, "Okay."

Millie dragged him through the kitchen where Mr. Lester and Miss Cora were cleaning up. "Hey, y'all. Mr. Lester and Miss Cora, this is Alex. Alex, this is Mr. Lester and Miss Cora. See y'all tomorrow." Mr. Lester and Miss Cora paused in their work, turned, looked at each other and stifled a laugh.

By now out of ear shot of Miss Cora and Mr. Lester, Millie kept up the chatter, "Come on, Alex. It's a real twisty stairway, don't you think, Alex?"

"Uh, huh."

Once in her room Millie turned to Alex. "Here, put this thing on your manhood while I take off my dress."

Alex stood there dumbfounded, looking down at the package. "Uh, Millie, I don't want to do this."

"Oh, you better because I do not plan on havin' a baby after what we do tonight, understand?"

"No, Millie, what I mean is I don't want to have sex with you. I mean, not because of you. You are very pretty. I'm just not ready for this. It was my daddy's idea. He thinks before I go off to college, I need to have this experience. I'm not ready. I'm so glad you're the one I ended up with. Maybe we can pretend that we did, you know, do it. Could you lie about this if you had to? I mean 'entertaining' a man doesn't have to mean that you slept together, does it?"

Millie just stood there with her hands on her hips, then asked, "Wanna go sit on the back porch and watch fireflies?"

Alex's handsome face lit up, his warm brown eyes shining. "Yes, I do."

Again, they navigated the twisty back stairs, giggling as they went, Millie dragging him by the hand. They stumbled into the kitchen. Mr. Lester and Miss Cora were almost done tidying up.

Millie stopped suddenly, Alex bumping into her back. "Oh, Miss Cora, Mr. Lester, y'all need any help. Alex and I can help clean up." Alex, busy nodding his head, added, "I'm real good with a broom."

Millie continued, "We were going to sit on the back steps and watch for fireflies, if there are any. That's the way Alex here wants to be entertained. Right, Alex?" She turned to look him in the face, a face that was grinning, a head that was nodding.

Miss Cora and Mr. Lester were speechless. Finally, Mr. Lester spoke, "Naw, Millie, Cora and I got this. You young folks go on out and enjoy this beautiful evening." Again once Millie and Alex were out the back door, Mr. Lester and Miss Cora looked at each other and again in unison said, "Millie!" and laughed out loud.

It was a perfect Southern evening, just enough warmth left from the day to bring out the fireflies, the last of the late summer, early fall.

For a few minutes Millie and Alex just sat there listening to the crickets and the trucks gearing up and gearing down as they barreled through downtown Mason. Just two young folks being together on a warm October night in the South.

Alex turned to Millie. "Millie, I never thought this night would turn out like this. Thank you."

Millie just nodded and smiled. They sat in silence. Miss Cora and Mr. Lester had gone home and soon their lights were turned off. And Millie and Alex just sat and watched the fireflies, listened to the crickets and the trucks.

Finally, Alex spoke, "Millie, I'll be going to college next year, University of Georgia. I'm gonna be a lawyer one day and maybe even a judge."

"That sounds good, Alex. I know your family will be proud."

"I'll be so glad to get away from Mason. Do you understand that?"

"Yes, I do. I left my home last month. It was really a matter of have to. My husband left me and now he's come back and gotten our daughter and taken her to Savannah with him. Ma's still there but says she's not long for this world. I guess someone will let me know when she goes on to be with Jesus."

"Sorry, Millie."

"It's okay, Alex. Nothin' I can do about it now."

They sat quiet again. The hours were passing and soon it was midnight. Alex spoke, "Millie, I guess I can go home now. I'll tell my father I was with a lady at Miss Sarah's. It won't be what he thinks, but it will be the truth." Alex stood, so did Millie.

Taking her hands, he kissed each one on top. "Thank you, Millie, thank you. I'll never forget you and the fireflies."

Millie watched him walk across the yard to the driveway and he was gone. "That was an easy $4.00," Millie muttered on her way through the kitchen and up the back stairs.

She continued, "I'll have $6.50 on Monday, plus the one other dollar so that makes $7.50. Now if I just had time to spend it. Maybe Buck will come through and I can send some money to Ma." Too much to figure out tonight. She shook her head and made her way to the bathroom. She had started her period, but Lucy had shown her how to use the belt and disposable pads, so Millie was enjoying one more luxury of city life, or in her mind, life at Miss Sarah's.

She wound and set the alarm on the little blue clock. She thought back on the evening with Alex. In her mind he was such a boy, a child. Money seemed no object for him. All he had to do was dream, plan. Money was an object for Millie. What she had to do was survive. She fell asleep with that thought. Survive.

Chapter 14

By six o'clock Sunday morning she was clean and wearing her oldest dress, the one she had come to Mason in, planning to change to her church dress after breakfast. Finding something to eat when breakfast was not being made was one of Millie's favorite things to do in Miss Cora's kitchen.

She started with the refrigerator. Inside she found a dish of sliced tomatoes, a ground beef patty covered in onions and a real prize, a two-day old piece of lemon meringue pie. So, there it was, her breakfast: sliced tomatoes, cold meat patty and onions, plus the pie.

Thinking that the patty and tomatoes needed something more, she spied a jar of Duke's mayonnaise, something Miss Cora used when making the cole slaw. Millie got a spoon and began dropping globs of mayonnaise on first the tomatoes, then the onions, then the meat patty. When she got to the lemon meringue pie, she paused. "Ain't never thought about it on pie. Maybe I'll leave it off for now."

But everywhere she had globbed the Duke's was a hit, especially on the cold onions and meat. Millie finished up her Duke's-enhanced meal and climbed the stairs to her room. She had enough time to read Psalm 23 again before she set about getting herself gussied up. She read the final verse aloud, "Surely goodness and mercy shall follow me all the days of my life…" She stopped there. She wondered aloud, "'Follow me' but does it ever catch up. What I need is some 'goodness and mercy' right alongside me."

She closed the Bible and started getting dressed for church. By ten o'clock she was ready, had pulled on her gloves and made her way down to the kitchen and out the back door. The October sky was showing off her blue beauty and the sun was so bright that when Millie looked up at the white frilly clouds floating by, she had to shield her eyes.

"Hey, there Millie, you look ready to go." It was Magdala dressed in a light green dress with a broad white collar trimmed in lace, her shoes just a darker shade of green. Miss Cora and Mr. Lester were not far behind and this Sunday, Mr. Lester's bowtie matched Miss Cora's dress, which was a bright kelly green. She had on a black broad-billed hat with a kelly green satin ribbon. She held her black gloves in her hand with her Bible, her purse handle across an elbow.

With the same precision as before the four stuffed themselves into Mr. Lester's truck. "And we're off," Mr. Lester announced.

Millie looked forward to church at First Baptist. Lots had happened in the week since last Sunday. To her now the crowd seemed familiar and even jolly. She found herself, like the Butterfields, speaking and nodding to those around her. The day was not as warm as last Sunday, so sitting by a window did not matter, but Millie did find herself searching for the little old woman she had sat by and shared a hymnal with last Sunday.

Millie saw her in that same spot, back row by a window. She caught her eye and waved. The old lady nodded and raised her hand toward her. Mr. Lester was doing his usual politicking around, flashing his big grin, nodding, patting shoulders, shaking hands, and at times laughing a bit. He found a row with enough seats left for the four of them. They got settled just as the song leader rose to start the service.

Millie and Magdala shared a hymnal, smiling as the organ began with an introduction to "Lily of the Valley." Then they sang, "Have Thine Own Way": "You are the potter; I am the clay." Millie looked at Magdala. They both shrugged. What in the world did that mean?

The choir sang "Amazing Grace," Millie's favorite. But their version was nothing like the Gaston Methodist Church version. This choir swayed, moving with the rhythm of the song, repeating phrases. And the organ grew louder with each verse. "Amens" began to break out all over the congregation. "Sing on, sing on." And they did, singing the last verse again: "When we've been there ten thousand years, bright shining as the sun, we've no less days to sing God's praise than when we've first begun."

Millie wasn't singing with them but felt exhausted from just listening. It was almost as if the choir sucked the air out of the room and then blew it back out over the church. Millie closed her eyes and let those heavenly voices blow across her face.

Now it was time for the sermon. Reverend Edwards stood and announced his sermon topic: "Joy in Trials."

He began with the reading of the text from James 1:2-6:

"Listen now brethren, be still and listen:

"My brethren, count it all joy when ye fall into divers temptation; knowing this, that the trying of your faith worketh patience.

"But let patience have her perfect work, that ye may be perfect and entire, wanting nothing. If any of you lack wisdom, let him ask of God, that giveth to all men liberally, and upbraideth not; and it shall be given him."

Reverend Edwards began, "Brothers and Sisters, I start with a question: How many of you have asked God for more patience?"

Heads began to nod and folks began to mutter things like, "too many times to count."

Reverend Edwards continued, "And how many times have you prayed 'oh, Lord, give me just the right thing to say, give me wisdom'?"

More nodding and muttering.

"So, how do we get patience. How do we get wisdom. Listen now. It's when we go through diverse temptations. What did you say, Reverend. I get wisdom by going through temptations. But chillen, it's this testing because that's what a 'temptation' is, it's a test. You ever had a test — and I'm not talkin' 'bout in school. I'm talkin' 'bout in life. Ever had a test in life? Tell me."

And now the call and response began. "Yes, Reverend, yes."

"And did you go through this 'test' with a smile on your face. Be honest now, chillen. Did you go through this test with a smile on your face?"

"No, Reverend, no."

"But what does Brother James say, and you do know that he was Jesus' brother. What does he say?"

"Well, tell us, Reverend."

"We are to consider this testing to be a joyous thing. You don't have to like the test, but look at the reward, PA-TIENCE." And now the organ was cranking up with a chord.

"And we'll come back to this patience thing, but I want to put one more piece of meat on the grill. What about wisdom. Did you hear what I said. What about wisdom?"

"What, what, Reverend?" Organ chord and a run or two.

"All you have to do is ASK. Did you hear me, chillen. All you have to do is ask." With that the organ really began to participate and have a say by herself.

The congregation was now fully engaged, so Reverend Edwards could bring them along through the rest of his sermon, but Millie was stuck back at asking for wisdom and being happy about tests. She'd have to think on this a bit. As she had done last Sunday, Millie was in her own head reviewing her week, thinking about Tom, Louise, and Alex, waiting for it all to settle, all to fit together somehow.

So, goodness and mercy are following me. I'm going to have tests, but I should be happy about that. And if I need wisdom – I don't even have enough wisdom to know when that would be – all I do is ask? Millie was pondering it all. But then another thought crowded all of that out: I wonder what Miss Cora has fixed for dinner. I sure hope we have cold fried chicken and potato salad again. Oh, and strawberry short cake.

And then the service was winding down with the final hymn. Magdala had already turned to the page. "Just As I Am." After five verses, Reverend Edwards gave the benediction, and everyone began to move toward the door. Magdala was speaking to friends from across the pew, but still keeping close to Millie and her parents. All they really had to do to reach the door was to lean into the folks ahead of them and not resist the push from those behind.

The October blue sky greeted them once they reached the door. Reverend Edwards was shaking as many hands as he could. "Well, well, Millie, you came back."

"Yes, Brother Edwards." That's how Millie would have addressed the reverend back home in Gaston. "I'm interested in that wisdom you preached about today."

"Well, Millie, just keep being 'interested' in her and she'll find you."

Millie furrowed her forehead and moved forward. Didn't know wisdom was a 'she.'

Another trip home in Mr. Lester's truck and they all spilled out in the driveway. Miss Cora immediately started giving directions. "Millie, we'll have strawberry short cakes like we did last week. You go on back in Miss Sarah's kitchen and find that leftover pound cake. I'm gonna let you and Magdala make 'em this time."

When Millie returned to Miss Cora's kitchen, she and Magdala had already set the table and begun to place platters on it. Millie was not disappointed. Included in the spread this week with the fried chicken, potato salad, and tomato slices were deviled eggs, perfectly filled with boiled egg yolks made soft and gooey with Duke's mayonnaise. Millie and Magdala made the dessert, dropping globs of sliced strawberries on the pound cake and then being a bit too generous with the vanilla ice cream, which completely covered the strawberries and spilled over the sides of the cake. When Mr. Lester got his piece, he took his fork and lifted the ice cream just enough to see under, asking, "Any strawberries under here?" Millie looked at Magdala and they both giggled.

Another happy Sunday at the Butterfields. Millie helped clean up and then excused herself saying, "Well, I need to do some washing and ironing so's I'll be ready for next week. Thank you for another wonderful Sunday."

"See you in the morning, Millie," Miss Cora said. Mr. Lester just nodded.

"It was fun sitting with you at church," Magdala added.

Once in her room Millie changed out of her church clothes, donned her oldest dress, and went to work. She'd decided to clean her room and bathroom. She thought it best not to borrow the broom, mop, and bucket from Miss Sarah's parlor, so she rummaged around in the kitchen closet finding what she needed there.

Last Sunday Millie had slept all afternoon and all the way to Monday morning, so this Sunday was her first Sunday to enjoy her own time. The house was quiet as if empty of all except Millie. She worked in this stillness, this soft space, cleaning her room and bathroom, then going to the kitchen to wash her sheets and towels and to iron the one dress she had washed and hadn't had time to iron.

Like the house, all the rest, the mop, broom, rags and now the washing machine, seemed to yield to her touch willingly. "Potter and clay," Millie remembered the words from the hymn. On this Sunday afternoon in October 1927, in Mason, Georgia in this house on Maple Street, Millie felt like the potter, all yielding to her touch.

Millie decided to start with the ironing, setting up the board, plugging in the iron. She felt in command of these modern conveniences she had never known. Rhythmically she flattened the wrinkles with the heat of the iron.

She returned the dress to its place on the rack in her room. Now to the wash. Again, the moving of the washer, the set-up with the hose and the sink. All done with confidence. Soon she had a basket filled with clean damp linens. Out in the backyard she stretched the sheets across the line and then carefully hung the towel and wash cloth using wooden clothes pins.

Back in the kitchen Millie returned the washer to its place on the porch, just as she had done with the ironing board and iron. Then, she just sat down at the kitchen table and listened to the nothingness of a Sunday afternoon. She let out a big sigh, as if expanding into the space she now inhabited, the turret room, this kitchen, Miss Sarah's rooms, the guest rooms, the parlor, and the dining room. She breathed in and out and sighed again. This place was her home now. She felt settled.

It was almost six o'clock and the sun was beginning to wane. She found a biscuit from Saturday's breakfast and began to break off pieces and nibble them. She had done a full day's work in just a few hours. Suddenly she felt bone weary. She poured herself a glass of cold milk.

The sun was beginning to set now, so she took the milk

and the biscuit and went to the back steps. No fireflies tonight, but she could hear the birds putting themselves to
sleep with short tweets and coos. She sat there until the first
stars came out. "It was a good day," she said aloud.

She washed her plate and glass, then took a bit of Crisco
from the can and rubbed it onto her hands like Miss Cora
had shown her, to soften them. Finally, she made her way to
her turret room. Five a.m. would be here soon. She bathed
quickly, wound the little blue clock, and lay down. The sweet
fall breeze slipped through the open window, floating over
Millie as she drifted off to sleep.

Chapter 15

It was Monday and Millie's workday began early as usual. After kitchen duty she headed up to Miss Sarah's floor. She was done with all the rooms except Miss Sarah's study, where her employer was working. "Miss Sarah, I can come back later," she said.

"That would be good, Millie." Miss Sarah paused, then added, "Millie, I will give you the bill to repay once the replacement Buttercups come in." She never looked up from her desk.

"Yes, ma'am, Miss Sarah. And, Miss Sarah, what about the guest rooms. May I clean them after I do the dining room and parlor?"

"Yes, Millie. All our guests checked out after breakfast."

Millie stood in the hallway, tears flowing. I'm doin' the best I can, but I'll never have any money for Louise, if I don't stop breakin' things. She wiped her eyes with the back of her hand, squared her shoulders. Then she stowed her cleaning equipment and made her way to her duties on the first floor. Taking the main stairs brought her to the second floor and the girls' rooms. As she made the turn to head to the first floor, Gladys was just coming out of her room. "Oh, Millie, come to our parlor after you're done. Lucy has given us some exciting news, and we want to tell you all about it."

Millie finished up her first-floor cleaning and decided it was time for dinner. She set a place at the kitchen table, placing her plate with biscuit and bacon there. She filled a glass with Miss Cora's sweet tea, got a linen napkin and sat down. She had decided to act like a lady even when no one was looking.

As she ate, she pretended that she was at the dining room table and began a conversation with an invisible guest. "No, I haven't been here long. Really about a month. What line of work are you in? Really. And in your spare time what do you do?" She nodded as if she had gotten an answer. Then copying what she had seen the girls do, she raised her hand and giggled slightly behind her fingers.

She decided to go to her room before she went to the girls' floor. She brushed her teeth, fluffed her hair, and put the $6.50 Miss Sarah had just given her into the side drawer of the dresser. It could just rest there, but once the bill for the broken china came in, that $6.50 would belong to Miss Sarah again. She counted her money.

Millie scampered down the two flights of stairs to the girls' floor. The door to the parlor was open. Corine and Gladys were sitting on the sofa and Hazel was sitting on the floor nearby. Millie looked around. Lucy was missing.

Corine looked up. "Millie, come on in. We have some exciting news to share. Here, sit down on the sofa." So Millie squeezed in next to Corine and Gladys.

Not able to contain themselves, they spoke almost in unison, "Lucy's getting married!" Millie just looked at them.

"Just guess who, guess," Gladys said.

"Uh, Joe?" was Millie's response.

"YES!" they all squealed.

"And guess what?" Hazel continued the tale.

"What?"

"Right this very minute they're applying for their marriage license," Corine answered.

"Soooo, the wedding will be Thursday at the courthouse and we're all going. Don't know about Miss Sarah or Miss Cora, but WE'RE going. Can you believe it?" Gladys this time.

Millie relaxed a bit and answered the question. "Yes, I can believe it. I saw how they look at each other."

"Yes, indeed," Gladys grinned.

"So," Millie began, "that means Lucy will be moving out on Thursday and Miss Sarah won't be able to entertain but three gentlemen."

The room went quiet and all three of them now looked squarely at Millie. "Uh, Millie," Hazel began, "I don't know for certain, but I think that's where you come in."

Millie gasped. "I can't do all the cleaning AND do entertainin' too!"

"Well, we don't know for certain," Corine picked up where Hazel had left off, "but I believe Miss Sarah will find someone else to do the cleanin'."

Millie just sat there quiet for a few seconds. "Well, I guess I'll wait until Miss Sarah tells me."

And with perfect timing Miss Sarah was standing at the door to the parlor looking in. All four girls looked up. "Oh, hi, Miss Sarah," Gladys spoke first.

"Hello, ladies, may I borrow Millie for a bit. Millie, will you meet me in my office. Just give me five minutes to get there before you head that way." It was apparent that Lucy, maybe along with Joe, had told Miss Sarah about their plans.

Millie looked at what were now the three angels. "Well, ladies, I guess I'd better head on to Miss Sarah's study." The other three just nodded. Gladys also patted Millie's arm, "It'll be okay, Millie. We'll be here when you get done. Just come on back."

Millie took the back stairs so it would take longer to get to Miss Sarah's office, then she stopped at the door, "Miss Sarah, you wanted to see me?"

"Yes, Millie, come on in and have a seat." It felt like that first week when the day after she had arrived, she was seated there listening to Miss Sarah offer her a job and a place to stay. What she had told Buck she wanted as they were on the way to Mason.

"Millie, I know that the girls were telling you about Lucy getting married. I guess it'll be on Thursday. She won't be able to stay here after that. In fact, her work here is done. She won't be entertaining any more gentlemen. I've asked her to be completely moved out by Wednesday. Joe tells me that he can use his truck. Lord knows I don't think she has that much to move. None of the furniture is hers." Miss Sarah paused, looked at Millie and shook her head. "This really puts me in a bind, but it's to be expected. These girls are young. Our guests get romantic ideas after a night here." She paused again and tapped on the stack of papers on her desk, trying to gather her thoughts.

"Millie, I want you to move into Lucy's old room once she is out. I've asked Alice, you know the colored girl who does the wash for me. I've asked her to work with Cora in the kitchen and do the cleaning. Just take over for you. She has a place to stay, so she won't be using the turret room. That gives you plenty of time to move your things. But, Millie, I'll need you to start having gentleman guests in your room for entertainin' starting Thursday. Until then you'll do your same chores. Do you understand?"

Millie just nodded, thinking, I don't really have any other choice under the circumstances.

"Ask Gladys to tell you what to do. I guess you know a little after that boy Alex — you entertained Saturday night. You can get more condoms from Gladys. She can give you some tips and also tell you what to expect. What to allow and what not to allow. I don't ever want my girls hurt. Understand?"

Millie nodded again. Last week when she learned about Tom taking Louise to Savannah, she had gone to a secret place in her head and stayed there for what had amounted to an evening and a night. Now she felt herself drifting back to that place, a place where she could live, could be, when her body was, well, otherwise employed.

"Do you have any questions?" Miss Sarah asked.

"Yes, ma'am. So, Miss Sarah, so this week I'll get paid for the cleanin', cookin', and entertainin', right?"

"That's right, Millie. And by the way, Millie, the bill for the replacement china has come in. You'll need to give me $6.50. Hope you haven't spent that."

"Yes, ma'am, Miss Sarah. I mean, no ma'am, I haven't spent it." It was almost 3:30 p.m. "Miss Sarah, if it's all the same to you, I think I'd better go on down to the kitchen to help Miss Cora with supper."

"Certainly, and Millie, thank you."

"Yes, ma'am."

Millie left Miss Sarah's office and without even thinking she was walking down the front staircase muttering as she went, "I don't know anythin' about entertainin' men. The last one, well Alex, we just looked at fireflies. Well, I've got three days to figure it out. Cover your manhood is all I know. Cover your manhood. Wait until I lie down. Get it done, then go back to your room. That's all I know."

She had kept walking, talking to herself when she realized she was on the first floor, and there was Buck just coming through the door.

"Oh, Buck." Without even thinking she ran and gave him a hug.

"Millie, glad to see you, too."

"Oh, Buck, Lucy's gettin' married and I'm going to be a wh...., a pros...uh, I'm gonna entertain men." Millie was waving her arms.

Using both hands Buck lowered Millie's arms. "Whatcha tryin' to tell me?"

So, Millie told him, starting with Lucy's matrimonial plans and ending with her moving into Lucy's room. Buck glanced around and finally leaned in and said, "Well, Millie, maybe I could, you know visit YOU next Monday when I'm here in Mason." Millie's eye popped open. Entertain Buck?

Buck had picked her up on the side of the road, brought her to Miss Sarah's, had taken the dollar to her ma. He even helped her hang out her wash, told her to get it in before the dew fell. Maybe he'd behave the same way in her bedroom. Not a chance, he's a man.

Millie took a breath, backed up, smoothed her dress, and composed herself. "Okay, Buck, well, I don't know." She paused, threw her shoulders back and stood taller. Giving her hair a toss, licking her lips, she nodded and added, "Okay. That would be lovely."

"Millie, I gotta get ready for dinner. Bathe and all that. See you in the dining room."

Buck left her there in the foyer. Millie shook her head, turned, and walked to the kitchen. "Entertainin' men. All I know is fireflies. I never had to 'entertain' Tom. He just threw me down and entertained himself." She was still mumbling when she got to the kitchen.

Miss Cora was chopping the turnips at the counter and humming a tune. Millie stopped at the table. "Miss Cora, Lucy's getting married and starting Thursday, I got to entertain men. Miss Cora, I have no idea what to do. But I'll make twenty dollars a week. That's all I know. Twenty dollars a week. And I get to move into Lucy's room."

"Sit down, Millie." Miss Cora brought the bundles of

turnips over to the table. "And start chopping. I've got to get the banana puddin' made."

"But, Miss Cora, didn't you hear me. Lucy's gettin' married and I have to start entertainin' men."

"Yes, Millie, I heard you. You're at a crossroads."

"Crossroads?"

"Yes, Millie, a place where you have to make a decision about what you're going to do next. Usually, a pretty big decision."

"But, Miss Cora, there's only one decision here. I can't go back to Gaston."

Miss Cora just looked at her and shrugged.

"Well, then, I guess you'll have to go into the 'entertainin'' business starting on Thursday."

"Humph." Millie started chopping turnips and muttering, "Don't know nothin' about entertainin'."

"Millie, all that muttering isn't gonna get the turnips chopped or the supper done. Keep choppin'. I've already got the water boiling with the fat back."

Soon the pile of turnips was in the pot of boiling water and fat back. And the earthy smell of turnips and roots mixed with pork fat back was filling the kitchen.

"Millie, we're going to smash the sweet tators tonight. I've already baked 'em, so all you got to do is pull off the peels and start smashin'."

Magdala came in after Millie's muttering stopped and joined her at the table with a big bowl and her own share of baked sweet tators. She and Millie began smashin'. Once they had a bowl full, Miss Cora dropped half a stick of butter into each one. The sweet smell of yams mixed with butter wafted up and married the earthy turnip smell. This was going to be another fine meal from Miss Cora's kitchen.

It was time to set the table. For once Millie was glad to leave the kitchen and Miss Cora's "crossroads" talk. "I ain't goin' back. I'm just puttin' my foot down to that," Millie muttered and for effect stomped one foot. By now she could have done the table setting in her sleep. But, every time, and this time was included, Millie did enjoy looking at a freshly set table.

A warm breeze fluttered the curtains at the floor-to-ceiling windows. Millie stared ahead, not really looking at anything. I'll be makin' $20.00 a week. And I ain't goin' back to Gaston. She turned and headed back to the kitchen.

It was after five o'clock and the gentlemen, cleaned up and smelling good, were making their way to the dining room. Some laughing, some just chatting about their day. Just a warm rumble of male voices. And from the kitchen, Miss Cora's voice giving directions with an "O, Lord," every now and then. Miss Sarah's on a Monday afternoon, but everything for Millie was changing.

Millie stood at her post by the china cabinet watching the girls as they smiled and cooed to their gentlemen, especially Corine, who was paired with Buck. Caught up in watching them, Millie began imitating all she saw, turning her head this way and that, casting her eyes toward the ceiling and then smiling. She was well into this role play when she caught Buck's eye and he looked questioningly at her, his freckled face lighting up. He knew what she was doing and could barely contain himself, but he just raised his glass, "Hey, Millie, could I have a bit more tea and maybe some ice?"

Coming out of her role play, Millie answered, "Oh, of course, Buck." She poured his tea and then dropped a few chips of ice into his glass. Looking around the table and in her best citified voice she asked, "Do any of you other ladies and gentlemen need some more tea. I'm right here ready to serve you." She finished with a rapid batting of her eyelashes. Miss Sarah looked up.

"Why, thank you, Millie," Miss Sarah smiled. She knew exactly what Millie was doing. She had seen this transition before. She went back to her pork chop.

Soon supper was over, and all these ladies and gentlemen were rising from their places and going to the parlor. Millie watched them leave. I'll be doing that on Thursday, she thought.

Back in the kitchen Mr. Lester was cutting up his second pork chop. "Cora, you've done another fine job with these pork chops. I think two better be my limit or I won't be able to squeeze behind a toilet. But I can't not have some of that banana puddin'."

Millie came through the swinging door. "Hey there, Millie, come here and have some supper with me," Mr. Lester said as he tapped the chair next to his.

So Millie made her plate and sat down. Miss Cora did the same, taking a break from the cleanup. What a fine plate of food: the dark green turnips with one white root, the dark orange sweet potatoes, a square of yellow cornbread and a bowl of banana puddin' with meringue on top. Millie just sat there for a moment and admired her plate.

"Miss Cora, you ever thought about the color of food. I mean this here plate, just look at it, the green, orange, and yellow. Why, Miss Cora, it's all just a work of art, don't you think?"

Miss Cora reached over and patted Millie's hand. "Millie, it is indeed, a work of art. That makes us a couple of artists, I guess."

As happens with folks who are comfortable with and accustomed to each other, the three of them fell silent and just ate, enjoying the flavors and colors of a fine Southern meal.

"Well, ladies, I hate to eat and run, but I will," Mr. Lester said, rising and winking at Miss Cora and Millie. "See you later, Cora. May read a while when I get home. That's where you'll find me, in my chair."

"That's where I'll find you asleep, in your chair," said Miss Cora, and popped him on the shoulder with her dish cloth as he left.

Millie cleared the table and shook out the tablecloth outside. Back in the dining room, she smelled the pipes and cigars being smoked in the parlor. Hope my gentlemen don't smoke in my room. That smell, especially cigars, is real hard to get rid of.

Back in the kitchen Miss Cora was washing the Buttercup china. After breaking a stack of the Buttercups, Millie would never have the honor of washing them. Miss Cora barely trusted her to bring a stack of them from the dining room. Millie looked around the room. "Miss Cora, anything else you need?"

"No, Millie, go on up to bed. See you in the morning."

"Yes, ma'am." With a surprisingly heavy heart Millie trudged up the back stairs. That kitchen was like her home. She'd be leaving home again. And her little turret room, she'd be leaving it, too.

It had been a very long Monday. Millie decided to soak in the tub a while and then read her dictionary. After her bath she decided to look up the word, "crossroads" and took her dictionary to her bed.

There it was, but missing that last letter, "s."

Millie read aloud, "1. road that crosses a main road or runs between main roads; 2. a place where roads meet, usually used in plural; 3. a crucial point where a decision must be made, usually used in plural."

She stopped and then read the third definition again. "'A crucial point where a decision must be made." But what does 'crucial' mean?"

She flipped forward a few pages and found it. Again,

reading aloud, "Decisive, important, significant." Well, I guess, it's 'important,' but I ain't goin back to Gaston, so it ain't a crossroad, it's just a road. That Psalm says that 'goodness and mercy' are following me, so they'd better keep up because my 'road' leads to the second floor." That was that and the day was done. Millie wound the little blue clock and lay back in her bed and watched the stars come out and tonight there was a full moon and it shone right into her face. "Mr. Moon, look-a-here, I'm tryin' to sleep." She turned to her other side and did just that.

Chapter 16

Tuesday morning came early as it always did with the little blue clock ringing her head off. Millie stretched and sat up on the side of her bed. "Well, today is Tuesday. That means I have two days left before I start movin' downstairs and entertainin'. Not gonna think about it. No. Time to make those biscuits!" She decided to wear the hand-me-down dress Miss Sarah had given her that first morning. Can it be only two weeks ago.

She took her time taking the twisty stairs down to the kitchen. She loved this time of day. Fresh fall breeze coming through the open windows, the smell of bacon, the pot of bubbling grits, the cracking of eggshells. All of it.

"Good mornin', Miss Cora. Did you sleep well last night?"

"Well, Millie, yes, I did and good mornin' to you."

Millie was soon at the kitchen table with the flour, soda and salt, and a bottle of buttermilk. Not long now and that first batch of biscuits would be in the oven. And then another. And then another.

When those two baking pans were lined up side-by-side on the kitchen table. Millie could start setting the dining room table and just generally making certain everything was just right.

It was only six o'clock and breakfast would not be served until seven. Millie was setting out plates and coffee cups when she heard her name. "Good mornin', Millie." She looked up to see Buck standing in the doorway of the dining room.

"Well, good morning, Buck. Did you rest well? I mean, you look wide awake." Blushing slightly, Buck smiled and nodded his head, "Yes, I got a good night's rest. And I'll be heading back to Savannah today. I have other routes, so I have to load my truck up again in Savannah."

He paused, then said, "I checked with Miss Sarah and she's going to match me up with you next Monday."

Millie set down the Buttercup plate she was holding, straightened the front of her apron, licked her lips, and looked squarely in his eyes, "I'll look forward to that, but I want to warn you that I won't have had much experience bein' entertainin' and all."

"But, Millie, it's not like that. I mean, not like you think. Aw hell, Millie, I'd just like to get to know you better. You know, talk."

Millie shrugged her shoulders. "Okay, Buck." She had finished setting the table and turned to head to the kitchen. When she got to the door, she paused and turned back to face him. "Buck, you've been real kind to me up 'til now, so I hope that'll be the same next week."

Buck blushed. "Oh, Millie, you can count on that."

Soon Tuesday had flown by and was almost over. A routine that had become familiar: cleaning, cooking, serving, cleaning, bathing, and to bed. And now winding the little blue clock and falling asleep.

Chapter 17

And then it was Wednesday, just one more day before the move to Lucy's room. Millie decided that it would be a good idea to talk with the girls today; after all she would be joining them tomorrow. Maybe even Lucy would be out of the room, and she could start moving in.

Feeling the weight of the transition, Millie walked slowly down the back stairs to the kitchen. "Good mornin', Miss Cora. Today's my last day to work with you."

"Good mornin', Millie. Guess you didn't notice Alice over there at the sink washin' dishes." Millie looked that way and saw a young colored girl, hair wrapped in Millie's orange scarf. "Oh, good mornin', Alice."

"Hi, Millie. Hope you didn't mind me using this scarf. Miss Cora said that you had been usin' it, but after today you won't be workin' in the kitchen. If you want me to take it off I will." The words tumbled out with no stopping in sight. Dark-skinned and round-faced, Alice's face lit up when she smiled and her teeth (Millie really admired a good set) were set in two dazzling white rows, evenly spaced. She was taller and rounder than Millie; her apron, barely covering her dress, was easily tied without the double wrap Millie had to do.

"That's okay, Alice. I won't be needing it anymore." In her mind Millie was thinking *I'm getting replaced*, followed immediately by, *I don't want to leave Miss Cora's kitchen.*

"Well, better get to making the biscuits." Millie gave her head a slight shake and began mixing the flour, buttermilk, salt, soda, and a bit of cold bacon grease.

"Millie, once you've gotten the biscuits going, please take Alice to the dining room and show her how to set the table," Miss Cora said over her shoulder.

Soon that first batch of biscuits was in the oven and Millie was cutting out the rest and putting them on the two additional cookie sheets. "Okay, Alice, wanna go to the dining room now?"

Alice was an eager and attentive student, quickly catching on to Miss Cora's table-setting standards as described by Millie. Soon the table was set and Millie, as she usually did, stood back to admire their work.

"I like to just take it all in. Ain't the Buttercup china beautiful? But I broke three bags full and had to pay Miss Sarah $6.50 for it, so be real careful."

Alice did not quite get the purpose of the survey but responded, "Ah, yes, oh, yes, Millie, it sure is."

Back in the kitchen Miss Cora outlined the course of Alice's training for the day. "Millie, Alice will go with you today, so she can learn where you keep your broom, mop, and all that. Give her any advice you think might be helpful. Now, let's get this breakfast on the table!"

"Yes, ma'am," Millie and Alice said in unison, smiling.

Alice was step-for-step with Millie, at times coming up behind her too quickly and once almost running into her as they came from opposite directions from and into the kitchen. The good thing about having Alice tail Millie all day would be that Millie would be distracted from the fact that the pleasant times in the kitchen with Miss Cora, Mr. Lester, and Magdala were coming to an end. And maybe even trips to First Baptist on Sundays.

Breakfast and clean-up were now done. "Come on, Alice, ever been up the twisty back stairs?"

"No," Alice giggled as she bumped into Millie on the first turn.

At the third-floor landing Millie stopped. "Now, Alice," she said, enjoying being the senior member of this team, "down this hallway are Miss Sarah's rooms." Millie pointed as she talked. "First her parlor, then her bathroom, bedroom, and office. If Miss Sarah is in her office, you'll just skip that one." Entering the parlor Millie showed Alice the closet where she could find the cleaning equipment, including the vacuum cleaner, which Millie decided was the place to start.

"Alice, have you ever used a vacuum cleaner?"

Wide-eyed, Alice just shook her head, no.

"Well, I'm going to show you the most important part. See that plug over there? I'm going to plug 'er in. But, before I turn 'er on, I want you to practice pulling that plug out. I killed this here vacuum cleaner my first week here. Miss Sarah was kind enough not to charge me for its repair. I'd still be workin' for nothin' if she hadn't been so kind." Alice plugged and unplugged the vacuum cleaner a few times. "Okay, Alice, plug 'er in."

Alice did.

Then Millie turned on the machine and demonstrated the correct way to vacuum the room, starting in the center and working outward.

"Understand, Alice?"

Alice nodded. Millie stood at the rim of the rug and Alice began the in and out motion from center to rim; rim to center. All was going well, until Alice got her foot tangled in the long electrical cord. As Millie attempted to assist, Alice ran the vacuum cleaner over Millie's foot, causing Millie to lose her balance. When all the chaos had ended both Millie and Alice were on the floor in the middle of the rug with the vacuum cleaner bottom up and growling like a wild animal.

Getting to the plug to turn the thing off was impossible, but Millie was able to reach the switch. The quiet was palpable. Millie couldn't be angry with Alice. She had done worse. All they could do was look at each other and laugh. Millie spoke first, "Well, Alice, this time the thing tried to kill us! But thank goodness, we won."

The rest of the cleaning of Miss Sarah's rooms went on without further drama. Miss Sarah had been in her study and Millie had checked with her about the status of the guest rooms. Empty. So, Millie and Alice went to the first floor, using the main staircase this time.

On the way down they ran into Lucy and Joe, each carrying a box overflowing with Lucy's things. Breathless but smiling, Lucy told Millie that she and Joe were right that minute carrying out the last two boxes and Millie could start moving into her old room any time.

Millie looked at the two of them, Lucy and Joe, standing there smiling big radiant smiles. They looked like a couple, her short blonde bob just inches below his dimpled-faced head.

"Gotta go, Millie. You know we're gettin' married tomorrow. Lots to do. Hope you come along to the courthouse with the girls, you're one of them now, you know."

"Good to see you, Millie," Joe added, his eyes twinkling. Then they were gone down the back way.

"Hey, Alice, this won't take but a minute. Let's look in Lucy's, I mean, my room."

"Sure, Millie."

The room, while not as large as Miss Sarah's bedroom, was just as elegant, starting with the four-poster dark wood bed, neatly made with a golden brocade fabric bedspread. Across from the bed was a fireplace over which was hung a large gold-framed oval mirror. In one corner were two lady chairs, between which was an elegant, mirrored chest of drawers. There were two area rugs, smaller, but similar to the ones in Miss Sarah's third-floor parlor and the first-floor parlor. The wallpaper was a multi-colored floral pattern against a cream-colored background. The room was simply breathtaking to Millie.

"Oh, Alice, and this is my room now," Millie sighed. There were two windows with shades up, so the morning light was streaming in. "Perfect, Alice. It's just perfect."

Millie paused. "We better get down to the first floor. Oh, I almost forgot. Are you hungry. Let's grab a cold biscuit and some tea before we start on the first floor."

She and Alice snooped around the kitchen, and each made a plate of biscuits, bacon, and apple pie, plus Miss Cora's sweet tea. Millie showed Alice how she always set a table, pretending to be a grand lady. The kitchen was comfortable, the October fall day acting like she should and not blowing hot. Alice asked questions about cleaning Miss Sarah's room as they ate.

They washed their dishes and put them away and then headed to the hallway where Millie's first-floor cleaning equipment was stowed. "And, Alice, look, you've got a sink in here and Oxydol soap on the shelf."

Millie told her about the incident with the bucket and the fresh-acting guest. "Be prepared, Alice. And swing that bucket if you need to."

Alice just nodded. Millie continued the orientation through all the first-floor rooms as they cleaned them, thinking to herself that Alice would have to deal with her own mistakes. Millie had.

They were all done now, and it was close to 3:30. "Alice, you go ahead on to the kitchen. I'm sure Miss Cora is already there. Maybe you can learn how to make mashed potatoes or as Miss Cora calls it, 'smashed' potatoes. Oh, and Alice," Millie continued, hand slightly across her face, as if sharing a secret, "The sheriff will probably come through the back door Thursday night. He visits with Miss Sarah about twice a week. But remember, as Mr. Lester says, 'He was never here'." Millie winked. Alice looked confused but didn't ask what that meant. Alice figured the other colored folks in the kitchen, Miss Cora and Mr. Lester, would help her understand.

Alice moved toward the kitchen. Millie said, "Alice, I'm going up the main stairs. I need to see the girls for a bit. I'll see you in half an hour. Good job today." Millie knew she was certainly not the same country girl who had landed on Miss Sarah's front porch two weeks ago.

She made her way to the girls' parlor. They were all in their usual places, except now Lucy's spot on the sofa was empty, though the stack of *Redbook* magazines remained. Hazel looked up, "Hey, there, Millie. Lucy said to tell you that you can keep those *Redbooks*."

Both Corine and Hazel paused in their painting and piano playing and greeted Millie, then turned back to their art and music. Millie began, "Ladies, I have just thirty minutes before I have to go to the kitchen to get supper ready. I have some questions about entertaining men. I won't have to do any cooking or cleaning tomorrow, so I plan to move all my belongings to my new room in the morning. And maybe before entertainin' time y'all could help me get as gussied up as is possible for me."

They, each one, stopped what they were doing and clustered themselves cross-legged on the floor in front of the sofa where Millie was seated. Gladys began, "Oh, Millie, we'll help you." Corine and Hazel both nodded.

Then Corine spoke, "Millie, first of all you need to have a

place in your mind where you can go while you, well, let the man do what he likes to do with a woman. My place is filled with nature, a butterfly, a flower. Well, filled with what I want to paint. You just close your eyes and stay in your secret place, until it's done. Then, the man goes to your bathroom and cleans himself off and flushes the condom down the toilet. Then he leaves your room and goes back downstairs to his." Both Hazel and Gladys nodded in agreement.

"So, I let them touch me anywhere and do whatever they want to do, while I stay in my 'secret place' the whole time," Corine continued, her dark pageboy bangs swinging with every movement of her head.

Then Hazel spoke, "Millie, do not let them hit you or tie you up, or talk to you like a dog. Miss Sarah won't allow that. That's why she makes them bathe, eat at a fine table, and spend time in the parlor. She's trying to turn these Georgia hicks into gentlemen."

Millie pondered what they were telling her. But there wasn't time for more. "I need to get to the kitchen. Maybe we can talk again tomorrow."

"Oh, and Millie, we're going to fix you up tomorrow, make-up and all. And we'll lend you some jewelry, too." It was Gladys this time.

As Millie reached the door, she turned and added, "Tell Lucy I'm real happy for her. I won't be able to go to the wedding at the courthouse. I have too much to do."

"Of course," Corine smiled. Hazel and Gladys just nodded.

Finally, Millie added, "And thank you."

It was meat loaf night. When Millie entered the kitchen Alice was already getting a tutorial on smashin' potatoes. Magdala was there as well, so the smashin' was going well.

"What you need me to do, Miss Cora?"

"Well, Millie, why don't you check on the table, make sure it's set right. Then, come on back here and you can start washing the dishes in the sink." *Finishing where I started two weeks ago. At the sink. Not a bad place to end my kitchen career.* Millie turned around and headed to the dining room.

The tablecloth needed some smoothing, so she started there. She took her time, making certain it all looked perfect. Buttercup china, silverware, linen napkins. It had started to drizzle, so the smell of rain, fresh, clean, drifted through the dining room. Millie stood and breathed it in. *This room, these smells will be part of that "secret place" Corine described,* she thought.

With a big sigh, a resignation to the circumstances she was now under, Millie returned to the kitchen to the sink which she filled with hot water and Oxydol soap. A few bubbles floated above the water and Millie caught one in her palm and blew it across the sink. *Another image for her "secret place." And Louise. She'll be there with the bubbles.*

"Alice, you and Magdala help me serve the table. Millie, you keep cleaning those pots and pans."

Millie was still at the sink when Mr. Lester came in. "Well, Millie, I see you are back where you started. This your last night workin' kitchen patrol?"

"Yes, suh, Mr. Lester. And I have to say, it sorta makes me sad. I do love bein' in here with you, Miss Cora, and Magdala." She sighed.

"Well, we'll be around here, Millie. You can drop by any time."

Mr. Lester made himself a glass of tea, got a plate and cut a slice of the meat loaf in the pan on the stove. There were still some green beans in a pot on the stove, so he spooned some onto his plate. Since all the mashed potatoes were still in the dining room, he might have to eat them with his dessert. No matter.

"Millie, if you need any help moving your things to your new room, just let me know."

"No need, Mr. Lester. I have all day tomorrow to do that. I'll start first thing tomorrow at 5:00 a.m."

"Guess you could sleep a little longer. But, hey, maybe I'll see you at breakfast tomorrow."

Supper time in the dining room was ending and Miss Cora, Alice, and Magdala were bringing the serving platters back to the kitchen.

As Miss Cora passed him with the bowl of mashed potatoes, he grabbed her arm. "Hey, Cora, I'll take some of those."

"Well, Lester, you can have the whole bowl," Miss Cora said as she placed the bowl on the kitchen table.

Millie was almost done washing the pile of pots and bowls. Soon Miss Cora would take her place to wash the Buttercup china and the silver with a fresh sink filled with hot water and Oxydol soap. The window over the sink was open and the cool evening breeze gave Millie a chill. She shivered.

"Millie, come make yourself a plate and eat with us," Mr. Lester said as he patted the chair nearest him. Millie wiped her hands on her apron and started fixing herself a plate. Soon it was four of them at the table: Miss Cora, Mr. Lester, Alice, and Millie. Magdala had already eaten and gone home.

Alice, eager to share all that she had learned about housework at Miss Sarah's, chatted them up. All Millie had to do was smile and nod. It was coming to an end. These days of kitchen work. They cleaned their plates, and each had a big slice of apple pie. Miss Cora even brought out vanilla ice cream to go on top.

Now Mr. Lester was pushing his chair back and walking toward the back door. "Good night, ladies. Thanks for your company tonight."

"'Night, Mr. Lester." Millie felt tears welling up in her eyes. She had to keep brushing them away. She ran to the door and almost knocked Mr. Lester down wrapping her arms around him.

"Now, now, Millie. I'll be around. Remember that. I'll be around." He paused and then started down the stairs.

It was time to finish cleaning up the kitchen, but with three of them it went quickly. Millie hung up her apron. Then she asked as she always did, "Miss Cora, need anything else?"

"No, chile, go on to bed. You've got a big day coming tomorrow." Miss Cora was at the sink washing the Buttercup china. She didn't even turn around. Alice had gone to the dining room to finish up there.

Millie paused at the foot of the back stairs and looked around the room. Then she ran to Miss Cora and hugged her tightly from behind. "Oh, Miss Cora, thank you, thank you, thank you." And then she began to really cry. "I'm scared, Miss Cora."

Miss Cora wiped her hands on a dish towel and turned toward Millie. "Millie, read that Psalm again tonight before you go to bed. Let it roll around in your head, you hear? You're gonna be all right, Millie. You gonna be all right."

Millie nodded, wiped her face with the back of her hand, crossed the kitchen, and started up the back stairs.

Miss Cora mumbled to herself, "Lord, take care of my Millie." And then she began to sing, "Some glad morning when this life is o'er, I'll fly away…"

Up in her turret room, Millie let her gaze fall first on the clothes rack with her new clothes, then on the little table with her dictionary and Bible, next the little blue alarm clock by the bed, the dresser with her money in one drawer and finally her bed, thinking of what good rest she got there every night. She hoped her new room would feel as safe and cozy as this special place. She had her doubts.

She followed her usual routine, stretching out in the tub, soaking for a while. Soon she was back at her bed seated with her legs folded under her, Bible in hand. She opened to the place Miss Cora had marked. The words that caught her eye tonight: "I will fear no evil; for thou art with me…"

"'For thou art with me' even when I move down to the second floor. You'll be with me? I thought I'd start moving tonight. But all that cryin' has plum wore me out." She wrapped up in the sheet and fell asleep.

Chapter 18

Five a.m. and the little blue clock announced a new day. I'll sure need to reset this clock tonight. Or maybe I won't set her at all, Millie thought as she decided what she would wear this morning, concluding that probably the dress she came to Miss Sarah's in would do.

After dressing, Millie began taking her new clothes from the rolling rack and laying them neatly on her bed. She decided to make a quick trip down to her new room. She picked up her Bible, dictionary, and the little blue clock and headed toward the door. Pausing, she turned around and went to the little desk. "Think I'll find a safe place for my money, first thing," she said aloud.

When she opened the door, there were two cardboard boxes with a note taped to one. She read, "Thought these might be helpful." It was signed, "Lester." She took the boxes back into her room and set them on the floor near her bed. She decided she would carry her clothes on hangers across her arm. The two boxes could be filled with everything else. She sighed, "Mr. Lester. I may just have to start calling him 'Papa Lester'."

It didn't take many trips down to the second floor and back up to move all her belongings. The last thing she moved was what she had in the bathroom, her toothbrush, tooth-paste, and a bar of soap Miss Sarah had left for her the first week she was there.

One last walk through the turret room and she was done. It was only 6:30, so she decided to go down to the kitchen, the back way of course.

Alice and Miss Cora were in their usual places: Alice at the sink, Miss Cora at the stove. Miss Cora hasn't taught Alice how to make biscuits yet, but she will soon, Millie mused.

Mr. Lester was at the table, a fresh biscuit, two fried eggs, two strips of bacon and a nice mound of grits on his plate and a steaming cup of coffee by his hand. "Well, lookie here, Cora, Millie's back. Grab a biscuit and eat breakfast with me," he said, patting the chair nearest his.

"Is that okay, Miss Cora?"

"Yes, chile, you're not part of my kitchen crew anymore. Get yourself a plate and I'll give you a biscuit. Maybe even eggs and bacon." She winked at Millie.

"Mornin', Alice."

"Mornin', Millie."

Millie got a plate, took a biscuit from the pan on top of the stove and sat down at the kitchen table. "Oh, Mr. Lester, thank you so much for those boxes. I'm already moved. Didn't have that much. But I certainly have more than what I came with. That's for sure."

"Well, Millie, you've got a whole day to spruce up your room before supper," Mr. Lester replied as he lifted a forkful of grits and eggs.

"I thought I might go to Lucy's weddin' now that I'm done movin'. Figured I'd check with Gladys about that once she's up."

"That'd be nice, Millie. I'm sure Lucy would appreciate that," Miss Cora turned as she spoke. "Yes, that'll be nice, real nice."

"I don't have a gift. Maybe I could just give her a dollar. Whatcha think about that, Miss Cora?"

"Millie, maybe just go to the wedding, save your dollar." Miss Cora had turned back to her bacon frying.

Soon Mr. Lester was finished with his breakfast and had slipped the plate into Alice's sink full of suds. "Ladies, I'm off to the world of stopped up sinks and clogged toilets. But-terfield's Plumbing Company to the rescue. I bid you adieu." With that he strolled toward the door, but not before stop-ping by the stove and giving Miss Cora a peck on the cheek.

"See you tonight, Lester. Salmon croquettes, plus lemon meringue pie."

"Now, Cora, that's something to work for!" And he was out the door.

It was getting close to seven and Millie knew that Miss Cora and Alice would start taking platters of food to the din-ing room and she would be in the way, so she said one more "thank you" for her breakfast and headed up the back stairs, this time just one floor up to the second floor.

She went into her new room. She looked into the bath-room she would share with Gladys and saw that it was exactly like the bathrooms on the first floor, modest, but adequate. She was glad it wasn't too elaborate. She remembered that she would have to help Gladys clean it each week.

She walked around the bedroom again, finally taking a seat in one of the lady chairs. It was then that she noticed the stack of *Redbook* magazines, piled high alongside the chair.

Millie knew that Lucy was leaving these for her, so she picked one up. It was the September 1927 issue with a beauti-ful dark-haired woman in profile on the cover. Millie opened the cover and began to page through the magazine, seeing an ad for Wrigley's Double Mint gum, one for Ipana toothpaste which warned the reader, "Don't wait until your toothbrush turns pink," and then the table of contents that listed "serial novels" and "short stories" and "the spirit of our day."

There were titles like, "What You Want in Life" and "When the Gods Smile." And ads for Coty perfume and Lucky Strike cigarettes, plus pages and pages of classified ads, some for various sorts of schools, an ad on one page offering a course in French. Millie kept flipping the pages. She determined that reading would definitely be part of this new leisure life, time spent other than entertaining gentlemen.

She heard the toilet flush and the water in the tub start in the bathroom. "Gladys is up," she said aloud. "I'll knock on her door when I figure that she's done in the bathroom."

There was plenty of time. Millie decided to read the article titled, "The Independent Woman." Some of it made little sense to her, but there was a part that described a game played at a party attended by successful businesswomen, writers, and artists, along with "two rather colorless, fluffy little ladies." When the men attending were asked using slips of paper to rate the women as to which had the most sex appeal, the "fluffy" ladies got the most votes.

Millie pondered, Why wouldn't I want to be "fluffy"? She simply flipped the page and went on to the next article. Bouncy and fluffy, that's what I want to be, bouncy and fluffy.

She looked at the little blue clock. It was now nine o'clock and she no longer heard water running in the bathroom, so she figured Gladys was out. Millie left her room and knocked on the door next to hers. Gladys answered wearing a peach-colored silk robe with wide lace trim.

"Oh, Millie, you've moved. Come on in." Gladys's room was identical to Millie's, but instead of a stack of *Redbook* magazines, Millie saw a stack of what appeared to be textbooks of some sort, piled high next to the lady chair on the opposite wall.

"Come sit down, Millie." She took one seat and Gladys

took the other. Gladys continued, "Since you're all moved in, you can go to Lucy's wedding with us. Don't you want to go?"

Millie thought for a moment. "Well, yes I do, and I guess I can wear my Sunday dress."

"Wanna try some makeup. I can fix you right up." So, gussying up began. After washing her face Millie took a seat at Gladys's vanity. Gladys lined up the face powder, the rouge, the mascara, the eyebrow pencil, and most important, the bright red lipstick.

"Millie, the first thing we need to address are your eyebrows. They need shaping, so I've got to do some pulling." Gladys grimaced. "You want me to make you some movie star brows?"

Millie nodded. She was so fascinated with the process that the tugging of eyebrow hairs didn't even bother her. Gladys paused and Millie looked at the results. Reflected in the mirror were two of the most perfect brows Millie had ever seen. Now Gladys was dusting her face with powder and then applying just a bit of rouge. She added penciled lines to Millie's eyebrows and then showed Millie how to apply the mascara. "You'll blink too much if I do it. Better do it yourself. You can get your own at Zimmerman's. But 'til then you can borrow mine any time."

Millie finished with the mascara, only sticking herself in the eye once. And now for the lipstick. Gladys leaned in near Millie's cheek. "Now Millie, do you want to have Clara Bow lips? You know, the 'It Girl'?"

"Glady's, I want to have lips like yours."

"Then, you can be an 'It Girl', too!" Gladys replied.

And so, Millie learned how to make the heart-shaped lips she had so admired that first Monday, when she was just the country girl from Gaston. She looked in the mirror. She could not believe what she saw. She turned her head creating the profile look she had seen in the *Redbook* magazine. Wow. Now all she needed was her beautiful blue dress and she'd be ready for Lucy's wedding.

"Thank you, Gladys," she said, smiling at her new friend.

"You are welcome," Gladys replied. "Now, Corine and Hazel will be in our parlor at 10:00. The wedding is at 11:00. Go put your dress on and I'll meet you in the parlor."

Millie nodded and headed out the door to her room. She had just enough time to dress and then admire the results in the large mirror over the chest of drawers. She noted that she also had a small vanity tucked in one corner. Maybe soon she'd have a stash of makeup just like Gladys's.

At 10:00 the girls, now including Millie, were assembled in the parlor. She had on her sky-blue dress and tee-strap dress shoes. The other girls were dressed as they had been that first day she saw them and labeled them angels: Corine with her dark-haired pageboy wearing deep orange, Gladys in purple with her marcel-waved light brown hair, and Hazel wearing navy blue, her tight red curls bouncing whenever she tossed her head. All three wore cloche hats, each one a lighter shade than her dress. And Millie wore her cloche hat. What a picture. And gloves, each one had lacy gloves that matched her dress. And Millie had gloves, too, covering her now Crisco-softened hands.

"The wedding's at 11:00 so we have no time to spare. Gotta catch the streetcar to get to the court house in time." Gladys was always the planner, the leader.

They left by way of the front door, walking quickly down the sidewalk to the streetcar stop. The October morning had started cool, but the promise of a warmer afternoon seemed to lie in the bright sun that kissed their faces as they hurried along the sidewalk.

Millie was now one of them and yet still their audience. She studied every gesture, every tilt of head and flick of the wrist. She thought about their painted fingernails inside their gloves. Now that Millie would no longer be cleaning rooms and washing dishes, maybe she too could have painted nails. Crisco was already giving her soft hands.

She could see the streetcar coming when she realized that she had no money. She didn't even have a purse. Gladys touched her arm, "Millie, this is on me."

They found seats and the streetcar began to lurch forward. Millie sat near a window. She watched the houses and then store fronts as they rattled by. She had never been on a street-car, but after three weeks in Mason, new experiences were becoming a daily expectation. She thought about where she was four weeks ago at home in Gaston with Louise. She was so far from there now. Unexpectedly, tears began to pour down her cheeks.

"Millie, Millie, what's wrong?" Gladys asked.

"I'm just thinking about how far I am from home and my baby Louise, who's even farther away now. Last week I was too busy to think. It took all I could do to get all that cleanin' and cookin' done. Now I have time to think. I'll be okay, Gladys, just not right now."

Gladys did not have time to make a response because they were now in downtown Mason and the courthouse was in sight, but she opened her purse and gave Millie a lace-trimmed handkerchief. Millie took it and lightly dabbed her eyes, leaving mascara on it. "Great!" She murmured.

They jumped off at the corner across the street from the courthouse. As they waited for the light to change a car slowed down and the driver hollered out, "Hey, there Corine. I'll be seeing you tonight. Wear somethin' pretty or nothing at all."

Ignoring the driver, Corine just looked down and kept her head down as they crossed the street.

As they climbed the courthouse steps, Corine asked, "Where do you think we're supposed to go?"

"Which floor?" Hazel added.

They were on the main floor now, looking around, when Lucy and Joe sailed through the door. "Oh, girls, you all came. And Millie, too." Lucy rushed to them, and they all giggled and hugged.

"We wouldn't miss this for the world," Hazel cooed.

"Hey, Joe," they all, except Millie, greeted him.

Lucy was resplendent in a white silk dress with a lace inset around the neck. She wore a simple strand of pearls. She had on a brimmed hat with a pale blue hat band. And Joe looked the part of the bridegroom, hair slicked back and dimples showing every time he grinned. His shoes were polished to a sheen that reflected any face that came near. He carried his boater.

"Let's go. It's almost eleven," Lucy was in charge now, leading the way up the marble stairs to the second floor. Joe was bringing up the rear, but he didn't seem to care. Being the only man surrounded by such beauty, such glamor, brought a big smile to his face.

A bailiff sat just outside the courtroom door. Lucy walked right up to him, "Sir, this gentleman"— Joe had quickly made his way to her side — "and I are here to get married. Is Judge Culpepper ready for us?"

The bailiff's face lit up, "Well, yes, ma'am. I heard somethin' 'bout a weddin'. Y'all can come on in. I'll let the judge know you're here."

Lucy and Joe marched arm-in-arm to the bar and stood there waiting, while the girls found places on the first row of the public seating.

The bailiff stood by a door just to one side of the bench and when the door opened shouted, "All rise." The girls jumped up, smoothing down their dresses and tossing their hair as they did. Judge Culpepper strode into the room in a rush, his black robe swinging. He took the bench.

"Well, now. I see two young folks standing outside the bar who look like they want to get married. Come on up. Bailiff, show them to the bench." All smiles, the bailiff came forward, pushing the low gate forward, and ushered Lucy and Joe in.

The judge spoke again, "Now I see you've brought four witnesses today." Looking at Gladys, Corine, Hazel, and Millie, he motioned to them. "Come on up, ladies. You can stand behind this lovely couple as they take their vows." Looking out now at a gathering of five ladies and one gentleman, the judge asked, "Ready now?"

Lucy looked behind her at the girls and then at Joe, "Yes, suh. I mean, yes, your honor."

"Well, young lady I've heard from you, but I want to hear from the gentleman as well." Turning toward Joe, Judge Culpepper asked, "Suh, are you ready, too?"

"Oh, yes, suh, uh, I mean, yes, your honor, I am. Yes, indeed, I am."

"Good. I have your marriage license here. Everything is in order. Who should be your witness. Which one of these lovely young ladies will have that honor?"

Before Lucy could make a selection, there was a jostling in the row behind the bride and groom with lots of "You should do it, Gladys" coming from three of the four mouths. So, when Lucy turned, she just laughed and said, "Gladys will do it."

That was all the judge needed. He began leading Lucy and Joe in the giving and taking of vows, to love, honor, obey, in richer, in poorer, in sickness and in health until death separates them. Millie was asking herself, Why is this making me sad? At the same time, she knew that in abandoning her, Tom had broken the vows she and he had taken.

That was what was on Millie's mind, but then she looked to one side at Corine, who was beginning to weep, as were

Gladys and Hazel. It was catching, so Millie, too, began to blubber.

By the time they all had wiped their eyes, Lucy had a ring as did Joe and they were kissing like it was the first time, but of course all of them knew that was not the first kiss or the first of anything for the two. But something about the solemnity of this turned the page for this couple, and they were starting fresh. There would be many firsts on this new page.

Gladys went forward and signed the license, as did the judge. He wished them long life and happiness and just as he had come in with the black robe swirling around his legs and his arms flapping like a crow, he was off the bench and out the door.

After a few quick hugs, they were out the courtroom door and standing in the hall. It was Joe's turn to take the lead now that Lucy was his wife. "Well, ladies, thanks so much for coming to our wedding. We'll be leaving now for our honeymoon."

Something about his tone and directness as he took Lucy's hand made Gladys, Corine, Hazel, and Millie know that they were being dismissed. That Lucy was no longer one of the quartet. She was his wife now and would be off to a whole new life.

The four watched as Lucy and Joe leaned into each other and left the courthouse. Hazel spoke first, "Well, ladies, let's go find some dinner. What about Spillers. It's just down the street from here."

They retraced their steps from earlier, crossing the street and walking down the next block to a small restaurant. It was buzzing with business. Dinner time, or as some had come to call it, "lunch" time. The place was packed, but just as they came in a foursome left, so they were able to be seated at a table in the rear near the kitchen.

The menu was a simple one. Today was meatloaf. Thursday. But there was a long list of side dishes: beets, macaroni and cheese, cabbage, sweet potato souffle, and sliced tomatoes. Hazel explained to Millie that meatloaf was the only meat choice, but she could pick two other dishes as sides.

The waitress, chewing a big wad of gum, pulled a pencil from behind her ear and asked what they wanted. Corine, Gladys, and Hazel were quick in giving their choices. Millie was last and was beginning to perspire just thinking about the choices and which she should select.

The waitress began losing patience. "Well, honey, what's it gonna be? Don't have all day." Millie looked up. "Uh, cabbage and sweet potato souffle." But, instead of saying "soo-flay," she said "su-ful." The waitress laughed, "Where you from anyway. Don't you know it's pronounced, 'soo-flay'?"

Millie's face turned red. She looked directly at the waitress. "Well, it's none of your business where I'm from, but where I'm from folks ain't rude like you just was, tellin' other folks how to say certain words." And then with a glare Millie repeated the word as she had pronounced it, but louder this time: "Su-FUL."

The waitress left muttering Millie's pronunciation, "Su-ful." Hazel, Gladys, and Corine looked at Millie and then burst out laughing. "Oh, Millie, we're goin' to love having you on our floor. We never know what you're goin' to say," Gladys said.

Soon they had their food and enjoyed eating and chatting about the wedding and what the future might hold for Lucy and Joe. When the plates were empty, Hazel, who had a watch, reminded them of the time. "We'd better head home, it's almost one o'clock."

They were near the door to the restaurant when a man at a table looked up. "Hey, there, Gladys, remember me?" The three other men with him looked up as well. He continued,

"Maybe I'll see you soon. I really got my money's worth with you."

Gladys and the three girls kept walking. He pressed on, "Hey, Gladys, I'm speaking to you." Gladys turned. "I don't know you, suh."

"Well, you will remember me next time I see you at Miss Sarah's." And then he looked at his friends and laughed. Under his breath where only they could hear, he muttered, "Whore."

Out on the street they hurried to the nearest streetcar stop. Soon one came rattling up the rails. They boarded. The mood was somber. They all just sat silent, hands folded, at times looking out the window as the scene changed from stores to houses, finally to their stop at Maple Street.

The October day had turned warm, so all four were ready to get their shoes and hose off and put their feet up before supper. "Anybody want a glass of sweet tea before we head to our rooms? Miss Cora always has a fresh pitcher full in the refrigerator," Millie said. She was beginning to fit in.

In the kitchen they all flopped down in the four chairs at the table. Millie served the tea. They swigged it down. "Y'all go on upstairs, I want to wash these glasses. Don't want to leave a mess for Miss Cora." Millie told the other girls as she went to the sink, ran hot water, and sprinkled a bit of Oxydol over the glasses.

As she washed the glasses, she thought about all she had seen and heard that day, the rudeness of the waitress and the man at the restaurant, the way that made her feel. She was still pondering it all as she took the back stairs to the second floor. Am I taking the wrong road at my "crossroad." Or am I just doing the best I can "under the circumstances"?

Millie wanted to understand more about the man at the restaurant, so she tapped lightly on Gladys's door. Gladys invited her in and Millie asked about the incident.

Gladys began. "Millie, I did know that man. He came here last week and was a guest overnight. Most of our guests know better than to speak to us like that in public. He was being very rude. That's why I told him I didn't know him." Gladys continued, "Millie, what we're doing here may be wrong, but it's the best us girls can do. It's the best any of us has ever had it. Understand?"

Millie nodded. "Thanks, Gladys. What time will we be going down to the dining room?"

"Five-fifteen is plenty of time. You may not have noticed, but we each sit at the same place at the table every night. The gentleman on your left will be your guest for the night. You will take what had been Lucy's place. We'll take our seats first so you can figure that out."

Gladys continued, "We usually spend about an hour or so in the parlor and then we all go upstairs, for you know, the entertainin'. The men are usually pretty tired from work and all, so they don't last long. Everybody is pretty much done for the night by nine o'clock at the latest. Funny thing is there are times when we finish up before you all were done in the kitchen. Why don't you go rest in your room for a bit and then come back in here around, oh, four-thirty and we can freshen up your makeup. It's two-thirty now, so I'll see you in about two hours. If you want to take a nap, just set your clock for, say four-fifteen."

"Gladys, could I ask you a question?" Millie said, wrinkling her forehead.

"Of course, Millie." Gladys smiled.

Hesitating, Millie pressed on, asking, "Well, Gladys, how did you come to be here at Miss Sarah's?"

"Pretty much same as you, Millie. My pa believed in spreadin' his love around, if you know what I mean. He started with me when I was twelve. It's a miracle I never got pregnant. One day I just decided I'd leave. Caught a ride to Mason, just like you did. Saw the 'Miss Sarah's Boarding House' sign and thought I'd find out if she needed any help. Well, turns out she did. That was four years ago. I worked with Miss Cora until one of the girls moved, went to Atlanta where there's better pay for what we do. I like the money and sometimes when the man is handsome or sweet, well, I kinda like what we do. I'm saving my money so I can go to college."

Millie nodded. "Thanks, Gladys, thank you for everything," Millie said. "I guess we're all doing the best we can under the circumstances." With a sigh, Millie said, "right now, I think I'll go take a nap. See you around 4:30."

In her room Millie set the little blue clock for four-fifteen, took off her dress and hose and shoes and stretched out on her new bed. She had lots on her mind, but emotional exhaustion got the best of her, and she was fast asleep in a few seconds.

She dreamed that she and Louise were riding the streetcar to town and Louise kept hanging her head out of the open window to let the air blow over her face. And then they were in a restaurant and the waitress was kind and told Louise that she was such a pretty little girl.

When the little blue clock began chiming, Millie awoke, but confused about what day it was or was this 4:15 a.m. or p.m. that showed on the little clock's face. Then it all came back, and Millie knew where she was and what was ahead later that evening.

She dressed again and went to Gladys's room for a makeup touch up. Gladys showed her how to use the makeup, especially the red lipstick. Millie skewed the lip line a few times in her first attempt, so Gladys had to apply face cream and Millie wiped it off with Kleenex tissues and tried again. At last, she had the heart shape in red looking like the It Girl, Clara Bow. Gladys fluffed Millie's hair and added a jeweled headband that fit across her forehead.

Corine and Hazel joined them bringing jewelry to add: drop earrings and a long strand of pearls completed Millie's ensemble. "These belonged to Lucy. She wanted you to have 'em. She's a little housewife now. Won't need 'em." Hazel said as she handed her the jewelry.

"Come down to my room. I have a full-length mirror. You look beautiful," Corine offered.

Down the hall they went. Millie stood in front of the mirror just taking in what she was seeing. She had been transformed. She looked complete, beautiful. "One last thing," Corine added. "Here, just spray a little behind each ear." Corine handed Millie an atomizer filled with Coty perfume, just like in the ad in the *Redbook* magazine Millie had read.

"That smells divine," Millie smiled.

It was getting close to five-fifteen. Miss Sarah peeked in the door to Corine's room. "You ladies 'bout ready?" She paused. "Oh, Millie, I almost didn't recognize you. You look very lovely."

"Thank you, Miss Sarah."

"Time to go downstairs." Miss Sarah led the way with the girls trailing behind and Millie falling in last. She had decided that the smart thing was to walk slowly, so that she didn't stumble, but what that meant was that she came into the dining room last, as in dead last. It was almost as if she were making an inaugural appearance, which she was.

Pausing at the entrance to the dining room, she searched for the one empty seat which would be hers. And there it was, two seats from Miss Sarah's right. And seated at Miss Sarah's right was Millie's guest for the night, the tall, lean bow-tied shoe clerk from Zimmerman's, the man who had fitted her shoes.

As she rounded the dining room table he stood and pulled her chair back. She sat down. Trying to be friendly, he smiled and asked, "How are your shoes working out for you?" Millie just nodded and said, "Fine." She couldn't think of anything else to say.

It seemed odd to Millie to be at the table, rather than serving the table. Alice had taken up the role Millie had assumed before, tea pitcher in hand and ice bowl nearby. Millie nodded her way and smiled. With that acknowledgement Alice's face lit up. Millie did note that Alice was still wearing the orange head scarf.

It was Thursday so Millie knew the meal even before a single platter had been placed on the table: salmon croquettes, cole slaw, sliced tomatoes, and lemon meringue pie. Millie was still full from the dinner at Spiller's so she took small portions of each. She would, however, need to eat a slice of Miss Cora's pie or Miss Cora would give her the evil eye.

Millie thought Mr. Bowtie was not unpleasant. His Adam's apple protruded out of his neck and bounced a bit when he talked. For that reason, Millie had a hard time not staring at it. He had long tapered fingers and used them when he talked, at times flapping them about like bird wings.

He talked about shoes, women's shoes, men's shoes, children's shoes, shoelaces, shoe heels. And then he started up with a tutorial on how to measure feet. This was fine with Millie. All she had to do was eat and nod, with an occasional murmur of "You don't say!"

Then supper was over and again it seemed odd to her that she would be leaving the dining room. She guessed that Mr. Lester was in the kitchen eating supper at the kitchen table. Soon Miss Cora would be washing the Buttercup china. Alice would be shaking the tablecloth out on the back yard for Henny Penny and the other chickens. With a sigh, Millie allowed Mr. Bowtie to pull her chair back and they both headed for the parlor.

Hazel was already at the piano. Mr. Bowtie wanted to sit as far away from the piano as possible because he wanted to talk. And talk he did. Because he thought Millie might be interested, he told her about shopping trips he took to New York City as Mr. Zimmerman's representative to see new styles of shoes. To her surprise, Millie was interested.

He described how women's shoes had changed over the past ten years, becoming less bulky, more strappy. Millie was enthralled. She couldn't wait to tell the girls about her new-found shoe knowledge.

At eight-thirty Millie noticed that Hazel had stopped play-ing the piano and was standing and taking her gentleman's arm. Corine and Gladys did the same. So, Millie turned to Mr. Bowtie and asked, "Would you like to see my room?" He nodded yes.

Mr. Bowtie continued to talk about shoes and feet all the way up the front stairs and down the hall to Millie's room. Once in her room, Millie handed him a condom. "Please put this on your manhood, suh."

"Oh, no, I don't want to start there. I want to see your feet first."

So, Millie took off her shoes and hose. She sat on the bed and Mr. Bowtie squatted on the floor and examined her feet.

"Millie, you have very nice feet. Those walkin' shoes you bought have served you well. Try not to wear those tee-straps too much. Presses your toes in. Gives your feet trouble later in life."

Millie just nodded. Mr. Bowtie stood up. "Well, I think it's time."

Millie handed him a condom.

"Oh, I won't need that, but I'll wear it so I don't mess up your dress. I just want to make love to your feet. Just lie down and let me enjoy myself with your feet." Millie was confused, but complied, furrowing her forehead.

Millie lay down completely clothed except for her feet. Mr. Bowtie sucked on her toes and rooted around on her legs. With one big gasp he was done. Then he left for the bathroom to rid himself of the condom.

As he was leaving, he turned and said again, "You have lovely feet. I fell in love with them the day we met at Zimmerman's. Until next time, good night."

He loved my feet! What in the world. It had been a long day. Millie took off her dress and hung it and the slip neatly in the closet. She fell back into the bed and was asleep in seconds.

Chapter 19

The light coming through the window the next morning woke her. Millie sat up suddenly, trying to figure out where she was or what time of day it was. She glanced at the clock. It was six-thirty. She wanted to have breakfast with Miss Cora, Alice, and Mr. Lester, maybe going down around seven. That gave her plenty of time to soak in the tub and rinse out her underthings.

By seven Millie was dressed in her blue everyday dress and going toward the kitchen. The smell of bacon was drawing her and going the back way felt normal and comforting. Miss Cora was at her place by the stove and Mr. Lester was at his seat at the kitchen table, a plate filled with eggs, grits, bacon, and biscuit before him.

He looked up. "Well, well, well, lookie here. Good mornin', Millie."

Miss Cora turned. "Millie, good mornin'."

Alice was moving between the kitchen and dining room with a quick "Mornin', Millie" tossed Millie's way on one of her passes through. The house was waking up. Soon the gentlemen would be at their places ready to eat and then be gone.

"Have a seat, Millie." Mr. Lester touched the back of the chair next to him. By the time she sat down Miss Cora had put a plate of food in front of her with a "make yourself a cup of coffee."

Just being in this kitchen calmed Millie. She savored her plate of food, drawing the smells in, especially the bacon and biscuit, as she ate.

Too soon, Mr. Lester was getting up and pushing his chair back under the table. "Well, ladies, I bid you a fond adieu. The pipes are calling me. Tra-la-la-la-la." He winked as he pushed through the back door.

Millie finished her plate of food and her cup of coffee. She slid the plate, fork, and cup into the sudsy water in the sink. No more to do here. She made her way back up to her room on the second floor.

It was only seven-thirty and Millie realized she had nothing else to do, unlike the busy schedule she kept as a kitchen and house maid. *I'll have to get used to this new routine.* Back upstairs she took off her shoes and, fully dressed, lay back on the bed. She drifted off to sleep. This time she did not wake up until ten o'clock. She could hear Gladys in the bathroom they shared. Maybe once Gladys was done, Millie could ask her how she filled her day.

Millie was sitting in her lady chair reading a story in the September *Redbook* magazine when Gladys stuck her head in the door. "Hey, Millie, wanna go to Zimmerman's with me. We'll check with Hazel and Corine."

"That would be real fine, Gladys. I don't have enough money to really shop, but I can sure do some 'dream' shopping. You know, lookin' at what I want to buy next time I have some cash."

"Okay. Let's go. I think Corine and Hazel are in our parlor."

Millie and Gladys checked in the parlor. Hazel was at the piano and Corine was painting and neither of them wanted to go to Zimmerman's.

Gladys and Millie headed out the front door and down the block, turning left on Third Street, the same route Millie and Lucy had taken on Millie's first trip to Zimmerman's. Gladys did not walk as fast as Lucy had so Millie was able to keep up with her and ask questions.

"Gladys, where do you and Corine and Hazel get your evening clothes?"

"Oh, Millie, we buy a lot of things from the Sears catalog. I have one you can look at and I'll show you how to figure your order and pay for it. You just give your money to the postman. He gets it to Sears, then he delivers what you've bought."

"Gladys, when do we get paid each week?"

"Miss Sarah will slide an envelope under your door Sunday morning with your pay for the week."

Millie was already thinking about how she could spend her money.

Soon they had made it to Zimmerman's and were scooting across the street. Millie was relieved that this time her shoes did not fall apart. She was wearing her serviceable oxfords. Mr. Bowtie would be pleased that she was taking care of her feet.

"Millie, I'm shopping for underthings on the second floor. Why don't we meet back at the front door in about an hour or so. Sound good?"

Millie nodded. It was now eleven-thirty, so Millie had until twelve-thirty to dream shop. She started with the purses.

There were evening bags with short chain straps and shimmering tassels hanging from the base. A bit further along Millie found the leather bags and began looking at the prices. $2.34, too much. $5.00, way too much. Further along she found a leather purse with a tooled floral design on the flap. The price, $1.49, seemed reasonable. Next time I'll get you, little purse.

She then went to the perfume and makeup counter. She would wait until Gladys could help her, but there it all was: mascara, face powder, eyebrow pencil, and rouge. Millie eyes lit up. But there was more to explore on the first floor.

She walked through the men's ready-to-wear section, shoes, shirts, suits, everything a well-dressed man might need. The last section on the first floor was piece goods with bolt after bolt of beautiful fabric. Millie had never seen this much fabric. She walked by the rows of cloth, letting her fingers pass over the bolts of crepe, cotton, voile, silk, georgette. And then there were racks of colorful thread and displays of shiny black sewing machines.

Finally, she reached a section near the cutting boards and the drawers filled with patterns where a few shelves held books about sewing. One caught her eye, *The Art of Dressmaking* by Butterick, one of the pattern companies. Millie took the book and began flipping through the pages which showed step-by-step instructions on how to make a dress. Two-hundred plus pages of instructions. Corine has her art Hazel her music and Gladys her books. I'm going to have my dressmaking. Miss Sarah has a sewing machine. I've seen it in her parlor. I'll get her to teach me.

Gladys came up behind Millie and leaning in asked, "Would you like to have that book. I'll get it for you. Let's call it a 'welcome to the second floor' present."

"Oh, Gladys, that would be the bee's knees!"

"Consider it done."

In no time they were climbing the back stairs rather than taking the front stairs in case some of the evening's guests had already arrived. It was close to two o'clock. As they came into the kitchen, Gladys asked Millie if she was hungry. Millie thought about it. "If there's a cold biscuit, I'll take that." Gladys agreed. So, they set their packages down, fixed a glass of sweet tea each, and drank tea and ate their biscuits. After that they climbed the back stairs to their rooms. Then she went down the hall to the parlor, *The Art of Dressmaking* in her hand.

This would be the first time Millie had spent time in the girls' parlor as one of the girls. It was a pleasant room, afternoon light coming through the one window; Corine with her easel set up, brush in hand; Hazel working on difficult measures in her music. Millie just slipped in and took a seat on the sofa, Lucy's place. That was it, wasn't it. Millie was taking Lucy's place.

This little sorority had a culture, a pace, an ease. Gladys slipped in and took her place in her chair and opened a book. They would stay as they were for almost two hours, each one lost in something she loved. And Millie was discovering dressmaking as an art form.

The reading went slowly at first, but she had her dictionary nearby and with that friend she navigated the text. October was a warm month in Mason, but today it was mild, almost spring-like and a breeze was moving the leaves on the oak tree just outside the window. Millie sighed.

At four o'clock Gladys, ever the leader, spoke. "Hey, y'all, we better start gettin' ready."

"And I was just gettin' these runs goin'," Hazel complained.

"Well, I think I need to think about what colors I want to use in the sky, so stoppin' for me is good." Corine began cleaning her brushes.

One by one they went to their rooms. Millie dressed and fluffed her hair. Gladys again helped her with makeup, though Millie was getting better at crafting heart-shaped red lips.

It was soon five-fifteen and Millie could smell the fried catfish and hushpuppies. One of her favorite meals. Miss Sarah was in the hall and the girls soon joined her.

Again, they made a grand entrance, coming down the

stairs, Miss Sarah in her white lace dress leading the way. Millie looked for the gentleman next to what had now become her chair.

He was an older man, balding and pudgy. Millie wondered if he were the owner of the hairy chest she had heard the girls mention once in the kitchen at breakfast. Oh, well. I'm savin' for a sewing machine, mister, and you're gonna help me get it.

He stood and politely pulled her chair out and pushed it in after Millie got seated. But in his enthusiasm, he pushed so hard Millie bumped the table and Miss Sarah's glass of tea took a tumble. "Oh, I am so sorry. Please forgive me. The first time at your table and, oh, I'm such an oaf."

"Mr. Zappa, don't worry yourself. Just take your seat and enjoy your supper." Miss Sarah, ever the consummate hostess, patted Mr. Zappa's arm as he settled himself in his chair.

Millie looked at Alice who was at her post with the tea pitcher. Millie shrugged and Alice stifled a giggle. Millie guessed that Alice had made the trip to Mr. Willie's for the catfish. She wondered if Mr. Willie had asked about her.

Soon Miss Cora was serving the lemon meringue pie, and everyone was oohing and ahhing. Millie had enjoyed her catfish and hushpuppies and even made small talk with Mr. Zappa about the meal. He told her that he had recently moved to Mason from New Jersey and had opened the new movie theater, The Ritz. Millie perked up. "Maybe you and the other ladies would like to come see a movie some time. My treat."

"We really only have one day off. That would be Sunday. And right now, suh, I'd like to eat my pie."

"But I could open the theater for you. Meet you at the side door. Let you in," Mr. Zappa continued.

"Let's talk about it when we go to the parlor. This pie is so good. You really need to try it." Millie was feeling more confident, more in charge.

Mr. Zappa took Millie's advice and ate his lemon meringue pie. "You're right. This is delicious. And those fried round things. What are they called?"

Millie continued eating her pie, "Hushpuppies."

"Oh, I'll bet there's a story there." Mr. Zappa continued his attempt to be charming.

Soon everyone was finished with their pie and were starting to head toward the parlor. Millie and Mr. Zappa began moving that way. "Millie, you pick where you want to sit," He said. One of Mr. Zappa's shoes had come untied, and he tripped on it as they crossed the foyer. Millie grabbed his arm and led him into the parlor and to the closest chair.

Hazel was not playing the piano tonight. Instead, she was lost in conversation with a very handsome young man who seemed to hang on every word she uttered. Here we go again. Another wedding may be coming, Millie mused.

Mr. Zappa began talking about the movies he had been showing at The Ritz. Millie had heard the girls talk about movies they had seen. As was her custom, Miss Sarah always spent time with new guests, so she joined the conversation Millie and Mr. Zappa were having. Millie was relieved since she had never been to a movie.

Mr. Zappa began telling them about *Wings*, a movie starring Clara Bow, the "It Girl," Buddy Rogers, and Richard Arlen, which he was currently showing at The Ritz. "Oh, it's a wonderful story. Has plenty of action because the two leading men are fighter pilots. Oh, and love, too. Gotta have love if Clara Bow is in it."

Both Millie and Miss Sarah nodded.

"Tell us about some of your other movies, Mr. Zappa." Miss Sarah really knew how to keep a conversation going. Millie was taking note.

"How about you ladies meet me at the side door of The

Ritz on Sunday, say around three o'clock," he said. "I'll show you the movie for free."

Millie and Miss Sarah looked at each other, Millie waiting for Miss Sarah's response. "Mr. Zappa, I think that would be very nice of you. We'll plan to be there. Might just be Millie and me. But we'll be there."

Then Mr. Zappa told them about *The Jazz Singer*, the first talkie. He talked about Charlie Chaplin, "the little tramp," and movies that would come out in 1928 like *A Woman of Affairs* with Greta Garbo. Some of the movies would be talkies. *Our Dancing Daughters*, a story of two women, one a flapper, vying for the same millionaire, would be coming out soon.

Millie asked, "What's a 'flapper'?"

"Oh, you know, a girl who dresses in short dresses and does as she pleases, maybe even drinks whiskey and smokes."

"Oh," Millie looked surprised. I think I'd like to see that movie.

It was almost eight o'clock. Hazel and her gentleman were standing and heading toward the stairs. Millie looked toward Corine and Gladys. They were following suit.

Millie turned to Mr. Zappa, "Okay, Mr. Zappa, I've enjoyed our talk. Would you like to see my room?"

Miss Sarah rose as well, waiting until all her girls and guests had departed before she would take the stairs up to her third-floor suite.

Once in her room and without any fanfare Millie handed Mr. Zappa a condom. "Oh, indeed. Thank you, Millie. I'll put it right on."

Millie undressed, lay on the bed, and closed her eyes as Mr. Zappa unzipped his pants and covered his manhood and let his pants fall to the floor. Millie just lay there and let Mr. Zappa do his business. He didn't last long and was soon flopped by her side panting and sweating.

When he had gained his composure, he got up and went to the bathroom to dispose of the condom. When he returned, he thanked Millie as he walked to the door. "Don't forget about coming to see *Wings* on Sunday. You can get some fashion ideas from watching Clara Bow. You know the 'It Girl'."

Millie had had her eyes closed and was just returning from the secret place in her mind where she had been thinking about making clothes for Louise. She opened her eyes and watched as Mr. Zappa was leaving.

"I gotta have a bath. He sure sweated a lot," Millie muttered. She did as she had before, washing her body and her hair and then just lying in the warm water. "I may be goin' to hell for this, but not before I see that movie *Wings* on Sunday," she mused aloud. "Thanks to you, Mr. Zappa. What kinda name is 'Zappa'?"

Not tired, even though it had been a busy day, Millie settled in her bed and started reading *The Art of Dressmaking* where she had left off.

She didn't even realize that she had fallen asleep. She had failed to wind her alarm clock, but still did not sleep late, rising at seven o'clock.

"It's Saturday. Maybe Magdala will be at breakfast." Millie dressed and headed downstairs. Sure enough there was Magdala seated at the table with her papa. And Miss Cora was there too. Only one seat left.

"Get yourself a plate of food," Miss Cora pointed to the stove as she spoke.

"Smells so good, Miss Cora." Millie put a biscuit, two pieces of bacon, and a mound of grits on her plate. "I'm not workin' near as hard as I did workin' for you, Miss Cora. I'm gonna get fat."

"Well, Millie, a little meat on your bones wouldn't hurt," Miss Cora smiled. "Sit down here and tell us about your week."

Millie gave an edited version, focusing on her move to her new room and her trip to Zimmerman's. She also talked about *The Art of Dressmaking.*

Millie turned to Magdala, "Magdala, tell me what you've been doing this week." Magdala talked about school and basketball, also mentioning that Hazel was going to teach her how to play the piano. Like listening to a kid sister talk, she set her coffee cup down and just looked at Magdala and smiled. Millie looked at Miss Cora and Mr. Lester, both enjoying all their precious Magdala was saying. This is my family now. Millie nodded her head. My family.

When Millie got back to her room, there was a gym suit lying on her bed with a note. "Lucy wanted you to have this so you can play volleyball with us. We'll be playing today." It was signed, "Corine."

Millie changed into the gym suit, which was a little baggy, so she pulled the cloth belt in a bit tighter. By the time she got downstairs it was after eight and the girls were seated at the kitchen table eating cold biscuits and bacon. All the Butterfields were gone.

"Millie, have you ever played volleyball?" Gladys asked. Millie shook her head. "Well, you can be my partner against Corine and Hazel. You'll catch on fast."

It was a perfect October day in the South. The sky was a brilliant blue and a slight warm breeze was blowing, catching loose oak leaves and tossing them to the ground. The clothesline would be the "net." Gladys and Millie on one side, Hazel and Corine on the other.

Gladys started the game with a strong serve barely grazing the line and shaking the few dish towels hung there. Corine jumped up and spiked the ball down at Millie's feet. "We get the ball now," Corine announced.

Corine's serve sailed across the clothesline. It was Gladys's turn to spike the ball. Millie took a turn at serving and connected well with the ball which sailed over both Hazel's and Corine's heads and landed fair.

"We got a point," Gladys shouted and patted Millie on the back.

Back and forth the ball flew, sometimes spiked, sometimes missed. This went on for an hour. They were all beginning to grow weary, but with each well-placed volley, their energy surged.

Corine hit a driving serve, which was coming like a bullet across the clothesline. Both Gladys and Millie went for it hoping to spike the ball to the other side, but what happened instead was Gladys's elbow drove into Millie's left eye. Millie staggered backwards, grabbing her face.

"Oh, Millie, I'm so sorry," Gladys apologized. "Here, let me help you get inside. We'll need to put some ice on that."

Gladys led Millie up the back stairs into the kitchen with Corine and Hazel right behind, clucking like mother hens. "Oh, Millie, I hope you don't get a black eye."

Gladys sat Millie down in a kitchen chair, grabbed a dish towel and filled it with ice, before pressing it against Millie's face. When Gladys pulled the dish rag back, the three gasped. "What, what?" Millie shouted.

"Oh, it's gonna be a big one, Millie," Hazel reported.

"Yeah, it's starting to bloom," Corine added.

Gladys pressed the rag against Millie's face a second time. But all the pressing in the world was not going to keep the red from turning to purple and then to black.

"We've got to come up with a plan," Gladys announced. "I think make-up might work. Or maybe she could wear a patch."

"Let's get some tea and think about this, "Hazel suggested.

Millie felt like a child who had been in a schoolyard fight.

It was almost noon, so Corine set out four glasses of Miss Cora's sweet tea. Hazel rummaged in the refrigerator and found leftover pie and a few hushpuppies. That would be their dinner.

"Why don't we all get cleaned up and meet back in the parlor. Y'all bring all your makeup and we'll start working."

Tears began to run down Millie's cheeks. "I hope my gentleman likes black eyes."

"Oh, he'll love it when he hears how you got it. You know, being the active type and all." Corine tried to cheer her up.

Millie dug into her piece of lemon meringue pie. "But you know Miss Cora's pie makes everything better," Hazel reminded her.

And so back up the twisty stairs to their floor they went. As Gladys was passing Millie going to her room, she told her she could go first in the bathroom, since she was the casualty of the volleyball game.

Millie's first look at her eye was a shock. While it was red now, she knew it would continue to blossom in blue and purple. "Oh, I do look ugly!"

She stepped out of her gym suit, took a bath, and washed her hair. She even took the time to rinse out the gym suit and her chemise. She found a clothes rack in her closet and stretched out what she had washed. She dressed, fluffed her hair, put on the dress Miss Sarah had given her, and headed for the parlor. Only Corine was there at the window, paints out, working where she had left off.

"Hey, Mille, I'm not real good with makeup. I'll leave that to Hazel and Gladys. They like that kind of thing."

Millie just slumped on the sofa and waited for Hazel and Gladys. Soon they were there with their kits of makeup. They argued over what base to use, how much to apply and where. They leaned over Millie, busy with their ministrations. When they were done, Gladys said, "Go look, go look now. This looks pretty good."

"Yes, Millie, go look. I think you'll be surprised," Hazel added.

Millie walked down the hallway to her bedroom and then into the bathroom. What she saw was not especially encouraging, but it would have to do. The purple was persisting and anyone seeing it would immediately ask, "What happened to you!"

There was still time before needing to finish her makeup and dress, so Millie decided to write Louise a letter. She now had her own stash of Miss Sarah's Boarding House stationery.

Sitting down in her lady chair and using her *The Art of Dressmaking* as a desk, she began to write. This would be the fourth letter this week, one for every day of the week. By Monday Millie would have seven letters she would give to Buck whom she would ask to deliver to Nadine Youngblood, owner of the only general store in Gaston.

Millie had no idea how Nadine would get them to Louise in Savannah, but she just believed she should write them. Maybe one day Louise would understand why her mother left Gaston.

Each letter summarized what Millie had done that day. Today Millie would write about the volleyball game and so in vivid detail Millie told of her encounter with Gladys's elbow. She closed with, "Louise, you should just see your ma's eye. Try as they can my new friends couldn't cover up the bruise. I look beat up. But Gladys and I did win the game." And she signed it, "Your ma, Millie."

"There." Smiling, Millie stuffed this most recent epistle into an envelope.

Now it was time to get gussied up. Millie had become more skilled with makeup and in her opinion looked as good as any of the other girls, except for the black eye. At five-fifteen she joined Miss Sarah, who was standing in the hall. She looked at Millie with a shocked expression. Millie quickly

responded, "Gladys's elbow got my eye while we were playing volleyball."

"Well, Millie," she said, "I want you to announce that to
the room before someone thinks I slap my girls around."

"Yes, ma'am."

Millie had forgotten to tell the girls about Mr. Zappa's offer to see the movie *Wings*. As they came out of their rooms,
Millie told them that they would need to meet him at the
side door of the theater around three o'clock on Sunday.

Corine seemed to speak for the group. "That sounds like
fun. That's just the berries!" Hazel and Gladys nodded.

"Time to go, girls. We'll see about that movie tomorrow.
I'll be going, too." As usual Miss Sarah led the way down
the stairs with the transformed volleyball players falling in
behind.

They came into the dining room and as before Millie
looked for her seat and the gentleman just to the right. Millie could hardly withhold her shock. He looked old, feeble
even. When he smiled, he appeared a few years younger, but
not many.

Millie took her seat next to him. He introduced himself
as Harold Henderson, president of the Dixie Bank, a small
local bank. Millie nodded demurely.

Miss Sarah looked around the table and said, "Millie needs
to tell everyone about her black eye. I don't want any of our
guests to think that my boarding house condones any kind
of mistreatment."

"Uh, yes, ma'am. Well, you see. We were playing volleyball
in the yard and, well, Gladys and I were on the same team.
Well, that is, my eye just jumped in front of Gladys's elbow."

Everyone laughed and Millie did, too. Miss Cora and Alice
had stood there holding the platters of food waiting to see what
Millie's explanation about her shiner might be. The shiner was
still blooming and defying any attempts at cover-up.

Tonight's meal: fried meat patty, gravy, and mashed potatoes tasted especially good. And those turnips, she knew them, almost like old friends. Mr. Henderson must have been hungry too because he kept his head down and cleaned his plate.

It was time for Miss Cora's famous pound cake. They each got a healthy slice and Millie imagined that back in the kitchen Mr. Lester might get a slice twice that big. Oh, yes, and the sheriff would be here tonight. It was Saturday after all. And he'd get a slice, too.

Miss Sarah stood and began moving toward the parlor. Everyone followed, finding seats there. Miss Sarah announced that she had a special treat. "Gentlemen and ladies, while we do all know that Prohibition of alcohol is the law, I do on occasion come into possession of a distilled spirit that is just perfect after a fine dinner. And we did have a fine dinner tonight."

With that Miss Sarah went to a cabinet near the piano and brought out a bottle of brandy. "Hazel, will you hold this tray of glasses and I'll pour a small glass for everyone. Oh, and gentlemen, please feel free to enjoy a cigar, pipe, or cigarette." She pointed to two boxes on one of the side tables.

Now I'm really going to hell, Millie muttered under her breath.

"Hazel, play a pretty number or two for us. And then I believe some of you gentlemen let me know you'd like to have a conversation about our local economy."

So, Hazel took her place at the piano and played a Chopin waltz and prelude. Beautiful, flowing, elegant music. The front windows were open slightly, and the evening sounds drifted in, a few lazy crickets — insect violinists, Millie thought — added their notes.

When Hazel finished playing the gentlemen puffed and

sipped and chatted about the state of the Georgia economy, trade policy, state taxes and interest rates.

Mr. Henderson, Millie's gentleman, said he had some concerns about some loans he might have to call due. Some voiced concerns about Georgia's cotton in competition with the cotton produced by Egypt.

They puffed and sipped and shook their heads. President Coolidge, was he really good for business because good for business meant good for the country. Maybe Herbert Hoover, who at the time was secretary of commerce, would be a good candidate next year,1928, since Coolidge had said he wouldn't run for a second term.

The cigar smoke was beginning to burn Millie's eyes. She was carefully sipping her brandy and beginning to feel sleepy. She began pressing her fingernails into her arm so she'd stay awake. Will this ever end. I don't know nothin' 'bout Egyptian cotton and Herbert Hoover.

Finally, the talk was winding down and the evening's couples were slipping up the stairs. Miss Sarah climbed the stairs as well. The sheriff would be waiting for her in her upstairs parlor.

Once upstairs Millie led Mr. Henderson down the hall to her room. Perspiration was forming on his forehead, and he was huffing and puffing as he walked. He was still worked up about the swirl of issues discussed in the parlor, all of which might affect his bank.

In her usual matter-of-fact manner, Millie handed Mr. Henderson a condom. "Here, suh, put this on your manhood." Mr. Henderson took off his tie, shirt, and undershirt, unzipped and dropped his pants, letting them fall to the floor, removed his shorts, and did what she had asked. Millie took off her dress, chemise and step-ins and lay down flat on the bed. She closed her eyes and went to that secret place in her mind. Okay, Mr. Banker Man, let's get this over with.

Mr. Henderson did just that. After one thrust, he let out a sigh and fell flat against Millie. He wasn't moving. "Mr. Henderson, suh, you can get off now." She paused. "Mr. Henderson." Nothing. A little louder, "Mr. Henderson."

Millie pushed as hard as she could, rolling Mr. Henderson over on the other side of the bed. His mouth was open; his eyes, set. And there he lay, naked on her bed.

Oh, Jesus, I've killed him. What am I gonna do?"

Millie got up and quickly dressed. She ran to the bathroom door, went in and tip-toed to the door leading to Gladys's room. She heard the hall door to Gladys's room opening and closing, so she assumed that Gladys's guest was leaving. She waited a few seconds, listening for him to head down the hallway.

"Gladys," Millie whispered. A little louder, "Gladys. I need your help, Gladys."

Millie heard Gladys moving around in her room. She came into the bathroom tying her robe as she did and fluffing her tight red curls. "What is it, Millie?"

"Oh, Gladys, Mr. Henderson is dead. I just know it. Come see."

With Gladys leading the way they both returned to Millie's room. Gladys went to the side of the bed where Mr. Henderson, now quite obviously deceased, was lying. Gladys lifted one arm and let it drop. Then she ran to her room and returned with a small mirror that she held over his face. Nothing.

"You're right. He's dead, Millie. And we've got to get him back downstairs to his room and I need to let Miss Sarah know. Oh, God, the sheriff will be up there. One thing at a time. Let's get Corine and Hazel."

Now they both tiptoed down the hall and listened first at Corine's door. No sound. So, Gladys lightly tapped on the door. Nothing. Gladys opened the door slightly and looked in, then she heard water running in the bathroom.

Gladys and Millie went in and at the bathroom door Gladys tapped and called out, "Corine."

"Gladys, whatcha doing up?" Corine responded.

"Come here. We have a really big problem. Millie is here, too."

Corine came out of the bathroom, wrapping her robe around her. Gladys looked her square in the eye, "Corine, Millie's gentleman is dead and still in her bed. We've got to get him back downstairs to his room and then we have to tell Miss Sarah."

Corine's eyes widened, "But Miss Sarah is with the sheriff!"

"I know, but we have to tell her." Gladys was working on a plan. "Let's get Hazel."

So now the three of them, two in robes, Millie in one of her day dresses, went quietly down the hall to the last bedroom. Gladys leaned against the door. She heard a man's voice, and it sounded like he was getting closer, so they scurried down to their parlor, slipping in and closing the door. All three of them now leaned against the door listening for the man's foot fall. They heard him heading for the staircase leading downstairs.

The three crept out of the parlor and went to Hazel's room. Now instead of knocking, they all three just walked in.

Hazel looked shocked. "What's going on?"

"Mr. Henderson is dead and still in my bed," Millie said.

"Oh, God," Hazel whispered. "What are we gonna do?"

Glady spoke, "We have to get him back downstairs to his room and then tell Miss Sarah."

"But Miss Sarah is with the sheriff," Hazel responded, unconsciously echoing Corine.

"Don't tell me what I already know," Gladys shot back.

"Let's get to work. We can use the top sheet on Millie's bed. Each of us takes a corner. We can drag him down the stairs to his room. We need to move quick just in case some of those other men are around. And we have to figure out which room is his. I'm hoping he left the door open."

So, the four went back to Millie's room. Millie tossed Mr. Henderson's clothes on top of him. First, they all worked the same side, pulling him closer to the edge. He was a slight, frail old man, so pulling him over was not too hard. But he was dead weight, so once he started to roll, he kept going. Before they could stop him, he was face down on one side of Millie's bed on the floor.

"Well, I think this makes it easier," Hazel offered. The other three just looked at her and rolled their eyes.

"Yeah, all we have to do now is spread the sheet out and roll him over on it." Hazel continued.

They spread the sheet, rolled him onto it and then began dragging it toward the door. What they soon discovered was that they had to drag in unison or again he would roll off the sheet.

So, like oarsmen on an ancient ship with Gladys establishing the rhythm, the four began to transport the recently deceased Mr. Henderson.

"Pull, pull, pull," Gladys kept it up. Soon they were at the top of the stairs.

"It's going to get tricky now," Corine pointed out.

"Yes, I think we need three in the front and one in the rear now," Gladys suggested.

So, Millie, Hazel, and Corine took the down position and Gladys held onto the top of the sheet. Mr. Henderson was most compliant, but soon the pull of gravity took over and he was moving faster than Millie, Hazel, and Corine could manage and soon they were all in one pile at the bottom of the stairs, with Mr. Henderson. The girls quickly got to their feet.

"Listen, we need to find out which room is his, so let's drag him into the dining room for now," Gladys suggested and the other three nodded, with Mr. Henderson naked on the floor at the bottom of the stairs.

They rolled him back onto the sheet and dragged him into the dining room and back to a corner out of sight. Gladys left to go figure out which room was Mr. Henderson's.

"Have you ever been around a dead body?" Corine asked.

"No," said Hazel.

"Where I come from, we had sittin' ups where the dead person in his coffin was put in the front room of a house and we all would come through," Millie offered. "Of course that was after the funeral man had fixed 'em up. Ain't never seen the likes of this. Do you think I should shut his eyes?"

"Lord, no, Millie. Don't touch him. You might get into trouble," Hazel said.

"But, Hazel, he's already been all over me. I'm already in trouble," Millie answered.

Gladys was back. "I figured it out. Let's get movin'." So they began dragging Mr. Henderson into the main hall and to his room. They heard a cough coming from one room, so they pulled the sheet even faster.

Finally, they were at the room Gladys had found was his. They dragged him in and then with a one-two heft they lifted him onto the bed, pulled out the sheet and rolled it up.

Now there he was, naked, but in his own bed.

"What should I do with his clothes?" Millie asked. "I don't see how we can dress him."

"Oh, just hang them over the chair. Maybe he sleeps naked," Gladys said, and then added, "Y'all wait here. I'm going to get Miss Sarah."

It was nearing midnight by the time Gladys got to Miss Sarah's room. She heard talking so maybe the entertainin' was over. Gladys knocked at the door. Miss Sarah answered, hair down and an elegant red velvet robe pulled around her statuesque body. The sheriff was sitting on the side of the bed, wearing no shirt and in his drawers.

"Gladys, what for heaven's sake do you want?" Miss Sarah asked.

"Well, ma'am." Gladys whispered. "Mr. Henderson is, uh, well, dead."

"Dead! Are you sure?"

"Yes, ma'am, we're sure."

"Where is he?"

"Well, you see we, I mean Corine, Hazel, Millie, and me. We, uh, have dragged him down to his room and he is, well, laid out in his bed."

"Claude, you hear that?"

"Sarah, let me get my pants on first." To Gladys's great relief the sheriff moved from view.

Gladys continued, "Miss Sarah, he's naked and his eyes are open. Millie wanted to shut 'em, but I told her not to touch him."

Now the sheriff was at the door. "What's goin' on?"

"Claude, Gladys here says Mr. Henderson, you know the banker, Dixie Bank, he's dead lying in a bed downstairs, naked and with his eyes open."

The sheriff turned, grabbed his shirt, and finished getting dressed. All that was left was to pull on his shoes, which he did. Coming through the door, he looked at Gladys, "Take me to his room."

So, Gladys, Miss Sarah, and the sheriff headed downstairs to Mr. Henderson's room. Corine had turned on the light in the room, and she, Millie, and Hazel were standing one on each side of the bed, as if holding a vigil.

The sheriff pushed into the room ahead of Miss Sarah and Gladys. He spread his hands down his ample belly, smoothing his wrinkled shirt, leaned back, and slid each of his thumbs into a belt loop. He looked around the room for a moment and then took charge.

"Ladies, please step back from the bed." Millie, Corine, and Hazel complied. Now in his element, he stepped toward the bed and examined the body, sliding his fingers down the lids of the deceased, now giving Mr. Henderson the look of a man truly resting in peace.

The sheriff continued, "I'll take it from here, if you can show me to your telephone, Sarah. I need to have a word with the coroner."

Turning to the girls, he said, "Now, ladies, you've done enough. If I may have that sheet on the floor, we'll cover him with that for now. Why don't you all go to bed?" Eager to be done with the dead, the four quickly left the room, then convened upstairs in Gladys's room.

After speaking with the coroner, the sheriff gave more instructions to Miss Sarah. "Darlin', I've fixed things with the coroner, but you know I can't be here when they come for the body. You'll need to call Mr. Jones down at Jones & Sons. Before you do that, give me five minutes' lead time." Miss Sarah nodded.

He leaned in and gave her a kiss. "A most pleasant evening, my dear, even with a bit of added excitement. Never a dull time at Miss Sarah's." He winked and, slipping down the hall, left by way of the kitchen and out the back door. Miss Sarah did as he had asked and soon the funeral director had arrived, loaded Mr. Henderson up, and left.

Back upstairs the girls were reliving their harrowing experience. But, ever the practical sorts, they were also planning what to do next, starting with Millie.

"Well, I'm telling y'all, I am not sleeping in that bed tonight. I'll fumigate it tomorrow, but tonight I'm sleeping upstairs in my old room."

The others all agreed that that was the best plan.

Millie continued, "But what about the movie. Do y'all still want to go to that movie with me. I'll bet Miss Sarah won't, but what about the rest of you?"

"I want to stay in and paint," Corine said.

"I may sleep all day," Hazel added.

"I'll go with you, Millie. It'll be a good distraction. Let's leave around two o'clock so we have plenty of time to get there." Gladys said.

"Well, I'm ready for bed, y'all," Millie said as she walked to the door. The other three agreed. Millie took her dress off and instead put on a robe Gladys had lent her and headed up the back stairs to the turret room.

"Oh, it feels good to be back here," Millie said aloud as she wrapped the robe tighter around her and fell into the little bed. A light quilt was still on the bed and Millie wrapped up in that as well. She welcomed the cleansing coma of a deep sleep.

Chapter 20

The turret room window was slightly open, and a Carolina wren had decided to start her day in the big oak right outside the window. So Millie awoke to loud trills coming from that pert little wren body. "Well, thank God last night is over." Millie yawned and went to the bathroom where she splashed water on her face, peed, and then decided to go to the kitchen to find some breakfast.

The sun was just coming up, so soft October morning light was falling across the kitchen. Millie found a bottle of milk. She poured herself a big glass and seeing the pound cake on the counter, cut herself a breakfast-sized piece. She sat down at the table and did what she really hated to do, that is THINK.

And what popped into her head was: a sewing machine. "I need to figure out how much one of those costs. Once I know that, I can figure how much more 'entertainin'' I'll need to do before I have enough money to buy a sewing machine."

She knew that Miss Cora kept a Sears catalog in a drawer of the little kitchen desk, so she got that catalog and began to study the sewing machines for sale. She grabbed a sheet of stationery and a pencil in another desk drawer and began to figure just how much she would need in order to buy one.

She found the page with the Minnesota H sewing machines, complete with a cabinet. One was around $35.00, a treadle type machine that could run without electricity. Millie had seen one in her neighbor Miss Mildred's house back in Gaston. "Well, if I make $20.00 a week entertainin'." So Millie, not knowing how to multiply or divide, began to add $20.00 plus $20.00. Two weeks' worth made $40.00, so by November at the latest she'd be able to buy a sewing machine. Gladys could show her how to fill out the Sears order form.

Millie looked at the kitchen clock. It was only nine o'clock and it was Sunday. "Well, I'm gonna go to church," she decided. She cleaned up the dishes and went back upstairs. "I just have to get back here by two in order to go to the movies with Gladys."

Millie noticed that Gladys's light was on, so she tapped on her door.

"Come on in, Millie. I know it's you."

"Mornin', Gladys. I'm gonna go to church with Miss Cora, but I'll be back by two so we can go to the movies."

"I'm still in the bed and may stay here until you get back."

Millie decided to wear one of her day dresses, the blue one, so she could save her dress-up one for her entertainin'. She slipped on her dressy tee-strap shoes, fluffed her hair, grabbed her gloves and cloche hat, and went back down the back stairs and out the back door. She sat down on the top step and waited for the Butterfields.

Soon there they were all decked out in their Sunday best. Magdala ran to Millie. "Oh, Millie, I've missed you. I'm so glad you're going with us to church. You are, aren't you?"

Millie stood and smoothed down her dress. "Yes, I am, Magdala."

They took hands and ran to Mr. Lester's truck where he was holding the door open. "Good mornin', Millie, glad you'll be joining us." Miss Cora just stood there, hands on her hips looking pleased.

Magdala was full of school news, telling Millie about making all A's on her report card and scoring a goal in a basketball game. It was the same jolly time as it had been the previous Sundays.

As they entered the church, Mr. Lester and Miss Cora followed the same predictable routine, greeting, laughing, a little back-patting as they made their way to their seats. Soon the choir was singing a rousing version of "Blessed Assurance" and Millie was glad that she had come. Dead Mr. Henderson had almost left her mind.

Then Reverend Edwards was at the pulpit announcing his sermon topic: "Finding Wisdom Under the Circumstances." "Brothers and sisters, hear the word of God from the Book of Proverbs, found in the fourth chapter, verse six. Yes, one verse is all we need today."

Then he read, "Do not forsake wisdom and she will protect you; love her and she will watch over you."

He continued, "Have you ever said, 'I'm doing pretty good, under the circumstances'. I'm sure you have. I find myself using that turn of phrase quite often. 'Under the circumstances.' Well, do you know that that's a real place? 'Under the circumstances.' And THAT is where wisdom lives. Yes, she's there. That's her home. Now you'll say, 'Rev, what in the world do you mean?'" I mean that when you are struggling with something, pressed down by something, frightened by something. When you are there and call out to the Lord, He sends Wisdom. He sends her to you, right where you are 'under the circumstances'."

Millie was on the edge of her seat. Miss Cora had used that phrase when Millie got the letter from her ma telling her Louise was gone and when Miss Cora had talked about the crossroads.

So "under the circumstances" was a real place and that's where wisdom lived. Reverend Edwards was continuing to talk about the value of persevering through difficulties, even mentioning chapter one of the Book of James as he had the week before. He tied in the connection between perseverance and "Lady Wisdom" as he called her.

"Look for Lady Wisdom when you are struggling under the circumstances and doing the best you can."

Just as had happened those other Sundays the members of the congregation were agreeing and encouraging Reverend Edwards to preach it and to tell them more. He did indeed and went on for another hour.

Then the service was ending, the final hymn had been sung, and Millie was walking toward the front door with the Butterfields. When she reached Reverend Edwards, she asked him, "Brother Edwards, can I find Lady Wisdom if I'm not living like I should?"

He took Millie's hand. "My dear child, look for her. She'll show up in the most unlikely places, but you'll always find her when your circumstances are the most difficult, if you look for her."

Millie nodded and continued down the steps with the Butterfields. It was now twelve-thirty and Millie knew that, even if invited, she might not have time to eat with them. Miss Cora of course asked her.

"Miss Cora, I'm supposed to meet Gladys at two o'clock. We're goin' to a movie today. I'm not sure I have time to eat with y'all."

"Millie, how can you see a movie on Sunday?"

"One of the gentlemen callers owns The Ritz Theater and he's going to let us in through the side door and then turn the movie on."

"Chile, you be careful. And as far as dinner goes, we're having pimento cheese sandwiches and potato salad. You'll be done with that by one-thirty with plenty of time to meet up with Gladys."

Millie was so relieved. This day was turning out to be a good one. Being with the Butterfields always made things better.

Once back at the carriage house Millie helped set the table and pour the sweet tea. They all took their seats and held hands while Mr. Lester prayed. Oh, those sandwiches tasted so good. Millie decided not to tell them about Mr. Henderson. She just listened to the conversation, adding a comment here and there.

It was getting close to one-thirty so, after thanking Miss Cora and Mr. Lester profusely and hugging Magdala, Millie went back to the main house and up the back stairs.

She found Gladys in her room. "It'll just be me and you. Miss Sarah can't go. You know that Mr. Henderson thing and all. Let's go."

Millie had some change in her pocket left from her last streetcar ride. She could pay her own way. They hurried to the corner and jumped on the next one going toward town. It rattled along, making it almost impossible to talk. But Gladys tried. "Listen, Millie, when we get off the streetcar, I want to talk with you about Mr. Zappa,"

"Okay."

They could see the theater up ahead, so they got off at the next stop.

Gladys looked at Millie. "I'm a little uncomfortable about all of this. You know meeting Mr. Zappa in the alley way, being in a dark theater, just you and me and HIM. Let's make certain that we know where the exit is in case, we have to, you know, get out."

"Well, how will I know if you think we need to, you know, 'get out'?"

"I'll just say something like, 'Let's go, Millie,' Okay?"

Millie nodded.

"Now act like you know what you're doing," Gladys said.

"But what if I don't?"

"Well, Millie, that's what ACTING is. Just hold your head up, don't rush along, and look around well, 'furtively' like this." Gladys demonstrated by turning her head this way and that.

"Oh, I never knew about 'furtively'. Now I do."

When they came to the alley way, Gladys in the lead simply turned left and Millie followed suit. Sure enough there was Mr. Zappa, sticking his head out from an open side door.

"Well, good afternoon, ladies. I am so pleased that you came. But where is Miss Sarah. I thought for certain she would be here too."

Gladys spoke for both of them. "Uh, Miss Sarah, yes, she had some business to attend to. She's real sorry that she couldn't make it."

"Well, come right in."

Mr. Zappa led them into the theater. "Just sit wherever you like. I'll go get the movie started."

Millie and Gladys settled down in the section nearest the side door. They still had a good view of the movie screen. The lights went out in the theater and the movie started.

Clara Bow, the "It Girl" was playing the part of Mary, a beautiful girl whose affections were being vied for by two handsome young men, Jack and Dave, both of whom became fighter pilots in the Great War.

A gripping scene between Jack and Dave was coming up and Millie and Gladys were reading the dialogue aloud. Dave's plane had been shot down and he was lying on a stretcher when Jack found him. Dave was near death and Jack, with tears in his eyes, was expressing his deep affection for him, brother to brother.

Just as Dave was about to breathe his last, Millie felt a

hand on her breast. It was Mr. Zappa who was now seated in the row behind them. In a reflex action, Millie swung her arm up and her elbow connected with Mr. Zappa's chin with such force that his teeth clinked and his upper plate fell out.

He was doing the same thing to Gladys, who taking that hand away from her breast, flipped it backwards.

"Let's get outta here," Gladys whispered to Millie.

They felt their way along to the end of the row, waiting for the next fully lit scene of the movie. The door was straight ahead, "Now," whispered Gladys, and they rushed the door, which thankfully was unlocked. They were momentarily blinded by the daylight in the alley way. Squinting as they ran, they made it to the street.

"What a creep," Gladys hissed.

"Yeah, we should've known he'd do something like that, especially since Miss Sarah wasn't with us," Millie added.

"Well, let's go home. We can tell Corine and Hazel about our adventure. How we got 'zappa'ed'!"

They heard the clang of the streetcar as it came to a stop. They jumped on and fell into one of the front seats. "Well, we saw most of the movie. I got some ideas for my makeup from watching Clara Bow. She's so beautiful!" Gladys was still talking, but Millie was just looking out the window, thinking about Lady Wisdom and the lesson she had just taught her. Don't look a gift horse in the mouth, he might have rotten teeth or, like Mr. Zappa, no upper ones.

It was almost five o'clock by the time Millie and Gladys got back to Miss Sarah's and the sun was making a rush for the western horizon. They found Hazel and Corine in the second-floor parlor.

Gladys started, "Do we ever have a story to tell!"

Millie added, "Lady Wisdom taught us not to go to the movies on Sunday."

Corine and Hazel looked at her, foreheads furrowed, not

understanding what she meant. Gladys and Millie started out by telling them all about Mary, Jack, and Dave and about the war and the plane getting shot down.

"I wish I'd gone now," Corine said.

"Me, too," Hazel added.

"Well, you won't think that after we tell you the rest of the story," Gladys said, looking at Millie.

Then they told them all about Mr. Zappa's handsy conduct and their hurried departure.

"What a creep," Corine said.

Hazel nodded, then added, "Anybody hungry? Miss Cora usually leaves us something to eat in the refrigerator."

So, they all headed down to the kitchen laughing about their most adventurous weekend with dead bodies and handsy men. They found pimento cheese sandwiches and potato salad in the refrigerator and a note that read, "Look in the freezer for dessert."

While Hazel and Gladys set the table and put out the sandwiches and potato salad, Corine looked in the freezer. "We've got chocolate ice cream, girls!" she shouted.

The four of them settled down at the table and talked and laughed through supper. Millie thought about this room. Maybe it was this table that made whoever sat here find acceptance and family. She had three sisters, four counting Magdala, and maybe even five if she counted Alice. Millie felt content under these circumstances.

Millie knew Gladys's story and she really wanted to hear how Corine and Hazel had ended up at Miss Sarah's, so she just asked. "Y'all know how I ended up here and Gladys told me her story, what about you, Corine, and you, Hazel?"

What had been a jolly time now changed and like a cloud passing over the sun, the mood darkened, and time seemed to slow.

Corine spoke first. "I'm not 'from' anywhere. I don't even

know what town I was born in. I never knew my father. My mother was a stage performer and we moved from town to town whenever she was part of a show. She was so beautiful. She could sing, dance, act. She also taught me to draw, taught me about colors and paints. Things were okay for us, until she got hooked on dope. Cocaine, I think it was. Then, all she wanted to do was find it, use it, and then pass out.

"I was about twelve when she started letting men use me. I knew what they were doing to me was wrong, so one afternoon when she was passed out, I took money from her purse and hitchhiked my way to Mason.

"Can't remember how I ended up here at Miss Sarah's. But, like you, Millie, I started in the kitchen. I feel safe here. Safer than I've ever felt."

There was a pause and then Hazel spoke up. "My turn. I'm an orphan. Both my parents were killed in a streetcar accident in 1910. I was three when they died. My godfather was a well-respected concert pianist and piano teacher in Atlanta where I lived. He offered to take me in and teach me to play the piano. From the time I was a tiny child, I had shown an interest in music, singing, and every time there was a piano nearby, I'd try to play it, not banging, but making up tunes. No other family members wanted me, so it seemed like the right thing to do. He was kind to me at first, gave me piano lessons whenever he was home. I was a good student, spending hours practicing. I also worked in the kitchen with his cook and did some cleaning with his housekeeper. He traveled a lot, so I was usually there alone, except when I went to school. When I turned ten, he started coming into my bedroom at night and touching me. I didn't understand. I thought he was being kind and loving. Soon, he, well, you know, started that with me." She paused and tears began to roll down her cheeks.

When she had gotten control of herself, Hazel continued,

"When I turned fourteen, while he was away on a concert tour, I took some money. He always kept a zipper-bag of dollars in his desk, and I knew where it was. Both the cook and housekeeper were away that day, so I called a cab and went to the train station. I bought a ticket for Mason, just the next city south. Didn't want to go to some place tiny, figured Mason might be, you know, fairly civilized. When I got here, I got a cab and asked where I might find a place to stay. The cab driver brought me here. And like Corine said, I'm never, ever going back. I'm better off than I've ever been. I want to go to college, and I will one day." Hazel stopped and thrust her chin up.

It had been a long twenty-four hours and after eating a big bowl of ice cream each of them was feeling sleepy. They trudged back up the stairs, each one going to her own room. But as Millie and Gladys walked to their end of the hall, Millie stopped. "Oh, Gladys, I need some clean sheets. The ones in my room have Mr. Henderson all over them."

"Come here, Millie. I'll show you where our clean sheets and towels are stored, as well as mops, brooms, and a vacuum cleaner. We'll be needing all that tomorrow, 'cause it's cleaning day. I'll clean our bathroom this week and you can do it the next Monday. We take turns cleaning the parlor. It's Corine and Hazel's turn this week. We'll do that next week."

Gladys opened a door in the hallway across from Millie's room and sure enough it was identical to the one Millie had used on the first floor. Millie grabbed some clean sheets and pillowcases, pressing the linens to her nose. They smelled so fresh and good.

"Night, Gladys."

"Night, Millie. Sleep well."

Millie stripped her bed and remade it with the fresh sheets. It smelled clean now. It was her bed again. She wound the little blue clock and set it for 7:00 just in case she overslept.

She wanted to have breakfast at Miss Cora's kitchen table. She decided that she would bathe in the morning. After slipping off her dress, kicking off her shoes, and pulling off her hose, she finished up her bedtime preparation by brushing her teeth.

After that she fell into bed thinking about Lady Wisdom and all she had taught Millie. "Tomorrow's Monday, maybe I'll see Buck," she sighed and drifted off to sleep.

Chapter 21

For the first time Millie woke up ahead of the little blue clock. It was six-thirty, plenty of time for a bath and then to go downstairs for breakfast with Mr. Lester and Miss Cora.

As was her fashion, Millie filled the tub with hot water and then slipped in to soak. It felt so good to get clean. She washed real good from head to toe. October was beginning to give Mason some cool mornings and this was one of them. Millie shivered as she stepped out of the tub.

She dressed quickly, thinking as she did, I'm gonna need to buy a coat. Yesterday she had found the envelope from Miss Sarah slid under her door. Ten dollars! Not the twenty dollars she would eventually make after entertainin' an entire week.

She felt rich, but she knew she needed to save for a sewing machine. She had stuffed the money into the drawer of her vanity. For now, it would be her safe.

She skipped down the back stairs to the kitchen. Breakfast was being served and Miss Cora and Alice were bustling about. Mr. Lester was at his place at the kitchen table and patted a seat when he saw Millie, "Come on in here, girl, and eat a bite with me." Almost like a sleight-of-hand magician with cards, Miss Cora set a plate for Millie holding a biscuit, a fried egg and two pieces of bacon. Millie got herself a cup of coffee and sat down next to Mr. Lester.

Trying out her newly almost-acquired social skills, Millie spoke to Mr. Lester, saying, "Well, now Mr. Lester, what does your day look like?" When she dropped her head to break her biscuit, Mr. Lester cut his eye at Miss Cora and winked.

"Well, Millie, I'll be stopping by Mr. Cunningham's rental office. He always has a list of clogs I'll need to work on. Good money, but well, let's jus' say I wash my hands real good when I come home."

"Now, Lester, not at breakfast," Miss Cora chided.

Mr. Lester just winked at Millie. He was finished with his breakfast.

After kissing Miss Cora on the cheek, Mr. Lester tapped his forehead in salute. "By the way, Cora, did you see in the paper where Mr. Henderson, that old banker died. Said he died in his sleep in his own bed."

Millie sputtered out a sip of coffee.

Mr. Lester glanced her way and smiled on his way out the door.

"Millie, how was the movie?" Miss Cora had now taken a seat at the table and was eating a biscuit and a strip of bacon, while Alice was busy clearing the table and shaking out the tablecloth.

"Oh, Miss Cora, you were right." Millie leaned in whispering, "Mr. Zappa got handsy when the lights were turned off. Gladys and I high tailed it outta there. But we had seen most of the movie."

"Lord, chile, I worry about you and what you're doin'."

"But Miss Cora, it was like Brother Edwards said yesterday, Lady Wisdom showed up. I don't mean in the real, you know, but I learned from that. I won't ever go to a movie on Sunday!"

"Glad you learned something from that sermon yesterday.

Keep thinkin' that way." Miss Cora stood and started back to bustling about the kitchen.

"Well, Miss Cora, I'm gonna head back upstairs. I've got a book I'm reading called *The Art of Dressmaking*. And I'm gonna ask Miss Sarah to teach me how to use a sewing machine."

"That's a fine idea, Millie. Good luck with Miss Sarah."

"I'll check in with you later, Miss Cora. You have a fine day."

Millie climbed the back stairs to the second floor. She paused and then kept going until she got to Miss Sarah's floor. She threw her shoulders back and walked down the hall to the office.

Miss Sarah was there and looked up as Millie came in. "Well, Millie, you're not doing the cleaning anymore, so what brings you to my office?"

Millie plunged in, "Miss Sarah, I bought a book called *The Art of Dressmaking*. Miss Sarah, I want to learn how to sew. And, Miss Sarah, since you have a sewing machine, I thought you might give me some lessons. You can keep some of my pay for the time you give me, teachin' me."

Miss Sarah smiled slightly, remembering the frightened country girl Buck had brought to her just a few weeks ago. She had never met a girl the likes of this. This one, wanting to learn, always wanting to learn. Somehow it was hard to say "no" to her.

"Well, Millie, I believe I could do that. I can't spend a lot of time, so you'll have to pay attention and learn fast."

"Yes, ma'am."

"Meet me in my parlor every day at one o'clock. I'll spend about forty-five minutes with you, say three days a week, Monday, Wednesday, and Friday. I'll charge you fifty cents per lesson. How does that sound?"

"Oh, Miss Sarah, thank you. I'll see you at one o'clock today, right?"

"That's right, Millie."

Millie left Miss Sarah's office. She scampered down the hall and down the stairs to the second-floor parlor.

She read and planned until late morning. She had a couple of sheets of stationery left from her earlier letter writing and she already had a pencil. She began to list what she thought she might need in addition to the sewing machine, thinking, This'll be a start. She wrote: "Thread, small pieces of lots of fabrics." I want my customers to have choices.

Monday was cleaning day on the second floor, so Millie closed the book, sticking the sheets of paper inside the back cover. Back in her room, she made her bed. No need for fresh sheets, she had changed them out just the day before. She went down the hall to the storage closet and dragged the vacuum cleaner to her room.

Now that she knew how, she liked using that machine. She vacuumed her room, taking care to work from the center to the sides on the rug. She couldn't remember whose turn it was to vacuum the hallway, so she did that, too. By this time Gladys was up and met her in the hall.

"I'll take that now, Millie. Kind of you to do the hallway."

"I don't mind. Remember, cleaning was my job until last week. I don't mind cleaning our bathroom." And she did, replacing the towels after she had cleaned. It was going on to eleven o'clock and her room still needed dusting.

By noon her cleaning chores were over. She checked her dresses and decided all were good and ready for the week. She decided to go to the kitchen for dinner, but first she checked in with Corine and Hazel. Sticking her head in Hazel's door, she asked if she might want to go downstairs and find something to eat.

Hazel was cleaning her room and declined, as did Corine. But both said they'd see her in the parlor after lunch. "We need to plan another volleyball game or a trip to Zimmerman's," Corine told Millie. "Your eye is really starting to look normal."

Millie found some leftover pimento cheese sandwiches and potato salad. She took her time making her plate and setting it down along with a glass of sweet tea on the kitchen table.

At one o'clock she headed to Miss Sarah's parlor. Standing by the sewing machine Miss Sarah took on the teacher's role. "Millie, we're going to start with the sewing machine," she said. "Sit down here on the chair in front of the machine. Let's start with how you run the thread."

The forty-five minutes were spent with Miss Sarah demonstrating and Millie practicing what she had shown her. By the time her lesson was over, Millie knew how to get a Minnesota H ready to use. First steps.

She went back to the kitchen for a glass of sweet tea. Sitting at the table she began to think about Louise. Poor Louise, her ma left her. But, Louise, I didn't have any choice. And then there it was, that phrase and she thought it, "under the circumstances." It made her feel better.

Then Millie began to figure how old that child would be, today being October 10, 1927. Millie went back in her mind to when she had first met Tom Stapleton. She had just turned fifteen on February 25, 1925. He seemed kind and attentive. She really wasn't ready to marry, but her ma seemed to think it was a good idea.

It had not turned out to be what she had imagined. Once married, Tom Stapleton had made it clear that he would be running the household, but running a farm was not something he wanted to do or intended to do.

Millie wasn't certain where he got it, but at times he would go somewhere after supper and then come home staggering his way up the front steps.

Their house was a dog trot design with a long hall front to back with rooms coming off each side. On one side was the parlor, on the other a bedroom. A second smaller bedroom came off the parlor. The kitchen was detached and out behind the main house.

On hot summer nights they'd bed down on the dog trot porch just to cool off. The mosquitoes were bad, but if you covered your head, you might fall asleep unbitten. It wasn't long after they married that Millie realized that she was pregnant. She kept doing what she could on the farm, using their one broke-down mule to plant their vegetable garden and grow cotton, even though the price per bale seemed to drop every year.

Louise had been born April 27, 1926. She had been six months old when Tom left in October. That was a whole year ago, Millie remembered. So, Millie calculated, Louise is about a year and a half old. She's still a baby. And a baby needs her ma. Millie laid her head down on the kitchen table. "What have I done?" she asked aloud.

"Not sure, but maybe you'd better wash those dishes before Miss Cora comes in here."

Millie looked up. "Buck. I am so glad to see you. I have lots to tell you. I was just sittin' here missin' Louise. Ain't heard nothin' about how she's doin'. Can't think about it too much or I'd go crazy."

She jumped up and ran to him, wrapping her arms around his chest tight. Then she caught herself. "Oh, Buck, that's pretty forward of me."

"No matter, Millie, no matter. Listen, I've asked Miss Sarah for you to be my lady tonight," he said. Millie's brow furrowed.

"Now, Millie, not like that. I just want to talk to you. Get to know you better. Tell you somethin' about me. Things I want you to know. Maybe we could sit on the back steps or somethin' or even here at this kitchen table."

"That sounds fine to me, Buck."

"Well, I came by early so I could tell you, if I saw you. Looked in here first since this is where I found you last time. You must really like this here kitchen. Listen, I gotta go make my last deliveries here in Mason. I'll see you around five-thirty, tonight alright?"

"Sure, Buck," Millie said.

He walked toward the door leading to the hallway, but turned, and looked back at her. "It's real good to see you, Millie. I've been thinkin' 'bout seein' you all the way from Savannah."

Millie smiled. "Good to see you, too, Buck."

With a big sigh Millie cleared the table, washed the dishes she had used, and headed back upstairs to the parlor and her book. Gladys, Corine, and Hazel were at their usual places, reading, painting, and playing. Millie settled down on the sofa and opened *The Art of Dressmaking* and started dreaming about what she would make first.

"Hey, y'all, Miss Sarah is teaching me how to sew. If I made you some new chemises and step-ins, would you wear them? You could pick out the fabric."

They each one stopped what they were doing. "Outta any fabric?" Corine asked first.

"Why sure. Satin, silk, whatever you choose."

"We can be your first customers," Hazel added as she spun around on the piano stool.

Gladys set her book down in her lap, "I'll sign up. But, Millie, we should pay you. Once you get started, you'll need to decide what you'll charge for a garment."

The other girls nodded. Then each one returned to her painting, music, and book.

Millie too had a book to read. And plans to make. Soon

it was four o'clock. Not much time to get ready, so they each one left for her room.

Millie was intent on looking especially good. She liked Buck. He had been so kind to her, and she really wanted to get to know him better. Gladys had let her borrow some makeup. She was getting really good at it, plus she had watched Clara Bow for almost two hours, so she figured she knew just how to give her mouth that heart shape.

At five-fifteen they made their usual descent to the first floor, led by Miss Sarah. Millie knew who would be sitting next to her place at the table, but tonight Buck looked especially handsome, his red hair slicked down and wearing a clean white shirt and bright green bowtie.

He pulled back her chair and she seated herself like a lady. "You look beautiful, Millie. I like your dress and that head band makes your eyes sparkle."

"Thank you, Buck. You look very handsome tonight."

When she put her hand on the table, he put his lightly over hers for just a moment. Millie especially enjoyed the Monday meal, the first one she had helped make, could it have been only three weeks ago. Pork chops, turnips, sweet potatoes, cornbread, and banana puddin'.

She and Buck talked about the meal. How much they liked the combination of turnips and sweet potatoes. And how they liked dredging the cornbread in the turnip pot liquor or what bit of liquid was on their plates.

Soon the plates were cleared, and the banana puddin' was served. Millie licked her lips. She and Buck dug into their bowls of Miss Cora's delicacy.

With the meal over, Miss Sarah stood, so everyone else did the same and followed her into the parlor. She followed her routine from Saturday night, having Hazel play a few selections and then serving the brandy in small crystal glasses and passing the box of cigars. Soon the men were lighting up and sipping and the women were dutifully listening.

Buck and Millie had chosen the seats nearest the window, which was open a bit. Millie enjoyed just listening and trying to understand all the "business" talk. Buck seemed to be intrigued as well.

It was nearing eight o'clock when the parlor time was winding down and the couples were making their way to the second floor. Miss Sarah had already left for her third-floor retreat.

Buck looked at Millie and said, "Wanna go sit in the kitchen and talk. Might be better than the back steps. It's gettin' a bit chilly outside."

"That's fine, Buck."

At the kitchen table they took seats across from each other. Millie filled two glasses with cool sweet tea from the refrigerator.

"This is real nice, Millie. Real nice."

"I think so, too, Buck. Real nice. But before we start to talk, I need to run upstairs and get some things from my room. I've got letters I want you to take to Gaston for Louise. And I have a book I want to show you."

Buck shook his head. That girl. There's no one like her, man or woman, he thought to himself.

Millie was back in a flash, moving at her usual speed when excited.

She almost missed the seat as she came to a sudden stop and flopped down. "You go first, Buck. I'll go after that."

"Okay, Millie. I wanted to tell you a bit about me. You see, I've been married. I'm twenty-seven years old. I married when I was seventeen in 1917. Sweet girl. Her name was" — Millie blinked — "Yes, I said 'was'. Her name was Emma. We were so happy. I have a little place on farmland my ma and pa own, and I built a little cabin, just two rooms really. I'd help Ma and Pa farm when I could but started the delivery business like I do now right after Emma and I married. Pretty soon after we married, Emma told me we were going to have a baby and in early 1918 we had a baby girl we named Mary. Kinda old-fashioned, but we liked that. Don't imagine you'd remember, 'cause you were pretty young in 1918, but there was a terrible plague that swept through all of Georgia, and I hear the rest of the world, they called it the Spanish flu." Buck's voice grew thick with emotion. "Well, Emma caught it and so did Mary, her little body just couldn't fight it. I held them as they slipped away. Buried them just as they died, Emma holding Mary." With that Buck just put his head down and began to weep.

"Oh, Buck that is the saddest story I have ever heard. Just the saddest. I am so sorry." Millie reached and patted his hand.

Buck slowly lifted his head and continued, "Well, since then I've lived a day-to-day life, nothing mattered, even spending my money to be with a woman at Miss Sarah's didn't matter, no reason to be any better, no one at home to care. But then I met you that day on the highway. Millie, you're real special. Don't think you see that, you're so young and all. But you've got spirit, spunk and well, dreams, ideas. Just watching you figure things out has been a joy for me. I look forward to comin' to Miss Sarah's every Monday just to see what you've learned, what you're up to. I hate that you're having to do what you do to survive."

"Aw, Buck it's not so bad. I just close my eyes and pretend that I'm somewhere else."

"That, Millie, that right there is what I mean. You seem to figure things out and manage."

"Well, Brother Edwards told us Sunday that Lady Wisdom can show up when you're 'under the circumstances.' And she sure has been doin' that lately for me."

Buck just shook his head. "Millie, Millie. Okay, tell me about these here letters and this book."

"I thought maybe you could drop these by at the general store in Gaston and give them to Miss Nadine. You know Nadine Bloodworth. You left that dollar with her for Louise and Ma."

"I sure did and got another customer for the effort. I make regular stops there now. I'll be happy to leave those letters there for your ma. Happy to do that for you."

"Now I want to show you my new book, *The Art of Dressmaking*." With that Millie proudly turned the book around so Buck could see the front.

"Buck, Corine has her art, Hazel her music and Gladys her books. I want to have somethin' too when we have our time in our parlor, you know before we have to entertain the men. So, when I was at Zimmerman's I walked around in the piece goods section and felt the fabric, even rubbed some on my cheeks. And then I found this book. Gladys bought it for me as a gift for becoming one of the girls."

Millie opened the book and caressed a page, showing a woman sitting at a sewing machine. "I'm not real good at readin' and all, but I have a dictionary and Gladys, who's so smart and can help me if I come across a hard word."

"Anyway, I'm going to become a dressmaker. I'm saving my money. I've found the sewing machine in the Sears catalog that I'm gonna buy, the Minnesota H! I make $20.00 a week, so in about three weeks I can buy the sewin' machine and start makin' ladies clothes and maybe get out of the entertainin' business. Miss Sarah's gonna teach me how to use a sewing machine. Had my first sewin' lesson today."

Buck just touched his forehead in a salute. "Millie, you'll do all that; I have no doubt. Listen, I'm pretty much tuckered out, so I think I'll go on to bed."

"But, Buck, you didn't get the 'entertainin' part."

"Listen, Millie, if that time comes for us, I don't want you to close your eyes and go anywhere, but where we are."

That was a whole new thought for Millie. "Okay, Buck, okay."

They stood to go, and he leaned down and kissed Millie on the cheek.

Millie smiled. "Thank you for everything, Buck." Buck walked toward the hallway that led to the guest rooms and Millie climbed the back stairs to her room.

Once in her room Millie wound the little blue clock and set the alarm for six. She enjoyed having breakfast with Mr. Lester and Miss Cora, but tomorrow she would eat in the dining room with Buck. She slipped off her dressy dress, brushed her teeth and fell into the bed.

She had left her Bible on the table by her bed. She decided to re-read Psalm 23, the one Miss Cora had marked. As before, her eyes settled on the last verse, "Surely goodness and mercy shall follow me all the days of my life…." Millie read it again, and then added, "And Lady Wisdom. She's following me, too." She turned off the light, got back in bed and fell asleep.

Chapter 22

In the kitchen at six-thirty, Millie, ever her completely honest self, said, "I'm gonna eat breakfast with Buck today. He was my gentleman last night but didn't want any entertainin'. We just talked." Mr. Lester looked up and smiled. "Millie, that sounds like a man who has somethin' else on his mind, or should I say, somethin' on his heart."

Millie paused. "Why, Mr. Lester, what do you mean by that?"

"That's all I'm sayin' right now, Millie. Go on now. Have your breakfast with your man, Buck." He winked as he said that.

Miss Cora turned from her work. "Millie, keep lookin' for Lady Wisdom." Millie just shrugged and walked into the dining room.

Buck was already there and as he had done at supper before, he pulled her chair out. Before sitting down, Millie twirled around. "Recognize this dress, Buck. It's the one I was wearin' that day when you picked me up by the side of the road."

Buck really didn't remember but knew from experience with women it was best to recognize whatever clothing item they thought he might should. "Indeed, I do, Millie. It's a pretty dress, worn by a pretty lady."

Millie smiled and sat down.

The other gentlemen were intent on finishing their break-fasts so they could attend to the business of the day. Millie asked Buck about his plans. "Well, I'll be heading straight for Savannah except for that stop in Gaston. I'll probably check on my ma, too. Pa died last year. Ma has some sharecroppers who are loyal and work real hard, so the farm is doing well. Her main crop is cotton, but she may plant some tobacco next year. The price of cotton is way down." Millie preferred eating at the kitchen table, but enjoyed Buck's company so much, it was almost as nice in the dining room today.

Buck stood to leave. Millie, too. He took both her hands. "Millie, that was a good talk we had last night. I hope we have one of those talks again next Monday. I'll see you then." This time he kissed her on the forehead.

"Bye, Buck, see you next week. And thanks again for get-tin' those letters to Ma for Louise. I still don't know where Tom's taken her in Savannah."

Buck climbed into his truck and cranked her up. Millie was standing on the front porch as he left. She waved good-bye. He did the same.

Buck had so much on his mind. He believed he was ready to marry again, and he was beginning to believe that Millie would make a good wife for him, but she was still married, and it would be hard for her to get a divorce, especially not even knowing where Tom Stapleton was in Savannah.

It was a straight shot down US 80 to Gaston. Ever since his wife's death, Buck had avoided church or reading the Bi-ble. Like he told Millie he had just lived day to day. But now as he was considering a future with Millie, he began to pray. "Lord, it's Buck here. I know you haven't heard from me in a while. But you know how it's been down here. I stopped for that girl about a month ago and now I'm findin' her all wound up in my heart. Help me, Jesus. That's one broken heart that she's gotten into."

Buck almost missed the turn down Gaston Road, straight into what was hardly even cross-roads. Nadine Bloodworth's general store was coming up on the right, so Buck parked next to the store.

Nadine's store was the hub of the Gaston wheel. Folks knew that Nadine could tell them what a bale of cotton was selling for, where moonshine whiskey was being sold, and which husbands and a few wives were sleeping around. She knew it all. Kept some secrets, some she didn't. Her long brown hair was pulled back in a tight ball, so tight she appeared to be constantly squinting. Her store was kept in meticulous order which meant Nadine spent very little time anywhere else. She was tall and could almost reach the very top shelves but had a rolling ladder for the ones that were out of her reach. Her skin was pale from the lack of sunlight. She had been married, but her husband had died years ago and left her childless. After he died, she had sold the farmland and started this store, "Nadine's General Store," with the slogan, "If it ain't here, it ain't anywhere."

"Mornin', Nadine."

"Why, Buck, what brings you to Gaston on this beautiful October mornin'. You brought me a delivery yesterday. Didn't think I would see you until next Monday."

"Well, I'm here with a special delivery from Millic. I've got a stack of letters for Louise from her ma. May I leave these with you. Maybe you could get them to Widow Martin some time."

"Buck, you're in luck," Nadine said. "Louise is here. Tom brought her back yesterday. Seems he's real sick. He's got that TB. He stopped by here on his way out and he was a hackin' and a hackin'. I put my hand over my face and asked him to leave my store. Bad stuff that TB. We're hopin' little Louise ain't got it. Right now she seems fine."

Buck couldn't hide his shock. "But I didn't think Millie's ma could take care of a baby. Don't she have the TB, too? Louise is just a baby, not much over a year old."

"Remains to be seen. Here I'll draw you a little map. Her place ain't far." So Nadine sketched out a map for Buck and he left, reading it as he went.

He followed Nadine's map and pulled his truck into a dirt yard. He slipped from the front seat and started walking toward the front porch. At the base of the steps digging in the dirt, and based on the looks of her face, eating some as well, was a baby. "This has to be Louise," Buck muttered.

"Hey, there baby girl. How ya doin', Louise?"

Louise stood up and started toddling toward Buck. Any port in a storm, she even put her arms out to him. As he picked her up, he looked her over. Her diaper was soaking wet and muddy where she had been sitting in the dirt. She wore a dirty little shift that covered her bottom and was wet and dirty, too. But her little blue eyes sparkled, just like Millie's, and her curly blonde bob reminded Buck of Millie's curls.

He immediately thought of his little Mary, now dead and buried in her ma's arms. "Oh, you poor little baby," he whispered hoarsely. "I'm gonna get you outta here."

He entered the house. It appeared that no one was there, but he soon found who he thought was Widow Martin, there asleep in a bed in a room across the dog trot hall from the parlor. He just left her sleeping and wandered around the other rooms until he found some baby things in a satchel in another back bedroom.

Taking the satchel, he went out the back door and down the steps to the kitchen out back. Once there he filled the sink with water. It was cold, but he'd be quick. Louise didn't seem to mind. He stripped her down and washed her good, even washing her hair.

He found an old dish towel that looked clean enough to use and he dried her little body, putting on a clean diaper and the only clean shift he could find in the satchel. He figured she was old enough to drink from a cup, so he offered her some milk he found. She kept trying to bite the cup and stick her face in the cup, but she downed enough to satisfy Buck that she now had something in her little stomach.

He had some crackers in his truck. He'd give her those before they hit the road. Now was the time to wake Widow Martin and tell her his plan.

He made his way to the front bedroom. There she was as he had left her half an hour ago, a cup by her bed filled with a mixture of spit and blood, her skin the color of tissue paper. It was obvious that Widow Martin had the white plague, tuberculosis, the color having completely faded from her skin. She was not an old woman, but the disease was draining her of life, as it ate away at her lungs. Her gray-streaked hair lay limp on the pillow and the filthy bed smelled like a greasy, dirty body. *I can only help one of you,* Buck thought.

He tapped Widow Martin on the shoulder and woke her. "What, who are you? And why are you carrying Louise?" she said in a querulous voice.

"Miz Martin, I'm Buck Wilson. I deliver goods to Nadine's store, and I know your daughter Millie. In fact"—and at this point he began to lie—"I am here on her behalf. We have learned that Tom Stapleton, Louise's pa, is very sick, and he can no longer care for Louise, so Millie has sent me to get Louise, since I have a truck and all."

Widow Martin just nodded. "When Tom came for Louise, I thought that was best and then here he comes yesterday, bringing her back. I had no idee where Millie was, so's I just didn't know what to do. If you can get her to Millie, I'd be much obliged." With that she began to cough uncontrollably, only stopping when she took a sip of something in a bottle by her bed. Buck thought it might be whiskey. Then she just fell back on the bed and closed her eyes, still coughing.

"Well, that's exactly what I'm gonna do." With that he went out the front door with Louise and her satchel.

On his way out of Gaston, Buck stopped at Nadine's store and told her what he was doing. Nadine asked him, "Well, now, Buck whatcha want me to tell folk around here. They'll be asking about it. Nobody seemed to want to help, but with you snatchin' her up and all, everyone will have an opinion."

Buck paused. "Tell them Millie, this baby's ma, sent me to get her."

Nadine smiled. "That's what I'll say, Buck, if asked."

He also bought some canned milk and a baby bottle. Before he left, he went by the pump out front and filled the bottle halfway with water, cut a hole in the can of milk with his knife and finished filling the bottle with the canned milk. In the truck he fed Louise a package of saltine crackers and then gave her the bottle of milk.

He lay her down on the front seat with her little head in his lap. He covered her with his jacket and handed her the bottle. She greedily began to suck the milk down. Before he had reached the main highway, she had fallen asleep, and he had to grab the bottle before it fell to the floor.

A little over an hour later Buck turned off the main highway onto an unpaved county road leading to his mother's farm in Chatham County.

He pulled up in front of a simple, well-maintained, white-washed farmhouse, the place of his birth. He could see his cabin and outhouse off to the right. He had spent as little time as possible there since Emma's and baby Mary's deaths.

He turned off the truck, grabbed Louise's satchel, scooped her up, and strode toward the front porch. By the time he reached the first step his ma was there, wiping her hands on her apron and then rubbing them along the sides of her head in an effort to smooth any sprigs of hair that had popped out.

"Lord, Buck, what in the world do you have there?"

"Ma, I told you about that young girl I picked up by the side of the road a few weeks ago. Well, this is her baby. Ma, this child has been abandoned. I found her diggin' in the dirt at her grandma's house in Gaston. I'll tell you more once I get her inside and change her diaper and get her some real food. All she's had are saltines and a bottle of milk."

"Give 'er here, Buck." Ma Wilson took the baby and pulled her close. Louise awoke to the warmth of Ma's soft, ample bosom and the smell of fried chicken, sweet potatoes, and turnips. Louise looked up at her and smiled, closed her eyes, and drifted back to sleep.

Ma Wilson's home had a parlor, but the real living took place in the kitchen, so that's where they headed. She spread a clean towel across the kitchen table and lay Louise down. "Hand me a clean diaper, Buck. Let's get this baby's bottom cleaned." Buck smiled and nodded his head. Louise was in very good hands now.

In no time Louise was sitting on a Sears catalog in a chair at the kitchen table now cleared of the dirty diaper and the towel. Ma Wilson had set a plate before her with mashed sweet potatoes, cut up fried chicken, and a small pile of turnips. Louise reached out and grabbed the chicken and stuffed it into her mouth. "She's hungry, Ma," Buck said. Turning to Louise, he added, "Here, baby, let me help you. But let's not eat too much."

Ma Wilson cleaned Louise up after supper, but before putting her down in Ma's bed, Buck measured her feet and her little body, using the tape measure from his mother's sewing box. "I'm gonna buy her some shoes tomorrow, Ma. And diapers, a coat, and some dresses."

Ma patted Buck's arm. "You're thinkin' 'bout Mary, aren't you, Buck?"

"Yes, Ma."

"Well, you go on to bed now. I'll take care of this little bit. We'll make out just fine. I've got some fresh cow's milk I think she'll like. And then I'll put her down for the night. See you in the mornin', son."

So, things settled down for the night at the Wilson farm. Buck had told his ma that she'd need to tend to Louise until Monday, almost a week away. He'd take her to Millie then.

Back in Mason, the routine Millie had become accustomed to was again taking place. Grand entrance down the stairs and into the dining room, supper with a stranger; cigars, brandy, and men talking in the parlor. Finally, entertainin' upstairs. Millie did as before, closing her eyes and going to some place, a secret place in her mind.

Tonight, she thought about her sewing machine and making clothes, and about Louise, and about making clothes for Louise. After her guest had left, Millie took a bath, put on clean underwear and went to bed, really to bed. Soon she was sound asleep. Tuesday was over.

Chapter 23

Wednesday dawned clear and cool on the Wilson farm. It was mid-October and fall had decided to come to South Georgia. Up before dawn, Buck was back in the kitchen ready for some of his ma's bacon, straight from the farm. And her biscuits. Miss Cora's were flaky and soft, but nothing as good as his ma's.

"I don't think that child has had a good night's sleep in a while. Her diaper is soakin' wet and she is still out like a light." But as is always the case with babies, as soon as those words left her mouth, Ma Wilson could hear Louise crying. "You go get her, Buck. I'll fix your plate. You can share it with Louise."

"Oh, baby, now, shhh, shh, shhh. You're okay. You're safe," Buck consoled her as he entered the bedroom.

Little Louise raised her arms to be picked up. He lifted her off the bed, hugged her close, and then changed her diaper. Bouncing her in his arms as he made his way down the hall to the kitchen, he entered and announced, "Lookie here what I found, Ma!" He tickled her tummy and Louise giggled.

Buck sat down at the kitchen table, Louise in his lap. He ate a bit and fed her a bit. They cleaned a plate that had been filled with bacon, eggs, and grits. Ma Wilson offered milk for

Louise. "Buck, see if you can get her to drink from this coffee cup." Louise bent her head over the cup and sipped a little.

"Maybe we ought to go one more day with the bottle, Ma," Buck said.

Ma Wilson nodded, "I agree." She fixed a bottle of fresh cow's milk for Louise. The baby grabbed the bottle and began to suck, leaning back in Buck's arms as she did. Buck's heart swelled, remembering his baby Mary. How good it felt to hold this little one!

"Well, Ma, I need to go now," he said reluctantly. "I'll be back this evenin' around supper time." He set Louise down on the floor. "I'll have some surprises for you, little lady." And he was out the door, cranking up his truck, and heading for the main highway.

"Well, it's you and me, Louise. Let's see what the day holds. One thing I know, for your sake and mine, you'll be takin' a nap today," Ma Wilson said. She patted Louise's head and then set her down with two wooden spoons and some pots and pans. "And look-a-here, I've made you a doll baby." Ma Wilson handed her a doll made from three dish towels tied in a fashion so that it appeared to have arms, legs, and a head. Louise grabbed the "doll," stuffing it into one of the pots and telling the baby, "Nighty, night."

Ma Wilson whooped and slapped her leg. "You are what I've been missin', Louise!"

By week's end Louise had shoes, dresses, and a double-breasted Shetland red wool coat with a velveteen collar. The kitchen floor was strewn with toys: balls, dolls, and blocks. Each evening Buck would play with her after dinner, sometimes stacking up the blocks so she could knock them down. Then all three of them, Ma Wilson included, would laugh.

Tomorrow would be Saturday, and Buck had decided to do an extra run this week, just for the money. He wasn't quite certain what he was saving for, but somehow, he knew Louise would be in that picture.

And up the road in Mason, Millie was finishing up her work week. In two days she would have $20.00 more when Miss Sarah slipped that envelope under her door. And one more week after that she'd have enough money to order the Minnesota H sewing machine. Maybe Buck could help her fill out the order form.

Millie had had two more sewing lessons with Miss Sarah. With Miss Sarah's written directions, Millie had bought a pattern for a chemise and pale blue satin fabric. During one lesson Miss Sarah had taught Millie how to lay out the pattern on the fabric. They had used the hallway to stretch out the fabric, with Miss Sarah cautioning, "Millie, I don't want you cuttin' my rug."

Miss Sarah would give instructions and leave Millie to work. Forty-five minutes passed quickly, so Millie listened intently. Now Millie had a garment cut and ready to put together. She spent time in Miss Sarah's parlor working from the pattern directions and the general directions she was finding in *The Art of Dressmaking*. She believed that she would have a new chemise to wear soon.

Saturday came on the Wilson farm and by the time the sun came up Buck was gone on his last run for the week. He planned to load up his delivery truck for the Monday run and leave it parked through Sunday. Louise had settled in well. Ma Wilson had her take a short nap in the morning and a longer one in the afternoon with Ma joining her for the afternoon nap.

On Sunday in Mason and in Chatham County, both Millie and Buck got dressed up and went to church. In Buck's case that meant himself, his ma, and Louise. It was Buck's first time in church in almost ten years, the last time being the funeral for his wife and daughter.

Monday, October 17 dawned cool and crisp. Up before sunrise, Buck was in the kitchen eating breakfast. "I guess you can give me a bowl of grits to take for when she wakes up. Don't see no need to get her up now. I'll jus' wrap her up in one of your old quilts and lay her across the front seat. Like I did comin' home," he told his mother

"That sounds fine, Buck. You go ahead and get her up, change her diaper and all. I've packed that satchel of hers, lots of clean diapers, so it's already right here by the door. I'll be praying for you, son, 'cause I know what you're 'bout to do." Ma Wilson winked at him and patted his shoulder.

In the bedroom Buck stood over Louise watching her sleep before rolling her over and quickly changing her diaper. He pulled on her little coat over her pajamas. She didn't even seem to notice. Back in the kitchen he shouldered the satchel, hiked Louise a little higher in his arms and took the bowl of grits from Ma Wilson. She tenderly kissed the baby's head.

Out the front door, down the steps of the porch with Ma pressing her hands on her apron, Buck headed for the truck, Louise asleep on his shoulder. Gently laying her down on the front seat, he slipped in under the steering wheel, pulling her little head into his lap. She stirred and snuggled down against his leg.

The motion of the truck lulled her deeper into sleep. The sun was just rising as they rumbled up the road going north. In about an hour Buck turned left and drove into Gaston and to Nadine's store. She was at the door, just opening up. "Well, good morning, Sunshine. You're out early."

Buck scooped Louise up, grabbed the bowl of grits with a strip of bacon on top, and ambled toward the door. Louise lifted her head and looked around. "Hungry, baby girl?" Buck asked and patted her back.

Inside the store he sat her down near Nadine. "Mind feeding her these grits while I unload your order?"

"Course not. Come over here, Louise. Let's get you some breakfast," Nadine said. "Hey, Buck, bring me a clean diaper or maybe her whole bag."

Buck brought in Louise's satchel and then began unloading Nadine's order. "Hey, Nadine, I can tell we're comin' into the bakin' season, Thanksgiving, Christmas, and all. I've got your flour, brown sugar, white sugar, baking powder, baking soda, cinnamon. Well, everything you ordered."

Using a hand truck Buck unloaded Nadine's order. Louise had finished the grits and had a clean diaper when Buck took over so that Nadine could review her order and sign for it. "That looks good, Buck. Here's what I owe for this week and last week," Nadine said as she handed Buck a wad of bills. He stuffed them in his pocket, picked up Louise, and moved toward the door.

"Thanks for giving me some extra time to pay. Oh, and by the way, Buck, Tom Stapleton died last Thursday. He was buried Saturday here in the cemetery at the Methodist Church."

Buck stopped midstride and turned around, staring at Nadine, who was now standing behind the counter of her tiny store, a place filled floor to ceiling with anything you might need, if Nadine had time to find it.

"What did you just say, Nadine?"

"Buck, that baby's daddy is dead is what I said. She's only got a ma now. That's Millie. Don't know what she's doin' there in Mason."

"Thanks for that piece of news. Gotta go. See ya later, Nadine." Buck walked to his truck, then remembering that Louise might like a bottle of milk, retraced his steps buying a can of evaporated milk and fixing Louise a bottle for the road.

Positioning her as he had before, Buck cranked up the truck and headed out of Gaston, turning north at the main highway. He remembered the very spot where he had picked up that frightened country girl clutching her cardboard suitcase a little over a month ago. Louise lay back down against his leg and sucked her bottle.

Buck had deliveries to make in Kellyville, Eureka, and Montrose, before getting to Mason. He figured he'd get to Mason around noon, drop Louise off at Miss Sarah's and then finish his deliveries before heading back to Miss Sarah's for the evening.

Louise was sitting up now still pulling on that bottle. "Let's put that thing down for a bit, Louise, and sing."

Buck began singing "Jesus Loves Me." When he got to the chorus, "Yes, Jesus loves me, yes Jesus loves me," Louise looked at him and clapped her hands. So, he sang it again and again.

The routine was the same at each stop. Buck would ask the store owner to hold Louise while he unloaded their order. Not one of them refused. But to each one's relief, he didn't ask them to change her diapers.

He had a croaker sack in the back of the truck for the soiled diapers and it was filling up fast. Getting back into the truck at Montrose, he mumbled to himself, "I think I need to teach this baby how to use a toilet, rather than how to sing 'Jesus Loves Me'." And then he leaned toward Louise, "Don't I, baby girl?"

They pulled up to Miss Sarah's around noon. Louise, who had been resting her head in Buck's lap, sat up and looked out the window.

"Come on, Louise. I have a surprise for you." He paused as he lifted her out of the truck. "But I'd better get your satchel and what's left of your clean diapers, or you'll be the one wearing the surprise."

Millie was alone in her usual spot at the kitchen table, having foraged in the refrigerator for her dinner. She had a plate with leftover fried chicken from Miss Cora's Sunday dinner and some cold turnip greens from Saturday's supper. She knew that Buck would have stopped by Gaston and left her letters for Louise with Nadine at the store. Maybe he would have heard some news from Nadine about Louise or about Millie's ma.

Millie was lost in this reverie when Buck walked into the kitchen with Louise. Millie looked up. Her mouth dropped open. Unable to speak, all she could do was whisper, "Louise." Jumping to her feet she ran to Buck, wrapping her arms around both Buck and her baby.

"Oh, Buck, let me have her. Give her here and tell me everything. Oh, Buck, you are the best." Before he could hand Louise over to her, Millie had reached up and pulled him closer to her and kissed him squarely on the mouth. Then she sat down in a kitchen chair and patted her lap. "Put her here, Buck, right here." And to Louise, "You come here to your ma."

Louise recognized her and reached her little arms out toward Millie.

Millie just sat there holding her, running her fingers through her hair, touching her cheeks, looking at her tiny hands. Then starting all over hugging her again.

Buck was enjoying every moment of this. He had done the right thing, but he had to finish his day's work. "Millie, here's her satchel. There's diapers, toys, and clothes in here. She might want some dinner, but you know best. I have to finish my run, but I'll be back. Millie, we have a lot to discuss." He paused. "Millie, Tom Stapleton is dead and buried, died last Thursday and was buried Saturday."

Millie looked up into Buck's face. What he saw was profound relief. The man who had neglected and then abandoned her was gone, forever. Millie set Louise down, stood, and burying her head in Buck's chest kept saying, "Thank you, thank you, Buck."

Buck grinned, "Now, Millie, you know I had nothing to do with that rascal's death." Millie looked up and they both laughed. And Louise, who was watching it all, laughed, too.

"And Millie, you'll be my lady tonight, so just spend time with Louise, instead of, you know, gettin' all gussied up."

"Thanks, Buck," Millie said softly.

"Gotta go now, Millie. I'll see you tonight. Got lots to talk about, Millie. Lots."

"We'll be here, Buck." Practically running, Buck headed for his truck, eager to get his Mason deliveries done.

In the kitchen Millie got practical, "Well, now Louise, let's you and me have some dinner." So Millie and Louise nibbled on cold fried chicken and turnip greens. Millie did pour Louise a small glass of milk and after trying to bite the glass a few times, she got the hang of it and drank half the glassful.

"Let's put it back in the refrigerator for later, sweet baby. I want to show you to my friends."

Millie went up the backstairs to the second-floor parlor where she knew she'd find Corine, Hazel, and Gladys. She walked into the room and very formally announced, "Ladies, this is my baby, Louise, who has come to live with me. I've just learned that her pa is dead, so all she's got now is me… and Buck, who went and got her for me."

No painting, piano playing, or reading ensued, for the rest of the afternoon was spent spoiling Louise, who from sheer exhaustion from all the attention fell asleep on the sofa with Millie.

Around four o'clock Corine, Gladys, and Hazel left the parlor, going to their rooms to get ready for the evening. Millie told them that she would be Buck's lady for the evening, and he wanted her to spend time with Louise, not getting "gussied up."

Millie gently picked Louise up and took the stairs down to the kitchen. "Louise, I want you to meet Miss Cora, my Mason mama," Millie whispered to her sleeping baby.

Miss Cora was at the stove starting the pork chops. The banana puddins' had already been made and lay on the kitchen counter in all their meringued beauty. "Miss Cora, look what Buck brought me from Gaston!"

Miss Cora turned, "Oh, Lord, Millie, is that baby Louise?"

Louise lifted her head and smiled sleepily at Miss Cora. "Come here, baby. Wanna banana?" Miss Cora asked. Louise looked up at her ma questioningly.

Millie smiled, "It's okay, Louise. I'll be right here." Turning to Miss Cora, she said, "Miss Cora, just sit yourself down and I'll put her in your lap." Before sitting down Miss Cora grabbed a banana and cut it in half.

Millie handed Louise off to Miss Cora, who had peeled the half banana and laid it on the table. Louise was uncertain about it all, but her eyes lit up when she saw the banana. She leaned over and mouthed it, before Miss Cora had time to break a bit off. "Here, Louise, take this little bit." Louise ate the bite and smacked her lips. Millie, at the stove turning the frying pork chops, laughed. "We do love bananas, Miss Cora."

"How did Buck work this out, Millie?"

"Miss Cora, I don't know. Buck had to finish his deliveries before he had time to tell me. He'll be back soon." Millie turned back to the frying pan and Miss Cora continued feeding Louise.

"And here he is," Buck surprised them all as he strode through the kitchen door.

"Buck, you know I don't allow guests in my kitchen," Miss Cora paused, "but under the circumstances, get your cracker fanny in here and tell me how you got Louise." Millie turned from the stove and smiled.

"Well," Buck started as he sat down at the table and patted Louise's leg. "This here baby and I have had quite a week."

Buck started with his stop at Nadine's store in Gaston, then his stop at Widow Martin's where he found Louise sitting in the mud. He grinned, "That's when I started lying."

"No, you didn't," Miss Cora chided.

"Yes, I did. I told Millie's ma that Millie here had sent me to get Louise. Her ma was asleep when I got there, so I didn't even wake her until I had bathed Louise and dressed her. She had a satchel full of diapers, so I grabbed that and left. Widow Martin agreed that I should bring Louise to Millie…ah, based on my lie. I stopped at Nadine's store, bought a baby bottle and evaporated milk, filling it with a mix of water and milk and popping that bottle in this here baby's mouth." Buck looked fondly at Louise, "Didn't I, baby?"

Millie had stopped turning the pork chops and one of them was starting to smoke. "Millie, Millie, the pork chops!" Miss Cora stood and thrust Louise into Buck's arms. Knowing it would be best to let Miss Cora take over, Millie moved away from the stove and sat in the chair Miss Cora had just vacated. Meanwhile Cora did what most smart cooks knew to do. She simply removed the pan from the stove and gave the chops time to simmer down.

Always ready to cheer things up, Buck quipped, "I'll take the burnt one, Miss Cora." Without turning around, Miss Cora nodded her head.

It was almost four-thirty when Magdala and Alice came through the back door. Almost in unison they spoke, "A baby. Is that Louise, Millie?"

From the stove Miss Cora responded, "Yes, that's a baby and yes, it's Louise, but there's no time to explain or play with the baby. You two need to get to work."

"I'll help," Millie offered.

Miss Cora was quick to respond, "What you and Buck can do to help me right now is to," she paused, and in a little firmer voice continued, "GET OUT OF MY KITCHEN!"

Millie looked at Buck, who was already standing with Louise's satchel on his shoulder. "Come on Millie, let's go sit on the front porch. I'll tell you about my ma and Louise."

Millie nodded, "Oh, Buck, this is such a happy day. Thank you, thank you." Out on the porch Millie sat in one of the white wooden rockers and began to rock. It was October so the sun was already slipping toward the horizon and its nighttime rest. Millie rocked while Buck played with Louise in the yard, chasing her and tossing her up and catching her. She squealed with delight, her golden curls catching the final rays of the day. Millie clapped her hands, "Don't let him catch you, Louise. Run, run!"

The front windows were open, so Millie could hear the voices in the dining room. She knew from the sounds that the dinner was coming to an end. Then she heard chairs scraping as the guests and their ladies rose and began ambling toward the parlor.

"Buck, I think it's safe now for us to go to the kitchen. I'm hungry, aren't you. Let's go 'round back and come in the back door." Buck picked up Louise and followed Millie around the side of the house to the back steps and then up into the kitchen.

Mr. Lester was there, his plate piled high with pork chops, turnips, sweet potatoes, and cornbread. "Well, well, well, what do we have here. Come on in you three, fix a plate and sit down here now." Mr. Lester, his usual ebullient self, was grinning from ear to ear.

Magdala had finished her meal and was already at the sink putting her plate into the soapy water. "I've got homework, so I gotta go." She came over to Louise, ruffling her hair and patting her cheek. "But Louise, I'll get here tomorrow in time to play with you some. Good night, y'all."

Alice had already left as well, so there were enough seats for the four grown folk and one baby in someone's lap. Louise started off with Millie, but by the time the meal had ended she had been passed around and eaten off everyone's plate. She had even sipped from a glass, this time downing one almost filled to the top. Now her eyes were getting heavy, and she was slumped against Millie's breast.

Miss Cora had a plan. "Listen, Millie, Lester here is going to clean up the kitchen, aren't you, Lester?"

"Seems so," Mr. Lester responded and winked.

Miss Cora continued, "And I'm gonna put this baby down for the night at our place. I've got a rocker if she needs some encouragement. You two" — and now she was looking at Millie and Buck — have some talkin' you need to do, so go on into the dining room. Millie knows how to finish up in there. And then you two sit and talk. Don't worry 'bout Louise. She'll be fine until breakfast tomorrow."

Millie nodded. "Thank you, Miss Cora." She took Cora's hand and squeezed it.

"Now give me that baby and her satchel and get on into that dining room."

"Come on, Buck, I'll teach you how to finish up the cleanin' in the dining room," Millie said.

Buck dutifully followed her instructions, taking the tablecloth out to the back yard to shake. As he passed Mr. Lester at the sink, he winked at him and quipped, "Mr. Lester, I think we've been recruited, or did we just enlist?"

Mr. Lester responded, "Son, I enlisted many years ago and haven't regretted one minute serving in Miss Cora's army, if you know what I mean."

"Well, Mr. Lester, pray for me tonight, I'm hoping to do the same thing tonight. Oh, I mean enlist in Millie's army."

"I knew what you meant, Buck. Now get on to it. Shake that tablecloth out and get yourself back in the dining room."

"Yes, suh," Buck responded with a faux salute.

Back in the dining room, Millie had finished wiping the table off and straightening up. She also closed the windows since the night air was making the room a bit too cool.

Buck came back in and with a sigh pointed to two seats at the table. "Millie, please sit down. I have some things to tell you and some things to ask you." Millie sat down.

"First of all, Millie I have paid Miss Sarah for your time for the next week, and I'll do the same for the week after if necessary. I want you to have what you need to buy that sewing machine, but I don't want you to entertain men, as you call it."

Then, dropping to his knee in front of her and taking her hands, he finished, "Millie, I want you to marry me. I want you to be my wife."

Millie gasped, pulled her hands free, and covered her face. He watched her expression change as she thought of all she now knew about Buck Wilson, a collection of kindnesses. He had never done anything to hurt her, had always been kind to her, had even lied so that he could get Louise back to her. He loves me. That was the only conclusion she could draw, but then she asked herself, Do I love him?

Then she traveled the same route again, feeling now a deep sense of gratitude for all he had done for her. His love was evoking hers, which had to come from a place of disappointment and hurt. She was free now; Tom Stapleton was dead. She had proven that she could make it on her own. She had found a family in Miss Cora, Mr. Lester, and Magdala and she had sisters in Corine, Hazel, and Gladys and a teacher in Miss Sarah. Circumstances can change. Millie realized that hers were about to do just that.

She dropped her hands from her face, looked Buck straight

in the eye, then grabbing him around the neck whispered in his ear, "Yes, Buck, I'll marry you."

Buck sat down in a chair, a big grin on his face. "Well, now let me tell you my plan. Hope you'll like it."

"Listen, Buck, every plan you've had so far has been a good one, including bringing me here to Miss Sarah's."

"Right, well, let's see. Millie, we've both been married before and both our spouses are dead, so I believe we'll have to have a death certificate for each of them. I have one for Emma, but I'll need to get one for Tom. Understand?"

"Yes, Buck, I understand. Buck, I want Brother Edwards to marry us after the church service on Sunday at First Baptist. Can it happen that soon? And Buck, I need to tell Miss Sarah."

Buck raised his eyebrows. "Well, Millie, let's see if I can't make that happen. I'll be here tomorrow morning, so I thought we might go to the courthouse and see how we start on gettin' a marriage license. Maybe Miss Cora could keep Louise. We could ride the streetcar to town. Whatcha think?"

"Oh, let's do that, Buck. Let's do that." Millie clapped her hands. "And I can talk with Miss Cora about how to go about gettin' Brother Edwards to marry us."

Buck looked at his watch. "Millie, it's almost ten o'clock. Let's get some rest, you in your room upstairs, me in mine down here. But come Sunday evenin' we'll be together in one room."

"Oh, Buck, you go on now." Millie hit him on the shoulder, blushing a little. As they both stood to leave, he took her in his arms and pulled her close. "Millie, Millie."

She kissed him full on the lips, ruffled his curly red hair, pulled away, and skipped out of the room and up the stairs.

"What a girl," he muttered as he went to his room. "What a girl. I am one lucky man. Yes, indeed, one lucky man."

Everything was quiet when Millie got to the second floor.

It was such a relief for her to be out of the "entertainin'" business. She wound the little blue clock, making certain it was set for six. She wanted to get up and bathe so she'd be fresh for her Buck. Yes, he was going to be hers.

Likewise, Buck went to bed grateful for how it had all turned out. He fell asleep whispering the prayer, "Thank you, Jesus."

Chapter 24

Millie woke before the little blue clock had begun to chime. She punched in the alarm button saying, "Not today, little blue clock. You get to sleep in."

She quickly bathed and washed her hair. She squeezed the water out of her hair and fluffed it up and speaking to it as she looked into the bathroom mirror said, "Aw, you'll just have to dry the best you can. I don't have time to wait. I'm goin' to town today with my Buck. And I've got to get downstairs because my Louise will be down there."

And indeed, she was, sitting on a Sears catalog and tied to the chair with a dish towel. Miss Cora had put a freshly baked biscuit in front of her and she was grabbing pieces and what didn't make it to her mouth was on the floor.

"Oh, Louise, you're makin' a mess, but good, good morning. I'll clean it up."

She turned to Miss Cora, who was frying bacon, "Oh, Miss Cora, Buck and I are gettin' married. Do you think Brother Edwards could marry us after church on Sunday?"

Miss Cora turned and stared at Millie. "Well, Millie, you're like a daughter to me, so I have to ask, are you still in the 'entertainin' business?"

"Oh, no Miss Cora. Buck fixed all that. He's bought me for a whole week."

Miss Cora raised her eyebrows, "What did you say, Millie?"

"Oh, Miss Cora, you know what I mean. Buck has paid Miss Sarah like I'd be entertainin' him for a week, but I won't because we're gonna wait for that until we're married. And I won't close my eyes and go to that secret place in my brain."

Miss Cora raised her hand to stop Millie from explaining any more. "Okay, Millie, I understand." At the table Mr. Lester just shook his head and grinned.

Buck stood in the doorway. "What did you understand, Miss Cora?"

"Oh, Buck, your future wife can tell you later. She does have a way with explanations." Miss Cora just shook her head.

And then remembering Millie's question about Brother Edwards and the wedding, Miss Cora looked at both Millie and Buck, "Listen, you two, once you find out when that marriage license will be ready, I'll take care of Reverend Edwards."

"Oh, Miss Cora, you're the bee's knees!" Millie reached to hug her, but Miss Cora batted her away. "Millie, I'm frying bacon. I'll have to wait on that hug."

Soon the little kitchen table was just as full as it had been the night before; Mr. Lester was there and Magdala, who had stopped by for breakfast before going to school. Miss Cora was still making breakfast for the guests. Alice had arrived and was helping get all the platters to the dining room table.

Looking up from his breakfast, Mr. Lester offered, "The courthouse opens at eight o'clock. You two need a ride to town?"

"If it's not an imposition," Buck said. "But, before we go, I want to show Millie something." With that Buck left the room. When he returned he held up the perfect wedding dress for Louise, a soft pink, batiste cotton with pink ribbons around the empire waist.

"Oh, Buck, Louise will look like a little princess in that. Here, let me put it upstairs for Sunday." As she passed him, she stood on tiptoe and kissed him on the cheek.

When Millie returned, Mr. Lester asked, "By the way Millie, who's gonna walk you down the aisle?"

Millie looked at Buck and then at Mr. Lester. "You are, Pa." With that Mr. Lester slapped his leg. "What a day that'll be!"

Miss Cora chimed in. "Millie, go get one of the girls to come down and take care of Louise while you're gone. Time for them to get up any way."

"Yes, ma'am." Millie ran up the backstairs and soon returned with Gladys in tow, hair ruffled, and pulling her robe tighter. With a big yawn she greeted them all. "Good mornin'. At least I hope it is. Anybody got a cup of coffee?"

"Sit down here and eat this biscuit. Lester, get this girl a cup of coffee." Miss Cora was in charge. "And before you leave, Lester, get the baby's satchel at our place and bring it here." Mr. Lester nodded.

Gladys yawned again, "Okay, Millie, what do I need to know?"

"Well, Gladys, you'll need to check her diaper about every hour or two. Just stick your finger in a leg hole."

"Oooh, what if it's, you know, messy?"

"Well, you'll need to change the diaper. Just wipe her down good and put on another diaper. Easy, really. Buck bought her some toys. They're in the satchel. Watch what she puts in her mouth."

"Oh, Miss Cora I may need your help," Gladys moaned.

"Gladys, I can't do anything for you until breakfast is over, the gents gone, and the kitchen is clean."

Gladys ran her fingers through her marceled hair. "Okay, Millie. I'll do it until Miss Cora can take over. How long y'all gonna be?"

This time Buck answered, "Oh, maybe an hour or two." Millie nodded.

"I'll be right back," Millie said. "I have to go brush my teeth. I'll meet y'all at Mr. Lester's truck."

Mr. Lester and Buck looked at each other and nodded obediently. Mr. Lester grinned. "She's been trained by the best," he said out of the side of his mouth, pointing at Miss Cora, but not letting her see him.

Mr. Lester and Buck headed to Mr. Lester's paneled truck with "Butterfield's Plumbing" and "A Flush Every Time" emblazoned across the side, shining in the morning sun.

Both Buck and Mr. Lester got in and before they knew it Millie had stuffed herself in, sitting on Buck's lap. He pulled her close, smelling her hair. "Millie, you sure smell good."

"I know." Millie said, "It's that soap Gladys bought me." Buck just shook his head.

It was a short drive to town and Mr. Lester pulled up alongside the entrance to the front door of the courthouse. "I'm having to double park, so you two love birds jump on out."

Millie and Buck scampered up the steps. Inside the courthouse they were both looking around when a bailiff saw them and asked, "What y'all lookin' for?"

Millie began, "We're gettin' married, well not right now…"

Buck stepped in and summarized, "Where do we go to get a marriage license?" The bailiff pointed down the hall. "Probate court."

They entered the probate court clerk's office. A woman with silver hair looked up from a desk just beyond the counter. "Well, now let me guess. I'll bet you two want to apply for a marriage license. You two just look, well, ready."

 Susan Middleton

Buck and Millie looked at each other and smiled. "Yes, ma'am," they said in unison and then giggled.

"Here you go, just fill out this form and pay the $1.00 fee. That should do it. Hmm, have you two been married before?'

"Yes, ma'am," Buck answered for them this time. "Both our spouses are dead."

"Well, you'll need to bring death certificates before we can issue you a marriage license."

Buck started filling out the application with Millie answering questions, like her date of birth and address. "Just put Miss Sarah's Boarding House," Millie instructed. That caught the clerk's attention.

"You look real young. How old are you?"

"I'll be eighteen in February. February 25th. That's just a few months off. And I work. I work at Miss Sarah's," Millie caught the woman's expression, so she finished the sentence with "in the kitchen. It's a boarding house, you know. We serve two meals every day." She turned to Buck, "Right, Buck. You've stayed there and eaten twice each day." Buck's eyes widened. Millie caught herself, "That's all." She smoothed her dress, looked up and licked her lips. Buck just sucked in a breath. Something about this girl. He simply couldn't get enough of her.

"All right. I'm writin' that down 'Miss Sarah's Boarding House'."

Buck spoke up, "So, let me get this straight. The application can go through once we get the two death certificates to you. We would like to get married this coming Sunday. Will that be a problem if I can get the death certificates to you by Thursday?

"Shouldn't be. I'll be issuing the marriage certificate. I'll keep your application on my desk until Monday. If you don't get back with the death certificates by them, I'll tear it up." She spoke authoritatively.

Buck handed her the dollar. "May I please have a receipt?" The clerk got her pad with carbon paper and filled out the receipt and handed it to Buck. "We'll see you Thursday," he said formally. "Good day. Thank you for your help." Buck ended with an especially big smile and then, leading Millie by the arm, left the office.

"Oh, Buck, I almost blew that. If I hadn't started lying about what I do at Miss Sarah's, oh, my!"

"Millie, you do work in the kitchen. You almost burned the pork chops last night."

"Oh, Buck!" Millie smiled.

"Hungry?"

"Yes, I am, but Buck, I want to show you how to make a dinner right out of Miss Cora's, well, I guess I mean Miss Sarah's refrigerator. Funny thing, I guess Miss Cora actually has two kitchens. Let's catch the streetcar and go home. I can show you the streetcar stop."

"I'm ready, Millie. Let's go." Then he added, "Millie, I have to leave right after dinner, 'cause, I gotta start workin' on gettin' that second death certificate. I'll need to stop by Gaston and see if Nadine knows where Tom Stapleton died. I'm hopin' Chatham County, 'cause I know someone in the courthouse there."

They walked two blocks and caught the streetcar. Millie liked being close to Buck. They held hands and looked out the side window. They jumped off at Maple Street and strolled toward Miss Sarah's. Buck liked going in the back way, Millie's favorite entrance. In the kitchen, Millie, just as she had learned from Miss Cora, took charge.

"Now, Mr. Buck Wilson, you sit right down here, and you will not believe what I'll fix for you." She set a clean plate in front of him and put one next to him for her.

Millie opened the refrigerator and began pulling out what she found. She took out two cold pork chops, putting one on his plate and one on hers. Then she scooped up a serving of cold turnip greens for each of them. Then, she found one sweet potato which she put on his plate and then cut in half.

Finally, she found leftover banana pudding which she set in the middle of the table. "Only if you clean your plate," she announced.

She took her seat and then, remembering the sweet tea, jumped up, got two glasses, and filled each one with Miss Cora's best sweet tea. She also brought out the Duke's mayonnaise, saying, "This is real good on the turnips. Might be good on the pork chop, too."

Buck just looked at his plate. He had never eaten a cold pork chop and cold turnip greens, so as he had done before when Millie asked if he liked a dress he did not remember seeing, he smiled and said, "Millie, this looks delicious." And he found out, as Millie had, that Duke's mayonnaise can resurrect leftovers and turn them into fine dining.

They had almost finished their meal when Miss Cora came through the back door with Louise. "This baby's missin' her ma and pa. She was happy with me for a while, but I think she's tired of gettin' passed around," she said.

Millie reached out and took Louise, who had quit sniffling and was now eyeing the sweet potato. "Want some tater, baby girl?" Millie started feeding Louise bits of her dinner. "Nothin' better than taters and greens."

Miss Cora nudged Buck's arm. "Ain't nothin' better'n this, is it, Buck?"

"No, ma'am, it's not." He wiped his mouth and stood. "I'd love to spend this fine October day with you ladies, but I have work to do and a most important errand to run. I will be back Thursday. And Lord, willing, we'll be gettin' married Sunday. Miss Cora, I'll leave it to Millie to tell you the details."

He leaned down and kissed Millie on the lips and Louise on the top of her head. And he was gone.

Miss Cora said, "Millie, I'm gonna need that kitchen table for my cake makin', so maybe you and Louise could head on up to the girls' parlor and spend your afternoon there. You'll have the whole afternoon with your little girl.

Millie smiled. "Yes, ma'am. I should do these dishes though."

"No, chile, I'll take care of that. Hard to do anything and keep up with a baby."

"Yes, ma'am." Shouldering the satchel, Millie left with Louise.

In the parlor Millie sat Louise on the floor with her blocks, dishtowel doll, and a ball. Louise looked around. "I'll be right back, Louise."

Louise began to cry. Corine, Hazel, and Gladys almost fell over each other trying to get to her. Millie patted Louise's head. "I'll be back in a bit, Louise." Soon the baby was distracted by the girls, each one offering a toy.

Millie climbed that familiar flight of stairs and headed down the hall to Miss Sarah's study. The door was open, and Millie knocked softly on the door frame. Miss Sarah looked up. "Yes, Millie. I figured you'd be comin' by soon. Come in and have a seat and tell me what's on your mind.

"Miss Sarah, Buck and I will be gettin' married next Sunday. I know that he has bought me for the week, so you don't lose any money, since I won't be entertainin' and all." Millie paused to judge Miss Sarah's response. Like a poker player, she maintained the same expression Millie had seen as she entered.

"I apologize for not gettin' your permission about Louise and all, but everything's been goin' fast, Miss Sarah."

At this point Miss Sarah raised her hand, "Enough, Millie, enough. I'm glad for you, but as you must understand it does put me in a bind. But I have been at this spot before. So when will you be leaving?"

"First thing Monday mornin' and I'll be sure to straighten up my room real nice like."

"Okay, now if you'll excuse me, I need to get back to paying bills. Go see about your youngin'. If you've left her with the girls, she may be a squallin' mess by now."

"Yes, ma'am, Miss Sarah. And thank you, Miss Sarah. You've been real good to me."

"Go on now, girl. Go on." Miss Sarah said dismissively, indicating with the motion of her hand. But after Millie left, Miss Sarah said softly, "I'm gonna miss that girl. No one like our Millie."

When Millie returned to the second floor, Louise was indeed "a squallin' mess." Millie scooped her up, stuck her thumb in her mouth and settled down on the sofa and began rocking her to sleep. Gladys, Corine, and Hazel stood in awe as Louise settled down, asleep in her ma's arms.

"I'm her ma and she knows it," Millie winked.

At this time down the road Buck had taken the turn off to Gaston. He pulled up in front of Nadine's store, jumped out of his truck, and headed to the door. Nadine looked surprised, "Back already, Buck? You haven't given me time to sell what I bought yesterday."

"Jus' here for some information, Nadine. Do you know where Tom Stapleton died?"

"Well, Buck. That's easy. Chatham County. He was livin' in Savannah. From what I've been told, he went back there after he left Louise with Widow Martin."

"Thank you kindly, Nadine. I'll see you next Monday. I've got your order." Nadine just shook her head. "What in heavens name is that boy up to?" she asked as he ran to his truck.

It was early, only two o'clock and he was close to two hours from Savannah. He figured he would be there well before closing time at five.

Indeed, he pulled up in front of the Chatham County Courthouse around four o'clock. Bounding up the front steps, he found his friend who worked as a bailiff for the superior court. He directed Buck to the Chatham County Health Department in a small building next door to the courthouse, telling Buck that's where you get death certificates.

Buck entered the small, one-story building. He found the main office just to the right of the entrance. Similar in design to every other government office Buck had ever entered, it had a long counter separating the public from all things official.

One clerk sat at a desk in front of a typewriter. She was smoking a Lucky Strike cigarette and talking on the phone. When Buck walked up to the counter, she hissed into the receiver, "Gotta go. Got a customer."

She tapped the ash from her cigarette and lay it in the ash tray where it continued to grow more ash. "May I help you, suh?" she asked as she came to the counter.

"Why, yes, ma'am. I need a death certificate."

"Well, you look pretty alive to me. You sure?" She leaned on the counter and grinned at Buck.

"Yes, ma'am, I'm sure."

"Well, then, what's this dead man's name. I'm guessing man, maybe a woman."

"Ah, Thomas Stapleton. I believe he died last Thursday."

"Hope we've got that one here." She returned to her desk and opened a small notecard file and began fingering through the cards. "Yeah, here it is. 'Thomas A. Stapleton, died October 13th. He died of alcohol poisoning. Must've gotten some bad moonshine. Did you know this here Thomas A. Stapleton?"

"No, ma'am, I did not. I need to get a death certificate for his widow. You know, insurance and all." I'll stop lying once I get that marriage certificate back in Mason.

"Well, all right. Sorry for your loss." She sat down and began filling in blanks on the certificate based on the information on the card. She took a draw from her cigarette. "You know this here certificate has to be signed by Mr. Kip O'Brian. He's the head man here. I can put the seal on it and all, but Mr. O'Brian has to sign. Don't know that he'll be back in today. He's runnin' for mayor of Savannah. Think he's out politickin'."

Buck drew in a breath, determined to manage his anger. A man with a government job, not doing his job while trying to get another government job. Buck clinched his fists and smiled. "Do you think he'll be back in today. It's 4:30 now, and y'all close at 5:00, right?"

"That's right. No, I don't think he'll be back in today. Might not be in tomorrow. He's like that. Comes and goes." She went back to her typing.

It was 4:45 and the door swung open and a short, balding, heavyset man rushed in. "Gloria Jean, I forgot my briefcase. I need my briefcase. It has my campaign buttons in it." He rushed past Buck, pushing his way through the low swinging gate at one end of the counter.

"Mr. O'Brian, I was jus' typing up a death certificate for this gentleman here. Would you have time to sign it please?"

Mr. O'Brian did not slow down. He rushed toward a back office and returned swinging a brief case that had a big sticker plastered across the front, "O'Brian for Mayor of Savannah."

"Mr. O'Brian, did you hear me?"

"Not now, Gloria Jean, not now."

Now he was coming back through the swinging gate and close to passing Buck, who in one quick turn grabbed him by his arm. "Mr. O'Brian, I want you to know if I lived in Savannah, I'd vote for you. I do live in Chatham County, but not in Savannah. But, sir, I plan to marry Mr. Tom Stapleton's widow this coming Sunday, October 24, and you, suh, are going to take time to sign that death certificate, so I can get a marriage license. Understand?"

Mr. O'Brian, attempting to wrest his arm from Buck's grip, looked up into Buck's very determined face. With a little chuckle, he said, "Why certainly, Mr.… what did you say your name was?"

"Wilson."

"Why certainly, Mr. Wilson. If you will just let go of my arm, I'll go right over to Gloria Jean's desk and sign that certificate."

"No, Mr. O'Brian, I am not going to let go of your arm. I am going to escort you to Gloria Jean's desk and watch you sign that certificate, but only after I have looked it over and seen that it's correct. Do you understand?"

"Well, of course, whatever the public needs, I am your humble servant."

So Buck, his hand still around Mr. O'Brian's arm, led him to the clerk's desk and all that Buck had described got done. Buck handed Gloria Jean a one-dollar bill and held his hand out for a receipt, as Mr. O'Brian again made his way to the front door. "Good-bye all. And congratulations, Mr. Wilson. God bless."

Taking a final drag from her Lucky, Gloria Jean handed Buck the death certificate and the receipt for the fee. "Thank you, Miss Gloria Jean, hope you have a wonderful afternoon." Buck gave a nod and walked to the public side of the office and out the door. But he was too far down the hall to hear Gloria Jean shout, "She's a lucky woman, whoever she is."

Back out on the street Buck looked at the precious document again. He suddenly felt grateful for Tom Stapleton's death. "Thanks, Tom…for dying."

He jumped into his truck, putting the certificate in the

zippered bag he used for the cash and receipts he collected during his runs. He took his time on the ride to his ma's farm, relieved that the day was almost over and proud of all that he had accomplished.

Ma Wilson was standing on the porch when he pulled up into the yard. "How'd it go, Son. Did she say 'yes'?"

"Yes, ma'am, she did and we're gettin' married on Sunday and Monday mornin' I'll be bringing Millie and Louise home."

"God bless you, boy. Come here and let me hug your neck."

Buck strode toward her, and they embraced.

Ma Wilson continued, "You know, Buck, the sun doesn't shine on the same dog's ass all the time. I think yours is about to get some of that sunshine."

"Yes, ma, I believe you're right. Speaking of which, this dog is tired and hungry. Can't wait to see what you've cooked up for dinner."

"Well, I had a little extra time today, so I made a couple of apple pies. You know that apple tree your pa planted is full of fruit. May have to make some apple butter."

They walked into the house together. Buck had been the only one of her children Ma Wilson had seen grow to adulthood. Four died in infancy and one in France in the Great War. It was a miracle that Buck had not been drafted. Thank God that the war ended when it did, but then the epidemic came and took Emma and Mary. Yes, Ma Wilson knew loss.

It wasn't long before Buck was patting his full stomach and talking about going to bed in his cabin. Ma Wilson touched his arm, "Listen, Buck, you know I haven't used the big bedroom here since your pa died. I'm content in the small one across from the kitchen. Maybe you and Millie might like to use that big one, seein' as the bed in your cabin is where, well you know, you and Emma…and well, you know that was where Emma and Mary died. Fresh start and all, Buck. Think about it. But just in case that's what you want I'm gonna have that front bedroom spruced up for you by the time you get here next Monday. We'll have a second wedding celebration when you, Millie, and Louise get here."

At the door, Buck paused and turned toward Ma Wilson. "Ma, I think that's a fine idea. It's time to put that cabin to some other use, maybe a new smoke house or maybe a sewing room for Millie. Keep Louise out of all that."

"So, Millie's a seamstress?"

"Gonna be one." Buck headed for bed in his cabin. He was exhausted. Once he got his pants off, he just fell into the bed, pulled the covers up and was sound asleep before the moon came up.

Chapter 25

The next morning was Wednesday. Buck had one more day to get things done. He opened the cedar chest he and Emma had bought to keep their good clothes in. His dark gray suit lay on top. He lifted it out and hung it on a hook by the small dresser in his two-room cabin. The last time he had worn the suit was at the funeral in 1918.

He took his boar hairbrush and began dusting off the suit. He had spent good money on this suit, bought the best as a way to honor Emma and Mary. He brushed and brushed, and the fine wool responded, beginning now to look like new. "I need a fresh shirt and a bowtie!" he said aloud. "And I know exactly where to find it." Buck went to his paneled truck and opened up the back. He knew his remaining inventory. He grabbed a white shirt still in its brown paper packaging. Looking through a box of bowties, he found a bright blue silk one that made him think of Millie's eyes. "I think she'll like this one."

Back in his cabin he packed a small bag with a change of underwear, his shaving kit, a stick of Old Spice, and the clean shirt still packaged. He covered the suit in a spare bed sheet. He wouldn't fold it, knowing he could hang it up in the delivery truck.

Almost forgetting, Buck paused, opened the cedar chest again and took out a small, zippered bag and pulled out Emma's death certificate. It seems a lifetime ago, he thought. I was such a boy. But that boy died, too. I buried him with Emma and Mary. I left that cemetery a grown man.

He took the suit, small bag, and the death certificate to the truck. He hung the suit in the back. Opening the door on the driver's side he tossed the small bag over to the passenger seat. Sitting down in the driver's seat, he opened the small, zippered bag that he used for his work. Pulling out the death certificate for Tom Stapleton, and laying Emma's on top, he patted them both. "All done, finished." He put both death certificates back in the little bag.

Reviewing his schedule in his mind, he knew the first thing he had to do was drive to Savannah to restock his truck. He had worked out a route that would still get him to Mason by late afternoon. Then he would bathe at Miss Sarah's in time for supper. Getting to Mason on Wednesday meant he and Millie would have all day Thursday to get the marriage license, and he also needed to buy a ring for Millie.

Buck climbed out of the truck and ran up the steps of the farmhouse. "Mornin', Ma. Sleep well?" he greeted his mother as he entered the kitchen.

"Yes, Buck, come on in and have some breakfast."

"Gotta eat and run, Ma." Buck gobbled the fried eggs, grits, and bacon, washing it all down with a cup of black coffee.

"Starting a new life, Buck," his mother said fondly. "I'm so happy for you. You know it's time."

Finished with his meal, Buck stood, kissed his mother on the cheek and went to the door. "See you on Monday, Ma, a married man."

Left standing in the kitchen, Ma Wilson looked skyward, "Thank you, Jesus. You've answered my prayers. You've sent him someone real special, a little firecracker from what I hear."

Back in Mason, Millie was following her usual routine of getting up around six o'clock so she could have breakfast in the kitchen. This time she had Louise in tow, so it took a bit longer to get ready. She had bathed Louise the night before, so all she had to do was change her diaper and dress her. Louise was a compliant, happy baby. Millie talked to her as she dressed her.

"Louise, you're going to have a new pa, Buck. He's gonna take care of both of us. 'Course, I'm gonna help, because I'm gonna be a seamstress. But we're going to be a happy family and live in Chatham County, that's near Savannah. I'll take you to Savannah one day. Louise, we need to buy you some books. Think you might like to go get some books today, Louise?"

By the time Millie got to the kitchen, breakfast preparation was in full swing and the safest place to be was at the table. She sat down quickly and pulled her legs and Louise's around in front, so that nothing could deter the comings and goings of Alice and Miss Cora.

Mr. Lester was there, but by this time he was finishing up the last bite of his biscuit. "Good morning, ladies," he said, tweaking Louise's button nose.

"Don't get up, Millie, I'll put a plate down for you and bit of extra egg for Louise," Miss Cora ordered.

"Yes, ma'am."

"Well, Millie, when do expect to see Buck again?" Mr. Lester said as he wiped his mouth and stood to leave.

"Mr. Lester, Buck will be gettin' here this afternoon. We plan on going to the court office to get the marriage license tomorrow. Since we've both been married before, he had to get those death certificates. He already had one for his wife, but he had to get one for Tom. Not sure where he died. I'm hopin' it all worked out."

"I'm sure it will. Well, I'll be going now. See you ladies tonight."

"Bye, Lester," Miss Cora leaned over toward him, and he kissed her cheek as he passed.

Alice was bringing platters back from the dining room. "Alice, get yourself a plate and sit down with Millie. You can finish up after you eat. I nibbled on some bacon while I fried it, so I'm not hungry anymore," Cora instructed.

Millie and Alice chatted about the upcoming wedding as they ate, feeding a bit to Louise from both their plates. Miss Cora wiped her hands on her apron and joined them, a cup of coffee lightened by a sprinkle of milk in front of her.

"Millie, I checked with Reverend Edwards and he's ready to do the wedding after church Sunday," Miss Cora said. "It won't take long, so he's goin' to ask everyone to just keep their seats. Also, Millie, he wants to meet with you and Buck on Saturday. He does this with all the couples he marries. He did it with me and Lester. Jus' wants to talk about Christian marriage and all that."

Millie looked at Miss Cora. "Miss Cora, I don't know anything about that, but I do like Brother Edwards, so whatever he wants to tell us, we'll listen. We've both been married before, but it's goin' to be different this time. I jus' know it is."

Miss Cora patted Millie's arm and cheek. "I believe you're right, Millie. I think Buck proved his love by bringin' back your baby," Miss Cora patted Louise's cheek, too.

"Well, I guess I'll go back upstairs and see what's going on with the girls," Millie said, but just then all three, Corine, Gladys, and Hazel, came bounding down the stairs.

"Any leftover biscuits for us?" Hazel asked.

Both Miss Cora and Alice gave up their seats. "Come on, Alice, we've got to finish cleaning up the dining room. Help yourself, girls. What's left is wherever you can find it, on the stove, on the counter."

The three grabbed plates and picked up a biscuit each and a couple pieces of bacon. They sat down with Millie and Louise and began to nibble as Millie had seen them do before.

Corine looked at Gladys and ordered her, "Tell her, Gladys. Tell Millie what we want to do."

Millie looked at Gladys. "Well, Millie," Gladys said, "we want to buy your wedding ensemble."

"What's that?" Millie asked.

"You know, a dress, and shoes, and maybe some lace gloves. Somethin' like that," Gladys explained.

"And a little white dress for Louise," Hazel added.

"I don't want to be ungrateful about the dress for Louise and all, but Buck has already bought one and it is just divine. It's pink!"

"We could go after breakfast," Gladys continued, as if she hadn't heard. "We could get there right when they open at nine, so the store is less crowded and maybe Louise won't get fussy."

Millie's brow furrowed. "I thought I'd jus' wear my best dress, the one I wear when we entertain gentlemen."

"But, Millie, you need somethin' brand new, somethin' that'll make Buck's eyes pop," Gladys said.

"Yeah, make Buck's eyes pop," Corine repeated.

"Okay, thank you," Millie said gratefully. "That's real nice of you. We can ride the streetcar. Louise'll like that."

"Let's meet back down here at eight-thirty sharp. Sound good?" Gladys was taking charge as usual.

They all nodded.

"I want to get Louise some books," Millie said. "Does Zimmerman's have books for children?"

"Oh, Millie, Zimmerman's has EVERYTHING," Gladys cooed.

They left at eight-thirty as planned. Millie had Louise in her arms. It was a mild October day, but Millie had chosen to dress Louise in a long-sleeved shift just in case it got colder. Buck had done a good job picking out dresses for her. His experience with stocking small town general stores was paying off.

They made a jolly group heading down the street. They didn't have to wait long for the streetcar and chose seats across from each other, so they could continue to chat. The girls wanted to know how Buck had proposed. What Millie said, what he said. So, she told them.

Millie pointed out Zimmerman's to Louise. "Louise, that's the big store that has everything. We're going to buy you some books and me a new dress."

They hopped off the streetcar and crossed the street to Zimmerman's. "Second floor is ladies ready-to-wear and shoes. Let's start there," Gladys suggested.

The store had just opened so the four and one-half of them fit easily into the elevator. They bounded off at the second floor. "Let's find your dress before we buy your shoes," Gladys directed.

"And this is our treat, do you hear," Hazel reminded Mille.

The ladies' clothing section had rack after rack of dresses in dark fall colors, magenta, navy, dark brown, and patterns, too. But nothing white, nothing looking like a wedding dress.

"Maybe we should go to the wedding dress section," Hazel suggested.

"No, I'm an ordinary country girl and I want an ordinary dress," Millie spoke up.

They all just stood there thinking. Gladys looked around. "Where did Corine go?"

"Come here. Come over here!" Corine was standing near a rack of dresses marked "Sale." Included were dresses that had been front and center in the summer but had now been relegated to the sales rack now that the season had changed.

In the back of the rack Corine had found a lovely long-sleeved cotton voile dress, a picture of femininity. It was delicately embroidered up the front from hem to neck in a broad pattern. Then along the arms was more scattered embroidery. There were narrow cuffs at each wrist and a deep hem weighing the dress down so that it hung beautifully on the hanger.

Millie looked at the dress, eyes sparkling. "It's perfect. Oh, I hope it fits!"

"Go try it on, go try it on," Hazel and Gladys squealed.

Corine handed Millie the dress and Hazel took Louise.

Millie made fast work of changing into the soft, white dress. She looked in the mirror and liked what she saw. She twirled once and fluffed her hair, then she went out for the girls to see.

"Well, what do you think?"

"Oh, Millie, you look beautiful!" Gladys said approvingly. "Just beautiful. But you will need a slip, so we'll find that for you. And you know what, with the right slip you won't need a wedding night gown."

Millie's eyes widened. She had never heard of such, but there was so much she didn't know, especially about fashion. And if she was going to be a seamstress, she'd better start learning. NOW!

Gladys paid for the dress, and they went to the lingerie department which was next to the ladies ready-to-wear. The girls made quick work of finding just the right slip. They insisted that Millie needed to try on the slip, so she appeased them by stripping down in the dressing room and trying it on. Looked fine to her. The girls, having squeezed into the dressing room, nodded their approval. Corine paid this time.

Finishing up Millie's ensemble they picked out t-strap shoes. The choices were: black, brown, red, or beige. And

Corine the artist assured them that beige was the best color with a white dress.

Grateful that Mr. Bowtie was not on duty, Millie got fitted in the shoes and Hazel paid for them. That was all that was needed for the ensemble. The girls had mentioned gloves, but Millie didn't want to have to pull off a glove to have Buck put on her ring. With her luck she would hit his hand and the thing would go rolling under the pews. So, no gloves.

They had noticed the book department near the front door when they came in, so they all packed into the elevator and once they got to the first floor they headed to the front of the store. Millie and Gladys, the only serious readers in the group, began looking at the books, Millie at children's books, Gladys at the latest fiction.

Millie bought The ABCs of Animals and a book of Mother Goose rhymes. Loaded with their prizes, the four and one-half left the store for the streetcar stop. Louise was starting to get restless.

They boarded the streetcar and sat as before, two on one side, two and one half on the other. Millie was seated next to Hazel. They had not gone long when Hazel wrinkled her nose, saying, "Millie, what's that smell coming from Louise. I think I'm gonna be sick."

"Hazel, she's just had, well, you know, done a job in her diaper."

"Oh, God," Hazel gasped, holding her nose.

Now Louise was beginning to really fuss. By the time they reached Maple Street, she was wailing like a fire engine siren.

As Millie passed the other passengers heading to the door of the streetcar, she kept saying, "Sorry, sorry. Needs a diaper change." And the passengers, like Hazel, were beginning to hold their noses.

In no time at all they were stumbling up the front steps at Miss Sarah's with Millie in the lead with the screaming, stinky baby. Millie sprinted up the stairs to her room. Dashing to the bathroom she snagged a towel and spread it out on her bed. "Now, Louise, let's get you cleaned up." Millie's hands moved quickly and soon the screaming baby was cooing and smiling. "Let's get you some dinner and then, you're going to take a nap."

Millie passed the parlor as she went to the kitchen. She stuck her head in. "Hey, girls, I'll get my things as soon as I feed Louise. And thank you so much. You are the bee's knees."

In the kitchen, determined that Louise would learn to drink from a cup, Millie used a coffee cup rather than a glass. Louise drank greedily and looked up at Millie with a milk mustache. Millie filled the cup a second time and Louise finished that one as well. "Not gonna let you just fill up on milk," she said. "Let's find you something to eat in the refrigerator."

Millie found leftover fried potatoes and fried chicken. She fixed a plate with one chicken leg and a few potatoes. She and Louise finished up the chicken leg with Millie pulling off the skin and stripping the leg of the meat. Louise enjoyed holding a fried potato and feeding herself.

"Now it's time to clean you and our plate." Millie wiped Louise's mouth with a clean dish cloth and set the plate in the sink. "Maybe Alice won't mind washing one extra plate. I'll try not to make a habit of it."

By the time Millie reached the parlor, Louise had laid her head on her ma's shoulder and was falling asleep. Millie settled her on the sofa and popped Louise's thumb into her mouth. "You go to sleep now."

Gladys, Hazel, and Corine were at their usual spots. Gladys looked up. "Millie, we put your things in your room, but we left Louise's books in here. Thought she might like to have them read to her some time."

Millie smiled, "Thanks, Gladys. Would you mind watchin' her while I go up to Miss Sarah's parlor and sew a bit. I'm workin' on a chemise and think I might get it finished today. I could wear it under my slip, under my wedding dress."

"Sure thing, Millie. We'll watch her."

It was getting on toward four o'clock when Millie returned and the girls tiptoed out and down the hall to their rooms. They would be getting ready for the gentlemen guests who would be downstairs at five-thirty.

Louise was beginning to stir. She sat up. Millie asked, "Wanna go sit on the front porch and watch for Buck?" Millie scooped her up, made a trip to her room to change Louise's diaper and then went down the front stairs to the front porch. She had picked up the two books as she left the parlor and also had Louise's satchel of clothes and toys.

It was a beautiful afternoon. The temperature was mild, and a slight warm breeze was pushing the limbs of the willow in the front yard up and down. Millie sat on the floor with Louise and opened *The ABCs of Animals* and started to read, showing Louise the pictures. "Oh, my, Louise, look, it's an aardvark." Millie chuckled at the thought of her dictionary and learning that strange new word.

Miss Sarah opened the door. "Millie, I just got a phone call from Buck. He's runnin' late. Says he'll be here 'round eight o'clock."

"Thank you, Miss Sarah. Louise and I will go eat in the kitchen. Get out of your way." Millie picked up Louise and her books.

Miss Sarah made an elegant move to one side and pointed her arm toward the hallway, leading to the kitchen. Millie and Louise went that way.

In the kitchen they found Mr. Lester. Miss Cora was too busy to even acknowledge them. "Just take a seat. I'll fix your plates. Keeps you outta the line of fire."

"Better do as Cora says. Don't want to end up with mashed potatoes on your face." Mr. Lester was good at interpreting Miss Cora's moods.

Millie and Louise sat down, the baby in Millie's lap. "Buck's runnin' late. He won't be here until 'round eight." She gave Louise a long string bean to gnaw, so Millie could at least get a start on her food. There was plenty of meat loaf, mashed potatoes, and string beans for both of them.

Mr. Lester leaned over to Millie, gesturing with his head, and said, "She's got two apple pies over there. May have some ice cream to top it off."

Millie patted Louise's head. "You'll love Miss Cora's apple pie, sweet baby."

"So, did you get that marriage license?" Mr. Lester asked.

"We will tomorrow. Buck had to get Tom's death certificate, he already had his wife's. We have to have both, since we've both been married before." Millie got up and got Louise a cup of milk.

After supper Miss Cora began serving the apple pie with ice cream. Millie spoke up, "Miss Cora, I'll share one piece with Louise. Gotta think about my honeymoon."

"Chile, you ain't got nothin' to worry about."

"Miss Cora, could you and Mr. Lester look after Louise for a bit so I could go to Zimmerman's tonight. I wanna get Louise a pair of dressy shoes for the weddin'. Buck got her a pair of good walkin' shoes, but I want her to have some slippers, you know, to go with her pink dress Buck bought."

"Well, Millie it's gonna be dark soon, so if you want to go, you'd better head on now," Miss Cora said.

Mr. Lester spoke up. "Millie, you give her to me. I'll take her home. Might even give her a bath."

"Thank you, thank you, Mr. Lester."

Mr. Lester was already feeding Louise some of his ice cream and apple pie. She hardly noticed Millie leaving. Millie caught the streetcar at the intersection of Maple and Third. The streetcar wasn't crowded. Most folks were home by now having their suppers.

Zimmerman's was magical at night, with lights outlining the roof and the store windows fully lit. Millie scampered across the street up the sidewalk to the front door. Children's wear was on the second floor not far from ladies ready-to-wear. Millie had brought one of Louise's shoes so she would know how to find the right sized slippers. This was the first time Millie had shopped alone for Louise. It made her feel like a real mother. She took her time, examining almost every pair of shoes on display.

Finally, she found exactly what she wanted, white satin shoes with soft pink ribbon bows on top. "These are for my baby," she told the clerk. "She's goin' to a weddin' on Sunday. Here's one of her shoes. Please tell me if you think these'll fit her."

The salesclerk took both the satin slippers and Louise's shoe and compared, after looking inside for a labeled size. "These look like they'll fit just fine. Not good shoes for every day, but certainly perfect for a weddin' since she won't be wearing them all day."

Millie pulled two dollars from her pocket and handed them to the clerk. There was added tax, so she handed the clerk another dollar and got the change and stuffed it in her purse. Now Millie had a Zimmerman's bag with Louise's wedding shoes. She hurried for the front door as the store would be closing soon.

The sun had set and it was dark, but the streetcar was still running, so she jumped on the first one that stopped at the corner. She took a seat near the front, near the streetcar operator. It would be good to get home. Maybe Buck would be there. She had never been out this late and suddenly found herself feeling anxious about being alone on a streetcar at night.

After Millie settled down in her seat, she looked around the streetcar at the other passengers. To her horror, she saw seated a few seats back on her same side the man she had hit with the mop bucket. The man who was trying to grab her at Miss Sarah's. The man Miss Sarah had banished from her boarding house. He stared at Millie, his gaze burning into Millie's face. He knew who she was.

Millie wilted under his gaze and stared at her own lap instead of looking his way. The streetcar was coming to Maple Street and Millie had to get off. She didn't know anything else to do. She would run, run as hard as she could for the three blocks from the streetcar stop to Miss Sarah's.

At the stop she clutched the Zimmerman's bag. Getting off the streetcar, she did not look back. She began to run, run as fast as she could, her breath coming in gulps. She could hear foot falls behind her. He was behind her, catching up. Now he was shouting at her, "You bitch! I'm gonna get what I wanted that day you hit me with your damn bucket. I'm gonna take what's mine. Bitch, whore, bitch."

Millie was running as fast as she could, but a broken piece of sidewalk caught her foot and she stumbled, giving her assailant enough time to catch up. He grabbed her and started dragging her to an alley scraping her legs on the sidewalk and tearing her stockings. Millie was afraid to scream, fearing he might kill her if she did.

In the alley he pushed her to the ground through shrubbery that tore at her arms and face. First, he grabbed the front of her dress, ripping it down and exposing her breasts, which he roughly pawed. He grabbed her skirt, pulling it up. And then he was tearing at her step-ins. All the while he was whispering in her ear, "You bitch, you whore." Millie was trying to go to that secret place in her head, that safe place, but she was so afraid, she just felt numb, uncaring about what was happening to her, about anything. Her mind was no longer working. Her body was no longer hers.

And then he was pushing himself into her again and again, with each thrust scraping her body along the gravel on the ground until he was through. Millie held onto the Zimmerman's bag to herself saying, Not my baby's shoes. I'll die before you take my baby's shoes.

He stood over her as she lay there broken, humiliated. The bastard stood, and spitting on her, hissed, "I taught you a lesson, whore." And zipping his pants, he ran up the alley away from Maple Street without looking back.

When she could no longer hear his footsteps, Millie slowly stood up. She was shaking, so numb she was not even aware of her bloodied arms and legs and the pain coming from her privates. I've got to get home. Buck will be worried.

Almost robotic, Millie kept walking in a stupor, head down as she sobbed. She covered her exposed breasts with the Zimmerman's bag.

Coming from the other direction was Buck, who had just arrived and checked in with Miss Cora and learned that Millie had gone to town.

"Millie. Millie!" He was running toward her. She looked up and then just collapsed on the sidewalk. In seconds Buck was at her side, scooping her up in his arms.

"Oh, Buck," she moaned, "a man had his way with me. He called me a 'whore' over and over, but he didn't get my baby's shoes."

"Now, now, Millie. I've got you." In a rush he carried her to Miss Cora's and Mr. Lester's home. Busting through the door, Buck was panting, "Millie's been hurt bad."

Mr. Lester sprang from his chair. "Let me help you, Buck." Soon Miss Cora was also at her side. "Oh, God, Millie, chile, what's happened to you?" They set her down in a dining room chair near the pallet where Louise was sleeping soundly. Millie slumped into the chair pulling her torn clothes together the best she could.

"Lester, get that bottle of whiskey you keep." Miss Cora ordered. "Millie could use a shot."

Mr. Lester opened a cabinet below the kitchen sink and came out with a pint bottle. He grabbed a small glass, pouring out a stiff drink for Millie.

"This, here Millie, is doc-ordered whiskey. Cora had an awful cough last year and the doc wrote me a scrip. But when I got home with it, Cora refused to take a dose. So now I keep this pint for when I need"—Mr. Lester give a fake cough—"a dose." He winked as he poured the drink.

He handed it to Buck who urged, "Millie, just take a sip. It'll calm you a bit."

Millie took a sip, coughed, and then looking at them she said, "Miss Cora, it was that man I hit in the head with the mop bucket. He called me terrible names." And she began to sob again.

"He had his way with you, chile?"

Millie nodded and then started crying again. Putting her arm around Millie's shoulder, Miss Cora took charge. "Come on, Millie, let's go upstairs and let you soak in the tub. Get cleaned up."

She continued, "Lester, get me a paper bag. These clothes are goin' in the trash."

Turning to Buck, she said, "Buck, I know it means going to the second floor in Miss Sarah's house, but you're gonna get Millie some clean clothes. Get her some underwear and her robe. We're gonna get her settled down and in the bed with her baby."

"Yes, ma'am." Buck was out the door, not even asking if they knew which room was Millie's.

Miss Cora took Millie upstairs to the bathroom in her house. She filled the tub with warm water, sprinkling some bath salts in. She helped Millie strip down. Millie stepped into the water and lay back like one dead, sinking into the water, which now completely covered her head. The warm, soapy water stung her back, arms, and legs, but she surrendered to it.

"I'm gonna let you soak a while, Millie," Miss Cora said when Millie's face broke the surface. "Buck will be back with clean underwear and your robe. Then we're gonna put you to bed, you hear?"

"Yes, ma'am," Millie said meekly. "Thank you, Miss Cora."

Millie closed her eyes and lay back into the water. She felt completely lost. Someone would have to help her find a way back.

As Miss Cora scooped up Millie's torn and bloodied clothes and stuffed them into a brown paper bag, she kept muttering, "Gonna burn these, just like I hope whoever you are who did this will burn in hell."

Buck was back with clothes for Millie when Miss Cora came downstairs. "Here, Miss Cora. How is Millie?"

"Well, Buck, she's just gettin' clean and soakin' in the tub."

"Miss Cora, is she gonna be all right?" he asked, his face taut, his eyes moist, his voice resolute.

"Buck, Millie is a smart, strong, fierce young woman. You are offering her a new life, so yes, Buck, she will be all right. You have a plan. Stay with that plan."

"Yes, ma'am." He paused, stricken. "What do I do now?"

"I'm gonna go back up and check on her. Give her these clean clothes. Then, you need to take her to her room with Louise and put them both to bed. Rest is the best medicine, even in times like this."

Mr. Lester spoke up, "And Buck, after that join me on the back steps and we'll share what's left of this bottle." He held the whiskey up for Buck to see.

"Yes, suh." Buck collapsed into a chair. "If I could find

that son-of-a-bitch I would kill him, but only after he'd suffered, and oh how I would make him suffer."

When Miss Cora got back upstairs, Millie was drying off, ready for a clean chemise and step-ins. "Here you go, Millie." Miss Cora opened the door and handed the underwear and robe to Millie.

Dressed, Millie came down the stairs. Looking at Buck, she said in a small voice. "Buck, I'm ready to go to bed now. Will you help me with Louise?"

"Of course, Millie. Let's go get you put to bed," he said tenderly.

Buck picked up the sleeping Louise and lifted her onto his shoulder. Millie slipped into her shoes. She took Buck's arm and, moving like one sleepwalking, made her way from Miss Cora's to Miss Sarah's, up the back stairs to her room. Buck led her to the bed, lay Louise alongside her, tucked them both in. Turning out the light, he went back to the kitchen and through the porch to the back stairs.

Mr. Lester was already there when Buck arrived. He sat down next to Mr. Lester, who handed him the bottle. Buck took a swig and handed it back to him. Then they sat in silence for a few minutes.

"Mr. Lester, you ever felt…well, powerless?"

"Buck, you ever been black?" Mr. Lester took a swig and handed the bottle back to Buck.

"I want to find that son-of-a-bitch and beat him within an inch of his life," Buck said, taking another swig from the bottle, then handing it back to Mr. Lester.

"I know, Buck. But, right now, you need to get back to the plan you and Millie worked out before tonight. Remember?" Mr. Lester just held the bottle.

Again, they sat there in silence for a longer time. Buck

took the bottle from Mr. Lester, took one final long swig, and handed it back to him.

"Thanks, Mr. Lester. I'm goin' to bed now, so I can be ready to get back to the plan. Night, suh. You've been good to me, to us tonight. Won't ever forget this." Buck reached for Mr. Lester's hand. With that he climbed the steps, walked through the kitchen to the hall and then down to his room.

Buck wasn't expecting to fall asleep. But pure exhaustion took over, he fell into the bed and drifted off.

Chapter 26

Thursday morning in Millie's room little blue clock, still set for six-thirty, began to sing. Millie opened her eyes. Jumping up and heading to the bathroom, she looked at her face in the mirror. Yes, last night had not been a bad dream, as the scratches on her arms and face and that raw feeling in her privates confirmed.

"Today we will go to get our marriage license and rings. I need to come back to our plan," Millie said to the mirror.

She started running the water and went back to the bedroom for Louise who was just beginning to wake up. "Hey, baby."

Louise looked up and said distinctly, "Mama." Millie picked her up.

"Did you say, 'mama'?" She hugged her tightly. "Let's get a bath. I had mine last night, but you need one. I smell a stinky diaper."

Millie ran some hot water until the tub was full and then ran the cold water to make it just warm, not hot. She bathed Louise quickly, washing her body and her hair and then wrapped her up tightly in a long towel. "Let's get you all dressed and ready for the day." Millie diapered and dressed Louise and then dressed in the only new everyday dress she still had, the blue one. "Let's go get some breakfast, Louise." With the baby on her hip, Millie headed to the back stairs and down to the kitchen.

At the final step she heard voices, Buck's and Mr. Lester's. "Good morning, gentlemen. May Louise and I join you for breakfast?" she asked.

Buck jumped to his feet and pulling out one chair, bowed and greeted her, "Have a seat, my lady and my little lady."

Mr. Lester grinned, "I think Buck's got this." And went back to his grits and eggs.

"Millie, let's take Louise with us to town. You said that she likes the streetcar."

"I was just thinking the same thing, Buck. We need to spend time with her before Sunday. Miss Cora and Mr. Lester will be keeping her from the time church is over until Monday morning, right Miss Cora…and Mr. Lester?"

"That's the plan," Mr. Lester smiled and turning toward Miss Cora, verified, "Right, Cora?"

Placing a plate of food in front of Millie, Miss Cora smiled, "That's right, Lester."

For a few minutes they all settled into finishing breakfast. Louise had gotten better using her fingers with eggs, but the grits still got gummed up in her palm and between her fingers. Millie filled a coffee cup with milk, and Louise drank it down, twice.

"Buck, I found that little sweater that you put in her satchel. We might need to put it on her. I'll go get her satchel."

Buck only had time to nod, and Millie was gone back up the stairs.

Without even looking up, Mr. Lester said, "Buck, she seems to be trying to be normal. Might want to be extra gentle with her today if you know what I mean."

"I believe you're right, Mr. Lester. I'm gonna try."

Millie was already back, declaring, "I'm ready to go now."

"Well, we are, too," Buck said as he lifted Louise, took the satchel from Millie and slipped it over his shoulder. He gently pulled Millie toward him and slipped his arm around her waist. "Ready to go, my future wife?"

Mr. Lester was up and headed toward the door. "Looks like you are following the plan, Buck." He winked and patted Miss Cora's fanny as he passed her at the sink.

"And what's your plan, Lester?" Miss Cora spoke without even looking his way.

"You'll see, Cora. You'll see."

"Get on now, Lester. You get on."

By that time Millie and Buck were walking down the front steps and down the street. Millie was stiff but forced herself to keep up a steady pace. As they boarded the streetcar, Millie grabbed Buck's arm. "Buck, something came over me just now, remembering last night," she whispered urgently.

"Take your time, Millie. I'm right here."

On the streetcar, Louise sat between them on the bench seat up front, looking from one and then to the other as Millie and Buck chatted about the day.

"I'm looking forward to gettin' rid of these here death certificates. I guess you could say they're burnin' a hole in my zipper bag here."

"I'll be really glad when we actually have that marriage certificate. You can put it in that bag for safekeeping until we deliver it to Brother Edwards on Saturday," Millie said as she smiled.

Millie leaned back against the seat and Buck put his arm around her. She looked out the window and sighed. The day was overcast and just a bit chilly. Buck noticed that Millie didn't have on a sweater.

"Millie, let's buy you a sweater when we go to Zimmerman's to shop for your ring."

They were nearing the courthouse, and the streetcar was

beginning to slow. People were on the sidewalk waiting to board, so Buck, Millie, and Louise left by way of the back door.

Buck bounded up the courthouse steps, taking two steps at a time, even carrying Louise. He had to wait at the top for Millie. "Come on, Ma."

Millie took her time, "Yes, Pa."

Now they knew where the probate court was. The same clerk came forward when they entered. "I remember you two. You were here Tuesday. I still have your application on my desk and your dollar."

"Well, I believe we have the rest of what you need." Buck unzipped the small canvas bag and handed the clerk the two death certificates. She took them to her desk and picking up the marriage license application, she compared that information with the death certificates. Millie reached for Buck's hand. He squeezed it reassuringly.

The clerk's head furrowed. She clipped the death certificates to the application form and picked up another document from her desk. Opening her desk drawer, she pulled out an embossing stamp and squeezed it on the bottom corner of that document.

Coming to the counter, she reached out and handed the now completed marriage certificate to Millie. "Just give this to whoever will be officiating at your wedding. He'll know what to do with it and how to file it with us. Do you know who that will be?"

Millie spoke up, "Oh, yes, ma'am. Brother Edwards at First Baptist will be doing the marryin'."

"First Baptist on Hill Street, the white church?"

"No, ma'am, the one on New Street, the black church."

"But you're white, aren't you?"

Millie looked at Buck and then back at the clerk. "Why,

yes, ma'am, I guess we are, but Brother Edwards will be doin' the marryin' for us, right Buck?"

"Yes, he will." Buck smiled down at Millie. "Yes, he will."

The clerk rolled her eyes. "Well, all right. You got what you came for." And with that she went back to her desk to answer the phone, "Probate Court."

Millie, Buck, and Louise left. Once outside in the hall, Millie said, "Buck, give Louise to me, so you can put this marriage license in your bag. You've been to too much trouble for me to lose it now."

With the two death certificates now replaced by one marriage license, they left the courthouse and strolled down to the streetcar stop two blocks away. Next stop, Zimmerman's.

The jewelry section was near the front of the store. Big glass display cases held watches, necklaces, bracelets, broaches, and rings. Buck asked the store clerk to bring out the tray of wedding rings. Millie knew exactly what she wanted, something simple. "There Buck, let's see if they have that thin one in my size." After two tries Millie found one that fit perfectly.

"Buck, I know you work with your hands a lot, so if you don't want to wear one, thinking you might get your finger cut off or somethin', I'll understand."

Buck ignored her and speaking to the store clerk, he pointed out a ring similar to Millie's but just a bit wider. One try and he now had a wedding ring. The clerk put each one in a small case; Buck paid for the rings, and the clerk gave him a bag emblazoned with "Zimmerman's."

"Now let's find you a sweater before you start shivering." Millie knew where to take them, second floor ladies ready-to-wear. They found the sweater section and Millie, ever the practical one, picked a black one. It did however have a nod to fashion with an open rolled collar and wooden toggle buttons. Buck paid for the sweater.

"Here, hold Louise. I'm gonna put this sweater on now." Buck took Louise and chuckled. "Where to now, Millie?"

"Let's go home, I mean to Miss Sarah's. Louise needs some play time. Plus, she's gettin' heavy."

As they were walking up the sidewalk to Miss Sarah's, Buck told Millie that he had some deliveries to make, so he'd be gone until supper time. "Well, I'll just go on upstairs to the girls' parlor and let Louise play some," she replied.

At Miss Sarah's, Buck saw them both into the house and then left to take care of those deliveries. It was just a bit after eleven o'clock so Millie dropped by the kitchen and foraged for dinner for her and Louise. There was always something in the refrigerator, so soon Millie had a plate with cold meat loaf, a biscuit, and a piece of apple pie. Millie drank a glass of sweet tea, and Louise swigged down two cups of milk.

Soon they were ensconced in the upstairs parlor, Louise with a clean diaper and toys and Millie with her book *The Art of Dressmaking*. Louise slept while Millie read. Gladys, Corine, and Hazel had headed for Zimmerman's earlier and wouldn't be back until four o'clock.

Millie enjoyed this quiet time in their parlor, especially after what had happened to her last night. Her mind drifted back to the assault, the pain, the humiliation. She put it aside just as she had learned to do when she was entertainin' men for Miss Sarah. She hoped nothing she had experienced would affect her being able to receive Buck's love on their wedding night.

When the girls got back, each one in turn showed Millie what she had bought. Millie talked about her day, getting the marriage license, buying the rings and the sweater. Millie decided to leave out talking about the rape, though the girls had all heard about it by then.

At four-thirty Louise was up, so Millie changed her diaper and went downstairs to the front porch. Buck would be back soon.

Routines. That's what Millie needed right now, routines. Buck coming home, supper in the kitchen, salmon croquettes tonight. Laughter round the table. Mr. Lester's hilarious tales about unclogging a toilet after a child had flushed a stuffed animal. Buck also had a funny story about hair pomade and trying to find what the store owner wanted to stock.

Buck, Millie, and Louise had another quiet evening at Miss Cora's and Mr. Lester's while they waited for the "entertainin'" at Miss Sarah's to end.

Buck carried the sleeping Louise back to Miss Sarah's with Millie walking alongside. In the kitchen Buck asked Millie to sit down. He said he had something he needed to talk with her about.

"Millie, I believe you know the man's name who raped you. He had been a guest, right. Was he your guest?"

"No, Buck." Then Millie told Buck the whole story about the bucket and the angry guest. "The girls told me his name, Buck. It's Jack Jones."

"Millie, tomorrow instead of taking Louise to the park, we need to go to the police station and swear out a warrant for Jack Jones's arrest. Understand?"

"Buck, I don't know. Do you think they'll believe me?"

"Millie, you have to try. I'll be there with you. You can do this. I believe in you." Buck held her face in his hands as he spoke.

"Buck, you don't understand. Lately, my body hasn't belonged to me by my choice, but last night that man took something from me. Something deep inside me, deep in my body. Arresting him won't give that back to me."

Buck searched her face for a moment, and then sighed. "Okay, Millie. Why don't you sleep on it. We can talk again in the mornin'." Buck wanted to accept what Millie was saying, but in his mind, in his heart, he wanted that man, that monster, to suffer, to hurt.

"No, Buck. I don't want to talk about it again. This is just too much. I want to take Louise to that park you found out about. Like a family. Sleep won't change my mind."

"Okay, Milllie." Buck took her hands and kissed them, then he kissed her tenderly, lightly on her lips.

Chapter 27

Friday came and after breakfast in the kitchen, Buck, Millie, and Louise left for the park with their picnic dinner of boiled eggs, pimento cheese sandwiches, apples, and tea.

They caught the streetcar headed downtown and then transferred to one running north. Buck had learned about a park located at the northern end of the north-south streetcar route. Seeing the high-end residential side of Mason was a treat. Millie kept whispering, "How do they keep that big ole place clean?" And Buck kept responding, "They have lots of help."

At the park Millie spread out an old quilt Miss Cora had given her and settled Louise down on it. The day would be spent chasing Louise, feeding Louise, changing Louise, and finally watching Louise sleep. Buck could not remember the last time he felt so content. He lay back, putting his head in Millie's lap and fell asleep alongside Louise.

They had eaten all the sandwiches and boiled eggs, saving the apples for the ride home. Back on the streetcar, they rode home in silence. It had been a perfect day; no words were needed to describe it. Buck and Millie nibbled on the apples with Millie biting off pieces without skin on them and sharing them with Louise.

By the time they got back to Miss Sarah's the sun was beginning to set, and supper was on the table. They settled in at the kitchen table and ate fried catfish, hushpuppies (which Louise especially liked) and talked and laughed about the day. Tomorrow would be Saturday, the day Buck and Millie would meet with Brother Edwards and Miss Cora would look after Louise. Another day coming to a close, bringing them closer to their new life.

Chapter 28

Saturday morning Millie rose early, the little blue clock having announced the time. She ran a bath for her and Louise and somehow managed to wash their bodies and their hair at the same time.

Back in the bedroom, she realized she now only had two good dresses, the blue one she had just worn and her dressy, entertainin' dress. She did have two other dresses, the one she had worn when she came to Mason from Gaston and the one Miss Sarah had given her that first day, but they were not serious dresses. And she wanted to look serious. "It'll have to be the blue one again," she sighed.

She diapered and dressed Louise. She would hand her off after breakfast to the Butterfields. As it was Saturday Magdala and Mr. Lester could help Miss Cora watch Louise. By the time Millie reached the kitchen, Buck was already there joking and laughing with Mr. Lester. Millie loved that sound. She could also hear Miss Cora occasionally adding one of her zingers.

Their appointment with Brother Edwards was at eight-thirty at the church. He had told Miss Cora when she made the appointment, that he devoted his entire day to sermon preparation and he didn't want that block of time to be broken up, so starting early fit his schedule best.

At quarter until eight, Buck turned to Millie. "Ready to go, Millie?"

"Yes, I am, Buck."

"I've got the license right here." Buck patted the small, zippered bag he had placed on the table.

Louise didn't even seem to notice when they left, enthralled as she was with the funny sounds and faces Mr. Lester was making as he held her on his lap.

On the street Buck opened the door of his truck for Millie and she climbed in. "This reminds me of the day I met you, Buck."

"Yes, that's a day I'll always remember," he said with a grin. "Ready to go meet the Reverend?"

"Yes, Buck. I am."

Mr. Lester had drawn Buck a map to help him find the church. Buck was accustomed to finding places in a strange town, so in no time he had pulled up and parked alongside the sanctuary. Reverend Edwards had told Miss Cora that they should enter through a side door. It was easy to find, as the words "Church Office" were written on a sign over the door.

Buck opened the door for Millie and followed her into what was a reception area. No one was there, but they heard a voice calling, "Children, I'm in here, come on into my office."

Buck and Millie looked at each other and shrugged. They found Reverend Edwards behind a huge desk piled high with books, each of which had been tabbed with short pieces of paper.

The Reverend stood and came around the desk. He reached out his hand to Buck, first saying, "Reverend Elias Edwards." Buck shook his hand, replying, "Buck Wilson, Reverend."

Reverend Edwards turned to Millie, taking her hand, "And Millie, it is so very good to see you."

"Yes, suh. I'm glad to be here."

"Sit down. Sit down, you two."

Buck opened the zippered bag and handed the reverend the marriage license. "Reverend Edwards, here's the marriage license. I'll tell you it was a relief to finally get it. We've both been married before, so I had to provide two death certificates in order to get one marriage certificate. I'd call that a real good trade."

"Well, Buck, I'll take that off your hands," the preacher replied. "This is all I need for Sunday. Now speaking of Sunday, let me get some details out of the way before we have a little talk about marriage. I'll have the congregation sit down after the final hymn. I'll explain what is about to happen. I want you, Buck, to slip up the aisle and take a seat on the deacons' bench, so you'll be close to the front and ready to stand up when I start the wedding ceremony. Understood?"

Buck nodded.

"Then I'll ask Millie to come forward escorted by Lester. Right, Millie?"

"Yes, suh, Reverend, suh."

"Now," Reverend Edwards clasped his hands, "Let's talk about marriage."

He looked directly first at Buck and then at Millie. "I could read from the Bible right now, but I know from past experience that what you're thinking about is the honeymoon and reading from the Bible will not get your mind off your wedding night. So, let's start there. That passion, that fire, that you'll experience tomorrow afternoon and night is the flame you must tend. But there will be times when you will be angry with each other and not even want to sleep together. Don't let those times frighten you. It will take a lifetime to know each other, so be patient."

Buck and Millie nodded, and the Reverend continued.

"Tomorrow you will start your life as a team. Not a one melded human being, but a team. Like a team of horses pulling a wagon. Try to find a rhythm, a pace you can each keep." As children raised on farms, Buck and Millie knew just what he meant, and they nodded again.

"Learn to hold your tongue, learn to listen, never stop finding each other fascinating. Always find a way back to each other's arms. Always, always, be willing to say, 'I'm sorry.' Listen tomorrow when I speak to you about sickness, health, richer, poorer. Think about what that means. And, finally, don't go to bed angry. That's pretty much it. Do you have any questions?"

Buck looked at Millie. They smiled at each other. Then they both looked at Reverend Edwards and in unison said, "No, suh."

"I'll see you tomorrow." Reverend Edwards stood as he spoke. He shook Buck's hand and squeezed Millie's. He walked them to the door and waved good-bye. At the truck Buck opened the door for Millie and got in behind the steering wheel. "Do we need to do anything else, Millie?" he asked.

"No, Buck, let's go back to Miss Sarah's and see what Louise is up to."

"Millie, before that, would you like to go to the pharmacy across from Zimmerman's and get ice cream?"

"That sounds wonderful, Buck!"

So they headed toward town. Buck parked his truck in front of the pharmacy. He hurried around to Millie's door and helped her out. Inside they took seats at the counter and ordered ice cream. Millie ordered chocolate, Buck, strawberry. They finished up the ice cream and walked to the door. As they did Mr. Zappa, the owner of the theater next door, passed them as he came in.

He stood stock still "Millie, remember me, Zappa, the theater owner. You came and saw a movie after I visited you at Miss Sarah's."

Millie blinked, feeling the mood change, feeling heavy, sad. Buck stepped between her and Mr. Zappa. "Excuse me, sir, I don't think I've had the pleasure. I'm Buck Wilson. This is my wife-to-be. I hope you have a pleasant afternoon. Come on, Millie."

With that Buck escorted Millie out of the pharmacy and to the truck. In the truck Millie put her face in her hands and said, "Oh, Buck, I've done some things I'm so ashamed of. Maybe I deserved what happened to me the other night." And she began to sob.

Buck reached over and took her hands, "Millie, I've done things I'm ashamed of, too. But are we gonna let that ugly past stop us from having a happy future? Indeed NOT. And you, Millie, did nothing to deserve what happened to you. You are innocent. You hear me? INNOCENT!"

"Oh, Buck, I love you." She reached over and hugged him. After a few minutes he cranked up the truck and they headed to Miss Sarah's. They spent the afternoon on the front porch followed by another supper shared in the kitchen. Louise got a few spoonsful of Millie's mashed potatoes and beef patty. As they had done the evenings before, Buck and Millie waited at Miss Cora's and Mr. Lester's while the entertainin' was going on at Miss Sarah's. Magdala was there and not doing homework, so they chatted with her about school and basketball. Buck had played in high school, so he had plenty of questions about her team.

As it was getting late, Buck and Millie walked back to Miss Sarah's house, Buck carrying Louise, who was sound asleep on his shoulder. They parted in the kitchen. "Millie, this is the last night we have to sleep separately. Are you glad?"

"Yes, Buck, I'm very glad. Good night." She leaned in for

a kiss, took Louise and climbed the stairs to the second floor. She was weary. She tucked Louise into the bed, then going to the bathroom, she peed and brushed her teeth. She checked to see if her blue clock was wound. There'd be no breakfast in the kitchen tomorrow, so she'd have to forage for something to eat for her and for Louise. But, right now, she just wanted to lie down.

Downstairs Buck was busy straightening the room and setting out the flowers he had bought. Daisies. He had bought two bunches yesterday. Two bunches and two vases. Daisies. Made him think of Millie. Their bright yellow centers lightened up the dark little room. A one-night honeymoon was the best they could do for now. Maybe next year they could get Ma Wilson to keep Louise and they'd go to Savannah.

<h1 style="text-align:center">Chapter 29</h1>

Sunday, October 24, 1927, dawned fresh and cool. Millie rose even before the little blue clock had time to chime. "I am so excited; I just can't sleep anymore!" she told the clock.

Gladys had promised to watch Louise while Millie got dressed for church and her wedding. She had said to tap on her door. Louise was still asleep, so Millie wrapped her faded chenille robe around her and tiptoed through the shared bathroom to Gladys's bedroom door. It was six in the morning and Gladys rarely rose before nine.

Millie tapped on the door, whispering, "Gladys, Gladys." Nothing. More tapping, more "Gladys." Nothing.

"Dagnabit, I'm goin' in."

Millie pushed the door open. Sleeping on her back, mouth open, Gladys was wrapped up in the bedclothes like a mummy. Millie went to the bed and started shaking her. "Gladys, Gladys." Louder this time.

Gladys finally opened her eyes. "What are you doing in here, Millie? I'm trying to sleep."

"And I'm trying to wake you up. You promised to watch Louise while I get ready for MY WEDDING."

With that Gladys sat bolt up in the bed, one marcel wave

over her left eye. "Yes, that's right. I'm awake now, Millie. I'm awake."

"I've got to check on Louise. Get your robe on and we'll go downstairs and figure out something for breakfast. Can't let Louise go hungry."

Soon the three were descending the back stairs to the kitchen. At the last turn in the stairway, Gladys and Millie looked at each other, Gladys speaking first. "Do I smell bacon frying?"

Millie sniffed, "You do. Someone is making breakfast!"

By this time Louise's tousled blonde head was up and she too was waking up to the bacon smell. When they reached the kitchen, they found Buck wearing an apron and flipping bacon in Miss Cora's iron skillet.

"Good morning, ladies. Will you come take your seats. Breakfast is almost ready. And just so you know, I did get permission from Miss Cora."

Gladys and Millie looked at each other. Then Gladys looked at Buck, asking coyly, "Say, Buck, do you have a brother?"

Buck laughed and said, "Here you go, you two." He set a plate in front of both Millie and Gladys. Millie's had two biscuits, one for Millie, one for Louise. Louise clapped her little hands. Each plate had a serving of scrambled eggs and bacon.

"Biscuits, Buck. You are one talented man," Gladys cooed.

"Learned from my ma. Always have loved workin' in the kitchen with her, 'specially after Pa died and it was just the two of us. And here's your coffee, ladies, and a cup of milk for my little lady."

"Thank you, Buck. What a lovely way to start our wedding day," Millie said, patting his arm.

"May I join you?"

"Of course," Gladys said, and added, "If no brother, do you at least have a friend?"

They laughed about Louise stuffing the biscuit into her mouth. Louise laughed, too, and the biscuit fell out. So, the laughter started again.

It was getting close to eight o'clock and Millie knew she'd need to get going if she wanted to be dressed by ten-thirty and be back here in the kitchen to load up and head to church. She had put a folded dress on the kitchen counter. Standing, she handed Louise to Gladys and turning to Buck she explained the folded pile on the counter. "Buck, please put that dress in your room. It's got clean underwear folded in it. I don't plan to wear my wedding dress while we're loading the truck, so I'll need this change of clothes for tomorrow after I have a bath."

Buck blinked. He had only gotten as far as the honeymoon in his planning. This little slip of a girl was already ahead of that, planning the packing up.

"And, Buck, I've got two cardboard boxes that Mr. Lester gave me to use when I moved to the second floor. I'm gonna start filling them now, so they'll be ready for you to put in the truck first thing tomorrow morning. Can you believe it, Buck, we'll be a couple of ole married people this time tomorrow?"

Buck smiled, "Yes, we will, Millie."

Millie turned to Gladys, "Gladys, it might be good to let me slip up the stairs before you follow. That way Louise won't start hollering. She's gotten real attached to her ma."

Louise was now fingering the scrambled eggs on Gladys's plate and didn't even notice that her mother was about to leave. "Corine and Hazel are going to help, too. I'll get Louise's dress and satchel once they come to the parlor. When do we need to meet up in the kitchen?" Gladys asked.

"Ten-thirty," Millie replied without even turning around as she climbed the stairs.

Back upstairs, the first thing Millie did was bathe and

wash her hair, so it would have plenty of time to dry. She started to pack while her hair began to curl up as it dried. She decided to leave the stack of *Redbook* magazines for her replacement, whoever she was. *The Art of Dressmaking* and her dictionary were now placed on top of her shoes in one of the boxes. She'd put her extra pairs of step-ins and chemises in the second box. Buck could hang her extra dresses in the back of the truck.

Millie looked at each dress, remembering that first trip to Zimmerman's with Lucy. Millie smiled. Once I get my Minnesota H, I'll be making my clothes and Louise's, she thought. Miss Sarah had already left the envelope for the week and Millie placed it in one of the boxes. This is really Buck's twenty dollars, but he said I could keep it. I have enough now. I can buy my sewing machine.

Mille pulled on her garter belt and stockings over her best step-ins and chemise. She looked at her body, giving herself a verbal critique. "I do hope he likes my bosoms. They're kinda small, but they're round and stand up, not like Ma's, hers really sag. Mine'll be like that one day, too. Good thing I'm marryin' him now before they sag!"

She slipped on her new beige t-straps, the white slip, and the cotton voile dress. She applied lipstick, drawing a Clara Bow mouth, but afterward changed her mind. "Nope, that's not the girl he picked up on the highway. That's not the 'Millie' he'll be married to," she said to herself. She went back into the bathroom, wiped the lipstick off with toilet paper and washed her face. "I'll give this makeup to the girls."

It was now ten o'clock and Millie had thirty minutes before she needed to be downstairs, so she decided to sit on the bed and read her Bible. She turned to Psalm 23 and read part of verse six: "Surely goodness and mercy shall follow me all the days of my life…"

"Well, Goodness and Mercy, I think I see you following

me," she said. "Is your name 'Buck'?" She closed the Bible carefully, pressing the book against her chest. "I'm gonna miss Miss Cora. Maybe Buck will bring me to see her sometime. But I have this Bible to remember her. Miss Cora, you'd be real happy to know that I'm readin' it on my weddin' day."

Time to go. Millie skipped down the hallway and at the parlor stuck her head in asking, "You ladies ready for church…and a weddin'?"

"Oh, Millie, you look beautiful." Corine was the first out the door. "But don't you need some makeup?"

"No, I want to be the 'Millie' Buck first saw. But a grown-up 'Millie'."

Looking at her daughter, Millie cooed, "Oh, Louise, look how pretty you are. Come here."

Louise reached up for her mother. Millie picked her up and walked toward the stairs with Corine, Hazel, and Gladys following her, like a trio of bridesmaids.

Millie made the last turn into the kitchen and Buck saw her. "Oh, Millie, you are so beautiful, and you are, too, Louise. Let me take her so she won't wrinkle your dress."

"Oh, Buck, there's no way to avoid it. You seein' me before the weddin' and all. You know it's supposed to be bad luck, groom seein' the bride before the weddin' and all. But I'm countin' on Goodness and Mercy to follow us, not luck, good or bad." With that she winked at him.

The little company moved toward the kitchen door and then down the stairs to the driveway. Miss Cora, Mr. Lester, and Magdala were ready and radiant. Mr. Lester was sporting his purple tie with his gray suit and Miss Cora wore her dark red dress with the sheer sleeves. Her broad-brimmed hat had a purple hat band. "Here they come, Cora. All that praying paid off." Mr. Lester leaned into his wife, giving her a peck on the cheek.

Also standing with them was Miss Sarah, in an elegant

navy dress, a large sapphire and diamond brooch on her left shoulder. Her Chevrolet sedan had been cleaned and waxed and stood sparkling in the driveway. Hazel leaned over to Corine and Gladys, and said, "You know I was wondering how we were going to get to the church."

The girls joined Miss Sarah at her car. Gladys called to Millie. "Millie, could you come here for a moment?"

Millie looked at Buck and said, "I'll be right back."

When Millie got to the girls and Miss Sarah, the three, Hazel, Corine, and Gladys made a circle around her, wrapping their arms around her as they did. Gladys spoke for the group. "Millie, we — that includes Miss Sarah — want you to have this." She handed Millie an envelope so full of dollars the flap could not be closed. "We know what happened to you. We're so sorry. If we could we'd hunt him down and cut his, well, we'd hurt him real bad. We want you to get that sewing machine. There's enough here for the sewing machine AND some fabric. We want you to make us chemises."

"Not me," Miss Sarah interjected and winked.

Millie just stood there speechless, tears welling up in her eyes. "I don't know what to say but thank you." She then hugged each one individually, including Miss Sarah.

She turned and walked toward Buck, but pausing she looked back at them and added, "You're gonna get those chemises, 'cause you've paid for 'em. Buck'll bring them to you." With that she turned and walked to Buck.

Mr. Lester spoke now, saying, "We are a fine-lookin' group. Time to go." He walked toward his truck.

Buck followed his lead and turning to Millie and Louise, repeated, "Time to go." They headed toward Buck's truck parked at the curb.

Miss Sarah followed suit, walking to her sedan and calling out, "Come on, girls. Load up. Time to go."

Everyone laughed as they climbed into their vehicles.

Buck opened the passenger door for Millie and handed Louise off. Soon he was cranking up the Ford and pulling in behind Mr. Lester and Miss Sarah. Millie looked his way, "Buck, I didn't tell you how handsome you look," she said. "That blue bowtie and all. And your beautiful red hair. I love it." She reached up and patted his head.

Mr. Lester led the way and found spots in the parking lot at First Baptist where three cars could slip in. Then they were all out of the cars, the ladies smoothing their dresses, the gentlemen settling their hats on their heads.

This clutch of white people following the Butterfields caused a slight stir. The reaction, however, was more one of enthusiastic welcome than dismay. Most of them knew the Butterfields, some knew of Miss Sarah's boarding house, and a few even knew about the business other than the rental of rooms which went on there.

As this little assembly from Miss Sarah's climbed the front steps, hats bobbed, heads nodded, and even a few fingers pointed their way. Corine, Gladys, and Hazel were taking it all in. To them it was a fashion show. The broad hats with feathers and satin hat bands. The dresses with sheer sleeves and frilly skirts, in a rainbow of colors, or in Corine's eye, a painter's palette. The gentlemen in their three-piece suits and bi-colored shoes. So much to see, but the wave of parish-ioners kept moving them forward.

Mr. Lester was in the lead and looking for a pew that could accommodate ten. He decided to break them up, pointing to one pew for Millie, Buck, Louise, and his family and then putting his hand on the next pew indicating a spot for Miss Sarah and the girls.

The organ had begun to play and now the song leader was at the podium, announcing the first hymn, "Holy, Holy, Holy." Buck wiped the bottom of Louise's shoes with his handkerchief and then let her stand in the pew between him and Millie. "Holy, Holy, Holy, Lord God Almighty…" The choir was weaving and singing, adding a descant sung by the sopranos. "Early in the morning, our song shall rise to Thee…" And rise it did, as the voices of the congregants filled the air.

Millie looked at Buck and whispered, "I just love it here." Buck grinned. Millie was soon lost in thought, remembering her first Sunday here, the little wizened woman she sat next to, remembering sharing a hymnal with Magdala, remembering parts of sermons. Peter getting out of the boat to walk on the water to Jesus. She was about to do that. Get out of the boat.

The service was a blur to her. Louise fell asleep, then she woke up and fussed, then she fell back to sleep. Reverend Edwards seemed to drone on and on. Millie just couldn't bring herself to really listen.

And then he stopped. And Millie heard these words, "Brothers and Sisters, we're about to sing our final hymn and while we sing, I have two young people who're going to come forward to be married. After the hymn is sung, I want you to take your seats for the weddin'. Now, I know you have chicken at home that needs fryin'. This won't take long, but hear me now, Christian marriage, the Christian home is fundamental to our faith. And you, church, are the family of faith. Today two of your children, our children, are coming before us to make a lifelong commitment to each other. All right. song leader, let's sing that final hymn, 'Amazing Grace'."

"Buck, that's my favorite hymn," Millie whispered.

"Meet you down front, Millie," Buck said as he stepped into the aisle and began walking to the front of the church. Then something wonderfully spontaneous happened as church members reached out, women patting his arm and men shaking his hand.

"Through many dangers, toils, and snares, I have already come."

Millie and Mr. Lester moved out into the aisle, and they walked down the aisle to the words, "'Tis grace hath brought me safe thus far, and grace will lead me home." Folks smiled as Millie and Mr. Lester walked by. Some were saying, "Good job, Lester!" Others, "She's a right pretty daughter, Lester."

Millie looked up at Mr. Lester. "Thank you, Pa."

Then they were at the front of the church with Brother Edwards, as Millie called him, facing the church and Buck standing to his left. Mr. Lester brought her to Buck and leaning toward him whispered, "She ain't needin' anybody to give her away. She knows what she wants. And, by the way, you're a real lucky man. And, uh, Cora put a picnic dinner in the refrigerator for you, you know for later." With that he left, taking the side aisle, and going back to Miss Cora.

Buck's face broke out into a smile.

Reverend Edwards began without even referring to a text. "Brothers and sisters, we are gathered together in the sight of God to witness and bless the joining together of Millie Stapleton and Buck Wilson in Christian marriage."

Millie and Buck looked at each other and with every question, heartily answered, "I will."

Then came the exchange of rings. Brother Edwards took the rings from Buck and held them high for all to see. "These rings are the outward and visible sign of an inward and spiritual grace, between Jesus Christ and his church."

They exchanged rings as a sign of their vows. Millie couldn't resist holding her hand out and looking at hers. Then she looked up at Buck and licked her lips and parted them. Dear God, was all he could think. I'm not supposed to be thinking about that right now. Buck just smiled at her. No one like her.

Reverend Edwards pronounced them man and wife, declaring "those whom God has joined together, let no man put asunder."

Then he gave the benediction, "Now to Him who is able to do exceeding abundantly above all that we ask or think, according to the power that works within us, to Him be glory in the church and in Christ Jesus to all generations forever and ever. Amen."

The organ began to blast a lively version of "Come Thou Fount of Every Blessing," giving Reverend Edwards time to get to the front of the church. He had told Millie and Buck to stay where they were until the service was really over.

When the service ended, a congratulating wave of people began coming toward them, but Buck was determined that they would somehow make their way to the back door. Miss Cora would have Louise, so there would be no need to try to reassemble outside. Everyone was on their own at this point.

Millie was enjoying every minute, but trying as hard as Buck was to move toward the door. They were halfway down the aisle when they saw Mr. Lester coming toward them opening up a passageway through the crowd, proclaiming, "Now you folks, give them some space so they can get to their honeymoon."

So what had been a force keeping them in the church now became a wave moving them to the front door, with men patting Buck on the shoulder and women cooing to Millie, "He's so handsome."

Finally, they were at the truck and Buck was helping her into the passenger's seat. Once inside as Buck was cranking up the Ford, Millie shouted, "We did it, Buck. We did it. We got married."

"Yes, we did, dear wife."

Soon they were pulling up to Miss Sarah's and racing to Buck's room, their one-night honeymoon spot. Buck lifted Millie into his arms and carried her over the threshold. Millie saw the two vases of daisies. "Oh, Buck, daisies. I do love daisies."

"Millie, you ready for this or should we wait?"

"I'm ready, Buck. Whatever happened a few days ago has nothing to do with us." With that she pushed him onto the bed.

Soon their fine clothes were in piles on the floor. And they hungrily and greedily loved until exhausted and giddy, they fell back on the bed.

Later it had begun to rain, and the steady patter lulled the sweet couple to sleep in each other's arms. Around five o'clock Buck awoke and seeing that Millie too was awake, leaned over, kissed her lightly on the lips and said, "Let's go see about the dinner Miss Cora put in the refrigerator for us, the one Mr. Lester told me about when he brought you down the aisle to me."

"But, first, Buck, I want you to know I didn't close my eyes and I didn't go to any secret place in my head. Understand?"

"Yes, Millie, I understand."

"And, Buck, you were so kind. I've never had it like that. It was, well, pleasant."

"I'm glad, Millie, real glad. Now let's go get something to eat."

"Sure, Buck."

So, they put on some of what lay on the floor and went to the kitchen, Millie's favorite room.

"Buck, you made breakfast this mornin', so I want you to set yourself down and I'm gonna find you some supper." Millie already had her head in the refrigerator and was finding what Miss Cora had made specially for them: pimento cheese sandwiches, potato salad, apple pie, and sweet tea.

"There, Buck. Almost like magic. I made your supper."

"You are magic, Millie, pure magic. You are, you are my inspiration."

"Aw, Buck, now I do have a stubborn side."

Buck was already stuffing a sandwich in his mouth. "Millie,

you needed that stubborn side, or you wouldn't have survived here in Mason. I like that about you."

They ate until they couldn't eat anymore. And then they talked and talked and laughed. It was nearly seven o'clock when Millie had a thought.

"Buck, I only have two boxes of my things upstairs. Why don't I go ahead and bring those down. I also have some things that'll need to get hung up in the truck."

"I'll help you, Millie."

"Well, I guess that would be okay. We'll just be real quiet going up and coming down. I don't know what the girls might be doing."

They moved stealthily like a couple of burglars and were in and out of Millie's room in no time. Millie looked back one last time, "Good-bye, second-floor room. I won't miss you." And with that Millie and Buck headed downstairs, each with a cardboard box and Buck with the dresses slung over his shoulder.

The rain had stopped, so they went out the front door to the truck. There was a full moon, so seeing their way wasn't a problem. They put the boxes and dresses in the back of the truck and returned to their honeymoon room.

This time the lovemaking was tender and deliberate. Buck even took the time to caress every scratch and scar on Millie's back, on her arms, and on her legs. Taking the time to love each other. A lifetime together, so no need to rush.

It had been a long week and an exciting day, so when the little blue clock showed ten o'clock, Buck looked at Millie and asked, "Ready to call it a day, dear wife of mine?"

"Yes, my sweet husband. I am."

Again, they fell asleep in each other's arms and were still there when the little blue clock began to chime at 6:00 a.m. Letting Buck sleep a little longer, Millie slipped out of the bed and went to the bathroom. She filled the tub with hot water and stretched out like she liked to do and soaked.

By six-thirty she was dressed and ready for the day. "Get up, sleepyhead. We need to go home." She shook Buck's shoulder. So Buck took a turn in the bathroom and then the two of them went to the kitchen. Two boarders had checked in during Sunday afternoon, so Miss Cora was busy making breakfast in the kitchen when Buck and Millie showed up.

Louise was there, dressed and sitting on the Sears catalog, tied to the chair with a dishtowel, but not seeming to mind, stuffing pieces of biscuit into her mouth. "Well, look at you," Millie greeted her daughter.

Louise looked up and said, "Mama."

"Oh, Buck, did you hear that?" And, pointing to Buck, she asked, "Louise, who is this?"

"Papa."

Mr. Lester was there taking the last bite of a strip of bacon, "Well, how about that. You got married and now your baby starts talking."

Miss Cora turned from the stove. "Good morning, Mr. and Mrs. Wilson. How did you like the honeymoon dinner I left you? I saw your tracks in the refrigerator as well as your dirty dishes in my sink."

As always, she was giving the orders. "You two take a seat, so you're outta my way. Come on, Alice, we've got to get this breakfast on the table."

Buck and Millie took seats and Miss Cora served them breakfast, so they'd stay seated. Louise reached for her ma, so Millie untied her. Bringing Louise to her lap, Millie then began to feed her some bacon and eggs."

"When you plannin' on leaving, Buck?" Mr. Lester asked.

"As soon as we finish our breakfast, Mr. Lester. And, suh, I can't begin to tell you how much you and your family mean to me and Millie and, of course, Louise."

"Glad to help. Hope you three will keep in touch. Letters are always good, but a visit now and then might be nice, too."

Things began to get quiet as they do when the thought of leaving a place and person who have become dear, will always be dear, gets closer. And now it was time. Buck stood and took Louise from Millie. With tears rolling down her cheeks, Millie stood, hugging Mr. Lester and then Miss Cora.

She looked first at Mr. Lester. She hugged his neck. "Mr. Lester, you are 'Goodness'." Then turning to Miss Cora, "You are 'Mercy'." Miss Cora was wiping tears from her eyes and Mr. Lester was looking away.

Millie continued, "Psalm 23 says that goodness and mercy will follow me all the days of my life and I will dwell in the house of the Lord forever. I will never forget you. Whatever 'goodness' and 'mercy' I find, I will know it started with you, both of you."

Mr. Lester finally spoke, "Well, I've got to go to work. Good-bye, Millie, Buck." He shook hands with Buck.

Then Buck said, "We need to go, Millie."

"Miss Cora, please tell, Hazel, Corine, and Gladys good-bye for me, and Miss Sarah. I'll write them letters when I get to Buck's home."

Buck smiled, "To our home."

And there it was, Millie leaving as she had come, wearing the same dress, the faded cotton dress she had worn when Buck brought her to Miss Sarah's. Endings are never completely endings; they always have a beginning wrapped up in them.

Opening the passenger side door, Buck helped Millie and Louise into the truck. Louise happily took her place between them, her parents. No one was on the porch to say good-bye. All were busy with their Monday lives. Buck cranked up the Ford and turned her south.

About the author

Susan Middleton is a retired lawyer/educator who lives on Jekyll Island, Georgia with her husband of forty-six years and two beloved dogs. She is a church pianist and active participant in the arts at Jekyll Island Arts Association.

9 781955 095372